Kevin Maher was born [...] g to
London in 1994 to begin [...] the
Guardian, the *Observer* [...] the
Face until 2002, before jo[...] [...]even
years he has been a feature writer, critic and columnist.

'The story unfolds like an action film with the beating heart of an
intellectual rom-com. Jay's journey from young man to proper
grown-up is told with tight, witty prose and deeply felt emotion'
Melissa Katsoulis, *The Times*

'Maher writes with an exuberance and inventiveness that makes his
characters joyous things to behold ... the novel is as delightful and
challenging as it is heart-wrenching and honest' *Esquire*

'Kevin Maher's adrenalin-fuelled prose shifts constantly between the
funny and the heartbreaking, the satirical and the tender – often in
the same paragraph ... The verbal fireworks – while thrilling in
themselves – are at the service of such old-school satisfactions as a
series of interlocking plots, the importance of love and the creation
of characters who are impossible not to root for. At times, in fact,
the result is not unlike a winningly unhinged version of David
Nicholls's *One Day*. It also ranks among the most enjoyable novels
of the year so far' James Walton, *Reader's Digest*

'A rowdy, compelling love story ... At its heart, *Last Night on Earth*
is the story of two people who are very much in love and should be
together, but whose marriage buckles under the strain of having a
baby who may or may not have a disability. Jay and Shauna's
struggle makes for compelling reading, and their anxiety over the
welfare of their precious child will find resonance with every parent.
Maher writes most powerfully when he is depicting the big emotions,
love in particular – romantic love, filial love, parental love, the
love between friends' *Guardian*

'An auth[...] word wizard ... this punchy read takes you where

'On page 1, in 1996, Bonnie tumbles chaotically into the world; reflecting this, Maher's prose has a frantic, uterine echo of Eimear McBride's Girl ("birthy splatlets and baby driplets") but quickly gives way to Jay's voice. And what a voice: the book pivots around him, and from the moment he opens his mouth Jay is a whirling dervish of a character. Kinetic, relentlessly verbal and hard to dislike, he is a memorable rogue ... Last Night on Earth thrums with energy; the dialogue is slickly moulded, making music of expletives and colloquialisms, and may owe a debt to the fact that Maher is also a film critic. This is a very funny picaresque, unafraid of its emotional core. Jay deserves a place on the big screen' Irish Times

'Exhilarating ... the extraordinary love Jay feels for his daughter Bonnie tethers the story, and as Jay gets further mired in disaster, it's not so much the clock ticking down to Millennium Eve that builds the momentum but the question of whether Jay will be able to remake his family' Daily Mail

'Maher handles his myriad ingredients with an impressive lightness of touch. Last Night on Earth is an old-fashioned, plot-heavy sort of book, the kind of novel that speeds by in a rush of incident and vividly-rendered characters. You look up and a hundred pages have gone by, almost without you having noticed ... Last Night on Earth is a big, warm-hearted book, funny and touching ... bursting with anecdotes, gossip, flashbacks, bedtime stories, confessions, jokes, and allusions to movies and philosophers: entertainment, in other words. This is very impressive work from a writer to watch' Sunday Business Post

'Extremely funny but between the comedy and verbal gymnastics, there are moments which are intensely moving and Maher accurately captures the thin line which most new parents tread between overwhelming love and complete terror. This funny, witty and compelling novel is a rollercoaster of a read' Daily Express

'Wonderful ... written with a wicked sense of humour that almost, but not quite, disguises the fact that at the heart of this fabulous, funny, sad, crazy journey is a love story' Good Book Guide

Last Night on Earth

Kevin Maher

ABACUS

ABACUS

First published in Great Britain in 2015 by Little, Brown
This paperback edition published in 2016 by Abacus

1 3 5 7 9 10 8 6 4 2

'Boom, Boom, Boom, Boom!!': Vengaboys, Positira, 1999.
By Benny Anderson, Danski, Wessel van Diepen and Bjorn Ulvaeus.

A CIP catalogue record for this book
is available from the British Library.

ISBN 978-0-349-13977-7

Typeset in Sabon by M Rules
Printed and bound in Great Britain by
Clays Ltd, St Ives plc

Papers used by Abacus are from well-managed forests
and other responsible sources.

MIX
Paper from
responsible sources
FSC® C104740

Abacus
An imprint of
Little, Brown Book Group
Carmelite House
50 Victoria Embankment
London EC4Y 0DZ

An Hachette UK Company
www.hachette.co.uk

www.littlebrown.co.uk

For Rosemary Margaret Cumberland

And what rough beast, its hour come round at last,
Slouches towards Bethlehem to be born?

W.B. Yeats, 'The Second Coming'

ONE

1

Bonnie, August 1996

Apologies for the speed, up front, from the start. But big hurry is upon me. Great hurry. For I am to be born. Right now. No joke. No feckin joke, as Dadda Jay might say. Or just, like, totally, totally, as Momma Shauna might add. But she won't add, Right now, because right now, as the soon-to-be Bonnie of a Dadda Jay and a Momma Shauna, I am, right now, to be honest, I am crowning.

Shheeeeeeeeeeeeeeeeeeeshhhhhhhh! she says, Momma Shauna says, as I, and she, and we together push like crazy, from inside and out, both beating blood together, her thumpety-thump and my wuchoo-wuchoo-wuchoo, pushing my greasy noggin to the edge of the world and through a skin stretch that's nothing less than rippy, teary, burny red and makes Momma Shauna go Shheeeeeeshhh through her teeth, but not Jesus, or Fuck, or Shit, or screamy gimme some drugs, gimme some drugs, like they do in the fillums when the mommies-to-be, all hot and wet and angry faces, scream out fuck and shit and try to punch the daddies-to-be, to make sure that the fillums are funny for all.

But no, Momma Shauna, brave and strong, four-floored in the bedroom, hands and knees style, on rich cream carpet with old undersheet cover to catch birthy splatlets and baby driplets, she

3

just says, hot head against mattress edge, she just says, Sheeeesshhh through her teeth, as I crown, and as rippy, teary, burny red opens and parts, opens and parts, and licks soft afternoon air on the tippy top of my greasy grey noggin.

And I know in my soul that Dadda Jay is scared. As scared as Momma Shauna is brave and strong. Scared and alone, standing and barking, holding ringback in hand, then crouching on coversheet carpet with us. And no feckin *doula*, as Dadda Jay says, with such anger, such fear.

No feckin *doula*! Should've got a real midwife! Said it all along! Every second of the way! No feckin *doula*! Call waiting, me arse!

And I want to say, Be not afraid, like they do in the good book, like Dadda Jay's Momma Dee read to him, soft and kissy, sing-songy, to him, when he was big-eyed and small. And her, all whisper warm and cuddle close, jumper tight, and going bible crazy and giant land-crack Jesus this, and Armageddon deathwave that, but always be not afraid, be not afraid, and her own eyes liddy with love-tears, and be not afraid, *me auld segosha*.

Doula, me arse! I'm calling the ambulance!

Momma Shauna says, Please! Jay! Please! It's not in the birth plan!

Feck the birth plan!

Jay! Nooooo!

And she means it, and she grits, and she digs nails, mattress deep, while he kneels beside her. Eyes terror wide.

Shheeeeeeeeeeeeeeeeeeesh!

Inside she pushes, so brave and so strong, a huge rushy-red push that squeezes my half crown to full crown. Then stop. Head out and hanging, outside for first, in the soft summer-world air, while body, my Bonnie body, stays tight, tight and fixed for sure, in the crush of inside.

And I know that I, my head, lolling out of skin stretch with body tummy crushed inside, I am death grey to the world. Alive,

4

just about, but not looking good right now. Like totally freakin crazy in a not-good way, as Momma Shauna might say.

But Momma Shauna, still four-floored and mattress-gripping, reaches down, low beneath, love-tapping, spider-light, all around my lolling, metal-grey, death head.

Love-giddy, she cries, What's she like? What's she like?

Dadda Jay, at the action end, looks at me, at my grey metal noggin, with eyes ripped terror wide in panic. Be not afraid.

A pause. A breath held. Mine and Momma Shauna together. Then ...

She's beautiful, he says. She's really beautiful.

And reach goes his hand, finger-twining Momma's, and together gently, hand cupping together, my head they hold, hands cupped together, with such tears and such tenderness that shamed am I for not yet knowing this precious warmth, this ancient strength, this now and forever, this Momma Dadda love.

But the big one is coming, and it's starting to show.

Sheeeeeeeeeeeeeeeeeeshhhhhh!

The big one. Big red. Final red. Building pressure behind me. Inching me forward, for the final body whoosh, from tummy crush to summer world.

Jesus, fuck, goes Dadda Jay.

What? yelps Momma Shauna.

Dadda Jay has seen the cord. The cord, double wrapped, a slither-tight purple scarf.

Jesus, fuck. The cord! The fucking cord!

But Momma Shauna is, like, totally, totally, like soooo not worried.

Normal! she says, not to panic, not to panic. Just pull it off! Over the head! Before the contraction!

And fuckin what the fuckin what! is Dadda Jay, with terror eyes and screamy thoughts! The fuckin what?

My heart, body crushed in tummy heat, is now doused in pain,

5

and, fuckin shit, going wuckity-choo wuckity-choo, instead of wuchoo-wuchoo-wuchoo. And Momma Shauna, my Momma Shauna, so brave, so strong, is saying normal to Jay, to calm Jay, and normal again, and no worries to Jay, but my heart pain is dousing, and fuckin the what, the wuckity choo.

Oh Jeeeeesus! The fuckin, the fuckin, the feckin, the fuckin! Dadda Jay screaming and finger-digging the cord, the slithery scarf, while trying not to scrape Momma Shauna's rippy, teary, burny bits.

And pull it! my momma says.

And I can't, Jay says, tiger tight, it is, fuckin the shit, around the neck, and while we're at it, she's grey as fuck, and I'm worried, I'm worried!

All normal! Now pull it! Pull hard! Before Shheeeeeesh, contraction, comes. Pull it off!

More digging, finger scrapes, and slither scarf yanked an inch only, because tiger tight like you wouldn't believe, and Dadda Jay doing tug-o-war yank, and Momma Shauna screams, yelps, Oh fuck, that's torn it, something within, womb deep within, where red rushy blood comes roaring down around me, yummy hot, turning me into a big rushy-red head, red fountainhead.

Oh fucking mother of good fuck! Dadda Jay shoots backwards across carpet, half covered, half caught, in red-splattered cover sheet.

Momma Shauna, no calm, no more, says we're ripped, inside. And worse still, sheeeeeeeeshhhh, the final contraction is here, she can feel it now, gushing from womb within, big red rush, past Bonnie head, on rich carpet cream, while wuckity-choo is painy and sore, and painy and slow. And I know in my soul, with my tiger-tight cord, that bad is the end, the early end, for bad baby Bonnie, and in bad rush of red the end is right now.

Be not afraid.

And yet.

Dear Mammy,

I am writing this to say sorry about the big fight, and to let you know that I am grand. As you probably guessed, I am in London. After all the *shcales* through the years from Auntie Maudie at Christmas hoolies about the fur coats, the jewellery, the big tippers and all the feckin city streets paved with the gold of happiness, prosperity and unlimited human ambition, it seemed like the obvious place to go.

I couldn't find a single trace of her, hide nor hair, on either Hemstal, Dynham or Cotleigh Roads, although this seriously decent landlady who comes from Castlerea, a big round wan of a thing, called Finula, a bit like moody Una Houlihan from Grey's hardware, but without the mini-moustache, let me have a room near by, as long as I could pay the deposit and a month's rent in cash, up front, which I did, with the savings that I took out from Drury's post office on the morning after the big fight, when I ran off for ages and you were all worried and crying in your hospital bed in Sligo Town, drugged up to the nines, waving your stump around, bawling your heart out to Fr Francis, worried for me and where I was, and how I was, and how I had reacted to your big showpiece demo, and asking him if I was ok in myself, with yourself and with the big news, when, unbeknown to you, and the father, and the whole feckin lot of them, I was actually sorting out me ferry ticket in Egan's.

Anyway, as I say, I am sorry for the pain.

Finula's trying her best to be my adopted Mammy, and made a big to-do about my age, and me being a right baby-faced chisler, and wasn't satisfied that I was nineteen-nearly-twenty until she held my passport in her hand. She says that we all have to stick together over here, especially at the moment, because of all the brouhaha and the bombings and the so-called renewed campaign, and that she knows a little ginger fella from Cashel, County Tipperary, who wandered over Earls Court way last month, on the same sunny day that the 'RA blew a massive hole in the visitors' bog of the Stock Exchange and brought the whole city to a big sweaty and angry standstill, and that the little fella got dragged into the jacks of some mouldy pub opposite the tube and was beaten senseless by a load of other fellas in red braces, nice shoes and proper city clothes, who said that they were fed up with all the micks in London who were ruining life here for all the non-micks and that we were all just a load of horse-killing, burger-bombing bastards. Finula says that she's going to put her 'feelers' out, and see if she can't get me a decent sweep-up gig on the sites.

And don't try to send Claps, or The Fox, or Mickeleen, or any one of that snickering, sneering booze-sodden Strandhill crew after me. I am doing fine. Being looked after, grand. I made myself spaghetti bolognese tonight, but with onions instead of meat, and Ragú instead of sauce. And I will write as soon as I get a job, so you won't have to worry, and be crying, and howling out to everyone about the fate of your one and only.

Give Bowsie a hefty clip round the lug from me, as well as my portion of the Thursday fry-up. And don't forget his flea drops – they're on my locker.

I'll write to Fr Francis too, to tell him to keep an eye in.

Good luck with the paintings. You were coming on something magic the last time I checked.

Love always,

Your Right-Hand Man,

Jay

2

Home-Flash Mini-Mental Breakdown, August 1996

I am in London. I am in London. I say it again. To reassure myself. I'm having one of those moments. Like all of us lads do. The London lads. Having a home-flash mini-mental breakdown kind of a thing. It's where you catch yourself, like. Where you've been thinking about, I dunno, feckin *Baywatch* or Daniel Day-Lewis going full throttle in *The Crucible*, 'Because it is my naaaaaaaaaaaame!' Or else you've been lost in rememberings, and wondering if that lad on the St John's Wood site, back in the day, Titch, the lad that got the metal shard shot into his eye from the jackhammer ever got better again, because you moved on real quick like, before he was out of the hospital, even though youze and him was bestie buddies, and the rest, and were always shooting the shit at lunchtime, and him telling you about taking drugs and dropping acid, and doing 'e' while riding the arse off some poor young wan, and you nodding along goodo, like a right gob-shite, as if you're Al-feckin-Scarface-Pacino himself rather than the lad from back-a-beyond who burst out crying over in Shauna's Notting Hill flat when you smoked hash for the first time and got stuck in her bath, surrounded by scented candles, with your whole body paralysed from the dope and the water level up to your nose, and you thinking that this was the end and that drugs were for other people, glamorous people, fellas and girls in fillums mostly, or them feckers at last year's inaugural, and super-flash, and mind-blowingly decadent, *Screen Grab* Christmas party, where they had the girls with the silver trays of cocaine sashaying about the room, taking twenties from punters and letting them snuffle and puffle away to their hearts' content.

Of course, I didn't actually see the trays myself, but everyone at the party said that they were there, and that the coke girls, like the ladies of the harem of the court of King Caractacus, were just passing by, just out of the corner of your eye, just over there. And Shauna kept nudging me from the dance floor, while I was doing my best floppy rappy dance, and pointing me up to the balcony area where the VIPs were, and saying Look, look, do you see the coke, the coke?

And it makes us feel all cool and young and hip and magic because we work in telly, and we're talking about coke, and we're surrounded by coke, and we've finally become adults who'll make our mams and dads look small-time and backward-assed because all they had in their day was Bill Haley and 'Rock Around the Clock' and fellas with greasy hair and flick knives ripping up cinema seats, and they were never at a big London telly party with VIP balconies and trays of cocaine. And I'm so thrilled with myself that I start the next letter in my head, while I'm bopping there with Shauna on the floor, and it goes, *Dear Mammy, guess what, I was at a party last night with trays of cocaine,* but instead Shauna pulls me close and glares into my eyes, a big beaming American love smile, and mouths the words of the rappy floppy song, 'I Like the Way You Move It', and then we kiss, and we kiss, and all is well.

As I say, the home-flash, mini-mental breakdown thing happens just like that. When you're thinking about all this stuff, and

11

deep in it, lost it in, and you're trudging out of the London tube, and it's a manky winter night, and it's dark and rainy on the London streets, and the cars, the London cars, are racing by in the rain, fast tyres through wet tarmac like freshly ripped sellotape. And it's that noise, that tyre noise on its own that wakes you up, snaps you out, and for a second, a split second, you look around, and the noise, the wet-tyre-tarmac noise, tells your soul, not your mind but your soul, that it's school nights back in Ballaghaderreen, in County Roscommon, walking home late from the Strandhill bus, with Claps Connolly in the rain, being passed in the dark by the evening rush of Ford Sierras and farm-friendly Hiaces. And Claps is punching you in the shoulder, and calling you a bender, trying to grab your jocks' elastic, for wedgies, the works.

And for a second, for a split second, your soul tells you to look around for Ballaghaderreen and Claps and the lads, and yet your mind finds nothing, you recognise nothing around you, the streets make no sense, the cars, the signs, the shopfronts mean nothing. You are, officially, nowhere, trapped between soul and brain. And at this very moment, this nanosecond of ache, while your brain is battling, and trying to beat back your soul, which has deviously dumped you somewhere between Roscommon and Reality, all you want to do is scream out in panic at the top of your lungs, Day-Lewis style, 'Where in feck's name am Ieeeeeeeee, like?'

And just when you think that you're going to go mad, and implode, and turn into feckin Lear on the bog, or some aul head case from back home who'd barricade herself into the bedroom, and wrap the hair curlers in newspapers and hide them under a shoe-pile in the hot press because the priests were coming to take them away; and just when you think that you're going that way, with Alzheimer's, dementia, and all the head-case specials, and that your mammy might as well go ahead and book you the place in Ballyhaunis convalescent home for mentlers, suddenly, finally, the brain gives the soul a right root in the bollix, and it all clicks into gear, and the buildings find form and function, the streets fling forth their names, the cars and the shopfronts too, and you sigh to yourself with relief as your London reality rushes inwards, tip to toe, flooding you, filling you with the force of knowing, for now.

And I don't have them that often. I'm not a total gom. But I'm having them now, on this day, in the hospital, where I'm saying to myself, to reassure myself, I am in London, I am in London, because the hospital seems so strange with the walls, and the lights, and the blinking and the noise. And the faces of everyone, looking in pity. It's things like that, you see. Triggers. When you get lost in the mind. And the soul craves home. It's the eternal return, like. Which is a thing that I cogged from the front of Shauna's favourite book, *The Unbearable Lightness of Being*. With that one, I thought, best case, if I got past the boring bit at the start about the eternal return itself I'd get to some seriously raunchy-like sex sessions, such as there were in the fillum version, where all the wans were into suspender belts and bowler hats and riding the arse off Daniel Day-Lewis. Ah jaysus, there he is again. Feckin gets around, that boyo, I'll tell ye.

Anyhow, I'm more into fillums and Shauna's more into books and art and paintings. And that's why she reckons we make such a killer couple, and why we work so brilliantly together in the *Screen Grab* offices, despite our very personal connection. Any book she's read, and she's read millions, before she's barely got the name out of her mouth, I can tell her about the fillum version, and why it's usually better.

Of course, we have big noisy hair-pullers about this all the time, where Shauna and the *Screen Grab* lot, after a few gargles in the back booth in the Dog and Duck on Frith Street, gang up on me in a jokey way, and fire titles at me, to see if I'll crack. They go, like, *The Godfather*? And I say, Five hundred pages of unmitigated shite! Feckin super *schonawn*, though!

Schonawn is, like, a Gaelic word for movie or fillum, and I use it only as a joke, because Shauna thought it was so funny when I told her, and it's become, like, a cracking gag between me and the whole team. Although we're always doing that, me and Shauna. Like when I told her out on the smoking steps on the corner of Marshall Street that *bookill dawna* meant bad boy, she practically ran back into the office, and into the conference room and told everyone there, even Jane the boss wan, even though they were working on a proposal for the Dani Behr Christmas Special, that I was a *bookill dawna*, and then she burst out laughing.

Other words that she thinks are dead funny are *shcale* for story, *mawla* for bag, *coopla* for a few, *labba* for bed, *kyoal* for music, *kyun* for head, *timpishta* for accident, *gon doubt awoyne* for without a doubt, *seshoon mah* for a decent aul snog, and, best of all, *ree raw ogus roola boola* for an argument. Oh, and she especially likes the Gaelic word for word, which is *fuckill*, which is, she says, just brilliant.

And it's not like she's slagging me rotten, or calling me a gom. In fact, she's always telling everyone, at the drop of a hat, that I'm fierce smart, which is, in fact, smarter than I actually am. Sometimes, depending on who's around, she announces at parties and pubs that that I'm an autodidact, which is both a posh word for a fella who left school without doing his Leaving Cert, and a way of making me sound interesting when all the other fellas start moaning on about their school days, and the time when Basher Finsey gave them a right good ragging for failing A-level Latin, or when they start banging on about freshers' week in Oxford, Edinburgh and Manchester, or life in the dorms, and how Kipper Meeks Montagu Scott topped himself because of the pressures of final exams and because he only got a 2.1 in his thesis about the deconstruction of masculine identity in the novels of Saul Bellow. At which point Shauna usually squeezes my hand and pipes up and says that I'm an autodidact and I can speak Gaelic. And then she goes, Go on, say something.

And you'd think, naturally, that we'd be doing it in the bedroom, you know, sexy-like. And that Shauna would be going, all panting and breathless, Go on, say it! Say it! And I'd be like, *Fayack air muh leeroydee! Guheentock, nock ah?* Which is Gaelic for *Look at my balls! Amazing, don't you think?* But we don't, because it's not our style. And besides, I'd say that only because I don't know the Gaelic for donger, and that's probably because there isn't one in the first place, because the lads who made up Gaelic were priests and monks, or Irish Revivalist feckers like Yeats and Maud Gombeen who thought that Ireland should be pure and ancient and all bows-and-arrows shite, and nothing to do with sex, even though Yeats was a right aul dirty fecker himself, who once had an operation to insert monkey balls into his stomach in order to make him more attractive to younger wans who were fed up listening to him blathering away about the metaphysical significance of the title characters in 'Circus Animal's Desertion'.

But, as I say, I'm in hospital, and I'm going, 'I am in London, I am in London,' and I'm trying not to lose the plot. But it's hard, because I've been awake for nearly thirty hours straight, and my head's thumping, my ears are ringing, and my eyes feel like they could just plop out of their sockets and onto the floor at any minute.

I'm walking the corridors of St Mary's in Paddington like a zombie ghost lad who's using every bit of strength he's got left in his terrified limbs just to stay upright and keep shuffling forward and back, forward and back, stopping, and standing, and rocking on the balls of his feet, the *leeroydee* of his feet, forward and back, just rocking. Because I'm waiting for our slot, in the X-ray

15

room, and everyone's been really kind and doing sad faces at me, and coming up and having a peek, and telling me not to worry. Because in my terrified arms, wrapped in a soft white blanket that was purchased with picture-book cuddles in mind, sits curled and silent, startled and unblinking, my newborn baby, my fresh-born love. My Bonnie.

And she's in bits.

And I'm in bits. And I don't want to cry. But I'm holding her, and looking down at her, and I'm being a dad. My hands are huge, and I'm cupping her, and she's breathing, quiet, and her eyes are huge; she's looking at me, unblinking, and I'm looking back, and I'm sorry that you've started this way, and I love you, I love you, till it ends me.

She's blotchy and red, her skin is red, which is a good thing, they said, which was the only good thing in a whirl of checks, and prods and pokes and pricks, and then sighs and scowls, and a whole rake of young doctor fellas turning to me and Shauna, and going, real snide-like, home birth, hmmm? As if they'd caught Myra Hindley and Ian Brady in action. Home birth? Nyyyeeees. And with a *doula* too? Indeed. Nyyesssss. And then more checks, and notes, and scribbles, and sighs, and then the youngest of the young doctor fellas, a real little twerp, the kind of fella who might've earned himself a good aul Ballaghaderreen Blindside (dazzle with the left and then, pow, take 'em out with the right!) back in the day, drops Bonnie back into my arms and gives us a big snarky lecture about how rubbish home births are, how *doulas* are nothing better than witch doctors, and how we're basically two big feckin eejits for going ahead with it, and then he lists all the things that are facing us in the road ahead with our recently brain-oxygen-deprived yet brand-new and possibly completely mental baby. It's all dyspraxia this, severe gross motor skill delay that, possible metabolic acidosis, Erb's palsy,

16

paediatric physiotherapy and learning support for the rest of her life on earth.

Of course, after the speech is done, Shauna twists around in the bed, shoves her head into the pillow and snorts herself into heartbroken hysterics. She's wearing a huge papery nappy-like thing, under the hospital nightie, in order to catch all the post-baby gunk that's still to come, and I can hear it crinkle and crunch under the covers as she shakes and shifts in teary-eyed agony. And in my head I want to scream at the doctor twerp, She's only just after given birth, you ignorant specky gobshite!

But instead, I say, like the cancer patients say when they're told the worst, or like my aulfella himself said when I was a tot and he heard that he had less than three months left to go, I go, Thank you, doctor, and then I cradle Bonnie even closer to me, right into my heart, while I lean over Shauna's rocking form and stroke her hair and tell her that everything will be fine even though I'm gagging with doubt and my stroky hand is shaking like mad, which makes it seem like I'm giving her the world's most ineffectual styling session at the singularly most inappropriate moment.

And it's not like we even have time for a snorty, tear-drenched group hug, because the specky fella is hovering around the edge of me, back in orders mode, pulling me by the sleeve, and pointing me towards the radiography wing. He shoves a scrunched-up piece of paper in my hand, and tells me to take myself and my newborn Bonnie off to the X-ray queue, and join a long line of the broken, the concussed and the quietly traumatised.

And so, I am in London, I say, as I trudge back 'n' forth, and as Bonnie looks, and I look, and I kiss, and I shake, and I kiss again. Close to my heart. To the very beat of me. Her, in the warm of me. And the ache.

I can't imagine anything outside these walls, this corridor, these humming, blinking, sci-fi strip lights. And I don't know how to say it, but I feel as if I could break apart at any minute, like there's two different atomic bombs of equal but opposite force going off inside of me. One of them is the raging never-known-before, all-consuming love I feel for this tiny, blotchy, big-eyed creature in my arms, and the other is the punishing fear and the sickening dread that I might ever lose her. That she might, already now or at any point in the future, be damaged beyond repair. Together these two bombs are exploding within. Feeding off each other, the fission and the fusion, splitting apart and blasting together. The pain and the love.

And Bonnie in my arms, it's one thing. I can just about make sense of it all. But when they get me to hold her down on the X-ray plate, her blotchy body all squiggling and wriggling, so small in the world, like a little mad animatronic alien, and her wide eyes looking and searching, it's too much. My throat burns, my lips wobble, and I start to snivel. The X-ray fella pretends that there's nothing the matter, as he asks me to shift Bonnie north again on the cold metal plate. Then hold her. Move her. Shift again. And the thing that floors me, is that she doesn't cry. No, she doesn't cry. Instead, she endures. She looks, she turns, she searches. And they'll tell you they can't see at that age, and that everything's a blur to their newborn eyes, especially in the dark of an X-ray room, but I'll tell you, and I know, that she is searching for me.

So I go, like, I'm here. It's me. It's Dadda, like. I'm right here, above you. I'm the big brutal fecker holding you down on the cold metal plate, in your tiny mini-nappy, because it's all X-ray beams and subatomic particles in here, and they don't want the doctors and the hospital technicians getting cancer, so they make the parents do the heavy lifting. And I want to bend down and stick my head right close up to Bonnie's face, right against the plate, and kiss her nose, and smell her, and tell her that there's

18

nothing to worry about because Dadda's here, face to face, now and for ever, world without end.

But the X-ray technician's got me standing to the side, at least two feet from the beam, and with an apron on that is fitted with its own heavy metal plate that hangs around my goolies, which feels strange, and makes me less and less confident about the actual safety of the whole situation when they've got newborn Bonnie casually squashed down backwards on a steel slab, like a frog in a school science lab, but are doing everything within their power, and pulling out all the stops, to make sure that they've guarded, covered and protected my feckin *leeroydee*. Not my heart or my brain or my kidneys, mind you. No, they can all go feck for themselves. It's just the *leeroydee* that are getting the royal treatment. Presumably so I can still pass on my seed when every other organ in my body is gone manky tumorous from the excess radiation, and the same technicians and specky doctor gobshites are wandering over to my dying bedside and saying, all patronising like, Well, you've still got your balls, isn't that something? And I'll say, Thank you doctor, while I think back to the day when they made me wear the apron with the metal plate and go, Thanks, lads, that was feckin brilliant of yiz. One in a million. How much do I owe ye?

I am in London.

We are allowed to bring Bonnie home after three more days of testing. Actually, a couple of hours of testing, and three days of queuing, stressing and staring blankly into space. And a couple of minutes of meaningless specky lectures.

We are told that Bonnie can breathe and can see. And that she can react to stimuli, such as a huge feckin torch beaming right into her eye, a loud kamikaze-style doctor's clap next to her ear, both ears, and, best of all, a sharp feckin needle stuck into the sole of her foot. I know. Ye'd think they'd never heard of a

19

feather, the feckin medieval bastards. She can swallow Shauna's breast milk too. Although that's a whole nother story in itself, and involves every sort of random hospital fecker just grabbing Shauna's boobs and ramming them into Bonnie's mouth. Everyone had a go. The serious young doctors travelling the ward in pairs and telling Shauna that, irrespective of Bonnie's brain condition, it's still all about stimulation and reflex. And so they roughly drag Shauna's nipples, swollen and painful, over Bonnie's top lip, up and down, back and forth, like a feckin magic marker, while they wait for Bonnie's jaw to drop slowly open, reflex style. And when it drops, they poke Shauna's nipple inside, and smile to themselves and pat each other on the back for being such brilliant breastfeeding masters.

Of course, it lasts only for about five seconds until Bonnie gives up, and the doctor lads are well gone by then, and this time it's the big, cuddly, old-school Jamaican nurses who simply grab Bonnie's head, crank her jaws wide open and shove as much of Shauna's boob as they can, like half the entire thing, into Bonnie's mouth, and down her throat. They laugh and chuckle kindly as they go, and they tell Shauna, who's wincing with the pain, that there's no secrets here, that Mother knows best, and that the little one just wants to be told. Naturally, you get about ten seconds out of that before Bonnie, who's probably still reeling from the subatomic X-ray blasts, spits it right out. And on it goes, with student doctors taking a turn next, and maternity nurses, and specialists, breastfeeding specialists, everyone having a shot. And Shauna's just there, like Bonnie, enduring, in the mad post-partum nappy, body open to the world, face frozen, and eyes telling of truck-impact trauma. And always exposed. Exposed and enduring. While everyone pulls and prods and yanks.

Although Bonnie, eventually, poos. This, more than anything, is why we are allowed to bring her home. She does a couple of black Bovrily-looking meconium poos, and then finally, on day three, a tiny scrambled-egg poo, which is the signal for our departure. This, we are told, is a result.

Our job now is to watch her, they say, during the brief farewell lecture from the edge of the bed. Monitor her every move, they say. Too early, yet, to tell if Bonnie will be completely mental-like for life, so we must instead watch out, first of all, for severe gross motor-skills delays. They give us a small green jotter, and tell us to chart her movements, her gestures and digestive habits, and plot them against a bell curve of a normal, yes, a normal baby on the opposite page. They smile when they say goodbye, especially the specky fella, and they look at Bonnie as if she is a rare species of lab monkey and act like me and Shauna should be dead excited, now that we've got a full-time scientific experiment on our hands.

We cry in the car park together, standing side by side, next to Shauna's ancient red Clio with the brand-new baby seat sat in the back. It is daytime, just after noon, and the sun is out.

It is Tuesday, 6 August 1996.

We are in London.

Shauna gently lowers herself into the front. And even though it is, officially, by all accounts, mental-dangerous, she refuses to place Bonnie in the baby seat, and instead wraps both arms tightly around her and orders me to drive. I pause to protest, taking just a breath, but before a word is even out, Shauna shoots me a look, right up from the primal abyss, and it's a new look that I've never seen before, a look that is the powerful flipside of the hospital-truck trauma face, as forceful and fulminating as that other look was passive and paralysed, and it's a look that tells me, in no uncertain terms, to back, the, feck, off.

Slowly, carefully, I touch the side of Shauna's face with the back of my hand, and tell her that, thankfully, we still have each other.

Yes, I say. You and me, like. We'll ride this one out together. Hand in hand. Heart to heart. We're stronger than this. We can do this. We can make this family happen. You. And me. And Bonnie. For ever.

We are divorced within three years.

3

Shauna and Dr Ghert

So, how do we begin?

How would you like to begin?

Oh please. I don't think I'm strong enough for that.

For what?

For the autonomy. I am not here to take control.

So why are you here?

I'm here because I'm depressed. And because I heard that you were the best in the business.

This is not for me to say, although I will tell you that my methods are unorthodox yet my results are unassailable. You have been diagnosed, no?

No.

Then what, my dear girl, makes you think that you're depressed?

What would you call it?

Call what?

Sitting in my room, on the edge of my bed, listening to my two-year-old daughter, banging on the door, wailing for my attention. Yet I do nothing. There are hazards all around her. Knives in the kitchen, glasses on the table, a gas cooker, eye-level access to bleach, sharp corners everywhere. And her, so clumsy, so fragile and quick to fall. And yet, for some reason, I do nothing.

Hardly extraordinary. We won't be sending for the men in white coats just yet. Hmm?

I do nothing because I'm frozen to the spot. Rooted to the bed. Unable to move, to reach the door handle. Because, somehow, I've fallen into a deep, dark manhole of my own making, where everything around me is black as night. And I know that I need to reach the handle but whenever I try to move, or even think about moving, or think about her, I drift further down, where the blackness becomes even more enveloping, and the door handle moves even further away until the very act of reaching it becomes a sheer physical impossibility. And all along the wailing rises and falls, and then rises again, with door thumps and kicks, until my husband comes home from work, three hours later, and finds our baby girl exhausted on the floor against the door. And, of course, he soothes her, and tells her that he loves her. He picks her up, comes into the room and finds me there, still frozen on the bed edge, like Mrs Dalloway on Quaaludes, unmoved from my pose hours earlier. And he says. Well, he says absolutely nothing.

This word manhole. This interests me. This word is very primal. A word from the id, no? Why do you think you use it? Why not, say, cave?

Because it's a manhole.

And what do you think of, really, when you think of the word manhole?

I think of a manhole.

You do not need to be polite, my friend, in this place. This space is safe, without rules or regulations. No laws here. No punishments, no wrongs. Just freedom to release what's inside. To be as free, as unburdened and as crude as you like.

I know.

So, I ask you again. Manhole, tell me all the things, all the

24

associations, this word triggers. What does the word inspire in you, in your darkest imaginings?

It inspires the image of a manhole.

And so you see the world from inside this manhole?

Yes.

You know the Classics, yes, the Greeks, yes? You are like the woman inside Plato's Cave, no? Watching the shadows of the world pass by from within the darkness, and trying to understand the world from within this manhole?

I guess.

But what if we turned around? What if we looked into this manhole, instead? What if we look at you alone there, frozen in the darkness? What would we see now?

We'd see a depressed woman.

Is this, my poor, poor child, the totality of your experience? Is this the sum of who you are?

You want the totality of my experience?

Of course. Were you not a different person before this, a younger person, a teenager, a girl, a child, even a baby? What do you know, for instance, about you as a baby?

Seriously?

Absolutely. What's the first thing you know about your own existence?

You're not kidding?

My good friend, I do not kid, not in this space. The entrance into life is as significant to me as the exit from it. Impressions and associations are created in the pell-mell of birth that last to this very day and beyond, to the day on which you eventually depart. Trust me. It matters.

In that case, I know that I arrived, according to my father, Paul, at exactly 4 p.m. on Sunday, 26 July 1970, in a private birth room at Wilmington General Hospital, Delaware, USA.

Anything else?

And that it was hot.

And that's all?

Seriously?

Absolutely.

Apparently Paul was down on the beach at the time, down on Rehoboth Beach in the sun. He was a hippie. A real artsy-fartsy guy. They say that this other guy, a store owner, Jack Burke from 'Burke's Bits and Bobs', broke the news by racing along the boardwalk and across the hot sands, screaming out loud that my mom had gone into labour.

And the birth, tell me about the birth. You are born, how?

I arrived quickly, I believe, with minimal fuss. No suction or ventouse, no drugs or nothing, just good, old-fashioned pushing power. Paul and Mom were seemingly so suffused with momentary joy that they threw open the windows and decided that I was to be called Summer, for obvious reasons.

A beautiful name. A beautiful word. So rich with connotations. You were a blessed child.

I was Summer for approximately one week, during which time Mom's mom, who was, according to Paul, a living nightmare, overruled the decision, claiming that she would not be made the laughing stock of Gibson Island.

And this woman, your grandmother, she had control of your family?

I guess. I once asked Paul why he didn't just tell Mom's mom to take a hike, but he said that it was complicated, and that Mom's mom covered the rent on the house in Lewes whenever Paul's so-called art failed to bring in so-called money. It was an arrangement that seemed, he said, to give Mom's mom carte blanche to treat Paul and Mom like total dicks, rather than people.

And the name Summer?

For a week after that, I was called 'Shaw', after George

26

Bernard Shaw, who was also born on 26 July, in Ireland. Paul's ancestors were Irish, and arrived in the US in the mid nineteenth century, having fled from what Paul liked to describe as tyranny, starvation, and the crushing jackboot of English imperialism.

You did not believe in these myths?

I believed it all right. I overdosed on it. Thanks to Paul. Up all night for half my childhood, listening only to Irish records, drinking heavily and weeping himself to sleep alongside an endlessly repeated chorus about the desecration of four green fields. Then, groggy over breakfast the next day, he'd retread the Irish war stories and give me and Mom lectures about the damages done to his family line in 'the old country'. Even took us to Ellis Island once. Dragged me, Mom, and my baby brother Chester around in front of endless walls of glass-covered registration documents, yet never found a single reference to the fortunes of his own embattled family.

And you were angry with him?

No. Not at all. He was like that, Paul. The Teflon dad. Meltdowns, mistakes, major familial faux pas, simply slid right off him. No repercussions. No questions asked.

And your name?

Mom's mom hated the name Shaw. Too masculine for a girl, she decided, at the end of my second week on earth. Give her complexes. Get her bullied by other girls. Paul eventually agreed to a compromise. Shawna. Paul was pleased, and announced it to friends and colleagues, even cooked up a hand-painted baby card with a caricature of two exhausted parents lying prone around a newborn, and giant chunky letters screaming 'Shawna's Here!'

And that was it?

No, Mom's mom hated the way they spelled Shawna. She said that, on paper, it made me look like a cheap Vegas dancer. Paul declared defeat, and I became Shauna. Just a girl called Shauna.

And this name has been good for you? How do you feel about it? What does it describe?

It describes Paul, slowly losing interest in Irish ballads and late-night weeping sessions, although not before he had forced me, aged eleven, to choose 'The Subjugation of Ireland and its Peoples' as the title of my summer-school project. I got an A for it, putting me in the top three of the class, but Paul's fingerprints were all over it. Entire paragraphs transcribed, in my hand, at the kitchen table, as he stood over me.

And you were ashamed of this?

I was asked to read it out at the summer assembly. It was either a sign of my own greatness or an indication that my uptight history teacher, Mr Sanderson, who sensed the guiding hand of a meddling so-called Fenian, planned to expose me. But I got through it. I stumbled over sentences. Some of the other girls, who had big cars and bigger houses and fathers who worked in Philadelphia, sneered as I spoke. Nicole Henson, whose father had once been interviewed on the ABC nightly news, said, right in the middle of my reading, and in no attempt to hide herself whatsoever, she said, as I was speaking, Provo!

This word was a bad thing?

Oh please! It means Provisional Irish Republican Army. Like a terrorist. The bombers? Hyde Park? Canary Wharf? A very bad thing. And when the bus doors opened at my stop that afternoon, in front of the Lewes library, my feet barely touched the ground. I practically flew all the way down West 3rd Street, and was already in through the front screen doors, and halfway through the opening line, 'Paul! Paul! You won't believe what Nicole Henson just called me?' when I saw it.

Go on.

The blood. Nothing spectacular. Just drips of it. Perfect circular splashes, some no bigger than a quarter, but dramatic and unmissable nonetheless, especially on the naked floorboards, leading from the door through to the kitchen where it climaxed in and around the sink, in a vivid crimson splash that half covered the draining board, and dripped, even as I watched, slowly down into the open mouth of the garbage masher.

4

The *Shcale* of the Tans

There is a story that is told by the Mother of Jay. A family tale.
A right *shcale*. She tells it best, the Mother of Jay, at the fag end
of a sweaty, woozy summer hoolie, or an intimate late-night chin-
wag in a low-roofed holiday lock-in on Achill Island, when the
red-eyed company has been reduced to whiskey shots and cheese
sangers, and sodden memories and imaginings of painful days
gone by. It's a hand-me-downer tale, they say. A real-life heir-
loom, set, as all the best Irish stories are, during the so-called War
of Independence, in the summer of 1920, around the police barracks of Rathmore, County Kerry.

The *shcale* stars Seamus Farrell, the maternal grandfather of
Jay, but only nineteen years old, nearly twenty, at the time. He's
a handsome boy, according to the Mother of Jay, and, she says,
blessed with big Bambi eyes. There is a photo of Seamus Farrell,
hiding in the darkness of a Roscommon attic that will prove the
point. A stern-faced hurling squad in front of gloomy school
buildings, snapped to attention, unexceptional but for a sharp-
focus outline of a smiling face in the front row, with a startling
pair of bright burning eyes and the beginnings of an early
twentieth-century fringe flick, locally known as a duck's arse.

Seamus and his best friend, Dessie 'The Rabbit' Moynihan,

also nineteen, are both hiding from the Black and Tans while crouched beside a squat mossy wall on Station Road, forty-five yards down the street from the barracks of the Royal Irish Constabulary. These two boys are like brothers, more blood than some real brothers, in fact. Been together in school, same class, same desk, since First Holy Communion. Elbow to elbow every day, joking and scribbling, nudging while reading, always on the edge of giggles, leaning in at times, shoulder to shoulder, always the warmth and the unspoken love.

Seamus and Dessie 'The Rabbit' ducked behind the low wall after spotting a straggling group of Black and Tans. The Mother of Jay, easily into her flow by now, will often digress, and explain that the Tans were the scum of the earth, a ragtag group of rapists, child molesters and cannibal killers, dredged up by a youngish Winston Churchill, Secretary of State for War at the time, from the very bottom of the English penal system and unceremoniously dumped upon a pristine and idealistic Irish populace who were famed worldwide for their love of freedom, drinking and *crack*, and for singing songs, while drinking, about the same. The Tans were mostly famed for committing heinous atrocities such as burning down orphanages, shooting babies, and torturing men of fighting age with rusty bayonets and deviously placed farming implements. And here she might add, Saving your presence.

In quieter tellings, the Mother of Jay has said simply that the Black and Tans were mostly made up of traumatised World War I veterans, still only boys themselves. Although in the public telling, with a wild island audience enthralled, a tame Tan version like this could provoke a furious volley from the elderly listeners in the corner with the cloth caps and carefully cradled stout. Traumatised, me arse! Tell 'em about the Ringaskiddy Six!

Either way, hiding from the Tans was not a good thing to do. Especially when the Tans have already seen you scrambling over the wall, twenty paces ago. But that August night in 1920 was tense and nervous, full of irrationality and high-pressure missteps. Hot for starters. Foreign hot and freakish. African hot. And the two of them, those boys, the pity of it all, on their hunkers in the undergrowth, twig-snappy and parched, with breaths held tight. Like hide and seek in days gone by, when everything was short pants and conkers, and killing was only in the soft-spoken thrill of a candlelit bedtime.

And neither are they entirely innocent, Seamus and Dessie 'The Rabbit'. They had, she says, dancing nicely over details, found themselves, earlier, in the midst of a fine rake of boys who pelted the RIC barracks with rocks and bottles while shouting inflammatory phrases such as *Airin guh braw* and Brits Go Home and The Black and Tans Have Relations with Their Mothers. Thus the sight of Seamus and Dessie's hopeless attempt at instant camouflage is nothing less than the proverbial red rag to the savage Tans who, true to their reputation, proceed to deliver a feverish, bloodthirsty beating to the bottle-throwing boyos.

The Mother of Jay usually allows the tale to hang there, to let the audience imagine the worst, before she engineers a crashing cut to take us right inside the barracks itself, where the Tans have expertly strung up Seamus and Dessie 'The Rabbit' via a deceptively simple rope-and-roof-beam system, and are whacking them to blazes, wanting to know all about their IRA contacts, and the whereabouts and the exact nature of their next IRA operation.

But Seamus and Dessie 'The Rabbit' were good boys. Card-carrying members of the IRA, yes, she says, turning to the people, her people, the people of the West, but back in them days who wasn't? Feckin right you are, Deirdre, comes the barked response from a sullen cloth cap in the corner.

So Seamus and Dessie, good boys that they are, handle the Tans like old pros. They speak only in Gaelic, and say the rabble-rousing mantra *chucky or law* around a million times, even when they're getting bashed in the mouth with the wooden butt of an Enfield rifle that belongs to Lance Corporal Charlie Briggs. He's a big human specimen, Briggs, and very much the villain of the piece. With an enormous black bristling moustache, Stalin style, and the huge arms of a pre-war docker, now exposed as he paces distractedly around the room, and thumps free from his two suspects every shade of shit known to man. Saving your presence.

At this point, sensing a rise in room temperature, and that her people are really lapping it up, the Mother of Jay goes out on a limb and does Lance Corporal Briggs in action. With a roughly emulated English accent, in the style of *My Fair Lady*, she delivers the lines, Cam on, you bleeding micks! Am ganna get the bleeding troof ah of ye summ'ow! So you baggas best pay me sam bleeding attention, and ansa my bleeding questions! Then she mimes the repeated shoving of a blunt object into a soft object. The crowd are loving it.

Thankfully, she says, nothing works. He's tried every card with the lads, Briggs, but nothing can get through the forcefield of incessantly chanted *chuckies*. Eventually, Briggs leaves the room and, after some muffled exchanges from behind a thick wooden door with a weary, sleepy staff sergeant, he strolls nonchalantly back inside and announces that the boys are free to go. Dessie 'The Rabbit' says his first words of English in hours, and thanks the Lord for small mercies. He half collapses with relief and turns to Seamus who responds only with a look of trance-like mesmerism on his boyish features.

Now, this is where the tale becomes to many ears, but not mine, a bit fanciful in the telling. And so the Mother of Jay, a consummate yarn spinner, and a human barometer for the moods and shifts in the hearts and souls of her listeners, will acknowledge this and explain that this is simply the way that the old

33

shcale has always been told, down through the years. And you really don't want to mess with that. In short, she says, dropping her voice down low in startlingly sombre seriousness for the first time in the telling, the story is bigger than just her, or just them: Because Seamus Farrell, the grandfather of Jay, had a religious vision, right there in the cell.

Like the visitation of the Holy Spirit in the village of Knock in 1879, or the angel fellas that take Patrick Swayze by the hand at the end of *Ghost*, this vision is a benign floaty presence that comes into the room from behind Lance Corporal Briggs. It's a glowing light, in flowing robes, humanoid in outline. Your classic religious apparition. It has a voice too. Apparently feminine. Soft and soothing. And it speaks these words. Three words. Directly to Seamus Farrell. Be not afraid.

Be not afraid.

The full speech, in fact, is longer than that. And here the Mother of Jay, highly theatrical in delivery as always, announces with a ghostly hush, Be not afraid. Be not afraid tonight. The light. You must wait for the light!

The light in question, in Seamus Farrell's mind, without equivocation, *gon doubt awoyne*, is simply the light of dawn. And thus the instruction to wait for the light was a warning from the heavens, meaning that the grandfather of Jay was to stay put, in the slammer, until the morning. And at all costs.

Typically, when he tells Dessie 'The Rabbit' that he is about to refuse the offer of freedom and instead remain in the enemy cell all night long, his bosom buddy is horrified. Torn between utter incredulity and muted hysteria, Dessie hisses through his teeth, in the presence of Briggs, Feck sake Farrell, are you havering? We need to get far away from these murdering *sassanocks* while we've still got the feckin legs beneath us!

But Dessie 'The Rabbit' has already lost the battle, and the nineteen-year-old grandfather of Jay, who is also, in his spare time, a fierce man for the prayers and one with an impeccable knowledge of Marian devotions and Seven Sorrows rosaries, is now officially on a mission from God, and will not be deterred. Nothing, not even the action end of Briggs's Enfield butt, will change his mind. He is staying.

Soon after 2 a.m., a decidedly exasperated Dessie 'The Rabbit' bids his bleeding friend farewell, and is released without charge, while the grandfather of Jay is given another foam-flecked punch-about by the apoplectic Briggs. He is then tossed into a tiny box cell, at the back of the building, from where he hears two large and unmistakable metallic bangs echo ominously through the still night air.

The Mother of Jay pauses there. The audience, her audience, her people, and her son, especially her son, all of them, in all times and in all tellings, all of them feel it, the gut punch to come. The Tans, she says in a whisper, let Dessie 'The Rabbit' make it as far as the main street. Under cover of darkness, they shot him twice. Once in the head. Once in the spine. Both from behind.

Seamus Farrell sat in his tiny, cramped and bloodied cell, and cried. He cried for Dessie 'The Rabbit'. And for himself too. He cried to his Holy Mother Mary, and said that it was too much for a lad like him to bear. Why him? Why had he been chosen instead of Dessie? For what reason had he been kept alive?

Seamus is collected the next morning by over a hundred aggrieved and deeply proprietorial villagers. They meet first at the church, and then turn up en masse, in order to guarantee that the dreaded Tans don't try anything untoward during the hand-over. Seamus, overnight, has become a hero. His survival is non-negotiable.

Seamus himself is, by the same token, as the poet Yeats would say, changed, changed utterly. He limps out of the cell, a mass of cuts, bruises and breaks, and, within weeks, leaves the Cork and Kerry region altogether. He moves north, and settles in Ballaghaderreen, County Roscommon, where he gets a job as a labourer on a dairy farm and eventually marries Mairead Dillon, a seamstress, and raises a small but devoutly Catholic family of two daughters, called Maudie and Deirdre. The latter eventually becomes known, to me at least, as the Mother of Jay.

And yet, all the way through his sad and unfolding life, Seamus is troubled deeply by this very real and very explicit intervention from on high. The questions never stop. Year in, year out. Why me? Why save me? What mission? Until finally, thankfully, the answer arrives in his sixty-eighth year, direct once more from God, clear as a bell on a cold spring Saturday morning in rural Ireland, just hours before the wedding ceremony of his young daughter Deirdre.

And the message from God, explicitly and boldly, states that Seamus Farrell was saved because he was carrying within him the secret of ...

'Jay!'

'Jay! Jay! Jay!'

That's Ree. He is whispering as loud as he can. It would, in fact, be easier to use his normal speaking voice. It's the small hours of the morning on Easter Monday, 5 April 1999, and Ree's head is jutting forward, between the two fragile glass doors, slightly ajar, that define the boundary between both bedrooms, and help bolster the illusion that Jay and Ree are actually occupying different living spaces.

There is fear in his voice. A brittle edge. It doesn't help that it's thundering outside, rain pouring down, with bangs and flashes in rapid succession. The atmosphere created is of the need to be tucked in button-tight, held close and safe, while the mind imagines and dreads the darkest, wettest, knife-flash world of black beyond.

Jay has been dreaming of Grandad Farrell, his demons and his deeds. He will later suspect that these dreams were sparked by that earlier evening's conversation with Fr Francis on the teatime telephone. By the father's quiet yet consistent demand, yet again, the umpteenth time in months now, for Jay to return home for the first time in nearly a decade of exile, to see the Mother of Jay. Finally, in his hour of need, without wife or child to his name, Christ-like indeed, to come back to the hearth, to return to the bosom of home.

Ah, come back to us now, *me auld segosha*, Fr Francis eventually says, half singing, when he knows that Jay is not biting. Not now, not ever. The idea of Jay ever coming back, seemingly impossible, and always so, from the start, from the very first word of the big fight. But while the conversation dries up, he is left with the seed. The very idea of home. The eternal return.

And so, the sights and sounds of the Farrell dream world – wild violent drama in firework bursts of bruise-blackened purples – drop away like stone the minute he hears Ree's voice. Jay. Jay. Riven with fear.

Someone at the buzzer! says Ree. And as Ree speaks, the buzzer sounds from the hallway. Eeeeech. Eeeeech. Always shocking, no matter what time of day. Like the children's board game, Operation. When one goes for the funny bone. But even more so.

Who? Jay asks.

One of yours! says Ree.

A mick?

Big time, he replies, adding with a slight snarl of confusion, says the name is The Clappers!

37

5

The Early Hours of Easter Monday, 5 April 1999

The Clappers? Jay repeats, aloud. Downstairs? At the door? Now?

Jay is not unaware, somewhere in the back of his mind, that he sounds like the Mother of Jay, at the start of the bad days, when the repetition of facts became loop-the-loop questions. He apologises to Ree, and to Wendy, and tells them to go back to bed, and that he will deal with The Clappers. Ree shrugs, still halfshaken, and tells Jay that he's lucky that Roo isn't here, because he'd crack some skulls over this. Jay says again, Sorry, and, keen to avoid a building-wide scandal, prances, quickly and barefoot, down the communal staircase in purple paisley Marks & Spencer boxer shorts and a bright green T-shirt emblazoned with the phrase, 'Emotional Boy Rock Can Save the Planet'.

Shauna bought Jay the T-shirt from a tiny stall in Camden Market, in the closing days of their relationship. She said that it was supposed to bring him out of himself, and transform his interactions with the world into a lighter, less onerous experience. He could tell that something wasn't right. He knew, for one, that those words were not Shauna's but were the second-hand cast-offs from the many psychotherapy sessions she enjoyed with the renowned North London-based but Danish-born psychotherapist Dr Ghert Rasmussen, BPsych (Hons), CPsychol BPS. Shauna had been seeing him, in a professional capacity, for over four months. Bonnie was over two years old, and struggling. As were Jay and Shauna. Having someone as special as Bonnie was comparable to the shock of having a normal child, times a million, Dr Ghert had once told Shauna. No relationship could withstand that. Jay was mostly silent on the subject of Dr Ghert. Occasionally, after listening to some more of the good doctor's advice, second-hand from Shauna, he would simply sneer the words, 'Dr Ghert Rasmussen, BSerious Feckin Bshit.'

Most of Jay's telly friends said that the T-shirt was the gayest thing that they'd ever seen on a straight man. And two sizes too small, at least, even though the label claimed that the Lycra material ensured that the size was 'Uni-fit'. 'Uni-fit for a feckin Munchkin' is how Jay described it first, standing there, spray-chested in the full-length bedroom mirror. But Shauna just swished up beside him and told him that skin-tight was all the rage, and that it was a statement piece, and that we were all metrosexuals now.

Jay has been living with Ree and Roo for nearly fourteen long and momentous weeks, since arriving at their door in a traumatic stupor at the end of December 1998, then in the midst of a dizzying legal assault from the solicitor of Ghert, who was pushing through the divorce of Shauna from Jay, decree nisi to decree absolute, in a breathtaking seven weeks. The Bonnie smell and Bonnie glow was still clinging to Jay's shoulder, to the crook of his neck.

He had looked into Bonnie's eyes, her soul-piercing saucer eyes, as if expecting, hope against all hope, at this moment of departure, a sudden word or a sound beyond the usual gasp, rasp or gurgle. He whispered to her his own words, Bonnie, Dadda loves you.

She said nothing, of course, her familiar half-smile of silence belying the monumental strains and stresses so far. The doctor visits. The clinic. The panic. The endlessly filled notebooks, documenting every gesture. The word-training, daily, cuddled down by the fireplace in the safe space of their pink-painted flat in Notting Hill Gate. And Jay, with all his growing Meeja Man pride, holding up apples, saying Ah-pil, ah-pil, into Bonnie's face, almost spitting out the sounds, as if, he said, she was a complete mentler, even though he knew, in his heart, that he was the eejit and she was the smart one, sitting in silence, just smiling, and knowing. And he'd catch it, that look in her eyes, all the time. That half-smile in silence that seemed to say that some day he'd know what she knew, but not now.

When he first told Jane about Bonnie's silence, she immediately went for the Greeks, and the river Lethe, the river of forgetting, the river, she said, from which we drink before birth. Jane said that maybe, such was the completely useless nature of Bonnie's birth, that maybe Bonnie had accidentally taken some of the infinitesimal pre-birth ever-space with her, and retained some of the primal knowing that is obviously manifested in her ongoing silence. Why speak, Jane said, when your awareness is total, from alpha to omega?

When Jay told Shauna, rushed at her with the news, the sheer silly optimism, the distraction, she was furious. Raging. How dare he discuss their daughter, and their problems, with that bitch? That pretentious bitch? That husband-kissing, marriage-wrecking bitch! And their birth too? Bonnie's birth? Shauna's trauma? With that bitch? Has Jay completely lost his mother-fucking mind, man?

It felt useless by then. Everything an aggravation. The relationship seemingly done and dusted. Broken down by gaps and silences from Bonnie care and Bonnie pain, hopes killed by a plethora of disappointments and blame, and painful lacks, and words unsaid over wounds so deep. Until finally, it was battered to death by the intervention of, according to Jay, a devious Danish bastard psychiatrist-cum-pervert with nothing but hubby-hate and hot young fanny on his mind. And so they ended, in record-breaking time, leaving Jay alone, standing there in front of Ree and Roo in the Yuletide season, smiling and shaking in the obvious stupor of quietly reverberating shock.

The flat-share is comfortable. Three bedrooms, off the Cromwell Road. A giant white terrace that appears all swish and Hugh Granty, but up close is flaky grey and mildew green, and inside smells of wet carpets and wino piss. When Bonnie came to visit for the first time, in mid-January 1999, Jay rushed her in and up the stairs, like it was a big game. He told her to hold her breath, and that they were actually swimming, underwater, all the way up to the flat door. She giggled in his arms and seemed to think it a hoot.

Ree and Roo are Africans, from Kenya, although they speak with the plummiest accents Jay has ever heard. In fact, Roo, for a joke, when he's being mock-shocked, sometimes says, 'Sink me!' in the fashion of the actor Anthony Andrews in *The Scarlet Pimpernel*. Roo explains that this is called 'being ironic'. To which Jay replies that he understands the concept implicitly because, after all, he works in telly, which is a very ironic place.

Once, Roo was demonstrating, on a rain-sodden Saturday morning, just before Bonnie drop-off, how to slice an onion the African way (into a million little cubes). As he practised his technique on a heavy breadboard in the cramped galley-style kitchen, he began to confess the tale of his latest romantic misadventure, which culminated with his 'unfortunate young paramour' expressing the opinion that she was owed more commitment from Roo than two phone calls and a single Sunday-night trip to the cinema. 'I mean, sink me, Jay!' Roo suddenly said, slamming down the vegetable knife with barely suppressed fury. 'I don't know where they get the nerve!'

Back home in Kenya, the Otienos used to be super rich, according to Roo, one of the most well-known families in the country, and certainly the bigwigs of the Machakos diocese, with servants and the works and a huge plantation just forty or so miles south east of Nairobi. But their dad lost it all when Moi was re-elected president in 1992, and became furious with Mr Otieno Snr for pillorying his campaign speeches in the local media and thus made sure that he was fired from his job as a high-flying brain doctor, and took away his house and everything he had. Roo, the older brother, a graduate of Oxford University who works in the City, says that the parents still have serious money hidden all over the place, and could have set up shop permanently in a large London mansion if they wanted to, instead of landing their two boys in a grotty Kensington flat-share.

The first words that Jay heard from Roo's mouth, as he shuffled blankly over the threshold, were, 'Is that the mick?' It was supposed to be an official interview for the free room, but was no more elaborate than Roo telling Jay that he was unusual, because not many single white men would share a flat with two blacks. There was a pause of uncertainty, after which Roo laughed, and then punched Jay in the shoulder, and told him to relax, he was being ironic.

On the first night Jay sat with Roo on the sofa and shared a six-pack of Roo's Diamond White cider. They discussed Roo's unconscionably early work hours, his potentially enormous Christmas bonus, and the thrilling reality of Jay's televisual career. They watched Jay's copy of *In the Name of the Father*, during which Roo was repeatedly outraged by the treatment meted out to Daniel Day-Lewis and all the other micks. Jay had yet to tell Roo anything genuine about his own existence, about his time with Shauna, or about the many weekends that Roo would soon be spending, however briefly, in the company of Jay's eccentric, limping, and groaning toddler, Bonnie.

Instead, they spoke about women, and dating, and joked about how important it was to take revenge on the evil legacy of imperialism through the subversive power of intercourse. They both recited lines that they might use on such an occasion.

Oh yeah, minority this babe! said Roo.

How would you like some oppressed Irish sausage for your troubles? said Jay.

And a bit of blacky, too, eh? Oh yeah! You like that?

And so they sat there, the two of them, sprawled out on the couch, drinking strong cider and making sex-related puns, until Ree waltzed into the room with his real-life girlfriend Wendy, and Roo stood up and announced that he was heading off into the West End to spend some of Jay's cash deposit on cocaine and white women.

Jay has a better relationship with Ree. He's softer, Ree. Quieter. He works in an accountant's office, and his room is separated from Jay's by a flimsy pair of double glass doors, over which are draped all manner of blankets, towels and rugs to give the impression of two genuinely separate living environments. They can, nonetheless, hear everything that happens in each other's rooms, at all times, with near-crystal clarity. Even when Ree is engaged in the art of intercourse with Wendy, and when Jay is desperately trying to rock Bonnie back to sleep at four o'clock on a Saturday morning.

Although, despite this, usually Jay can read, or listen to the radio, or stare sadly into space and think of Shauna's eyes without being entirely disturbed by Ree's intercourse. He's too much of a gent for that, Ree. Unlike Roo, who lives three rooms away from Jay but makes it sound like feckin sexual Armageddon whenever he's managed to secure some company for the night.

The women! says Jay, recounting these nocturnal episodes to Jane, and Stevie Fitz, and the rest of the crew. The women are, like, screaming their heads off, all, Jesus Christ! And, oh, my, fucking, God! And Roo's in the background, swearing and cursing, and calling them filthy names, mostly bitches, and telling them how much they like it.

But Wendy, says Jay, is too classy for that. She's a nurse by day, a right laugh by night, and totally political, and into documentaries, and always popping her head in through the double doors, with a knock first of course, to invite Jay into their room to hop up onto the bed and watch on Ree's prized video player a film about a kid on Death Row in the Deep South who was framed by the cops, or something about Chernobyl, or even a bizarre French entry that was nothing more than close-ups of insects pushing balls of dung through the grass.

She's taken Jay's side too, in the marital split, and is of the view that Shauna sounds like a tricky American fish all right, and that giving birth to a brain-damaged baby is no excuse for hopping into the sack with the first healthcare professional that comes your way, and that dads get a really rough deal in the courts these days, which is why Jay has been royally screwed and should be marching every weekend, or chaining himself to public monuments, or at least going to single-dad support groups.

Jay, as is his way, often struggles for words during these pep talks. He usually grunts, says that he's doing fine, that his relationship with Shauna is getting more civil by the minute, and that he doesn't want to make matters worse, with lawyers and the like, and that maybe, just maybe, there is some hope. For him and Shauna. Wendy pats him on the hand like a mammy and says that she understands, but Jay has heard her, through the glass double doors at night, whispering intimately to Ree and telling him that Jay is still in shock from the break-up, and that she knows what shock looks like, because she sees it, up close, every day on the ward.

Ree, inititally, was not very keen on the idea of using the flimsy glass double doors as a conduit between rooms. He felt it was over-friendly. In the early days he made a point of getting up from his bed, and marching out of his room and around to Jay's official bedroom door.

It was only something as unsettling as Bonnie's midnight croup that eventually forced Ree through the doors. He popped his panicked head inside and asked Jay if he needed an ambulance call-out, or the impromptu services of his half-sleeping yet highly trained partner. The sound of Bonnie wailing with throat pain, bawling non-stop in between intermittent bronchial barks – like a particularly portly seal getting thwacked across the back of the head – all in the small hours of a dark January morning, was seemingly enough to overturn any sense of household decorum.

After that it was open season. Practically every night. He'd come in, or Jay would go in. Or mostly they'd just leave the door ajar, and pass comments to each other, like two old washer-women on either sides of the Liffey in a Dublin long gone. Jay would moan about the day's filming duties, and the fact that the previous afternoon's tapes had been filled with everything other than actual interesting and arresting footage, while Ree would complain about tube journeys, office air-conditioning, and his desire to leave the world of accountancy for greater things.

At least you've done it! Ree would say. At least you're living the dream!

Thus, when Ree sticks his head into the room on the night in question, in the early hours of Easter Monday Morning, the action itself is nothing new. It is the words 'The Clappers' that throw Jay. The last words he thought he'd ever hear in this place.

And there are Easter eggs too. For Bonnie, two of them, one Yorkie and one Buttons. They sit on the junk-sale wooden desk, right next to Jay's new, and very first, home computer. The computer was Jane's idea. She said it was vital for his profile, and would make the meeja folk take him seriously. He didn't use it much, though. He liked starting lists and writing out running orders. He rarely sent emails. He tried watching pornography, mostly images on his monitor of unsmiling women in underwear who seemed to speak directly to impulses forged among the purloined catalogues and bathroom lock-ins of his own adolescence. Yet these images appeared so reluctantly, at such a sluggish rate of reveal, down the screen, pixellated line by pixellated line, like a kind of strange cyber striptease, that they produced in Jay nothing but apathy and a sickly, yearning remembrance of the beating eroticism that he once shared with Shauna.

He put the Easter eggs in the fridge on Easter Sunday afternoon. He was worried that the heat would soften them, and perhaps spread the dusty white lines of sugar damage over the surface. He didn't want, he decided, Bonnie's first experience of a proper honest-to-goodness Easter egg to be compromised in any way.

He got an enormous thrill from the very act of buying the eggs. He had to stop himself from standing in front of the blank-faced Sainsbury's girl and saying, They're for my daughter, she isn't really allowed chocolate, so this is a big deal. My daughter, love saying that, my daughter, makes me weak with pride, my beautiful daughter. Already, can't believe it, two and three quarter years. Can't wait to see her face, her huge eyes, when she sees all this chocolate, this thing that is never seen by her two-and-three-quarter-year-old eyes, because of the sugar, which might, or

46

might not, interfere with the painfully slow recalibration of minor motor skills that her so-called condition inhibits.

Shauna, my ex, has been on to the doctor and they've said that an egg or two won't kill her, not this time, just this once, and then we had the chat, where Shauna decided that I could be the one to give her the eggs and I nearly cried with happiness and nearly told her that she was a good woman and that I still loved her, a thousand times yes. We were on the phone so she couldn't see my red flushing face, and I just said something thick like cool, or like no probs, but inside I was going fecking ace times a million, and had to stop myself from running to the shops straight away, then and there, to buy the eggs themselves, but here I am now, buying these eggs, and I have a place all ready for them at home in my flat, in my room. I can't wait to get them home and put them on my desk and stare at them, and imagine Bonnie's face when she sees them first, and when I tell her, dead-casual style, that they're for her, all for her, a Yorkie and a Buttons egg, all for her.

Jay apologises to Ree and to Wendy, and flounces down the stairs in his giant M&S boxer shorts and spray-on T-shirt. Not that he is bothered at all about how he looks as he steps across the cold, cracked marble floor of the front porch, and reaches slowly down towards the double-door locks, like a man condemned. He watches The Clappers in silhouette through the steamy security glass, a hefty shadowy form rocking excitedly from side to side, as Jay clunks and unclunks his way towards their reunion.

The door, at last, swings open. There is no lightning flash. No thunderclap. Just rain. And The Clappers. Standing there, storm-soaked to the skin, yet beaming like a child. And after ten years and not a single line, or word, of communication between then, this is what Jay gets:

'Who the feck have you come as? The feckin jolly green bender!'

No surprises there.

She hasn't changed a bit.

Guess what, Mammy? I'm a feckin builder. How's that for progress? A builder! Technically, for now, I'm more of a sweeper-upper. But, well, good aul Finula from Castlerea came round to the flat in early January and, real mysterious like, just gave me a scrunched-up piece of paper with a phone number on it. And, Mammy, I have to say, it was a bit like finding yourself in the middle of a drug deal from *Miami Vice*, because when you rang the number all you got was a scratchy English voice who told you to be at the entrance to Green Park tube station at six the following morning. And when I got there, still in the dark and dusty early hours, didn't I find a load of other lads like me, in new boots, rubbish jeans and wide eyes, all staring at the floor, and not making eye contact, except for the moment when a big white transit pulled up with a blond-haired Paddy in the front who shouted out, 'Well? Who wants to work?'

The blond fella, Darren from Dublin, who's quite the Jackeen, clearly took a shine to me and a lad called Titch, who's Australian and dead chatty, because he kept us in the van right until the end of a million different drop-offs. At each one Darren would just jump out, reef open the sliding door, look in at all us anxious lads, and say, 'Ruy, youze two, ow now!' in that real rough Dublin way they do, like Brendan Grace doing The Bottler, only each time he'd glare at me and Titch and say, 'No! Not youze two!'

And so, for the next ninety minutes, I listened to Titch blather away about the skills he'd already collected on site (drilling, cracking, sweeping and forklift driving), while I stared through the transit's tinted back windows and watched the enormity of London roll by in a choppy montage of exotic-sounding street signs, from Golden Square to Prince Albert Road, St Pancras Way to Seven Sisters Road, to Hampstead, Highgate, Hendon and Mill Hill, until it all kicked off on Elstree Road when Darren leapt from the front seat and battered this posh lad's white beemer to pieces with a feckin hurley stick because the posh lad had cut him up twice, and made filthy hand gestures out the window each time.

You should've been there, Mammy. Terrifying stuff. Darren's whacking the side of the beemer and screaming, 'Don't you fuckin mew-ev, or I will, on my fuckin daddy's life, give you such a dig, that you will fuckin die!' He stops whacking and warns the posh lad that he knows some 'serious Brit-killing bastards' and if the posh lad even thinks of calling the cops he'll send the Brit-killing bastards round to blow off the kneecaps of anyone found alive in his house – man, woman or chisler. He then marches back to the van, jumps into the driver's seat as if nothing's happened, and barks in through the wire mesh, 'Alruy, lads?'

After arriving at Hunton Bridge, North London, Darren informed us that we were about to indulge in a bit of off-the-books gardening at his own, frankly massive gaff. Although when he said gardening he really meant removing, by spade and back power alone, an enormous alpine-sized pile of builders' rubble from where he'd dug out an Olympic-sized, outdoor-yet-indoor swimming pool, with sauna and jacuzzi attached. He left us with two spades, and a pickaxe, and said he'd be back at around five with some cash and a train ticket back to Green Park.

And that was that. We dug, we axed, we tipped, we chopped, we tipped, we dug, we scooped, non-stop, no break, no food, no water, all day. Occasionally, we slashed. But just into the bushes. It was savage work, and by the early afternoon even Titch had stopped talking. By then I knew everything about him, though mainly about his mam with no money back in Melbourne, his no dad at all, and his incredibly good luck with the ladies. A new girlfriend every week, he said. Big time.

He asked me about my luck with the ladies and I said nothing much. I told him that I hadn't had a wan in ages. Which turned out, on reflection, to be gas timing. Because at the end of that very day, with hands ripped to pieces in welts and blisters, and back nearly broken on me, I met a wan who I kind of fancied at first sight, and who I thought, then and there, eye to eye, might yet become my first real actual girlfriend in England.

Her name is Diana, like the Princess. She's originally from Morocco, so she's super-tanned and drop-dead gorgeous (picture Whitney Houston mixed with Ann Doyle, and you're almost there). She works for Darren, and I met her that day, at five exactly, when she arrived in a Fiat Uno with a couple of train tickets and some small brown envelopes (for me and Titch, thirty-five quid each – pretty handy for a day's work, ha?).

We started chatting immediately, or at least she started chatting to me, about how interested she was in Ireland, because her aunt married an Irish fella who was always bringing Galtee cheese and Tayto crisps over to Agadir when she was a teenager. I was dead cool during these early bits, and made a brilliant joke about the Gaelic translation for Galtee Cheddar being either Hard Cheese or Tough Shite. She was mega flirty too, like a proper wan that you'd see on, say, *Falcon Crest*, all hair-swishy and smiley and that. She wrote her phone number down on my pay packet, super classy, and the last thing she said, as she swooped down, real glamour-puss style, into the Fiat Uno, was, 'Use it!' Meaning her number.

Darren was thrilled with the amount of old shite that we dug out of his garden, so he kept me and Titch on as his star pupils. He dropped us off the very next morning to a cushty hospital-conversion gig in Watford and boosted our pay packets to forty pounds a shift, and promised goodo that he'd only break our legs, rather than kneecapping us, if we ever displeased him.

Meanwhile, I did indeed use Diana's number, calling it a couple of times, to tell her about growing up in Ireland, and how it was all just non-stop *crack ogus keyole*, and how *crack ogus keyole* was a popularised ancient Irish phrase for 'fun and partytime', which best described the essence of life on the island of Ireland for most of its existence. At the end of the third call, however, I went all quiet and pausey, and cleared my throat around twenty times, before grabbing the bull by the horns and inviting her to the fecking pictures. On Titch's advice, I chose the Odeon, Ken High Street, and a picture called *Ghost*. Titch said that it was dead romantic, with Patrick Swayze and Demi Moore, and that he'd already brought three wans to it, and that each time he'd ended the evening up to his tonsils in the wans. Not that I was planning to go anywhere near Diana's tonsils at that early stage in the courtship. As you know yourself, Mammy, I'm not exactly a playboy when it comes to the wans. I've only had, say, roughly, one almost-girlfriend, and that's if you include Mairead Ni Davitt. My main overriding fear was that Diana would be expecting all sorts of sophisticated sexual shenanigans on our very first date, and that I'd be forced, at the action end of a bra strap, into revealing my hand as a complete romantic novice, and that it would all fizzle out in a series of mal-coordinated grabs and rubs and squeezes. Or worse.

Well, Mammy, it was worse. An absolute disaster. And don't get me wrong. It had great potential, and a fablas beginning. *Ghost*, for instance, was a triffic picture. Although, I'm learning quickly that they don't actually call them pictures over here like the way the Irish and the Yanks do. Instead, they call them fillums. Either way, Titch was right, and *Ghost* seemed to be one of the best possible fillums to which you could ever take a wan, on a first date.

In a nutshell, you've got this lad, Patrick Swayze, who gets shot and killed, and his girlfriend, played by Demi Moore, is in bits. She's normally happiest alone at night in her pants doing pottery. But whenever she and Swayze can't sleep they just stick on this super-smoochy love song on an ancient jukebox record player thing and start, well, having a *seshoon mah*, right in the middle of her midnight pottery session. It kind of makes a shag of the flower vase she was doing, but because her hands are all wet and mucky it sort of adds to the randy atmos.

I was morto during the entire *seshoon*, actually sweating too, and cursing Titch, the Aussie fecker, for sending me to such a filthy flick, and worrying that Diana was thinking that I was a real perv who wanted to get her in the mood with some arts-and-crafts-themed sexual hijinx. Thankfully, when the scene was done, Diana reached over and grabbed my hand, and gave it a light squeeze, which was her way of saying that everything was OK and I wasn't a perv. We held hands for the rest of the fillum, right up until the end, when the Swayze ghost solves his own murder with the help of this gas black wan, and finally, in the big ta-dah moment, makes a ghostly reappearance before Demi and tells her that he loves her, which was a thing he had hitherto been unable to do, for reasons known only to the scriptwriters of the fillum and the complex persona of the fictional Swayze ghost character himself.

After the fillum Diana drove me all the way from Kensington to the centre of London, the Soho area, to eat in a snazzy Italian restaurant called Pizza Express, where they play live jazz all the way through your meal, and if you don't want to have an actual starter you can have a plateful of lovely buttery bread lumps, called dough balls, just to, like, stuff you up goodo, so you feel nicely blocked to the back of the throat by end of the night.

Diana went on for ages about how moving it was to watch a fillum about the impossibility of a perfect love, and how she had been choking back the tears in the end, but hoping that I hadn't noticed. I told her that I was seriously moved too, and that fillums about the afterlife and couples not being able to be together always get to me. I rattle off a few of them, like *A Matter of Life and Death* or *Topper* with Cary Grant, and she goes all amazed that I know so much about the fillums. This makes me tell her, straightaway, about you and me and the fillum marathons we'd have every Saturday, and how we'd be cuddled up on the couch together, watching BBC2 through till midday, usually get two decent ones, definitely black and white, maybe an Ealing comedy, and then a break for lunch, followed by a switch to UTV and, mostly, a western, and you'd talk all the way through it, and tell me about Da, and how youze went courting almost exclusively to western fillums, and what a big cowboy fan he was, and how he'd sit me on his knee and bump me up and down while he was watching John Wayne and Gary Cooper and how he'd hand me back to you only when I got so screamy and distressed that I started ruining the fillum.

And the fairy cakes too. You'd never forget the fairy cakes. Make a right rake of them, twelve of them between us, just the two of us, halfway through the afternoon, stirring the arse off the mixture in a giant plastic bowl by your feet during the western, and then flinging them into the oven before the evening session begins.

I told her about the winter of 1987 too, when you returned from Dublin town with two massive feckin boxes in tow. One of them was a brand spanking-new Moulinex, which was the talk of the neighbourhood, and brilliant for whizzing stale bread into crumbs, cabbage into coleslaw, or, and this was the real clincher, making fairy-cake mix in a busy second. The other box was a Philips. A video player. For fillums. For watching as many fillums that we liked, exactly the kind of fillums that we liked. It was as if, in one fell swoop, our Saturday marathons were about to be taken to a whole new, industrial-strength level.

Diana's eyes popped out on stalks when I told her about the Philips and the Moulinex. She said that you sound like a brilliant mam, Mammy, and I went a bit coy and said, like, Oh, she has her moments.

Anyway, the night goes on like that. Totally brilliant. Tons of chat. Diana even offers to drop me home in her jammer – the same super-flash Fiat Uno, with a tape deck and everything. The upshot of which is that we stop outside my flat, engine off, seatbelts undone, and in my head, and I don't mind admitting this one bit, Mammy, I'm thinking, definitely, marriage material. She's just fablas, and the kind of girl I'd be dreaming of, all those years, up there, alone in the bedroom on the Cloonavullaun Estate.

I tell her that I'm dead sorry, but that part of the conditions of me renting out my own place from Finula from Castlerea is that I'm not allowed any visitor wans. She laughs, and leans over and gives the side of my head a long lingering stroke without saying a word. At this point I'll try to be delicate, Mammy, but we're all grown-ups now. Diana and I start snogging, a serious *seshoon mah*, right there in the Uno. In fact, it's not just snogging. We're baiting the faces off each other, sucking and chewing like there's no tomorrow and, as I say, I'm thinking wedding bells, serious wedding bells.

And then, just when it couldn't get any better, the most extraordinary thing happens. Diana reaches for my Budweiser belt buckle, the one that you gave me for my confirmation, Mammy.

I flinch, shoot bolt upright in the seat, and say nothing. I am hoping that she'll just be happy with opening the jeans, and won't go any further, like the way you might open a Jacob's biscuit tin for visitors on Stephen's Day, just, like, for effect, because you know that everyone's bloated from the turkey sangers and can't handle another morsel. Diana, fair play to her, can sense the sudden change in mood, and can no doubt spot the beads of sweat forming on my forehead. She tells me to relax, and that we don't have to rush into anything. She adds that we're just two people messing around in here, and that the last lad she was with, in the messing-around stakes, seemed to really enjoy, and God knows why, 'this'.

And this, Mammy, I'm afraid, is where you'll need a strong stomach and a decent cuppa to steady the nerves. For Diana's snake-like hand makes its way into my trousers all right, and into my feckin M&S boxers. But it doesn't stop there. It winds its way around the back and hovers dramatically over its intended target, before unleashing its secret weapon – a long probing index finger topped with a brutally unforgiving, varnish-coated fingernail.

Well, Mammy, I think you can get the picture. Sufficeth to say that I withstood the probing for fear of both offending Diana and revealing myself to be a completely unsophisticated gom who isn't yet up to date on the erotic traditions and localised customs of the indigenous peoples of North Africa.

Indeed, I tried, like the feckin gent I am, to return the favour, with a few politely delivered bum-pokes of my own, but as soon as I got me hand anyway near Diana's behind, she'd give it a right elbow out of the way. In the end, we finished up the kissing, and

Diana automatically removed her hand from my behind, like she was unplugging a dishwasher, and we just stared at each other for a bit, heads side to side on the seat rest, me flinching every time she tried to stroke my face with the pokey hand, and secretly thinking that I wouldn't mind meeting an old-fashioned girl, who was into mickeys and things.

Still, you can't go from marriage material to nothing at all in the space of one random arse-poke. I eventually broke the romantic silence by busily buckling up your belt and going, 'Same time next week?' At which point, Diana just burst out laughing, called me a big thick, and said she'd first have to run it by her boyfriend, Darren from Dublin.

Naturally, on the outside, I was cool as a cucumber, and went, 'Ah sure, I feckin knew that, Darren th'aul bollix, eh?' But inside, I was sick. I looked down at my kneecaps. Why did it have to be Darren?

Your Right-Hand Man,

Jay

Step Number Nine: Later in the Day, 5 April 1999

Jay and The Clappers are sitting in a rowboat, drifting down towards the central bridge-side barrier posts of the Serpentine lake, in London's Hyde Park. From a God's-eye perspective they are a speck among specks, defined by tiny imperceptible movements, and encased in a large, shapeless, green lake-splodge, like sun-kissed bacteria on a pleasant mid-afternoon petri dish.

The Clappers, naturally, is rowing. Rowing and talking. Talking incessantly. She is strong. A fine big girl. They called her that, a fine big girl, all her life, in the Land of Jay. Farmers, friends, uncles and brothers. Mostly men. It was a joke, at first, dished out during the early teen years, when a love of camogie, netball and water polo transformed her slender girlish frame into a thing, to me at least, of broad shouldered beauty, with the powerful legs and thick barrel chest to match. Sure isn't she a fine big girl, they'd say, always in earshot, while she stood on the makeshift podium, still in her togs and swimming cap, head bent for the gold medal, but eyes cast permanently downwards with shame, afraid to catch within the cat-calling crowd the disappointed frown of her own mortified mother.

Fine big girl. Another win for the camogie As. Fine big girl. Another St Aoife's netball trophy. Fine big girl. Runners-up in the county cup water-polo championship. Fine big girl. Until finally, during a tear-stained, Christmas-night confession, The Clappers was deemed due for a diet by the concerned yet inviolable edicts of that same anxious, occasionally distant, and noticeably slim-figured mother.

If I look like Mother, The Clappers would think, at least her inner mind would think, the one that rarely rises to the surface. If I can be more like Mother, then maybe she will love me. Really love me.

Diets begin, teams are abandoned, and greater unhappiness follows. The Clappers yo-yoes in size, is mired in sadness and self-hate, and eventually, triumphantly, refuses to relinquish the primal pleasure of pure physical power for the promise of approval that may never come. Broad and strong, a fine big girl, she finds solace in the salty rush of Feeny's batterburgers, the weekly dip in the icy North Atlantic, and the rowdy, boozy company of the Strandhill boyos – Jay, The Fox and Mickeleen – who rechristen her 'The Clappers', in place of Claire, and delight in her unbridled and unequalled strength, and tell her, with open smiles and uncruel eyes, that she has more balls than the lot of them put together. And for her, at least this is something, and so she grabs it, with both hands, and she goes, like the clappers, shaving her head into a blonde peroxide weapon, sealing her body within second-hand army fatigues, and drinking, always drinking, with the best of them, the last of them, under the table, onto the floor, and into McCloskey's car park for a late-night fist fight.

'Well, look the size of the colleen we got here, lads! Sure, aren't you a—'

SMACK!

Fine big girl, me arse.

Effortlessly, still talking, she heaves the boat through the water, and up against the bridge post with a single oar stroke. She is still broad, notes Jay, still strong underneath a Daz-white denim jacket, black leather trousers and biker boots. Although the blonde flat-top has softened into a sandy-brown skinner, and she wears make-up now, around the eyes, sky blue with a dash of turquoise, which deftly pitches her overall appearance into a fluctuating zone somewhere between Sinead O'Connor and the former wrestler and television entertainer known as Hulk Hogan.

The Clappers tells Jay, repeatedly, that she has made a fearless moral inventory of herself, that she has placed him, Jay, on the top of Step Number Eight, and that she is ultimately here for him, for Jay, to make it right with Jay, which makes this visit Step Number Nine.

I am here for you, Boss Man, she says, over and over. I want to make this right, like. I owe you, big time. You are my Step Number Nine. I am stuck and incomplete, in the face of God, as I understand him to be, until I make this right.

She ties the boat against the bridge post, on Jay's instruction. He comes here with Bonnie, almost every weekend, weather permitting, Mother of Bonnie permitting. It's their treat. Row to the bridge posts, tie up the boat, and lie back cloud-watching in silence, her with head against his chest, him prattling away about the dogs, the dinosaurs, and the ballet dancers floating overhead in creamy-white cloud puffs, and holding her hand, pointing them out, tracing them, and her giggling, never talking, but giggling all the same, a blessing, and an affirmation of presence, and both lying back, and just the weight of her, the physicality of her, being enough for him. To feel her on his chest, to know the weight of her, is to know she exists.

She's coming, of course. Today. In less than two hours. For an Easter Monday stayover with Jay, to receive her very first Easter eggs – actually, Easter egg, singular, for the morning began with an hysterical reflex yelp, provoked by the sight of The Clappers tapping away on Jay's new personal home computer, studiously searching for a 'meeting' in the local area, while simultaneously munching her way through Bonnie's precious, yet-to-be-delivered, Cadbury's Buttons egg.

'What? You mean this?' said The Clappers, casually holding up the last fragment of chocolate delight. She dismissed Jay's exasperation with a wave of her hand, and announced that she was loaded with cash, could buy a million Buttons eggs this very day, and that, besides, she needed chocolate, for the rush, for the buzz, to deal with the deep inner sadness in her life, now that she'd finally kicked the booze. Oh, and it wasn't just her, she said. The whole country's at it.

Tellin ye, she said. It's all change, Boss Man. The place is flush with cash. Multinationals, pop stars, rock stars, fillum stars, Coca Cola, Hewlett Feckin Packard, Boyzone, Westlife, Mickey Flatley and Daniel Fecking Day-Lewis. Flush, with cash. Which, between you and me, and anyone with half a brain in their head, means process work. Seriously, what's the first thing you do once you've met your material needs? Therapy. What do posh people do? Therapy. It's that simple. And now it's like the whole country has finally met its material needs, and realised what it's like to be posh. And so they've gone into process. And it's a beautiful thing.

As for my own process, she began, launching herself into the intricacies of a mother-daughter bond that wasn't right from the beginning – she was a big baby, a nine pounder, and a disappointment to a well-dressed icicle who was then craving a son. And on it went, through breakfast, with a brief pause for salutations, handshakes and heartfelt apologies to Ree and Wendy for the clamour and the chaos, then out of the building, and up into Kensington Gardens, where Jay tried to lift the mood with a perambulatory diversion past the very gates where, he said, everyone went mental after Lady Di's death, with entire families falling around the place in floods, screaming, 'Oh Jesus, Lord, no, say it isn't so! Not her! Why her? She was the best of us! The best of us!'

Jay, half chuckling, poked The Clappers in the arm and told her about the zany so-called 'interstitial comedy bite' that was filmed by his production team on the day of the funeral, during which they paid a German stand-up comedian to be deliberately controversial and ironic, and to say that he was really going to miss Lady Di, because she was brilliant at going to the gym, and looking at people through her fringe, only nobody understood that he was being deliberately controversial and ironic, and instead all those who heard him simply thought that this was the German way of paying your respects.

The Clappers, however, wasn't entirely interested in Lady Di, but by way of compensation, consistently referred to Jay, to an almost worrying degree, as the Boss Man, and commended him on how well he'd done for himself, what with coming over to London with nothing but a handful of dud addresses, and then rising from the filth and dirt of the sites to the glamour of the box itself. You couldn't make it up! said The Clappers. It's like something from a fillum!

The Clappers continued, barely a breath drawn, and said that, of course, the Irish do well wherever they go. And then she was off, back into the paradox of being part of a nation in process, and being in deep personal process herself, and being put in a position where she must constantly observe the wavering state of her own emotional equilibrium through a complex salmagundi of breathing, reflection and fearless moral inventorialising.

Roo will later inform Jay that The Clappers seemed to be exhibiting the central fundamental symptom of mental illness, namely, incessant self-analysis. In fact, Roo explained, elaborating further, all mental illnesses, especially all the modern ones, should really be renamed talky-selfy-non-stoppy disease, which is a literal translation from a Swahili phrase that almost means madness but not quite, because they don't actually have a word for mental illness in Swahili. In fact, says Roo, they don't actually have mental illness back home in Africa either, because, he explains, if someone starts 'banging on' about themselves and their processes, like the way they do in the West, everyone in the village simply gangs up on them and screams, 'Shut up, you boring old shitbag! We've had enough of your moaning, now go out and find some effing water for the community and stick your emotional equilibrium up your effing hole!' Which, apparently, usually does the trick and instantly cures the patient in question of even the most severe case of talky-selfy-non-stoppy disease.

The Clappers, however, is in a league of her own. She dazzled Jay, all the way to the jetty, with the ups and downs of the Twelve Step programme. How she 'hit bottom' by driving her mam's car, hammered out of her box at eleven in the morning, in through the main glass doors of St Attracta's Nursery School in Carrickbanagher, and was saved from an immediate and lengthy custodial sentence only by a concerned call to the Gardai from her Uncle Frank, a Fianna Fáil councillor, and by the fact, miraculous in itself, that the school was empty on the day – courtesy of a seasonal visit up to see Johnny Logan in panto at the Gaiety, in Dublin city.

She said that she had to break, naturally enough, from the Strandhill mob – a right bunch of booze-sodden enablers if ever there was. And that it was only in the quiet sanctity of the tea-room meetings in St James County Hospital, Roscommon, that she found the space and the support to believe in a power greater than herself that would restore her to sanity.

They climbed, gingerly, into the boat. The cheery, fresh-faced lake steward, with a chivalrous nod, proffered the oars to Jay, but they were gruffly snapped out of his hands by The Clappers, who muttered under her breath the sneering rejoinder that they were not living in *Brideshead Fecking Revisited* any more. Once they were on the lake, her lower lip trembled, and she talked about turning her life over to the care of God. She mixed powerful oar strokes with long effortless glides, deftly adjusting course with a dip and a jab, port or starboard, whenever they veered too close to the tiny mounted duck sanctuary, or the many giddy tourist pairs, yanking themselves around in hopeless hysterical circles.

She told Jay that the god she discovered in AA is the real god, and not the one they've been teaching in Ireland for a million years. This god is a benign, all-powerful force that cares for each and every one of us, and wants us to be the best person we can be, and wants us to achieve, and to strive, and to be successful. This god wants us to work for Hewlett Packard. Or be the new Boyzone. This god is all about us, and our life, and our successes. But in order to achieve these successes, we need to become pure, and to free ourselves from all our flaws. And it's a process that begins, she said, beaming, not trembling, right here in this boat.

'This, Boss Man, is Step Number Nine!'

Buzzing with excitement, and wide of eye, and with a remarkable barrage of words which, even to her dumbstruck listener, bore the tightly-honed hallmarks of a speech well learnt, The Clappers, over the next two to three minutes, still rowing, explained to Jay that he had topped her Step Number Eight, a list, self-compiled in ascending order of grievous offences, to remind her of those individuals who had suffered most at the brunt of her whiskey-addled and often sinister malfeasance. The list was mainly filled with leery publicans, unlucky barflys, DJs, dancers and bouncers, all of whom, courtesy of a thoughtlessly fired off and disparaging remark on the nature of The Clappers' imposing physical appearance – 'for a girl' – had experienced the full force of her teeth-smashing, skull-cracking, face-pulping retri-bution. No mercy.

Jay, however, continued The Clappers, was an easy choice for the top slot. 'But?' interrupted her subject, with palms raised upwards, and head shaking slightly, brow scrumpled somewhere between confusion and disagreement.

'No!' barked The Clappers, brusquely, adding, 'This is hard enough for me, Jay! Don't!' And on she went, listing the wedgies given, every one of them, on the beach in Strandhill, right after swimming, when the togs were sandy and at their most chafey, or the amount of times she whipped the barstool out from under Jay, and he never complained, even when he cracked his head on the back of a table in Madigans, and they had to take him to Dr Shaw's for stitches. She, The Clappers, was always behind it.

The strip gags, the burnt underwear, and the tied shoelaces. And he never said anything, never protested beyond calling The Clappers an aul bollix. And even the big fight with his mammy? The one that sent him fleeing from home and hearth? That was her fault too, for standing by and doing nothing, and for bring-ing Mairead along even though she knew the shite was going to hit the fan.

'Of course,' continued The Clappers, not missing a beat, 'I did all this because I was in love with you. I know that now.'

Jay nodded, very slowly. The Clappers added that Jay should not feel too flattered by this piece of information, as she wasn't exactly spoilt for choice with the Strandhill mob, noting that Mickeleen, to this day, is still barely pubic.

She explained, too, that beating Jay, and goading him, and rip-ping his pants off whenever she could, were just desperate attempts to make a deep soul connection and were intrinsically wrapped up, she had since discovered in process, with her low self-esteem, and her craving for approval from a feminine source that was not her mother.

'But?' said Jay again.

'Sorry!' snapped The Clappers, right back. 'Because you are, aren't you? Kind of feminine?'

The Clappers concluded, just as they neared the wooden bridge posts, that she had reconciled this wounded need for mother-love within, and was ready to move on with her life under the eyes of the new modern God, but that in order to do so she must make amends, must execute Step Number Nine, and that meant making it right for Jay, making everything right for Jay. When she said that last bit, she shot suddenly upwards and leant forward, a movement violent enough to send the boat into a sudden hefty wobble. She bent down again, right into Jay, face to face, rested a powerful hand on his thigh, and squeezed tight, with strong, round fingertips digging deep, while the mouth smiled, the blue eyes fizzed wildly and the voice announced, in something close to a threat, I am here for you, Boss Man. I want to make this right, like. I owe you, big time. You are my Step Number Nine. I am stuck and incomplete, in the face of God, as I understand him to be, until I make this right.

Jay, tentatively at first, compliments The Clappers on the pro-cessing work, but, nodding to his watch by way of illustration, suggests that they should unhook the boat, get back to shore, say their goodbyes any minute now, and that Jay should return to the flat as soon as possible to prepare for Bonnie drop-off. As he says this he reaches for the oars, but The Clappers holds his thigh even tighter, fingers almost bone deep.

'No!' she snaps. 'I'm going to make this right! Tell me,' she says. 'I want the whole truth. The whole story. About you, and that Yank wan!'

Jay winces. What about Bonnie?

'I said the truth,' sighs The Clappers. 'Not the feckin director's cut. You'll get back in time for Bonnie! Just give it to me! Ten minutes max! The truth!'

Ten minutes?

'Not a second more!'

Righto. Here's the ten-minute version.

7

Shauna and the Two Wolves

You are composed? Ready? Remember, there is no shame and no rules in here. You can cry all you like.

I'm not crying.

I know.

Really. I'm not.

Did you know that women in studies who admit to regular crying have lower rates of cancer than those who stay predominantly dry-eyed?

I did not. What about the men?

They didn't study the men.

Figures. Did you know that Paul has spent the last twenty years in psychotherapy?

Has it helped?

Well, it helped him realise that excess liquor consumption, self-hatred through failure, and the derisive needling of a dissatisfied wife were a punishing combination. He hit her only once, he said. But it was enough.

And he feels no guilt for this, now? Because of therapy? And you are angry because of this, no?

I am angry because Paul discovered, through twenty years of therapy, that on that day, that drunken afternoon, in his subconscious mind, he was not punching my mom flat in the face, but punching my mom's mom, who was the focus of all of his rage, of all his pent-up aggression. It just happened that my mom's face got in the way.

And what do you think about what happened on that day?

On that day, after clearing up the bloodstains, Paul made chilli beans for me and Chester, with rice and tacos. We ate them on the sofa, all three of us, while watching the Friday-night family movie, which was *Airport IV: The Concorde*. It was the first night of the summer holidays, and we were supposed to be on Gibson Island, with Mom's mom. All of us. The family. Like every year.

And every year, you had been happy there. You remember this happiness. This was an idyllic place for you, no? A safe place, magical, and it has become more so over time, in memories refined. And memories are good. Memory is our friend. But it is never passive, never objective. Memory protects us, guides us, tries to shape us and, if we are not careful, memory becomes us. What does memory tell you about Gibson Island?

It tells me about late-night dips, for everyone, with pancakes ready on our return, and the grown-ups drinking scotch and loudly pronouncing its many benefits, and how it warms the body from the inside after a cold and bracing dip, and us falling asleep under crisp white sheets, listening to a deafening chorus of insects and amphibians outside, and watching fireflies floating by the big bay windows, blinking green, on and off, for us, it seemed, for us, celebrating our arrival.

It's a beautiful thing, and this touches me. And yet, go further back, back into the pain, and ask yourself what does memory tell you about the night that Paul struck your mother?

It tells me that my bathing suit was already packed when I got up to my room. The books in the bottom, school books for summer reading, Shakespeare's *Lear* and *Henry V*, to get ahead for next semester, and to stick it to Nicole Henson. And my 'Blondie' beach towel, neatly folded over the books, also at the bottom of the loose black canvas bag, waiting for the final touches of carefully pressed Mom-chosen summer clothes, strictly skirts, T-shirts, sneakers, and one single emergency sweater. Chester's *Sesame Street* carry case was also ready. Mom had packed that too, just before.

And this movie? What, do you think, is the significance of this movie to you, and to your memory of this day?

We liked it. Despite everything that had happened that day, that afternoon, we liked it. We especially liked the bit when the Concorde, suffering from sudden hydraulic failure, has to do a high-stakes emergency landing in Paris, but through, like, a dozen orange stretchy nets on the runway that spring up for such an occasion. Paul even laughed, he laughed out loud when this comedy guy, a black guy, who's supposed to be funny because he's cowardly and black, starts praying beside a wealthy elderly lady. She turns to him and says, 'Why? I thought you were an atheist?' And he says, real cowardly like, 'What do I gots to lose?' Paul hooted at this, shook his head and sighed. Chester was already asleep between us.

It was a strange kind of magic, bad juju, or momentary madness. Because for a split second there, for a split, for half a split, somewhere between Paul's laugh, the comedy black guy, and the hissing, burring, buzz of the TV screen, I felt, just for that half split, that none of this had happened, that we were free, and that the horror of the real had evaporated completely into the giddy flickering bliss before me.

But it didn't last?

No, Paul put me to bed. Knelt down beside the bedhead, hands shaky, and contrite as ever, elbows deeply down on the mattress for support, his breath still humming of stale booze. He tried, maybe five or six times in a row, to complete a sentence that began, 'Thing about your mom and me . . .' Eventually he gave up, and opted for *Romance 101*, announcing instead that relationships, all relationships, are tricky things.

This is true.

After which he added that you can push a man only so far. He then held both my hands in both of his, like some sort of official ceremonial exchange, and he said it again, solemnly, like he was nauseous with the pressure of the moment, he said that really, it's true, that you can push a man only so far, and that I was to remember this lesson when I grew up, and when it came time for me to choose my own man. I said nothing. He left the room. Meanwhile Mom, of course, never came back.

And so, you have these two memories, these competing stories of Shauna's summer. The blissful and the traumatic. Which one is truth to you?

Hell, I dunno. Both?

Maybe. Or maybe, and more likely, it's as the Red Indians say.

Isn't that a little racist?

There is no racism in this space. Only freedom. But you've heard the story of the Red Indian boy and the two wolves, yes?

Sorry. No.

Oh good. Because this story applies to you, and to your memories of Paul, and your feelings for men in general. And if you understand it, really understand and internalise it, we may unblock you yet.

And?

And the story speaks of a Red Indian boy who—

Do we have to call him that?

As I was saying, this Red Indian boy is approaching adolescence, about to emerge into manhood, but is feeling all the difficulties, the conflict, and the angst that this implies. He is getting into fights. He will not do chores. He sulks in the corner of the teepee, morning to night. Naturally, his parents send him to the witch doctor.

70

Naturally.

The witch doctor is a wise man, a village elder of many years, and after a minute or two with the boy he offers a razor-sharp diagnosis. My child, he says, right now, whether you know this or not, your body is a husk, and inside it there is a battle raging, to the death, between two wolves. One of the wolves is compassion, serenity, charity, understanding, kindness and altruism. The other wolf is rage, selfishness, greed, superiority, pride and regret. These wolves will fight until one is dead, and the other is the victor, and is free to take control of the husk of you. This is certain. The boy, visibly panicked, falls to his knees and begs of the witch doctor, Which one is going to win? Tell me! I can see it in your eyes! You know it! Which one is going to win? Tell me! But the witch doctor simply smiles and says, Whichever one you feed.

What. The. Fuck?

You can cool your jets, Mammy, because I still have the kneecaps. And the rest. Turns out that I spent the bones of a year dodging Darren for no good reason. Unbelievable. I made my own way on the tube every morning, no lifts required. I collected the pay packet from Diana once a week, without barely a word fired in her direction, killing that relationship dead for the sake of my legs. And I was head down with Titch, five days a week, sometimes on Saturdays for time and a half, with the ears and eyes out all the same, always scoping for that big blond Dublin bollix, in a state of nerve-shredding emergency to the point of near breakdown.

And in that time I learnt a lot about smashing and sweeping up hardened cement, I became more than efficient in the use of the jackhammer, I listened patiently to Titch's incessant bedroom stories, and I befriended an ancient fella from Cavan, called Frank, whose only job on site, as far as I could tell, was to make the tea. Scrio. He wore dirty denim rags, no hard hat, had a porter-stained beard, and emerged every day around elevenses, like a feckin wizard, from behind this massive metal urn that was standing on a rickety picnic table, and said absolutely nothing other than 'Tay?' 'Tay?' 'Grand job' and 'Tay?'

Anyway, I thought the coast was clear over the arse-poke with Darren's missus until one afternoon, when I'm running up to the fifth and highest floor to clear a rake of pallets so that the brickies can get to work, I hear an unmistakable guttural Dublin growl coming from below.

'Jay, ye deaf bollix!' he goes. 'Come the fuck down, ruy now!'

I think about hiding. There's tons of little hidey-holes on any site, lots of unfinished rooms, low walls, high walls, tiny darkened spaces. But mindful of the fact that there's nothing that makes an angry head even angrier than when the thing that made them angry goes into hiding, I trudge down to the ground floor to embrace my grisly fate.

Darren is waiting for me in the Portakabin, and when I step inside I'm half expecting two IRA lads in balaclavas to jump out from behind the door and shoot my legs to pieces. Instead, there's a wan beside him, called Jane.

'And the dead arose, and appeared to many!' Darren says, all smiles as I shuffle over to the desk. 'Jay, meet Jane!' he adds, and darts out the door before I've barely finished shaking her hand.

Jane is dead glamorous, Mammy. I'm telling ya. The style would take your eye out. Short croppy blonde hair, tight jeans, boots, and a short puffy jacket. I nearly have a weakness when she says, in the first few sentences, that she's feeling groggy today, because she's recovering from her own fortieth birthday party last night! Feckin forty! I play it dead cool like, and tell her that all the forty-year-old wans I know from back home in Cloonavullaun are wrinkly as shite, with dirty black farmer's fingers and feckin 'taches in the making.

She laughs, and tells me I'm a gas man, and then, real businesslike, lets me know the full *shcale*. Turns out, she's one serious media wan who, like her fella Matt, works in telly. She runs a company that normally makes award-winning documentaries but, for a bit of a nixer, they've been paid to shoot some mini-fillums about the comings and goings of life in the big smoke, to be shown on real-life telly, she says, in between the ads.

My one is going to be about the mad characters from all over the world that you meet any day of the week on a building site, and the funny things they say about living in London, and how brilliant everything is here. For my one she's chosen three of us – me, Titch and this Pakistani-English guy called Faisal who uses 'bleeding' the whole time when he speaks, which will, no doubt, make for great telly.

Although, in order to make sure that we're the right material for the box, and not just the first three names that came reeling off the top of Darren's thick Dublin head, she gives us a test, one by one, right there in the Portakabin. With me she's all, like, tell us what you love most about London? And I'm like, Going to the fillums. And then, she goes, And when you're at home in the bedsit, what type of stuff do you watch on telly? And I go, Fillums.

And the last time you went out socially? she says. With friends, in London?

Straightaway, I go, *Robin Hood: Prince of Thieves*. It's a fillum.

It seems to do the job, though, because I get the gig, and within a month I'm on the feckin telly! Not for long, mind you. It was just two shots of me and Titch and Faisal sweeping up on the site, and me stopping to wipe my brow. And then they cut to me in Leicester Square, on my day off, where I turn to the camera and go, like, 'London's the best, folks! Because if you work hard with the lads during the week, you get to play with yourself on the weekends!' And then I turn and point towards the main doors of the Odeon, and say, 'And there's nowhere I like playing with myself more than in the Odeon Leicester Square!'

Jane was thrilled with the fillum. Making it was a blast. And the people in telly couldn't have been nicer. All fellas and wans in

74

combat trousers, with a million pockets rammed full of important stuff, like tape and biros and batteries. Well, they were all nice except for this one Yank wan who kept barking at us, and ordering us about, calling us, 'You guys!' or 'Builder dudes!' Really rubbed me up the wrong way. Called Shauna.

Luckily, however, Jane was around to keep the Yank under control, and to make sure she didn't get above her station. Jane is brilliant like that. She can scan a roomful of people and see the sparking and scraping in any assemblage of differing personalities and get busy sorting it out, rebalancing the mood, and making sure nobody's nose is out of joint along the way.

On the downside, she's a mad aul whore in the sack. Seriously, Mammy. On the night of the wrap party she came waltzing into her own sitting room, where I was sprawled alone on the couch, and said that she was sorry, but she couldn't get to sleep alone in her big massive bed knowing that I was roughing it out here on the sofa.

It had been a mad night all right. In this flash bar, straight out of *Miami Vice*, but in Soho, with ultraviolet lights, and green cocktails on the house, and a huge projector down the end, where they showed all the mini-fillums together in one giant fillum. There was loads of bits with Pakistani fellas, working in chippers, and kebab shops, and corner shops. Then there was Italian girls working in restaurants, and below them in the basement, scrubbing pots, there was tons of Africans. And every time someone new would appear on screen they'd get a big cheer from themselves and their buddies in the audience, who were obviously pleased to see that they'd made it to the big time. My bit got a big cheer too, from Jane and the crew, and even a few extra punters in the bar area who came up to me later and told me that I was a gas man.

Jane's gaff is feckin smashing. Dead modern, all glassy and steely, and two floors above an old-fashioned pub in Soho, just a spit and a stumble from the wrap party. We had some oven chips and Jane sat me on the couch and gave me this long and brilliant speech about self-improvement, and asked me if I'd ever seen *My Fair Lady*, which of course I feckin had, like a billion times, and then said, if it was OK with me, that she'd like to start self-improving me by giving me the right books to read, and just chatting to me about literature, philosophy and shite.

So I go, just to like, call her bluff, go on then, chat to me about philosophy. And, Mammy, sure enough, she launches straight into the self-improvement lecture, pure Henry Higgins style, and goes right back to the start of all thinking with Thales of Miletus, from the seventh century BC, in Greece, who basically, way before Jesus was even a twinkle in anyone's eye, announced that he'd had enough of all this goddy stuff, and spooky religions, and decided that we were all the same, and united by the fact that, like everything in the cosmos, we were made of water.

Obviously, he really fecked that one up, the big eejit, but the way Jane tells it, like a master storyteller, gets me all excited, and imagining that Thales of Miletus is looking around at everyone praying and worshipping on their knees, and he goes, raging, Get your damn dirty paws off the ground and look at me with my big brain, because at least I'm making a feckin effort here!

Jane does two more philosophers – Pythagoras, who's a maths nerd, and Heraclitus, who's a bit rock'n'roll and says that everything's in flux, so why bother – before my head starts to hurt. She tucks me in, and says that this is only the tip of the iceberg, and then kisses me on the forehead and calls me her own sweet Eliza Doolittle.

So, when she appears in the sitting room, in the darkness, with the whole empty *labba* scenario going on, it's definitely a change in tone – like she's taken *My Fair Lady*, and mixed in some *Pretty Woman*, with just a tiny, delicate dash of *Fatal Attraction*. Now, Mammy, if this had been last year, and I'd been all innocent and with my fresh-off-the-boat head on, I might've gone skipping into her room, all high-voiced, like Aled Feckin Jones, going, Thank you very much, Jane, a good warm night's sleep in a big double bed is exactly what I require. Instead, thanks to my experience in Diana's Uno, and from listening to Titch's constant X-rated stream of London love stories, I knew that there might be more to it than a quick cuddle and some ancient Greek philosophical pillow talk.

So, I hit the sack with Jane and decide to go straight in for an aul smooch, keep it simple at first, no arse stuff at all. And it's feckin great. She's moaning. I'm moaning. I'm thinking that Diana was a freak mishap, and this could definitely be the one. But as soon as we get going in the big leagues, as in properly riding, as in actual intercourse, saving your presence, Jane goes a bit mental and asks me, in the nicest possible way, to give her a couple of digs. And not just digs either. But words too. Like she wants me to call her a right feckin bitch, even as we're doing it. And not just a bitch either. But, like, a prostitute, and a prostitute of low worth at that, like a real down-on-her-luck kerb-crawler, not like Julia Roberts. At this stage I still haven't said a word. I'm just doing the business as solidly and consistently as I can while listening to the menu of words from which I'm supposed to be choosing, and wondering whereabouts on her body I'm supposed to give her the dig.

Getting impatient, she starts yelling, and calling me Rough Boy, and Builder Boy, which I secretly think are rubbish names, like a backing vocalist from *Frankie Goes to Hollywood*. And she pinches me too, and really scrapes me, and barks at me, ordering me to feckin thump her and call her, like, the most worthless, hateful, useless, mickey-hungry streetwalker that ever lived.

So, thinking that she's only seconds away from flinging a feckin ashtray at my head, and kind of clearing my throat, and getting ready for my big moment, I give the back of her lower leg, just above the calf muscle, a nice decent slap, and I say, 'Get up out of that, ye big ancient aul cow!'

Well, Mammy, you wouldn't believe the effect it had. It was like a sex power cut. Jane just shot up in the bed, grabbed her fag packet and burst out crying. We stayed like that for a couple of minutes. Her crying, and fiddling with her fags. Me, frozen still, half-turned away from her, tensing up for a belt on the back of the head. And then she said sorry, and I said sorry, and we hugged, and we stayed there, in the bed, hugging while sitting up, hugging tight, her crying, me hugging, just both of us hugging, for ages, until Jane says, sniffling, that I really need to brush up on my sex speak.

I see Jane loads after this, but just as friends. She gives me her home number and her direct line at work, and says that I can treat her like a hot-line for lonely and depressed Irish labourers, and then tells me not to laugh because I am, in fact, part of the largest growing suicide demographic in London, and she's not going to have my death on her conscience, having shown me the highlife over the course of a couple of days' shooting and a wrap party, and then whipped it all away. We keep up the philosophy grinds goodo, and we even get as far as Foucault, Derrida and Habermas, a bunch of complete chancers, and then bleed straight back into medieval English literature, starting with Geoffrey Chaucer and 'The Miller's Tale' which is a right bawdy romp and features a famous scene where this onefella goes to kiss this gorgeous young wan, only at the last minute finds her beautiful face has been replaced by someone else's big hairy arse. Which, according to Jane, is both a seriously inventive gag and one of the high points of medieval writing.

As it happens, Jane ends that particular session by breaking the big one to me. She tells me that her company has been asked to cook up a proposal for a fillum show for the telly, big time, and she wants to know, seeing as I'm the resident fillum spod around these parts, if I'd like to become a member of the cooking-up team? Fecking what? Fecking A! Doesn't want me to quit the building work. But she does want yours truly to meet up with the fellas and the wans from her company this weekend, to discuss 'our' vision for the best fillum show ever. I said, That's grand and then asked, Just one thing, might not be important, but is that Shauna wan going to be on 'our' team? And Jane goes, Of course, why, is that a problem? What is it? And I go, Nah. Nothing.

Your Right-Hand Man,

Jay

8

Rage Like the Clappers: Slightly Later in the Day, 5 April 1999

'That. Fucking. Prick!'

That's how slowly she says it. The Clappers. She gives the boat a violent tug to the beat of each word, and stamps her left biker boot down onto the simple green wooden hull, almost pushing it through to the water beneath. Jay lurches right, and puts his palms out, fingers splayed, as you would, perhaps, to placate a rabid dog, or an escaped convict with a gun. Calm. Calm.

His story, the ten-minute version, has just concluded with the intimate coupling of ex-wife Shauna and her therapist Dr Ghert Rasmussen, in the latter's modest and low-lit Hampstead clinic. Shauna presented herself to Dr Ghert with a combination of post-natal depression, nervous exhaustion, cyclothymic disorder, and all-round listless apathia, being exacerbated and aggravated by nearly three years of complete sexual abstinence, broken sleep, stress-injected night trauma and the care of a baby girl who is still suffering the effects of an oxygen-deprived birth panic, and whose inability to utter a single human word in her third year would seem to suggest a negative appraisal of her developmental abilities so far.

Dr Ghert, in his mid-fifties, with greying beard, a comfortable red cardigan and strong dark features, has, after several fruitless months of standard cognitive therapy, suggested something far more radical to treat Shauna's condition – the latter nervous state being, he suspects and has explained repeatedly to Shauna, entirely rooted in her current state of sexual paralysis. The treatment, he informs her, while standing up and adjusted the dimmer switch to near darkness, is something he learnt very recently while on a weekend workshop retreat in Copenhagen.

Thus, gently, he repositions Shauna on the couch opposite him. She is wearing her traditional funereal garb of black leggings, enormous black sweater, black sneakers, all topped off with a messy brown backcomb and a dramatic, unapologetic, kohl-eyed stare. Dr Ghert lifts her physically out of a traditional therapy recline, and instead perches her on the very edge of the couch, with her feet flat on the ground, legs wide apart and facing him, elbows resting firmly on the knees, hands supporting the head at the chin, eyes staring into his. Dr Ghert mirrors this position exactly from his own chair, so that both sets of knees are touching, forming a diamond of open legs, with both faces separated by mere inches.

Dr Ghert announces that this is called energy pathway boosting, and that it sounds kooky and vague but, on the basis of what he's seen and experienced already, it really works. He repeats that Shauna's sexual senescence is the key to her condition, and that the young American-born mother of one is currently carrying an enormous and formidable energetic block in front of her vagina. A block that is as real to her as any object in the physical world, from a shield, to a door to a chastity belt. What he hopes to do, through a combination of breathing, energetic transfer, and visualisation exercises, is to blast through Shauna's vaginal block with the energy, the so-called kundalini energy, from his own sex centre.

And so they sit there, this pair, in near darkness, in a modest

Hampstead clinic on Rosslyn Hill, in their perfectly formed diamond spread, with their eyes shut, and him breathing aloud, sibilant inhales, huge blowy exhales, and half-whispered words in his deep Danish basso profundo, pushing her in and out of a near-hypnotic state, telling her to feel, to focus all her energy downwards, and to feel the energy flushing into her vagina, the heat, the heat on her vagina, as it fills and swells from within, finally released from three years of ice, now swelling hot and swelling wet, as the energy from his sex centre throbs and pulses, pushing forward, hard with heat, pulsing and pushing, always inwards, inwards and upwards, pushing and thrusting.

Can you feel it? he says, eventually, after an age, after a second, ordering, more than asking. Can you feel the pulse? The heat? The hot, wet, spread? Can you feel it? Can you feel it? Feel it!

Shauna's voice falters, caught between the shaking in her throat, and the rapid beat of her heart. Yes, she eventually says. God, yes. And then she adds, with the tiniest, almost imperceptible whisper, the phrase that Dr Ghert, secretly, in his wildest dreams, his darkest imaginings – ever since he spied her, signing herself in, glumly and nervously flicking long and unkempt strands of hair from her face, at the clinic's quiet reception desk – has been longing to hear.

'Fuck me.'

Naturally, they have sex.

Shauna is ecstatic when she arrives home, suitably late, after multiple sexual intercourses with Dr Ghert, bursting through the flat door in a giddy whirl of flowers, champagne and kisses. The latter are bestowed upon her so-called baby-love, Bonnie, who is sitting in her high chair, mashing fish fingers into her hair, while Jay toys distractedly with the baked beans on her plate. Jay tries to speak to Shauna, but she raises her index finger, first in the air, and then lays it directly onto his mouth, with a long sultry shhhhhhhh, while she indicates the champagne bottle in her left hand. She pours out two glasses, places one in front of Jay and now suddenly has to cover her own mouth with her hand, as if to stop herself from erupting into paroxysms of laughter.

What's got into you, *me auld segosha*? Jay eventually says, half joking, using the conspicuous Irish colloquialism to let her know that he is humouring her, and to remind her, quietly, of their once-loving bond.

Listen, hon, she says, taking the first sip from her champagne. I don't want you to take this the wrong way. And I still love you to bits. God knows I do. But, you and me, hon? We're done, relationship-wise.

That. Fucking. Prick.

The Clappers is fuming. Where does he live? she barks at Jay, repeatedly, now grabbing his shoulder, now jostling him urgently, as they march down through the park, out onto the high street, and south towards the Science Museum. Where does he fucking live? Because, I'll tell ye what, Boss Man, I am going to find out where he lives. And I am going to break his fucking neck! His. Fucking. Neck.

Again, Jay raises the hand. Calm. Calm. He knows The Clappers.

She once waited three weeks before beating to a pulp a fifth-year hurling star whose only transgression had been to steal Mickeleen's can of Lilt while on a school trip to Bundoran. She yanked the hurley stick effortlessly out of his hands, and the last thing Jay heard, as she gave chase, straight towards the technical drawing prefabs, was a high-pitched male voice screaming, in utter terror, 'I have asthma! I have asthma!' As if that would've stopped her.

Jay, inevitably, finally, manages to talk The Clappers down from the edge of madness and retribution. A flash of inspiration at the

83

junction of Exhibition Road and Cromwell Road is all that it takes. He glances at his watch. Forty minutes till Bonnie drop-off. He looks right, but points left, and announces, 'I want to show you something special.'

Two steps inside the archway and The Clappers raises her head towards the vaulted ceiling and gasps.

Jay leans into her ear and rests his chin briefly on the shoulder of her white denim jacket. He whispers a rhetorical Gaelic phrase of approbation.

Fecking *guhalling, nock ah?*

Sha, says The Clappers. *Gu-halling!*

She breathes deeply and, smiling, feels the rich smoky afterburn of holy basilica in her throat. The interior of Brompton Oratory, still slightly bruise-blackened from a midday squint, begins to ooze into focus. Dark marble pillars, velvet red along the walls, a dramatic gospel pulpit with high relief, and all attention on the centre altar, where an enormous wooden crucifix stands, with a purple cloth conspicuously placed around its base. The cloth is the resurrection, lying boldly beneath the feet of the risen Christ, where it has remained since the morning of Easter Sunday. Before then, right from the close of the Passion Mass on Good Friday, the cloth was the cloak, a painful covering, hiding the great wooden cross completely, a sop to the crucified death of the human man in Jesus. Its ceremonial removal, in front of Sunday morning celebrants, symbolises the glorious resurrection and the redemption of all mankind.

Jay and The Clappers know this. As if in a trance, good Catholics both, with Catholic codes and Roman rituals flowing freely through their veins, they shuffle up the aisle, genuflect, and choose a middle pew in a grand cavernous church that is now almost empty, but for a sprinkling of the aged devout, dotted throughout and slumped forwards with clasped hands and knotted knuckles.

Conceived of the Holy Spirit. Born of the Virgin Mary. Suffered under Pontius Pilate. Was crucified. Died. And was buried.

Jay and The Clappers sit in silence, staring at the cross.

Eventually Jay, indicating the stiff red prayer cushions at their feet, says, 'Well?'

Get to feck! hisses The Clappers.

For old times' sake? teases Jay, intimating at the existence within the mind of his female companion some rapid-fire flash-backs through cold Sunday sermons in St Lawrence O'Tooles on the Sligo Road, sour-faced school trips for pre-Communion pro-gramming, and all ears strained outside the flimsy confessional box while loud-mouthed Dennis McCarthy from Mrs Goggins's maths class sobs throughout his shame-filled recollection of venial self-pleasure and the sin of stolen knickers.

Well? says Jay. If not for me, then for the fallen boys in the GPO!

The Clappers gives a tiny shrug of confusion.

Easter Monday? Jay proceeds, with mock incredulity. In 1916? Padraig Pearse, Michael Collins?

Oh, that!

The Clappers rolls her eyes, groans, and remains entirely still. Moments pass. The pair eventually, slowly, awkwardly, without actual agreement or consultation, and due mostly to Catholic reflex and Catholic impulse, ease themselves forwards from their seats and down onto their respective prayer cushions. They loosely cup their hands, casual style, and flop forwards onto the pewback in front. They could be twelve again.

The Clappers shuts her eyes tight, and runs the Serenity Prayer on a loop inside her head. The things that cannot be changed ... the things that should be changed ... Taking as Jesus did ... This sinful world as it is.

Her lids remain shut tight, squeezed into two tiny wrinkles of uncluttered concentration, while her forehead is furrowed with sincerity.

Jay doesn't pray. He looks at The Clappers instead. Side on. Drinks her in. Before sliding along slowly, closer and closer. Close enough to plant a gentle kiss on her cheek.

Thanks for coming, Claire, he whispers.

She opens her eyes in shock, and threatens Jay with a half-hearted punch.

Straight up? asks The Clappers, double-checking, as the pair embrace through their farewells on the steps of the church. Jay confirms, a little impatiently, that coming over here to see him was a gesture in itself and that the redemptive work of The Clappers is henceforth completed. He asks her to pass on his regards to The Fox and to Mickeleen.

The Clappers demands, cuddling Jay now, and lifting him bodily from the ground with excitement and relief, that Jay return home soon, to Ireland, the Land of Jay, for a visit.

Jay nods.

This year, says The Clappers, shaking him roughly, rag-doll style, and reassuring him that nobody cares about all that Jesus shite any more.

I'll try, says Jay, calmly, before flashing his widest farewell grin, pointing to his watch and saying the words, Bonnie drop-off. He runs down the length of Cromwell Road, twisting his head back occasionally, to catch sight of his eccentric female friend, still outside the church, unmistakably still in mousy-brown crew-cut, white denim jacket, black jeans and biker boots, just standing there, looking.

Not moving.

The flat buzzer buzzes for Bonnie drop-off at exactly 2 p.m. on Easter Monday. Jay is already down through the hall and at the front door when it rings. He has watched from above, by the window, lathered in sweat, courtesy of an excessively speedy return from Brompton Oratory. He has seen the drop-off car approaching. He likes that. Even if only for a heated, sweat-lathered minute. To anticipate her arrival. Butterflies in his stomach sometimes, such is the excitement. It surprises him, still. Like he'll never get used to it. His own daughter. Just ummm-believable.

It's a new car this time, he notes, not without judgment. Flashy and black. He can see Bonnie in the back seat. And the hands of Ghert only – weathered and tanned against brilliant white shirt-sleeves, bright silver cufflinks and an enormous silver and gold Rolex – gripping the steering wheel. Hardly surprising, Jay thinks, at his rates.

But it's just talking! All you're doing is talking!

Jay, at his most obstinate, used to say that to Shauna, deliberately so, with a whiff of curdled humour, knowing deep down that it was more than talking. Just as his childhood confessions with Fr Hanrahan had been more than whispering. He had joked about it at dinner parties too. Risqué jokes, deliberately so. Around polished, glass-topped, Notting Hill tables.

Ah sure, I had all that shite on tap when I was a chisler! And I didn't have to pay for it either. As long as you don't include giving the bishop an aul blowjob every now and then!

Sometimes they laughed. Mostly, they laughed. But Shauna seethed. She explained, because Ghert had explained, that the money, the going rate in fact, for his level of professionalism had to cover two ex-wives and six ex-children. To which infor-mation later, much later, during the break-up, and directly into Shauna's face, in order to wound and to damage, and to avenge, and perhaps, hope against hope, to open her up to the light, his saving light – Jay would describe Ghert as a 'pervert', a 'sleaze-bag', a 'douche bag', a 'serial philanderer' and a 'dirty Danish gee-bag!' All the bags. And yet Shauna, at least in Jay's eyes, and infuriatingly so, even at the crucial moment of the interpersonal *coup de grâce*, always seemed entirely protected by the strange impenetrable glow of honeymoon love.

Bedtime for Bonnie on Easter Monday night is later than usual. No time for story. Jay apologises to her, sincerely, as he lies her down in a three-sided cot, tightly jammed against his single bed. Bonnie, dressed tonight in the huge, oversized, tiger-striped pyjamas that she chose herself with a grin, point and gasp, often rolls out across the divide, during the night, over onto Jay's side. Sometimes it's half and half, with legs remaining inside the cot, and body creeping over onto Jay's pillow. Other times the legs shoot out, crawl and drag, and pull the entire frame, leaving all but the head remaining, comically askew in the three-sided cot.

Storytelling was key, they were told, during their first appointment with the specialist, in the paediatric play department, at Imperial College, Royal Brompton. Talk to her all day, engage her all day, describe everything you do, and douse her, no, make that 'drown her', in your language, said the specialist, a beaming thirty-something from the Indian subcontinent with bright-red nail polish and a mellifluous, lightly accented delivery that seemed to inculcate hope and optimism into every utterance.

Story is the place to start, she said. Calmness, comfort, well-being and language acquisition? These are all rich rivers that are fed by the waters of story.

Jay began his very first tale nervously, with dry voice, like a poor public speaker or a sober groomsman. There was a father polar bear and a baby-girl polar bear, he said, tentatively retooling a recent nature doc. And the father polar bear had been shot by a hunter, just above the heart – serious, but not fatal. And while the father polar bear was nursed by the mother polar bear in the family's underground polar bear den, the baby-girl polar bear was forced to take tentative steps outside, into the big bad world, to find food for her family. And that, of course, said Jay, is where the fun begins!

Polar bears, inevitably, became his thing.

No time for polar bears tonight, Jay says, whispering and tucking in the cot corners. Instead, he retreads the afternoon's events aloud, and watches Bonnie's eyes slowly close with each advancing word. He starts with the tanned hands on the wheel, and how they, it transpires, actually belong to Grandad Paul, and not to Momma's new friend, Uncle Ghert the Pervert. Instead, Grandad Paul has been in London for some time now, for many, many sleeps, and he drives a lovely, brand-new big black vroom vroom, but has only just decided to show his face at Dadda's home, even though Dadda and Grandad Paul like each other so very much.

Grandad Paul and Bonnie, however, have seen each other so many times since Grandad Paul has been here, and they have such good fun together that today they thought it would be even better fun to see Dadda together, to come from Mamma's house directly to Dadda's house in Grandad Paul's brand-new big black vroom vroom. Because Dadda and Grandad Paul like each other so very much.

And, yes, Dadda was surprised to see Grandad Paul at the door, but also very happy. He invited Grandad Paul inside and, with Bonnie in his arms, the three new best friends ran as fast as their legs could carry them, all the way through the smelly, stinky, pee-pee hall and up into the home that Dadda shares with Friendly Ree and Kindly Wendy and Big Friendly Roo Who's Sometimes Big Moody Roo who tells us to stop crying in the night and even stopped Dadda on the stairs today and said that Friendly Ree and Kindly Wendy had told him all about the story of the big funny hullabaloo from the previous night with Dadda's funny

Irish friend. Don't let it happen again, said Big Friendly Roo, before saying a big smiley hello Grandad Paul and lovely Bonnie you, wishing us all a happy afternoon.

And, oh, what an afternoon, oh lovely little Bonnie you. We played games with Grandad Paul. We played hiding all over Dadda's home. And you were such a good hider, so good at being invisible, that Grandad Paul and Dadda couldn't find you anywhere, and thought you'd gone off all on your own, and climbed into Grandad Paul's big black vroom-vroom and driven away into the countryside for fun, or to see some cows, when in fact you were hiding under the bed all along.

And Grandad Paul was so pleased to find you there that he brought us both back up to the high street for chips, and he told us all about his life in America right now, and the clothes that he sells, and the money that he makes. And then he got sad, didn't he? He had a little sad time, didn't he? And he said that he loves Momma so much, and he loves Dadda too, and so he's having a lot of sad time when he thinks about Momma living in one home and Dadda living in another home, and Momma and Dadda not being such great friends as they once were. And then Grandad Paul had a bit of a forget, didn't he, and got very silly in the chippy place and held Dadda's hand, and gave Dadda a bit of a shake, and had a big, big sad time while he said that Momma and Dadda were going to live happy ever after, and that he was going to see to it, if it was the last thing that he did on earth. And this made Dadda a bit sad, then, didn't it? But it didn't make Bonnie sad, no, because lovely Bonnie had a huge, yummy, scrummy, strawberry ice cream for dessert, didn't you? And you ate it, and Dadda and Grandad Paul chatted some more, about adulty things, and then we all came back here to Dadda's home, and played even more hide and seek! And you were even better at hiding this time! And although you went straight back underneath the bed again we still couldn't find

90

you for hours. Until Grandad Paul decided that it was very, very late in the dark, dark night, and that it was time to say his goodbyes.

And so here we are, you and me, and your eyes are rolling slightly, and the lids are dipping down, and the angel face in repose so perfect in the softly humming lamp-light. The tiny frail frame is just a modest clump in the covers. I drape a heavy arm around you, to cuddle you close, protect you for ever, against anything and everything that might dare chance upon you through the rest of your days without blinding goodness and compassion at heart. You reach out and you hold my arm, between chin and chest, like a disembodied plaything, a snuggle toy, and you pinch, scrape and weed with tiny nails on tiny fingers the forearm hairs you find, while your eyes shut, my own eyes shut, and our breaths, in synch out of synch and in again, are all that remain, breathing as we drift through sleeplids of silence. Just breathing in dreams. Lovely Bonnie and me.

Jay! Jay! Jay!

Jay is sluggish and slow to wake, but when he does he props himself up suddenly, on his elbow, and squints into Bonnie's cot in the darkness, expecting the worst – vomit, a fit, faltering breaths or, no, a tiny corpse. Instead, she is dozing neatly on his pillow, angelic to the end under backward bush curls.

Jay!

Roo's head is sticking through the door crack. No fear or anxiety in his voice this time. Just a sizeable quantity of irritation, as the buzzer rattles incessantly in the background.

It's your friend, he says curtly, adding, with barely concealed annoyance, mostly at having to say these two ridiculous words in the first place: The Clappers!

She says it's an emergency.

Hot news from the land of telly. We're close, Mammy. I'm just back from another high-profile meeting with Jane's lot, where she told us that the show, which is now to be called *Screen Grab*, is only inches away from a feckin green light. A few more Ts to cross and Is to dot, and you could be the mammy of a real-life feckin telly star. No joke.

Although it wasn't really a meeting as such. More like a big shmancy evening meal, like the ones you'd do yourself, when you'd have the Sunday roast in the evening, instead of after mass, because Ollie Campbell was playing in the rugby, or Jigger O'Connor was putting Meath under the cosh in the hurling semis. Only this one wasn't scoffed goodo around a blue-topped kitchen table next to the sink, but on a massive, great big, long brown wooden mahogany monster of a thing, like the one Tarzan eats off, when they bring him back to the ginormous Greystoke mansion for the first time in his life.

It wasn't Jane who was cooking the food, but her mam and dad, who are dead posh, and dead English, and who invited us all over to their ginormous gaff in Notting Hill Gate to celebrate Jane's first ever documentary award (for a fillum about an Asian wan who jumped under a train after her hubby kidnapped her kids – dead depressing), and to encourage her, but in a jokey posh English way, to 'finally, now, get a proper job!' You're supposed to laugh after that bit. You go, Eh heh heh heh, which is what the posh English do when they want to say something that they can't find the words for, which is most of the time. They go, like, say, for instance, like Jane's mammy just did earlier, looking at me, And do we have ourselves a left-footer here? Eh heh heh heh! I go, Eh heh heh heh too, because I don't have a feckin clue what she's talking about, but can tell that she's kind of extracting the michael, which makes me think that I'd like to give her ancient posh arse a right boot for her troubles, with my feckin right foot, which is what I am, so I tell her, No, eventually, that I'm a right-footer, and always have been, whether it's soccer or Gaelic, it's always come naturally to me, to give the ball a right decent wallop with the right. She looks at me and goes, Eh heh, and turns away, and Jane later explains that left-footer meant Catholic, and comes from a time when all the posh bollixes in England came over to Ireland and stole all our potatoes and sold them back to the English at home while one and a half million micks died of starvation, and another million had to leave Ireland and remake themselves entirely in brutally unforgiving parts of England where the posh English bollixes slagged them off for being left-footers, which meant being Catholic, but actually referred to the use, by Catholic Irish, of cheap-arsed spades with only one side, the left side, for digging potatoes, compared to the posh English spades that had two sides for digging potatoes, at a time when they were digging for Irish potatoes that had already been stolen by the posh English bollixes in the first place.

Jane much later on, in the dark, out in the back garden next to a trickily ornamental fountain, after coffees and during smokes time, apologises to everyone about the meal, and the entire evening, and also thanks everyone for coming, and for being the so-called back-up and moral support. It's only me, Stevie Fitz, Jane's fella Matt and the Yank wan, Shauna, but it was enough, she says, to balance a full house of clowns.

And I'm telling ye, Mammy, you would've been proud of me, right there at a table that was positively brimming with local hobnobbers, vicars, mayors and magistrates. When they rang the dinner bell (Eh heh heh heh), Jane's mammy grabbed my arm wordlessly, and led me, in a vice-like grip, right up to the table, and to my place, which looked like they had emptied out a fecking cutlery factory all over it, and stuck a shmancy name tag on the top, with 'Jay' written on it, with the finger quotes and everything, rather than plain Jay, as if I have a madey-uppy name, like a feckin super-hero or one of The Jackson Five.

I was dead cool with the cutlery though, didn't flinch. I just looked over at Shauna, who was sitting opposite me, and kind of laughing, while mouthing back in silence to me the words, 'Outside, in!' She then pointed to the cutlery and moved both fingers slowly towards the centre of the plate. I gave her a nod of thanks, and thought that maybe she wasn't such an aul bossy boots after all.

The meal was a hoot, with Jane's dad making a speech at the start where he welcomes Jane, and congratulates her on the dead-Asian doc, and thanks her for bringing along her friends, meaning us, who are clearly a very 'colourful' bunch (Eh heh heh heh). He says that it's great to see so many different faces from so many different peoples, the Scotch, the Irish and the Americans, and then he adds, 'As Chesterton used to say, "I am never so inadequate as when I am universal; never so limited as when I generalise!"'

Everyone, especially the other posh oldies, goes, Well said! Well said! as if they have a fecking clue. Although me and Shauna look at each other, and she winks and giggles and does a wonky mouth that says a sneaky, 'Fuuuuuuuuck!' She is, I'm thinking, quite the goer.

We get through the first two rows of cutlery pretty smoothly. The aul poshies mostly blather about among themselves, about Neil

Kinnock's Kremlin connection, the evil of the Maastricht treaty, and how the best food and smartest service in Egypt are to be found not in Cairo, nor in any land-based hotels, but on the weekly Nile cruises that leave from Luxor and take in the Valley of the Kings and Abu Simbel. 'Abu Simbel!' repeats one of the aul wans, placing a bony bejewelled hand on her chest.

'Magnificent!' This starts a brief discussion about which is better, the temple at Abu Simbel in Egypt, or the one in the rocks at Petra in Jordan. And, Mammy, it will come as no surprise to you that the star participant of this particular debate was none other than yours truly, who completely flattens the chat into silence by taking a big slurp of my red wine and going, real funny like, 'Oh, the penitent man! The penitent man! The penitent man? What does he do, Indy!? He kneels before God!' And then I kind of make a big show of rolling out of my chair, like I'm kneeling before God and dodging two giant circular-saw blades while I'm at it!

The oldies don't have a clue, obviously, because they don't keep up with their fillums, unless it's some aul shite with Judi Dench and Charles Dance in a big house, or a fillum about life in the old days, when all the wans wore meringue dresses and the fellas wore top hats, and they'd waste the whole fillum just farting around at balls and tea parties, unable to say what's really on their minds because they hadn't yet been taught the words for shit, feck and fuck, and only knew how to say meaningless shite like, 'I shall absolutely expire, Miss Charlotte, unless you honour us with the pleasure of your company at this latest game of feckin cribbage!'

So I go, '*Indiana Jones*? *And the Last Crusade*? The one with Sean Connery? And the climax in the magic red temple, which is fillumed in, yes, are we warm yet? Petra!'

A few of them do a token Eh-heh, while Shauna practically chokes on her mid-course cold rhubarb and spinach mousse mouth-cleanser, but Jane's dad quickly moves the conversation on to the possible refurbishment costs of the Windsor Castle fire, and how Lady Di is nothing better than a common hussy, which, Mammy, you wouldn't expect, them being English and everything, and normally they would've loved Lady Di, and were big fans of her wedding day and the hair and everything, but the squidgy tapes and the book have gone and put everyone's nose out of joint and made them think, for the good of the country, that some things are more important than the happiness and sanity of a little blondie thing with a gym card, and so they're like, Ah, poor aul Charles, wouldn't your heart go out to him, married to that mad wan?

So, as I say, it's all going grand until the vicar, a real snowy-haired arse with veiny cheeks and a thin pointy nose, suddenly announces, out of nowhere, that the armed forces should catch and punish the bloody Irish savages who, only five days previously, injured a whole rake of innocent Christmas shoppers in Manchester City Centre with two taxi bombs. He's had enough of that lot, coming over here and wreaking havoc, he says, and Major should just bite the bullet, be the man that he is, and round the lot of them up, like the Yanks did to the Japs during World War II.

Now, Jane who, up until this point, has been pretty much invisible with shame, suddenly lifts her head out of her lamb cutlets and proves herself perceptive as ever to emotional room temperatures by doing a big conspicuous throat clear at the very mention of Irish savages, and flings her bulging eyeballs over from the Reverend Aitken's place setting to mine, and back again, repeatedly, even as he's staring at her in acknowledgement and saying the words, If you ask me, hanging's too good for them!

Thing about the Irish, he continues undaunted, is that they're a slippery, untrustworthy and superstitious race. And then he adds, with a huge comedy nod of his head, in my direction, Present company excluded, I'm sure!

Right you are, Rev, I say, and I tell him that I'm none of the above, and that Kevin the Foreman often gives me the keys to lock up the site on Saturdays, with the alarm code and everything, even though, if I was dodgy or slippery or untrustworthy, I could probably nick a few pneumatic drills, or throw an illegal rave on the second floor.

Oh, so you're a builder, so you are, says the vicar, real smiley-like, how fascinating?!

And as much as I want to let it go, and take all the praise for myself, I have to tell him no, that I'm not technically qualified enough to be a builder, and am just part of the site's hard-working USL force. You know yourself? Un-Skilled Labourer?

Quite! he says, still smiling.

I notice that the table has gone super-silent, and not even Shauna's looking up from her plate. Instead, everyone is just kind of listening to me and the rev's Q&A session. It's a funny kind of silence, Mammy, and one that I had not, until this exact point in my life, ever experienced before. It's the kind of silence that's deafening, screaming and scraping through your ears, with your heartbeat whacking around inside your head, and making you sick to your stomach all the same, even though you're supposed to be eating and having a whale of a time, quaffing and haw-hawing with the best of them. So, anyway, doing my damnedest not to throw up over the table, and kind of feeling sorry for the millions of posh English families in massive houses over hundreds of generations who've had to eat their evening meals while trying not to puke with tension, I decide to fill in the blanks with a more thorough description of my duties on site, starting with early-morning spill collections. I am only, however, through the first bit about me and Titch fighting over the jackhammer when the rev cuts me short with, And superstitious? What about superstition?

Naturally, Mammy, this opens up a whole can of worms between me and the rev that starts with me saying that I don't walk under ladders and all that crack, but it doesn't mean I believe in leprechauns and banshees, which makes him go, matter-of-fact style, Why not?

Which is the moment – while I'm struggling for the words to explain why leprechauns clearly don't exist, and can hear a few of the others, even Jane's Matt and Stevie Fitz having a giggle at how I'm tying myself in knots – that finally makes Shauna kind of snap with annoyance and turn to the rev and tell him that, surely, religion itself is the greatest superstition of all? Some of the other oldies do a little tut at this, and you just know they're thinking, Typical Yank, all mouth! But the rev's cool as a cucumber, and simply turns it back to me, and talks to Shauna and me at the same time, and tells me that the Catholics are great at marrying superstition to religion, and asks me if I've blessed myself today, or said a prayer today, or if I know what day today is, being 8 December?

Immediately, I go, like, dead classy, Feast of the Immaculate Conception! I always know that, Mammy, because it was my favourite day, 8 December, when I was yours alone, Mammy, because I always got the day off school, because it was a Holy Day of Obligation, and you and me, Mammy, we'd go to mass first, then you'd take me in the car all the way to Sligo Town, where we'd do a full day of Christmas shopping, and you'd buy prezzies for your sister, and for your own mammy, before she

98

died, and then we'd have lunch in McDonald's on Wine Street, and I'd have everything, large size, even a large Coke, and you'd just have an apple pie and tea, and you'd break the pie into pieces and let it rest in the cardboard packet to cool, because one of them pies once burnt you and gave you a tongue blister that turned into a mouth ulcer that lasted a fortnight and was the talk of the parish, especially when the goss turned to you suing Mickey D's for emotional distress and lack of earnings from the post office.

And after lunch, after you'd reapplied your lipstick and kissed a paper napkin, you'd look down at me, and stroke my cheek, and tell me, because not enough mothers tell their sons this, at least not until it's too late, but you'd tell me that you loved me, truly, with all your heart, which would make me cringe and flinch and want to hide under the table. But no bother, because after that we'd go to Carbury's toy shop, and this was the best bit, because we'd do a big tour of the toy shop and you'd ask me, real sly like, which were the toys that I liked the look of the most, and once I'd given you five or six answers, ranging from anything as varied as Grivvity Gravity to Action Man with Bomb Sweeper to Star Wars Millennium Falcon, you'd tell me to go and wait down near the Barbies, and you'd give me a Mattel catalogue to read, and you'd whizz around, doing your so-called secret shopping, and gab away with the wan on the till about 'his nibs', meaning me down at the Barbies, and niftily slip all your shiny new purchases, magical items all, cardboard boxes with cellophane windows, magically slipped into that big red clothy *mawla* of yours, the one that could've been made from aul carpets, and could hold a new fridge inside it without even a dent to the side, such was the strength of its carpety material, and of the rubber handles holding it upright.

And all the way home in the car I could hardly sit still, bobbing around in the back seat, knowing that the red *mawla* was in the boot, and that it was filled with unthinkable delights for me. Spaceships, hero cars, and soldier men with roaming eyes, left and right, left and right. And in the darkness of night, after beans and toast, homework and prayers, with you by my bed, kneeling low, and whispering sleep, I'd make you recite the day, recite in recap, from morning to mass to bed and back again, and I'd make you count, with me, the days until Christmas, until the wishes in the red *mawla* came true, and I'd make you say it, make you do the maths, again and again, until sleep fully, finally fell on me, on one of the best days of the year, ever, no doubt: 8 December.

Shazam! So, I'm like, Feast of the Immaculate Conception! Easy, next question! But the rev's having none of that. He starts going full Magnus Magnusson on me, really grilling me, like my specialist subject is Holy Days of Obligation and the Four Dogmas of Roman Catholic Mariology, and he wants to know what the Immaculate Conception actually means, really means, in the bible, rather than just a day off that Catholics get for Christmas shopping. Stevie Fitz, of course, who's a Scotty Proddy by birth, and Scotty posh to boot, and is a little fella with a super-neat goatee beard, has now had enough wine to dazzle his own senses and push past the puke-tension barrier and join in the conversation, so he launches himself across the table with a big dismissive swipe at the rev, saying that everyone and their wife knows what the Immaculate Conception is, because it's the moment when Mary conceives the baby Jesus immaculately, without any access to any, you know, actual slap and tickle. Fitz says slap and tickle in a real winky, jokey way, man-about-town-style, but I just groan, because Rev Aitken is already rolling his eyes, because he knows that Fitz has made a classic schoolboy error, and that the feast of the Immaculate Conception celebrates

100

the moment when Mary, the mother of Jesus, was herself conceived in the womb of St Anne, but conceived immaculately, which is to say, conceived without Original Sin, rather than without a father, who in this case, is none other than St Joachim, who was apparently super-rich, but dead nice to the poor, and is always depicted in saintly windows as tanned, and with really cool gear.

Whereas, the conception of Jesus himself, which occurred without an earthly father, and happened on 25 March, nine months exactly before Christmas Day, is celebrated by what feast day? The rev, at this point, nods to me and smiles, and calls me Our Good Catholic Friend, and assures everyone else around the table that I'll know the answer to this easy starter round question. Hmm?

Feast of the Annunciation, I say, quietly, not wanting to be a bighead about all the religious stuff I know, thanks to the years we spent, me and the gang, getting the heads bit off us by Fr Spitty-Face Hanrahan in St Cormac's. Feast of the Annunciation! the rev repeats, this time looking just that tiny bit mad, and determined, it seems, to catch me out on all the goddy stuff. But, thing is, Mammy, no more than I need to remind you, fillums and goddy stuff pretty much run the gamut of what I was learnt back home. Before I met Jane, and before she started making me better myself, fillums and goddy stuff was the only stuff I knew.

So I think the rev's on to a loser, and, sure enough, the poor bollix just gets angrier and angrier, as he's firing any aul catechistic shite at me, and I'm just trotting out the answers that are as natural to me as they would be to any English fella my age who's asked about the size of Isambard Kingdom Brunel's stove-pipe hat, how Britain became the workshop of the world, or the name of the politician who wouldn't send any aid to the Indians during the 1943/44 Bengal famine because he said that them dying of starvation was no biggie because they were only feckin Indians, and would be breeding like rabbits again within minutes! Actually, Mammy, that last one's a trick question I learnt from Jane, because the answer is Winston Churchill, and when you tell it to people, especially English people who love the war and the blitz and *Dad's Army*, they get really shocked and tell you to get shagged, because Winston Churchill was this lovely aul fatso with the cigars and the V-sign, and was like Santy for war people, and not some aul fat racist who was brilliant at making speeches, killing Germans and letting darkies die.

Anyway, so the rev's spitting lamb juice at me, simultaneously smiling and seething and calling me a Catholic non-stop, and we're having a grand aul game of verbal, with him going, 'The Annunciation, What book?'

And me saying, 'Luke!'

And him, 'What chapters?'

Me, 'Chapter one, verses twenty-six to twenty-eight!'

Him, 'And the angel came in unto her, and said?'

Me, 'Hail, thou that art highly favoured, the Lord is with thee. Blessed art thou among women!'

Him, reddening even more, 'And the angel said unto her, Fear not, Mary?'

Me, 'For thou has found favour with God!'

To be honest, Mammy, and, no boasting here, I've pretty much aced it, and have given Catholics all over the world a right good showing, when the rev changes tack completely, and stops doing religious knowledge questions and instead turns it into a mini-lecture on the values of Protestantism versus Catholicism, and how fablas it is to have a personal relationship with God, one that's not mediated by priests or bishops or the Holy Roman See, and how a Protestant man's belief is between him and his God, whereas a Catholic man has to toe the line and believe in what he's told to believe in, or risk going straight to hell.

And so? he says, turning back to me, more direct than ever, and silencing any objections from around the table (mostly groans from Shauna) with a wave of his hand, and he says, Do you believe?

And I go, In the annunciation?

And he's like, dead calm, Yes. The annunciation. And the virgin birth. Do you believe?

I know, Mammy, you couldn't make it up! You, especially, would've had a right aul laugh at that! But me? I just freeze, I stare at him for an age, and eventually, and for reasons known only to the big thick head on me, and possibly to the woozy combination of red wine and all-consuming, table-top puke-tension, I go completely into Fr Hanrahan mode, super-goddy style, real Forgive Them For They Know Not What They Do stuff, and I look right into the eyes of the snarky, snowy-haired, veiny-faced arsehole, and I say, real gentle like, not cheeky, not smart, more calm than anything else, 'Be not afraid!'

Well, naturally Mammy, the rev's eyes nearly pop out of his head, and he says, gasping, 'I beg your pardon!' as if I've just told him to go and give Prince Charles a reach-around on the steps of the Albert Memorial (I'll tell you about reach-arounds later – I only found out about them myself from Titch today). I say nothing back to him, not even half sure of what I said in the first place, or if the words had just come shooting automatically out of my mouth, like holy tongues from an evangelical nutjob, or rhubarb and spinach mousse from the young wan in *The Exorcist*. Either way, and straightaway, there's a lethal stand-off brewing between us, one that could've prematurely ended the entire nightmarish evening before we'd had a chance to sample some more mid-course liquidised shite, were it not for the timely intervention of a genuine miracle in the form of a gagging, choking, blue-faced aul wan.

Sure enough, just as me and the rev are locked into the aul Leone stare – eye to eye, lips twitching, trigger fingers flexing – and just as everyone, especially Jane, is about to positively burst with the tension, a feckin posh aul wan does just that. Yep, the same posh aul wan with the bejewelled hand, who had earlier professed a love for the Egyptian ruins of Abu Simbel, comes shooting forward in her seat, grabbing all the attention, suddenly coughing and gagging down onto her plate, making all sorts of guttural gutsy groans, like Bowsie when he's running, wild and distraught, around the kitchen table legs with the handle from the peg-basket stuck down his throat. She's spasming on the spot too, with each cough, and kind of hopping in her seat, with her mouth open, super-wide, and all sorts of silvery-greeny slime just dripping down, falling freely onto the plate in front of her.

But wait, Mammy, that isn't the maddest thing, not by a long shot, no. Because you'd think, really, that everyone would be like, screaming blue murder, giving her the Heimlich, or clearing the table, propping her up there, on her side, and bashing clean out whatever filthy obstruction she's holding inside. But no, it transpires that just as the poor aul poshies don't yet have the words for shit, feck and fuck, neither have they yet received instructions for how to react when anything shit, feck and fuck-ish erupts into their neatly planned, carefully coordinated world of shmancy crockery, glass, silverware, pewter dishes, aperitifs in the lounge, speeches at the table, hear hear, cling cling, clutter, munch, silence, haw haw, smile, die and repeat.

So, instead of reefing the aul wan out of her seat and slapping several shades of shite out of her gullet, Jane's mam simply puts her hand to her own mouth, and does a little cough, as if she's the wan choking and not the ancient wan opposite her, and she pushes her chair neatly backwards, rises to her feet, creeps slowly over to choky head, and whispers, 'That's enough, Evie,' as if she's feckin doing it on purpose. Jane's mam half lifts Evie up by the armpits, and the poor aul wan now has to walk, as well as choke, as well as catch her own slimy spit in her hands, while Jane's mam leads her outside, out of earshot, out to the kitchen where, no doubt, some butler fella administers a crushing blow to the back of the head with a polo mallet, while inside Jane's dad, with impeccable timing, simply turns to the mayor-type fella, who's actually wearing the big jangly-jewellery chain that mayor-type fellas wear in case anyone thought he was just a pompous aul prick, and he says, 'More lamb, Bernard?'

Which I thought was a brilliant joke, so I gave a big guffaw, but Bernard, the mayor-type fella, actually says yes, dead serious, and the two of them launch into a big loud chat about going abroad for Christmas, for the whole table to hear, to demonstrate to the whole table that everything's back to normal, that order has been restored, that the aul choky wan was just an aberration, and that we're back on track with holiday chats, clinking cutlery, mid-course mouth cleansers, and more wine, Vicar?

Naturally, Jane is morto when we all meet up in the back garden, like sneaky banditos, at the far side of the plinky decorative fountain for chilly late-night fags, and to have a look around at the backs of all the other giant Notting Hill houses and wonder are they too filled with posh mentlers who speak through their teeth while smiling at everything and yet are secretly gripping the edge of the table top for dear life. Jane apologises to me loads, for Reverend Aitken, and for the aul legal duffer on the other side of him who spent the rest of the meal, after they had shipped the choker off the premises, quizzing me about Ireland, but in the thickest possible way. Like, when they're talking about how Andre Agassi was spotted in Harrods, and he turns to me and goes, So, tell me young man, do they have tennis in Ahland? Or, someone mentions the scandalous love-triangle between Antonia de Sancha, David Mellor and Chelsea FC, and he goes, Now, tell me this, do they have football in Ahland? Or, best of all, and you'd love this, Mammy, when the desserts are served, I get a huge chunk of traditional Bramley apple pie on my plate, and as I look at it I can feel yer man looking over at me, and so I look back at him, and sure enough, he's smiling through his teeth, and he goes, dead serious, Do they have apple pie in Ahland?

I tell Jane not to bother with the apologies. She says that she'll make it up to me in our next lesson but then she stops herself short, mid-sentence, when she squints down in the darkness and sees my hand, which is fully entwined with the hand of Shauna. This is a big deal, Mammy. Because I had never done that before, reached out and held a girl's hand, just like that, without any warning. Bold as bedamned. But something happened during the meal, and I saw something in Shauna, in her defence of me, that made me want to be close to her. And so when we got the chance, and we headed out, all the 'younger people' as they called us inside, I walked the length of the garden with her, towards the fountain, and as I did, in silence, my silence and hers, I felt the bio-electrical crackle between us, and the backs of our hands kind of brushing off each other and off the other's hips as we walked, and so, bold as bedamned, without a thought but her in my head, I laid my hand over hers as we walked, and I clasped it close, and she said nothing, and I said nothing, but we squeezed and we squeezed and it was love, I tell you, it was love.

I walk Shauna home. It's no biggie. She also lives in Notting Hill Gate, only, like, half a mile away from Jane's folks' ginormous gaff. Shauna's is in what she calls the 'cool' part of town, up near the canal, with the black lads, the drugs and the like. She lives in a great big eyesore of a thing. Hilarious. Painted bright pink, it is. The only one on the street. Three storeys. All flats. All buried in pink. Nicknamed the Pink Palace. The colour, she says, was her brainchild, together with flatmate Jess, a girl, a student, also a Yank, who felt it would be the first of many, and a brand leader that would encourage the entire length of St Mark's Road to go completely multicoloured in reply. And so they got it done, on the cheap, over the long weekend, after shrugging apathy and indifference from the neighbours above and below, and now they're engaged in a long-running battle with the council over who's going to wash it all away, and when.

We don't kiss or anything, Mammy. And there's certainly no bum-finger action or premature bed-hopping. Instead, we just hold hands some more, and I tell her that I've got to be up at the crack for work, because Titch is picking me up in his new jammer, and she tells me that she thinks Jane is a controlling influence on my life, and that I should be my own man and quit the evening classes for a start. I tell her I'll think about it, but that we're just now getting to the best bits of the siege of Stalingrad, where the devious aul Ruskies train a load of dogs to run under tanks with mines strapped to their backs by feeding them for weeks only under mock-up tanks, so whenever the dogs see a real tank approaching the poor feckin eejits go darting underneath, looking for their latest bowl of Pedigree Chum, not realising that they've got a massive great big landmine on board and that they've got about two seconds to say goodbye to the bliss of canine life before they're blown to smithereens. It makes me feel a bit queasy when I think about Bowsie that way, and about how the Nazis, who soon copped on to the whole exploding dog-mine routine, would freak out whenever they saw a dog wandering across the battlefield and eventually began shooting dogs on sight, any dogs, any dog in the vicinity, from feckin chihuahuas to Great Danes, no mercy, and so, if you were unlucky enough to be a dog in Stalingrad between August 1942 and February 1943 the chances were that you'd end up pulverised by either a Nazi bullet or a Russian landmine.

Shauna says OK, but that after Stalingrad I should quit, and get my own library card.

I end the night on her doorstep, admiring the paint job under the orangey haze of street lights, and not even asking if I can come up for coffee and a bit of how's-your-father, but still holding tightly onto her hand, till death do us. I ask if I can see her tomorrow night, but she says no, because her father's over from the States, and it's a big deal. And what about Thursday? Same. Friday? Same. She must be able to read the disappointment in my face, or the wobble in my bottom lip, because she thinks about it for a sec, and then relents, and tells me that her pop's got a thing for the Irish, and I might be lucky, and she'll see if the lot of us can't get together for a Saturday-night knees-up, although it can't be boozy because the old man's a teetotaller and has been ever since he gave her mam a right belt in the mouth that ruined Shauna's childhood. She's brilliant like that, Shauna. Boof. Straight out with it. No messin about with the haw haw and the eh-heh-heh. So American. Just brilliant.

I tell her not to worry, and that we're in London, and there's a million things to do in London, of a night, that don't involve booze. A fillum, for starters? She crosses her eyes when I say this, super-funny style, and groans out the words, Goodnight, Jay. We release the grip on our hands, and we smile at each other, dead flirty like. Any other couple might've kissed. But we are not any other couple. I walk home to Kilburn, thinking all the way about Shauna, and about her dad, and what kind of man he is, and what kind of relationship they have, and is it as good as the relationship I have with you, Mammy?

9

Eye for an Eye

I fuckin kilt him, Boss Man. The shrink is fuckin kilt!

I am in London. I am in London. I am starting to panic. I can feel it, coursing through me. Where am I? I am in London, Boss Man. Yes, The Clappers. She is sitting on the edge of the *labba*, in total darkness, breathing manically, mere inches away from Bonnie, mere feet away from the flimsy glass door of Wendy and Ree, doing the worst possible whispering act imaginable, while bleating out one of the most important, and genuinely ominous, sentences that I have ever heard, or may ever hear again.

I kilt the fuckin shrink!

Now, I was robbed once, back in Ballaghaderreen, as a teen, in Bret's Garage on the Ballymote Road. Back then, it was Saturday evening in May, just after the gang had headed off to McGarrigle's in Sligo Town for a hop. And me only minutes away from locking up – switching off the pumps, sliding across the garage door, and bringing in the bins while all the time racing through the accounts, with an eye to removing my wages, cash money (a decent ten pounds), to be spent later on, in a smoky, noisy, pint-strewn back bar.

But it was not to be. The doors were kicked open by two complete feckin shoeless knackers in balaclavas, who punched me in

110

the noggin, pushed me to my knees and held to my throat, of all the weapons, an enormous antique sabre, Charge of the Light Brigade-style.

Empty your fuckin pockets! one of them barked, while the other kicked the register to pieces with his bare feet!

Quickly, quivering, I put everything I had on the table, while the cool of the blade nestled neatly against my throat. The barker went through everything, removed my tenner, and then grabbed, and held up, in fury and in horror, the remote alarm.

What the fuck d'ya call this? he yelled, elbowing the back of my head, while shaking in my face a hefty grey remote, the size of a spectacles case, with one single button in the centre, marked by the childish blue graphic of a flashing light, which, when pressed, would indicate the imminent arrival of the boys in blue.

Too late, of course. I had already pressed the fecker. In fact, the very first kick of the door from the first knacker had sent my hand shooting down into the pocket of the Bret's Garage overalls, and I had pressed the button manically, repeatedly, without thinking. It was reflex. Nonetheless, the reality of the fabulous, mobile, grey security system was nothing more than a tiny blue blip on the front desk of some wage-slave gobshite at the Stay Safe Security Company in Tobercurry, which, if spotted at all, would necessitate a speedy call to the Garda Barracks in Sligo Town, some 18.4 miles away, after which, on the off chance that they had two Garda fellas ready and waiting with car keys in hands, and who proceeded to drive at full feckin *Knight Rider* speed down the N17, still meant that I had a hefty twenty minutes left to wait in the company of two increasingly irate and outraged, sword-wielding knackers.

I'll slit ye! I'll fuckin slit ye! my one, the barker, was yelling now, after smashing the remote on the ground, and pulling the sabre blade even closer, proper deep into my throat.

I'll admit it, and not a bother, but I was scared that night, at that moment. Petrified rotten. Lost all feeling in my legs. Didn't know how to speak. Just frozen, traumatised, an absence of humanity, a hollow man. It was a low point for me, and it showed me, right then and there, the complete disjuncture that it was possible to feel between self and soul when thrust against the face of pure feckin terror.

And yet, really, genuinely, it is nothing in the slightest, not even a fleck of angst, when compared to the howling and unbridled evacuation of identity that occurs in me when The Clappers sits on the end of the *labba* and tells me that she has ended Dr Ghert's life with a single punch.

And it happens, I know. I have read it before. In the papers. Street brawls gone awry. Soccer louts unleashed. A drunken punch at closing time, and a poorly placed kerbstone. Then all that fall, and lights out for ever, and a youngfella in jail, and his mammy crying for the news, and a decent dad with an honest-to-goodness job leaving behind only bitterness and a rake of bawling babes.

But this is different. No. And I say it. No. Right into her face. No. That's all I can manage.

No.

And the funny thing is, I had gone to bed with such hope in my heart. After the day I'd had. With Bonnie's breath softly hissing away on the pillow next to me, and the many soothing words of American Paul, real calm stuff, like an adopted Yank dad, echoing within, and daring me to dream about the love that Shauna still held for me, and about the need, at our age especially, not to repeat his conjugal errors and instead to fight for the one thing that mattered to our very existence, despite all the barbed talk and the actual divorce. Which was, he said, love.

And Paul's no fan of Dr Ghert's either, naturally, at his age, what with the beard and everything, and with him being guilty of what Paul decided, unequivocally, was some seriously shifty feckin mind manipulation.

Just give her time, man! She needs the break, man!

His words of advice. Even at this late stage.

I drifted off with such soothing excitements in mind, picturing Paul's many suggested sit-downs, between me and Shauna and a healthcare professional, not Dr Ghert, but someone new, preferably a woman, young and recently graduated, who could beat back the briars of breakdown, and reform us again, in love and in vigour. These thoughts that I had, these drifting, dreamy thoughts of renewal, would invariably conclude, via scrappy, sleep-laden jump-cuts, with the humiliation, the rejection and the punishment of Dr Ghert, who would flee from the scene, wincing at the sight of my blinding love for Shauna, and be known for ever throughout the city of London, and in every corner of his own precious industry, as a sleazy seducer, a grab-handed creep, and a heinous abuser of trust.

But, no, never dead.

I say no, no, a lot, while The Clappers bangs on hopelessly about Step Number Nine, and a job well done, too well done, eh, Boss Man?

It's a funny thing that. The eruption of the real. There's no preparation. A veil is lifted, and you suddenly see, with cruel clarity, the coy charade that you've been playing, for so long, in every sense, in words, thoughts and deeds.

No.

The Clappers says thick things, mental things, in the heat of hysteria. All whispered, mind you, for Bonnie's sake, and for the sake of Wendy and Ree. And the thick things say that we'll have to go on the run, like. We will. We. Her and me. On the run. As if we're in a feckin *film noir*. A John Huston classic. From the

113

cops, like. Because it is we, and because I'm in it too, as the lad, you know yourself, like – who ordered the hit.

The hit?

No.

No.

No.

And she rambles too, The Clappers. Nervous giggles and almost tears, showing the scared and sacred softness beneath the bluster. No one means to do that *crack*. To be that strong, and to take life with a single blow. She taps her wallet and says that she'll spring for the flights. Dirt-cheap Ryanair jobbie, first thing in the morning. Back to Ireland. Deep cover in the old country. Just like 'RA lads on the run from the Brits in the old days. She says that we can bring Bonnie too. And then she nudges me roughly, and says that it'll be like my aul 'RA Man grandad, Seamus Feckin Farrell himself.

Again, no. And I hiss at her this time, and tell her that Seamus Farrell's partner in crime got shot in the back by the Brits. And I suggest that, given the completely freakish nature of the manslaughter, we should both hand ourselves in tonight, and explain that the hit was not a hit, the punch an unlucky punch, and that the end of Dr Ghert's life on earth was the worst accident imaginable.

True. It sounds weak, and I gasp when I say the words, 'the end of Ghert's life'. Gagging on the real, and sensing an awareness of the implications that this particular end of life will have for my own, and for the precious few relationships that it supports, and the other surrounding lives through which it intersects.

The Clappers rambles. I slide onto the floor. I know, in the darkness, that we are truly fecked. No escape. Distraught, I rest my nose up against Bonnie's cot and try to breathe deeply. The words of The Clappers are stumbling into self-righteousness. She denigrates Dr Ghert. Calling him an aul eejit. And describes how

114

she lay in wait at the famous pink-painted palace on St Mark's Road. And waited and waited. And after he had come, the filthy shrink gobshite, and gone inside, the pervert, and done his business with Shauna, the bastard, and then finally, after waiting and waiting, he had come outside again, and she simply leapt on the sneaky little gom and knocked his lights out with the one blow. That was it. Head back like a punchball, down onto the pavement. Nothing. Pulse gone. Breath gone. All life gone. Nothing. Broken neck probably, the big filthy wimp. And such a vain gom too. Like, the song goes, the oldest swinger in town, ha? What was he like, too? Who did he think he was? Feckin Tom Jones, with the silver cufflinks, and the massive silver and gold Rolex?

Sorry, Claps. Say that last bit again.

TWO

Woo! Woo! Woo! Aw, yeah! Feckin right I'm the man! You do the math, Mammy! TX-minus twenty-four shaggin hours, no less! TX, Mammy, in case you don't know, is media industry lingo for 'transmission date', which means the date on which you plan to broadcast your brand-spankin-new, high-profile, feckin television show! Yes, indeedy, *Screen Grab* is a go!

Seriously, Mammy, we're all guns blazing around here. I've got my own big pair of baggy green combats, with a million pockets and a clipboard hangin out the arse, and a mad aul bobble hat on my head like yer man in the 'Two Princes' video, even though it's feckin boiling outside, and I've officially joined the team, as one of the gang, down at th'aul swanky office on Dean Street in Soho, dead flash like, no more buildering hickory doo-dahs for me, no sir.

Although I left the manual labour pretty quick smart, literally on the feckin day. Was a big hoo-haw for me at the time, bit of *ree raw ogus roola boola* only hours after being knocked for six by the sight of Titch rolling around the ground, clutching his eye and screaming the head off of him, because he'd got a right nasty shard stuck good deep inside from using the jackhammer without goggles, the eejit. He was only seconds into starting when he suddenly smacks his own hand up against his eye and yells blue bloody murder. Drops the jackhammer and hits the floor himself. I'm guessing there must be a shard the size of a feckin pencil rammed into his brain because he's popping about on the floor, flipping flopping left to right in agony, and without

119

words, while some of the big English lads are trying to hold him down and get him to open his peepers, and Kevin the foreman's bopping about in the background, assuring him that the ambulance is on its way.

The whole place is in shock after that, and I'm just trying to keep my head straight and not go completely to pieces, when Darren suddenly appears, all respectful and funereal because of Titch, and says, dead quiet, that there's a call for me in the cabin, some wan with a snooty voice. Of course, it's Jane, and all she says, half giggling with excitement, spy-movie style, is how soon can I leg it down to Soho and get started in my new job.

I'm down in Dean Street within the hour, still in my building duds, but getting cheers and jeers from Jane and the assembled gang for being the last one to arrive, and for missing all the coffee and the tiny Portuguese pastry cakes. Everyone's sitting around a huge white table made of smaller white tables pushed together, and there's a big shiny whiteboard on the wall, with squiggly boxes all over it already, dividing the months ahead into weeks, and with fillums and names and ideas such as 'Horror Night' and 'Sex Special' scribbled into the boxes. And there's no niceties, no chit-chat or nothing, just straight in, knee deep, into the business of fillum. I'm telling ya, Mammy, you would've been in heaven. Just the buzz. Like Stevie Fitz being all in charge and shouting out, so, Jay-meister, what do you think for the first TX? *Indecent Proposal*? 14 May? You like?

And I know about *Indecent Proposal*, because the trailer was on with *Somersby*, and I know there's been a scan' about it in the States, with folk everywhere having conniption fits at the very idea of the fillum, which is about this ancient lad in oompa-loompa make-up, who's played by Robert Redford, and is like this dead suave billionaire who goes cruising around Vegas

120

casinos, looking for young wans who've lost all their money and who'll take a million bucks in return for a single night of fine dining and fine wines on a giant billionaire's yacht in the company of a fossil in oompa-loompa make-up with a shrivelled aul donger.

Jane thinks it's a fablas film around which to base the launch of *Screen Grab*. She says that it's the ultimate water-cooler movie. Everyone agrees, and starts congratulating each other on having their fingers on the pulse of popular culture, when Stevie Fitz, always on for a bit of gas, spots me in silence and says, really corny and really loud, So, Jay, how much would you take, in cash, to give Shauna up for the night?

I go puce, and say, Ah, would you feck off with yourself! And then Shauna goes puce too. And then everyone goes Oooooohhhhh, all sing-songy and long, and laughing at us, because they all know that we are, officially, lovebirds. And, Mammy, we are. As lovey as lovey as lovebirds could be.

It's feckin magic, and I wish you had, in whatever way you could have done, prepared me for it, Mammy. Not Mammy Love. Because Mammy Love, as you know well, is love like the covers on a cold winter night, it's love like warm porridge on the following morning, it's nourishing love, love through your veins that grows and sustains. But romantic love? Ah, Jayz, Mammy, that, as I have learnt and loved and am still learning this minute, this second, in my heart as it beats, is another feckin sport entirely. And I know, as you've said, and as I believe, that you and Dad weren't exactly Roberts and Gere in a rom-com dream, so I don't want to be going and rubbing salt in the wounds. But fecking hell! It's mental stuff! We just lie there. Sometimes for hours. Just lie there, just looking. Eyes to eyes. Staring. No words. Just looking. Hours.

And I know, because I'm supposed to be all smart now and cute who-ery from Jane's books, and because I've read the English version of Zizek's 1988 introduction to his Slovenian translation of Lacan, I know what the staring thing's really about, that it's two people, two lovers, staring into the blackest black pit of the other's dilated pupils and seeing nothing at all but a great black abyss, 'the' great black abyss. Possibly the greatest abyss of all. And it is in the reaction to this terrifying abyss that you find the heart of the woman, the man, the lover and the culture. Thus love, romantic love, so the man says, is simply a reaction to terror and not a thing in itself. It's an extreme fabrication. A dreamy, delicate bandage to cover the wound of utter human emptiness. We love, in short, because otherwise, with eyes truly open, we'd cease immediately from what we're doing and dive directly under the nearest tube train. Society would collapse. Humanity would implode. There'd just be an unfettered planet, devoid of *Homo sapiens*, with monkeys and rats and tons of unopened boxes of Cadbury's Milk Tray, all because the lady realises that love is nothing, and that existential horror is everything.

But, Mammy, I tell you, as sure as I'm here and you're there, and there's a cold blue Irish Sea rolling between us, I tell you I've looked into Shauna's eyes, stared at the pupils, the blackest pits, for hours on end. Silent hours. And as I've stared I have fizzled with life, with overflowing life, and shaking so, to the pit of my churning stomach. I have seen the whole world in those eyes. And what I have is the end proof of love. What I've seen in those eyes is the shadow of God.

Of course, it wasn't easy, getting it off the ground, the love thing, and we had fierce trouble trying to have a decent bit of the sex. Mainly because on, like, feckin date number three, Shauna announces that her head's throbbing off her on account of the amount of cocaine she's tooken the night before, which was just before she snogged the face off Jess, and watched an ancient gay fella called Jonathan take his langer out and do a cack-handed ham-shandy in her direction. Naturally, Mammy, I nearly fall off my stool when she tells me all this, but I keep it dead cool on the outside, don't want to put her off with notions that I'm not up to the job. I just nod, dead casual, and cast a few lazy glances around us – we're in this mad multistorey disco in Soho, down by the gay end, where they're repeat-playing 'I Feel You' by Depeche Mode on massive multi-screens on the wall behind Shauna, which makes it even harder to absorb and comprehend her nutty and seemingly limitless sex *shcales* because the front-lad fella from Depeche is shouting his face off on the screens, all angry like, while some model wan wanders around in her bra and everyone looks moody and in their flowers and fecked off about the fact that love and sex have become such a chore.

As I say, I'm trying not to give out any small-time sex signals, and instead project the sophisticated mien of someone who's hiding his own pretty scandalous love life up his sleeve, possibly a few completely gay encounters at midnight in Hennessy's cornfield, or maybe an aul gang-bang or two down at the swim club, or a fablas history of transgressive yet consensual intercourse with some crack-smoking clerics after mass. Inside, however, I'm terrified that I have been outclassed and outgunned in the sexual stakes. And sure enough, Mammy, despite my two lonely and quirky nocturnal encounters with Diana and Jane, when it comes time that very night, in the pink palace bedroom, to actually do the bold thing itself, my equipment, as you might say, has a total feckin freak-out, and recoils up into my body every time Shauna's fingers, hand or thigh makes the slightest contact.

And she's brilliant about it too. Because we've got a million candles going, and she's in her best black undies, and all the electronic choirboys from Enigma are giving it socks on the

123

stereo, and you'd expect it to be the most mammoth night of pleasure ever imagined. But instead, Shauna just kisses me real tender like, and says that sex is mostly overrated and that intimacy without sex can be a beautiful thing, and then she lets the moment hang there just for a second, before adding the comedy rejoinder that there are worse things in the world than having a totally useless mickey.

Naturally, Mammy, you'll be pleased to know that we eventually do manage to execute a decent bit of technically proficient how's-your-father, though not until we do some proper courting first, like the way you and Daddy might've done back in the day. Although instead of spending three and sixpence on a hop in Barry McGowan's barn, we'd be mostly hoovering our way through a Thai curry on Portobello Road, before retiring back to Shauna's room where she'd spend the night up to her elbows in monkey grease, while twanging the mickey off me in the vain hope of readying it, good and strong, for an encounter with the feckin Ollie Campbell of internationally capped vaginas.

At the same time, during the day, any time me and Shauna happen to cross paths in, say, an editing suite, or in the so-called staff canteen (a tiny boxy room with a kettle and a fridge), anyone who happens to be there at the time goes all giggly and pretends that they'd better abandon the room in case me and Shauna burst out into a bad case of instant shagging. While at night, back in the pink palace, we make, as the man says, piecemeal gains. Without, Mammy, wanting to get too mechanical about it, I soon manage to salute the flag for as much time as it takes to allow Shauna to get to work, with fingers, hands, feet and toes – everything, that is, except th'aul Ollie itself. Jess, of course, the little rip, knows everything, and is always real smiley around me, giving me the sneaky eye, and wishing me luck every time I head into the bedroom. Which kind of makes me feel bad that Shauna, clearly more troubled that she's letting on, has had to unburden herself of our manky secret, but it also makes me feel relieved that I'm not trying to do it with Jess, which would be like trying to force-feed my useless mickey into the vagina world's version of Hannibal Lecter.

Anyway, Mammy, I believe it was René Descartes who first said, in his early meditations on philosophical dualism, that the mickey has a mind of its own. And, well, now, I feckin believe him. For it seems that my own mickey was holding back, for my own sake, and for the sake of everyone on *Screen Grab*, until the first actual RX date, and until the first RX was done, before it was eventually ever going to perform, properly, goodo, its appointed sexual function. RX, by the way Mammy, is to Recording Date what TX is to Transmission. Indeed, our Recording Date was only yesterday and, thanks to a myriad of ongoing so-called technical 'snafus' (more media lingo – you'll get used to it!), we didn't leave the studio (get me, eh?!) until one in the morning, after which our presenters, Jiz and Liz, were in a right fouler, so we all piled back to Jane's gaff for champagne on tap and a wild sort of a hoolie that had cocaine and everything, although when Jiz, who's a gas man, took out the baggies of coke and started spilling it around, I had to give Shauna a right decent reef on the arm, because I could feel she wanted to lunge for the stuff, and so I had to make it very clear to her that I had seen enough episodes of *Miami Vice* to know the kind of godforsaken roads you go down when you start messing with the Peruvian marching powder.

The party is mental. One of those nights when everyone is so feckin wired with emotion and tension, like the summer school disco in St Cormac's, that the whole thing just kind of explodes into screaming factions, and tiny groups of the disgruntled and the inebriated, who run off into little corners for hugger-muggering, back-stabbing whispers, and to fix the make-up on the wan that's always crying because some other wan fancies her fella. In my case I'm staring at Jane and Shauna, thick as thieves over in Jane's library, arms interlocked and jabbering away to ninety, when Stevie Fitz, drunk as a lord, comes swinging into me, and decides to give me a nonsensical pep talk about how lucky I am to have snagged a job for meself in the media, although he keeps calling it the 'meeeeeja' as a joke, and using finger-quotes, and saying the eeee bit longer and longer each time until he finally sounds quite feckin demented. Anyway, the gaff is hopping off the hinges to this mad noisy disco song that goes, No, no, no-no, no, no, no-no, no, no, no-no there's no limits! And maybe it's the thumpety thump of the music, or the buzz of the coke he's taken, but Stevie Fitz's lecture starts to get a bit aggressive towards the end, and he starts telling me all about how I think that I'm real hot stuff, real feckin Diet Coke Break Man, strolling in off the building site and stealing all the fine-assed fanny from him. Oh yes, Mammy, he drops quite the bombshell. While rubbing a feck-load of cocaine residue from his nostrils, he tells me that, however hot and raunchy my love life with Shauna is now, it will only ever be known, to him anyway, as sloppy seconds.

You better believe it, Diet Coke Man, he says. I've been there. Deep dicking. Big time. And then he goes on, real aggressive like, about how Shauna wanted his babies, and to get married, and to meet his parents and everything. Oh yeah, he says, really enjoying the mad feckin pale look that must've been sliding all over my bamboozled noggin, Three words for you, my good Diet Coke Break Man friend. Three words: UK, Spouse, Visa!

Well, Mammy, long story short, we had the ride of our lives that night. I said nothing to her the whole way home, and she, also with a face like feckin thunder, said nothing back to me. We marched up the stairs, filled up a couple of glasses of water, went into the room, locked the door, removed our clothes, all without a

126

single fecking furious word, and then we bet the living shite out of each other, sex-wise. I mean, Michael Douglas, me arse!

After the session, with both of us lying there, somehow hooked together at the crotch, in some splodgy masticated mess, and both of us afraid to look down in case medical attention is required, but both of us nonetheless keen to avoid all the cuddly love shite, I finally break the silence, figuring this might be the last night we ever spend in the sack, and I say, Why in feck's name didn't you tell me about Stevie Fitz and the UK Spouse Feckin Visa?

I think I have her completely on the ropes, and am expecting tears and a big bawling Yanky confession. But instead, she goes harder than ever, harder than I've ever seen her, and says, And what the fuck is this about you being the second coming of Christ?!

Naturally, Mammy, it was dead awkward.

Will keep you posted.

Meantime, be sure to tune in tomorrow. *The Indecent Proposal Special*. Will blow you away.

Your Right-Hand Man,

Jay

10

Escape to Knock

On the plane from Luton, Jay is sitting in a catatonic stupor, in between Bonnie and The Clappers. He eventually speaks, explaining, haltingly, that all his life he has experienced recurring dreams of persecution and pursuit. Being chased across nightmarish cityscapes by relentless Nazis. Beaten down in abandoned warehouses by disgruntled prison guards. And once, even, no joke, he says, but whispering, for the ears of The Clappers only, he was chased around the dreamy topsy-turvy back alleys of Temple Bar by a giant disembodied phallus. You name it, Jay could be chased by it in his sleep.

He says, still whispering to The Clappers while Bonnie stares wide-eyed out of the window, that he is now the proud owner of an epiphany. Because the dreams, he says, were all part of him and all part of this. They were cell memories of an event to come, in a time-flattened, post-Newtonian sense. A quantum event, rippling backwards along the space-time fabric. An event so profound that it cannot be contained by the humdrum delusions and linear patterns of daily life. Then he shakes his head, and says aloud the single word, as if testing the sound of it – murder.

Thanks for the lecture, Mr Hawking, says The Clappers,

adding drily, I hope they bring your feckin wheelchair to the gate. She then grips Jay's arm, tightly, from underneath her own folded arm and warns him, in the meantime, to keep his fecking voice down. Or else he might scupper their plan.

Plan? says Jay, looking up at his friend, pleadingly into her face, as his own red, sleepless eyes moisten with emotion. This is not a plan!

Jay has been crying, intermittently, in sudden profound body-shaking bursts that leave as quickly as they arrive, since the small hours of the morning. The tears have punctuated his exchanges with The Clappers, emerging at the end of any practical rationalisation of their situation that invariably leads to a punishing moral reflection. Grandad Paul, dead. Bonnie. Shauna. Future. Past. Crime. Right. Wrong. All concepts, ideas even, to push Jay into paroxysms of shaking, broken despair.

The Clappers, on the other hand, like a wan on a mission, is incredibly focused. She has even slapped Jay firmly, across the face, and has pointed him, in the early morning darkness, towards Bonnie, in the hope of regrounding him, reorienting him towards a fragile belief in tomorrow.

Lie low, Boss Man, she says, in a soothing whisper. Lie low in the wilds. The wilds of the West.

The Clappers takes charge of everything. Packing. Taxis. Tickets. She even scripts Jay's answerphone message to Shauna.

'Hiya Hon ... Treat for you ... Deserve a break ... Me and Bonnie to Brighton ... Call you soon ... Treat yourself ... You and Dr Ghert ... Quality time ... You deserve it ...'

And then, suddenly, finally, erratically, and still decidedly *verklempt*, Jay drifts wildly off message.

'And Shauna. I just want to say sorry. I am truly sorry. For everything. And I love you. Always.'

The Clappers slaps him across the back of the head and says that he's not supposed to be reading out a fecking suicide note.

'Maybe she'd like to sit on Mammy's knee?'

This option is offered to Jay as he struggles to keep Bonnie's belt clipped shut, fully shut, on their final approach down into Knock Airport, far to the west in the Land of Jay. Bonnie has found much sport in opening and closing her own belt, clicking and clacking out loud, and does not yet understand, despite some tight-faced insistence from Jay, that it must remain closed. She smiles, she clicks, she smiles, she clacks. A woman with stern, tired features, wearing a blue and yellow uniform, tuts quietly from the aisle and, running quickly out of options, waves a baby belt in the air and indicates The Clappers, mistaking her for the mother of Bonnie, suggesting that she remedy the situation, quick smart, with some maternal nous.

Difficult birth, says The Clappers to the woman in blue and yellow, clutching her own stomach with a melodramatic wince. Oxygen deprived. Damaged the head. Would break your heart, *nock ah*?

Oh sha, replies the woman in blue and yellow, backing slowly away with baby belt in hand.

Jay doesn't even turn around. He's still struggling with the task in hand. With every one of his closing clicks, Bonnie responds with her own opening clack. Responds and smiles. Jesus, he thinks, looking at her beaming through unkempt curls, while echo-memories bounce about inside. Her, kicking away with wild hysterical laughter while he tries hopelessly to fit her flailing legs into green woollen tights, his mood teetering between syrupy adoration and unfettered rage. Her, flinging fries on the white-tiled floor of the Prince Bonaparte on Chepstow Road, their first day out, ever, as a family, at a meal, a public meal, and her in her own wooden high chair, not scribbling on the kiddie-friendly mats, not staring at the

130

kiddie-friendly books, not even playing with the kiddie-friendly toys. Just flinging fries on the floor. And Shauna saying, No, leave her until she learns, until she understands the words from our mouths. And Jay bending to pick up each chip. Back up to her high chair, and down again. Up, and down. Up, and down. Her giddy fits, his bendy back, his face half rage, half adoration. And with nappies too, always a sore point, her urge to wriggle before wiping is done. Eight, eight and a half, nine, nine and a half, nine and three quarters, nine and— And off she goes, flick, twist, and flinging herself out of his grasp, rolling over the crisp white covers, again and again, stamping away as she goes, a plethora of tiny yet pungent splodges of defiance. Him, cleaning. Her, smiling.

The Clappers releases a huge rousing cheer to mark the reassuring moment when the plane's undercarriage connects with the runway, and just before the *fawlcha go hairin* announcement. Bonnie flinches at the sudden noise, but then gurgles happily. The Clappers, encouraged by this reaction, cheers again, and says aloud, right into Bonnie's upturned face, the phrase, Home sweet fecking home, before immediately adopting the gregarious demeanour of someone who is conspicuously happy to be back in Ireland, most notably when she drops to her knees at the foot of the air stairs and kisses the tarmac, much to the bemusement, and some amusement, of her fellow passengers.

Thought the Peelers would've had us back there, in aul Eng-er-land for sure, she whispers to Jay, as they trudge in a dutiful line into the terminal building, a tiny fleck of concrete grey in a wide rolling sea of grassy greens. The airport is a strange anomaly, the crackpot passion project of a long-dead priest who believed utterly in the regional value of placing an international flying hub in the middle of a wide expanse of marsh and bog, and who regularly rehashed the catchy mantra of the 1989 baseball movie with a spiritual twist, *Field of Dreams* – if you build it, they will come.

131

This must be how the 'RA fellas feel, ha? continues The Clappers. When they arrive back safely home, from killing the Brits. Jay remains silent. He clutches Bonnie's hand tightly.

How's she cuttin, leds? asks The Clappers, of any and every airport official they pass, and informs them, before they can answer, Up the middle, like a plough, ha?

The terminal building is busy. Unusually so, for a lunchtime, on the Tuesday after Easter. Jay thinks this thought. It's the first thought he's had all day that is wholly unrelated to the death of Grandad Paul. And it feels like something close to relief. He looks left to right, and back again. He sees old people with sad anxious faces, more women than men. Some families. Rucksacks. Rain jackets. Not here for luxury. Barely here for holidays. They move, these people, these mostly old people, in great unified droves. Shuffling slowly around the concourse. They are led, Jay notes, by uniformed officials in fluorescent jackets holding up laminated signs decorated with stark black crucifixes that simply read, Knock 1, Knock 2, and Knock 3.

He remembers, as a child, visiting the holy shrine in Knock. You could kiss the wall, if you liked. Right on the stone itself. At the exact spot where the Virgin, and St Joseph, and Jesus as a lamb appeared. Mammy, his Mammy, was all over it. Snogging the face off the old grey brickwork. Moaning and muttering Mary this and St Anthony that. Jay couldn't do it. There was a queue. His turn behind Mammy, and a hundred mammies behind him. He lifted his head up. Leant forward towards the wall, and allowed his nose to make light, brushing contact. That was it. No kissing. On the bus home he and his mammy pored over their treasure-trove collection of Knock tea towels, Knock necklets, Knock rosary beads, fridge magnets, novelty lights and glow-in-the-dark Virgin Marys. It was some haul.

Jay is snapped to attention by The Clappers, excited and excitable, who has returned from a brief so-called 'grub run', arms overloaded, in the fashion of 80s TV staple *Crackerjack*, with crisps, sweets, fizzies, newspapers, a large frothy coffee for Jay, a large frothy chocolate drink for Bonnie, and an even bigger bucket of froth for herself. Jay does not thank her. Barely even responds. Just tugs lightly on the sleeve of her white denim jacket, nods over to the busy elderly droves in raincoats, and, wordlessly, gives a modest shoulder shrug of enquiry.

Oh, groans The Clappers. The fecking shrine! She lifts her hands upwards, and shakes them rapidly, as if impersonating a scared and superstitious supplicant. Ooooh the shrine! The shrine! Gods and monsters! Lord help us! Fecking disgrace!

She explains that the so-called holy shrine in Knock has been doing gangbusters business all year, courtesy of a cute whore diocesan letter from a cute who-er regional bishop, one Bishop Gannon, a right trendy aul get who wears shades in the church-yard, and sometimes indoors too, and who accidentally on purpose leaked his own diocesan letter to the Sligo *Herald*, and it went national from there, and was a big to-do in all the papers, and on the news, because it spoke, very cleverly, the cute who-er, of the End of Days and the Biblical Apocalypse at the dawning of the year 2000, and managed, very cleverly, to weave in the fantasies of some millennialist nutjobs, Zoroastrian eejits and a whole rake of computer nerds to let the country know that the entire place was about to be launched into hell in a hand-basket at the first stroke of midnight on New Year's Eve 1999, which will signal a rapid-fire line of global cataclysms. And – and this is the cute who-er bit – that only prayer and repentance at the holy shrine in Knock, complete with a generous if incidental influx of cash to meet the region's developmental needs, would save any and every honest-to-goodness Catholic from eternal, and instant, death and damnation.

I mean, hisses The Clappers, in a sudden falsetto of rage. It's feckin Stone Age stuff, Boss Man! Gods and monsters, lambs and virgins, floating ghosties, and the sudden dramatic flattening of the planet at exactly midnight on New Year's Eve instead of, like, just after breakfast the next morning. She shrugs, changes tack momentarily, and asks Bonnie if she's enjoying her Bay-B-Chino, then takes a generous swig of her own giant cup and, suddenly renewed, launches into a fulminating rant against Gannon and the like, and the fairy stories peddled by the Catholic Church. Visions, me arse.

Outside the terminal, Jay, for the first time that day, takes a slow, deep, chest-filling breath. He observes the world beyond him, and beyond his own throbbing, searing skull. At a glance it is landscape, undeveloped and predominantly rural, just as he remembered. He sees patchwork greens, brushstrokes of brown, broken splashes of lake blue, defined and contained by the furthest, faraway stretch of hazy mountain lines, and all cast against a stark cyan sky. Unexpectedly moved, he bends down and lifts Bonnie into his arms. He does a soft, slow swirl around, with his finger outstretched, tracing the horizon and describing as he goes, with schoolboy precision: Lough Roe to Lough Nanoge, Cloonacolly to Bella Bridge, Cornaveagh to Lough Gara and back again to Lough Roe.

This, he says to his only child, is Ireland.

Bonnie does not react. She lets her head fall gently into the crook of Jay's neck. There are thick chocolate lines rimmed around her lips. She is tired.

Instinctively, without thought, as it was in his message to Shauna, Jay whispers sorry into Bonnie's ear, and tells her that she's a grand girl.

Jay sits beside Bonnie in the back of The Clappers' indecently large vehicle, a jeep-van-truck-tank hybrid with tinted windows, chrome hubcaps and the spotless, blinding sheen of money. They are driving, apparently, and, according to The Clappers, to a safe house. They are far above the ground. They could be in a space-ship. Hermetically sealed from engine revs and the world outside, by thick soundproofing and heavy leather upholstery. Bonnie is lying prone on Jay's jacket. Jay asked for a car seat, but The Clappers laughed and said that they'd do it 70s style instead, and that not wearing seatbelts was good enough for them when they were chislers, and they didn't turn out too bad, ha?

Bonnie sleeps almost instantly, as soon as she lies down. She holds her arms outstretched for longer than normal. It's one of her birth quirks. Jay often has to fold them down, like the stubborn legs of a sun chair, or a stiffened tripod. Her other quirks include trance-like stares, coughing fits, a strange lolloping running gait, unnoticeable at walking pace, and a very occasional and wildly unflattering capacity for drooling. The doctors, who have never seen the drooling up close, suggest that it is connected to the coughing. But Shauna and Jay both know that it is connected to the words, the beginning of words, the backlog of words, waiting to come out.

Jay hates Bonnie sometimes. Her silence infuriates him. He can hear sounds in her breathing. Sounds in her laughter. Sounds in her coughing. On the night of Halloween last year, back in the flat after a desultory round of trick-or-treating, with Shauna collapsed in a depressed heap upstairs and Jay working grimly through a familiar pile of dishes, Bonnie emptied an entire bottle of ketchup on the kitchen floor and made smiles and sun-faces with negative lines in the huge splash of red. Jay, on his knees, cleaning again, finally cracked and screamed into her face, Speak, motherfucker, speak! Bonnie winced, and she shook with fear, and opened wide two terrified eyes. But she didn't speak. Jay stood up and made her pancakes, washed her, dried her, told her a story about the adventures of polar creatures, turned out her light, crept into his own bed, and then cried himself to sleep.

He cuddles with Bonnie now. Lies down beside her on the back seat, keeping her safe in an inverted spoon. The Clappers talks incessantly, and slurps from her giant paper cup. Her words are nonetheless soothing to Jay, as soothing as the delicate hum of the tank's engine, the rumbling road below, and the background radio rattle of velvety shockjock Gerry Ryan, discussing today, on his phone-in show, the most popular methods of toilet paper application for the nation's posteriors. Jay drops off, eventually, listening to The Clappers in mid-rant. She is driving with one hand – automatic, cruise control, she explains – while shaking a newspaper with the other. She's still on the Millennium Apocalypse. Planes falling from the sky. Cars crashing in city centres. Oil tankers smashing into each other. Feckin nukes loose from computerised silos. It's feckin science fiction. Don't you think?

Jay is dreaming in the back of the car. Half dreaming, half thinking, half remembering. Half listening to Gerry Ryan and The Clappers. He dreams of freedom, and flying. Floating above the earth. Hovering in space, dizzy with terror. Yet looking down all the same. And he remembers a double-bill, at the Rex in Castlebar, of *Superman* and *Superman II*, seen with his mammy, on a school night no less. And that night, late home, going through the films in detail, both films, scene by scene, with Mammy on the bed. Buzzing with excitement. He gripped her arm, and refused to let her leave the room until she named her favourite moment, hands down, out of both films. That's easy, she said, without seeming to think. It's the moment when Lois Lane sees Clark Kent as Superman for the first time. Sees who he is. Realises that the world's saviour has been by her side all this time.

Jay wakes with a start at the safe house. The journey is over. It is evening time, night is falling. The familiar roaring sound of breaking waves is the first perception. Jay looks around, confused, squinting through failing light.

Bonnie is also blinking back into awareness. She is crabby, and hungry. Her curls are matted with sweat. Her woollen tights too hot. She pushes Jay away. She misses her mother. He can see it in her eyes. Disengagement with him, a rejection of his caress and an aching plea for a return to the mammy, always to the mammy, the eternal return.

This? This is the safe house? asks Jay, with an incredulous flutter of his eyelids. The shed?

The Clappers shakes her tightly shorn head, and sighs, archly, 'Blessed are they that have not seen, and yet believe!'

She tells Jay to wait in the car, lights off, and then, on her signal, covert spy-movie style, walk briskly and quietly, with Bonnie in his arms, in through the back door of the so-called shed. Jay peeks through the gap in the open driver's door. The shed was once the only edifice along the sands of Strandhill, standing proudly in the dunes of Carrowdough, facing into the North Atlantic, and towards the deserted, wave-washed headlands of Skibbolecorragh and Carrowloughan East. Tonight, from just a momentary scan, Jay can see eleven, twelve giant, boxy, beachfront properties around it. Glass constructions, floor to ceiling, with intermittent stripes of black stone, while all else is chrome. Balconies too. More glass. More chrome. Fecking *Miami Vice*, he thinks.

Bonnie screams all the way to the shed. It's not a familiar child scream that one might easily recognise from playgrounds, shopping centres and nursery schools. It's more of a goaty sound, as if procured from somewhere deep inside of Bonnie, low down in the angst of the gut. Jay has heard this scream before. At bath times. At bedtimes. At mealtimes. At end of ice-cream times. At hospital times. At X-ray times. At blood-test times. Especially at needle times. And often at paediatric play specialist times. The same sound. A harsh, coarse, gravelly roar, almost braying. It is loud.

Security lights from either side of the shed blast the ground into bright bluey white. A man, middle-aged and balding, in black T-shirt and grey tracksuit bottoms, appears on the back balcony of an adjacent glassy beach box.

Claire, he says. Claire, darling, is that you, ya? He speaks with a long Dublin drawl.

Bonnie brays. Jay soothes. The Clappers appears, sheepishly, in the spotlight.

Yes, it is, Fintan, eh, darling, she says, tentatively. She looks at Jay and red-faced Bonnie, both frozen in the glare, then back up to Fintan.

Here for a viewing, she finally says.

A viewing?

The word seems to ignite a fire in Fintan. He warns everybody not to move, races down through his house and out into the sandy scrub, and launches himself on the trio, shaking Jay roughly by the hand, tickling Bonnie and promising Jay, face to face, eye to eye, and man to man, that any offer made for the shed will be doubled, straight off the bat, as the Yanks like to say. He's had his eye, and Claire knows this, on the shed for months now. Been discussing with the missus non-stop. The missus has plans. She's a great one for spending the money. Wants to knock right on through, turn the whole place into a den for the boys. You know what the lads are like, especially the 'Rock lads. Fond of a brewskie or two. Great lads all the same, solid men, some of them Leinster reserves. But then Claire here's been holding back on us, clearly, Claire. She can sell any old shoebox this side of the Mason–Dixon line, sand to the Arabs, but refuses to let go of her precious shed, until now, that is, Claire, ya?

Fintan clasps Jay's hand a second time and, shaking it more vigorously than ever, barks, Pardon my manners, Fintan Smith McGonagall O'Reilly. Solicitor.

Jay stalls. He remembers the joke – 'Help, help, my son, the doctor, is drowning!' He shakes hands again. He thinks, sadly, so this is it, this is life on the run. This is the eruption of the real. And then he says it.

Jack, he says. Jack.

He spots three surfboards stacked neatly in Fintan's back patio. A momentary flash of televisual inspiration.

Jack Lord.

The Clappers winces slightly.

Fintan, without missing a beat, asks, As in *Hawaii-Five-O*?

The very same. I'm in construction.

I knew it! says Fintan, excitedly, before turning back to The Clappers. You, are, devious! What are you, ya? De-vee-us!

The polar story tonight is brief. Jay tried to do some life story for Bonnie but his heart wasn't in it. We got up, so so early, and we flew on a big, big plane with Auntie Claire, and you had yummy hot chocolate and a big, big sleep in Auntie Claire's big, big truck-tank-car thingy. And Auntie Claire talked and talked and talked all about the end of the world, and then Daddy had to have a big, big sleep too, such were his stress levels, and the state of his confusion.

The shed, of course, is unrecognisable to Jay. Though the back and front façades of shrivelled silver maple remain intact, the entire interior, gutted, widened, expanded, raised, is now defined by blinding-white walls, tasteful nudes, blood-red couches, chrome kitchenette, centrepiece breakfast bar, and a balcony bedroom for Bonnie and Jay.

So, he says, staring into Bonnie's eyes, immediately abandoning the life story, exhausted from the effort, and beginning instead with an update on Penny the girl polar bear, who has been bringing home food, every night, for the polar den, to feed her weakened and wounded father, and her terrified mother. Bonnie's eyes beam. She makes a giddy gasping sound. She is wearing a warm Dalmatian bodysuit, with floppy black doggy ears, and short paw places for one-to-two-year-old limbs (her hands have ripped through to the wrist already). She pulls the sheets up to her chin and grins. Jay is pleased.

Penny's polar-bear father is very, very proud of Penny. He calls her the great hunter. Jay tickles Bonnie when he says the words, Great Hunter. She chuckles. Penny's polar-bear father marvels, each night, when she drags in a whole salmon, with barely a scratch on it, or four or five sea-trout, or an entire chicken, neatly plucked. Penny, however, has befriended the lonely son of the fearsome owner of a local Canadian restaurant, and at night, each night, the son meets Penny at the service exit, then plays with her, kicks ball with her, and hands over the best kitchen cuts that he can find.

On this particular night, nonetheless, when Penny arrives at the service exit she finds no trace of the son. She waits, she kicks the ball alone, and is just about to return home, and face a curious grilling from a disappointed father, when she hears a familiar voice coming from the alley next to the restaurant.

Penny! says the voice. Penny, down here! Down in the alley!

Bonnie begins to chew on her sheets.

Penny pauses and sniffs the air. She smells the son, but something else. Cigarette smoke, garlic, aftershave, fish guts, man sweat and, crucially, fear.

Hurry Penny! comes the son's voice, more insistent this time. I need your help. A load to lift, and only your strong paws can do it. Come on, Penny. After all the fish and the free food, I just need this itty-bitty piece of help.

Bonnie shakes her head.

Proud Penny lollops down the alleyway, dutiful above all else. The smells get stronger with every step, until finally, there, next to the bins, looking terrified and tearful, face battered and bleeding, she finds the son. Behind him, however, stepping out from the darkness, with loaded rifles in their grizzled hands, and cigarettes hanging from their dirty crooked mouths, are Penny's dreaded enemies, Tim and Tom, the polar trapper twins.

Penny flinches.

Bonnie flinches.

The son shouts for her to run for her life, and is smacked in the mouth for his trouble by Tom. But before she can even turn, and before the claws of her paws gain a millimetre of purchase on the slidey, slithery alleyway floor, BANG, she is shot in the leg by Tim. Bonnie flinches again. Penny hits the ground with a yelp. Tim and Tom march slowly over, with both rifles cocked. Tom strokes Penny's fur and coos happily to Tim, marvelling over the thousands and thousands of bucks that they'll earn for this pure, impossibly soft young skin. And with that Tom places his rifle up to the back of Penny's skull and says aloud, Sorry, you won't be needing this.

On Penny's polar-bear face is a quizzical frown.

Your life, my pretty, your life!

He puts his finger on the trigger.

Bonnie's eyes are out on stalks.

11

The Truth about Love and Truth

Where was I?

It was the night of the party . . .

The argument?

Yes. The argument. Where he tells you that he knows about the spouse visa, and you tell him that you know about him being the son of God.

Yes, I am aware of the argument you're talking about.

And?

And what can I say? It was one of those nights. It was the early days of the show. Everyone was on coke. Lips flapping, jaws working. Secrets spilling out left and right. And I was with Jane, who, as well as being my boss, and our producer, was this, like, fairy godmother mentor figure to Jay. Force-feeding him books, taking him for coffee, having 'intellectual discussions' with him. Pure Eliza Doolittle shit.

And you resented this?

Damn straight.

You resented her willingness to improve the internal and intellectual life of your future husband?

I resented her willingness to fuck my future husband.

She fucked your husband?

142

She half fucked him. But she apparently changed her mind in the middle.

And how do you feel when you think of Jane fucking your husband?

Oh, just dandy. I want to hop in and high-five her at the climax!

Hmmm. I find this –

—No. I'm furious. And I was furious then too. Especially that night. Because she lords it over people. Jane. Bleeding heart, my ass. And, 'Oh, didn't Jay tell you this? Hasn't Jay told you that?' And she knew that I was sensitive to that shit. I had told her that I found him quiet, that I was trying to bring him out of himself, to open up, to be brave, and not to be afraid to be exposed. I'm like, Don't be afraid, Jay! Open up! What's the worst that can happen? So when she talked like that, about their closeness and his seemingly constant confessions, she knew that it got to me. She must've known. Oh, Jay told me that yonks ago, darling, when we were studying our Ferdinand de Fucking Saussure and the importance of sign, signifier and signified. And then, of course, she drops the bomb. Has he told you about the mammy and the Jesus thing?

And had he?

What do you think? No! Never mentioned the mammy, beyond a grunt and a dismissive groan. But what do I say? I panic and I say, No, say, Kinda, sorta, the whole Mammy thing is kinda off the table, which it is, which it was, and she looks shocked, and coked up, and buzzy and black-eyed, and, like, what sorta woman am I that I can't coax outwards the one central, inalienable truth of this guy's being, a truth that he happily divulged to her some many months previously, casually over coffee and post-structuralist linguistic classes, so happily in fact, that she happily divulges it back to me, coked up and fizzy eyed, right there in her own library, the library so important to her ongoing and heroic education of Jay.

I notice you turn your face away from me when you say the name Jay.

I do?

You do. It is brief. But you look to the window, and then back again. Why do you think you do this?

Because it's painful.

This is true. What else?

Because it's really painful?

But why me? Why turn from me?

Why not?

Because you see me as an authority figure? Yes? Because you see me as the ... as the ... as the fffffff ...?

Oh. I see you as the father?

You ask me?

I see you as the father.

Excellent. You don't show the father your painful face.

I don't.

You need to be more bold. More open. More free. And yet these are the very things you wanted to see from Jay, no? What do you think about that?

I think I should finish Jay's mammy story.

Which is?

Which is mostly Jane, dropping a bombshell through my world, talking about the essential motor that defines my man, while Jay himself is totally scoping me from the hallway, throwing tiny little half-waves in my direction while this nerdy, needy, Scottish doofus, Stevie Fitz, the stupid midget, is hanging out of him, practically tonguing his ear, filling his head full of nonsense and cracked-up coke stories about me being a serial dater, and crazy shit like that.

And were you? A serial dater?

I was a serial dater if you were a small-town munchkin hick from the asshole of Edinburgh. To anyone else, I was a woman.

144

And you dated him too, this needy man?

Only briefly. Like, a couple of movies, and maybe a meal or two. And some sex.

Of course. And from that, you deduced that he was needy?

He was a cling-on. An A-grade cling-on. Give you the willies. We'd, like, do it in his flat, in his filthy room, with his books, magazines, newspapers and old sneakers scattered about, no sign of the carpet, the floorboards, or whatever the hell he was hiding under there. And he'd apologise in advance, telling me that it's the Malaysian cleaner's night off, but not to worry, because I was about to have my mind blown by some grade-A Scottish beef. Which was kinda depressing, but his way, I guess, of breaking the ice, doing the super-stud act, and kind of ironic too, because on the very second time, right in the middle of it, he said that he loved me, and that I was perfect. And then, his O-face? Christ, man, his O-face was a horror show. Literally, the cry-baby face. I swear I could see tears each time. He was definitely whimper-ing.

. . . Sorry, but—

O-face. Orgasm-face! Cum-face! Your face when you climax.

I see. And this face. This face is important to you?

Not important. Just interesting. Can short-cut a lot of small talk when you go straight to the O-face. You see so much in that face. Like reading a résumé. Some guys get their teeth out, and their eyes blacken, and they spasm with raw rolls of effing, and bitching, and cunting, spewing nothing but spite and anger, like they're craving your annihilation with each closing, spurting, thrust. And you just know, with these guys, with these O-faces, that the minute you've had that shower, and are barely towelled down, still soapy, you're out of there. No numbers, no baby talk, straight into the taxi. Boom. Foot down. Go! Go! Go!

I see.

The others get lost in themselves, in their own pleasure. The eyes roll back, shark attack style, the head flies back too, the mouth twists itself into a groaning rictus of unspeakably delicious agony. I used to like this kind. That was my preferred kind. Jay was that kind. Unforced, nothing to hide. Open and exposed for once in his life, for those few moments. When we did it, he was that kind.

And your kind? What does your O-face say about you?

Me? Shit. I haven't had an O-face in years. Not since I got pregnant with Bonnie.

And Stevie Fitz? Did you have an O-face with him?

Are you kidding me? No, I didn't have an O-face with Stevie Fitz. I didn't have any face with Stevie Fitz, other than the face that's trying to hide the fact that I've made a terrible mistake, and the face that's trying not to blow chunks after the twentieth time that he tells me that he loves me, and that he wants to take me back up to rural Perthshire to meet his midget mom and pop, and his midget dog.

The element of size, I surmise, is important to you, no?

No, the element of truth is important to me. And Stevie Fitz was not truthful. Not to me, or not to himself. He knew me for ten minutes, before he said he loved me. That is not truth. That is confusion. That is delusion. And that is as close to a lie as the real thing.

And you never lie.

Plus he told Jay, that night, the coked-up party night, that I had practically thrown myself at him, and wanted his babies, and that I was some sort of bunny-boiling psychopath who was using Jay in order to hoodwink him up the aisle and secure for myself that rare and elusive professional security known as a UK spouse visa.

And were you? Using Jay?

I don't know. Maybe.

But I thought you said you never lie.

146

No. You said I never lie. I said that truth is important. But at that time, even before that night, and before his confession, I knew that I loved Jay. I could feel it within me. Growing and spreading like a sickness. A strange, beguiling and, at that time, a beautiful sickness. A new sensation and a new emotional reality that I had not previously felt, honestly, ever. Awakened, I was. Like everything I had been through, all the guys, all the crap, all the sadness with Paul, it had all been part of some grand and tortuous testing process to get me to this point. With Jay. And with the softness of Jay. And the quiet care, and that instant tender embrace. But I also knew that my visa was almost up. And I knew that marriage was mostly bullshit, apparently defined by boredom and resentment and the very high likelihood that the man with whom you trotted down the aisle, like a moony-eyed cream-puff, would one day turn around and hit you so hard in the face that your lower jaw would break in three places, leaving you physically scarred, and emotionally deformed for life. So, screw it, I thought, yes. Do the visa. Be with the guy. It's no biggie. It's win-win.

And you told him this?

I told him everything that night. In bed. In his arms. No secrets left between us. Nothing to hide.

Because he had told you?

Yes.

About his mammy, and being the son of God?

Yes.

And you believed him?

I believed what he told me.

Which was?

The truth.

Which was?

The hardest thing he's ever had to say.

And you don't want to say?

I don't want to break his trust.

Look around you. This is not a police cell. There are no lawyers present.

I'm sorry. I need a moment.

12

Strandhill

A knee in the groin. That's how Jay wakes up. A pinpoint shot from the patella bone of a thirty-two-month-old child weighing just under twenty-nine pounds, and landing with some force from a modest height, no greater than two and a half feet in the air. The resulting impact catapults Jay's torso upwards and forwards, from the prone position, producing an instinctive and almighty yelp in the form of the holy exhortation, Jeeeeeesus!

Bonnie smiles. She does this a lot. The shock wake. The Dadda bounce. Or the Mamma hop. And it was, it seemed, funny at first. A rare, momentary, mark of pride shared between Shauna and Jay. A sign that this strange, wheezing, silent child with an occasionally lolloping gait was robust, spirited, and essentially healthy. The shock wake, they decided, was a small price to pay for a smaller comfort, and was thus generally greeted with a long comedy ooooooof, followed by a gentle hair ruffle and an enveloping arm that would pull her close, bodily, squealing excitedly, beneath the covers.

Bonnie was normally insistent too, straight after the shock wake, that life begin, that the day start immediately, moonlight be damned. You could cuddle all you liked, and breathe in deeply the warm sustaining air of heaven-sent sleep child, but she'd wriggle and she'd writhe, and she'd kick and she'd poke, until the parent in question, the one of least resistance, was up, out and down, and feeling the dull bracing cold of the wooden kitchen chair against the back of their thighs while the dawn barely broke outside.

She is different today, though. The initial wake-up shock is followed only by mild wriggling and writhing, and she is content, instead, to stay snuggled in her Dalmatian suit, on the covers, next to Jay, not venturing, not yanking, not even sure if Aunty Claire's kitchen, with its long strip of metal and glass in the corner, qualifies as such.

Jay should've known better, of course. The signs were all there. The sounds at least. He had heard the shuffling of sheets, the diminutive yawn, and then the neat and diligent double-rip, chhrrp chhrrp, of the night-time pull-up, followed by the soft near-silent thud as it hit the ground by the bed legs. But he was gone. Adrift in the black and woozy non-slumber that had defined his sleeping patterns since Bonnie's very first nights at home. Back then, in the early days, he'd thought it was a novelty aberration. Baby in the room, and all that. He'd share zoned-out, small-hour breakfasts with Shauna where, baggy-eyed and red-rimmed, they'd chuckle nervously in disbelief, and concur with the startling fact that they had not, in any verifiable form, actually experienced a single genuine wink of sleep over the course of the entire night. For four nights. Then five. Then a week. It was the practical joke that just kept on giving.

By week nine Jay announced, out of sheer desperation, that what was needed was a change in terminology rather than in sleep patterns. They needed to believe that sleep did not necessarily require actual sleeping, as the old, pre-partum definition would've explained sleep – the darkness, the letting go, the forgetting. Instead, they needed to see sleep in a new light (often literally so), and simply as the absence of daytime activities and

150

coherent communication combined with a sludgy grasp of consciousness within horizontal darkness and underwear.

And the other new parents didn't help, the NCT bunch. With their blissed-out tales of all-night dozers, or their lightweight confessions, over coffee, of tiptoeing into the nursery, bending down over the cot and just, well, listening, because, you know, just to make sure that they're still, you know, breathing? Shauna agreed, of course, and sympathised quietly. Yet she could not avoid feelings of rage and helplessness when reflecting upon her own nocturnal misadventures, lying bug awake, next to a tiny twisting, coughing creature, flipping and flopping on the spot, crying one minute, groaning the next, barking, wheezing, screaming the next. Minute by minute. Every hour. All night. And her and Jay, faking it, bluffing it, as minor medics in the making, buzzing around the bedroom like demented bluebottles, flicking through jotters and supposedly spotting dyspraxic tics, involuntary muscular spasms, and eerie dystrophical markers.

And the pain was the other thing. The pain that they held for this strange and innocent wounded thing. A pain so great that they felt, separately and together, that if they slipped for a moment, or let the side down, if they flinched in the face of it, they might simply, in the most literal, physical and existential senses imaginable, implode. And yet, bizarrely, the rage was great too, the boiling defiance. In this upside-down, inside-out world of extremes, Shauna's best day was found in some calming words from a visiting nurse, a toe-counter and pupil-tester, who told her, quietly, and without fuss, that it was fine and understandable to have the thought, the big thought.

What thought? said Shauna.

The thought, replied the nurse, that says that maybe it wouldn't be such a bad thing to pick up this baby and fling her out through those open windows.

Oh my God, gasped Shauna, covering her mouth and flooding

151

forth with tears of relief. She thought it was her dark and wicked secret to keep.

And they tried to be normal too. To be like other new London parents, the NCT bunch, smiling together, supportive as ever, wildly content and coolly controlled, with Baby Bjorns, and backwards strollers, and blobs of ice cream by the fountain in Queen's Park, and regular rat-a-tat media chats, while Baby coos quietly in pram, running through the highs and lows of final edits, first drafts, pilot scripts, production overruns, buyouts to sell-outs, floor managers to stage managers, designers, presenters, ten-percenters, three-shots, two-shots, tequila shots at Groucho's, head-wreckers, big buzzers, daily uppers, nightly downers, all nighters, no brainers, on-set complainers, real-life megalomaniacs, real-world tours, publicity whores, publicity hounds, marketing buzz to marketing mayhem, to read-through, to test card, test cut, final cut, final edit to first draft.

And so they tried. So, dinner over at ours? For the whole crew. Even Liz and Jiz. And don't be late! Organic bangers and mash, and some seriously spitballed ideas for season four. That was the theory. But bad Bonnie baby was awake all night, screaming and yelping through the nascent chat. Jay, drinking heavily and hopelessly, decided on an alternative tack. An impulse reaction. He lifted Bonnie up, out of her darkened room, and walked her through the kitchen, the noisy, boozy kitchen, holding her under the arms, puppeteering her into the company, feet inches off the ground, and giving voice to her thoughts with a broad American accent, in the vein of TV comedienne Roseanne Barr, or Bugs Bunny.

So, eeeeeeee, what you folks doin, heya? he began, bouncing Bonnie into a jolly canter across the floor. There was much laughter among the guests, especially Jane. Bonnie stopped crying. Shauna, silent, was seething. Drunken Jay the object of her hate. He continued, which one-a you folk stole my unda-cooked and ova-priced organic sausage? More laughter. More cantering. And then it happened. Jay stumbled forward, and clumsily stamped, full-force, on Bonnie's tiny ten-week-old foot, before collapsing on top of her in a panicked, leg-flinging heap. Bonnie froze in the open-mouthed silence of unthinkable agony. Then screamed. Then Shauna screamed. Then Jay apologised, to Bonnie, to Shauna, and to the assembled guests.

Was only having a bit of *crack*, like, he said, weakly.

Shauna and Jay argued, furiously, in front of their guests about whether or not to take Bonnie, still screaming, into St Mary's A&E, for X-rays and the full once-over. Jay, mildly addled and booze blurred, adamantly refused, saying that it would be like Orkney, from the news, all over again, with a crack team of social workers abseiling down through the ceiling to take Bonnie off their hands for good. Everyone knows, he said, that you don't report *crack* like this! It's the fecking dinner bell for the social!

Shauna called him an asshole-prick-bastard and marched off to bed, with Bonnie in her arms, still screaming. The dinner party was abandoned. Shauna and Jay stayed awake all night. Bonnie finally got some sleep sometime around three. She woke at five, for the day.

She is different today, though. She listens, in rapt fascination, to the deep sonorous rhythm, slow bass rumble and long treble retreat, of the waves outside. She leans languorously back against Jay, who has collapsed again onto his pillows, but with eyes wide open, staring blankly at the thick, black-lacquered beams above.

That's the sea, he eventually says, after an age. He strokes Bonnie's head, letting his fingers get lost in the tangles of her tresses. He stretches his left arm, and points from the balcony bed out towards the giant bay window downstairs. Out there! He says. Daddy and Auntie Claire used to swim in that same sea, when we were young young boys and girls, young like Bonnie.

153

Any chance we got, weekends, holy days, sometimes even after school on a scorcher, Daddy and Auntie Claire would grab our togs, run down to the high street, hop on the bus and we'd be up here, to this very spot, within the hour. We were fierce competitive too, the lot of us. Always racing, and always fighting about who got the head start into the waves. The others were, well, Uncle Mickeleen and Uncle Foxy. But Auntie Claire had the beating of us all, every time. She was like a fish. In through the breakers like a knife, or a torpedo. Nowadays it's all blondie surfer dudes, riding the barrels, wiping out and getting radical fecking point break, excuse the French. But you can never underestimate the purity of a body in water, sliding through the swell, lifted and embraced by all around. We couldn't get enough back in our day.

And after the races there'd be the chats in the dunes, the dares, and the tell-tales. Which was part of it, and often just as exciting. Little secrets that we heard, things that we knew, or rude stories that we needed to share. And then we got older and there were girls, and giggles, down in the dunes too, drinking a bit of pinched Cinzano to raise the stakes goodo. And they dared Daddy too, Auntie Claire dared Daddy to kiss Mairead Ni Davitt on the lips even though I'd only just met her that day, in the dunes, her up from Sligo, just that day. And because I did it, no problem, which wasn't normally like Daddy, but something made me do it, but because I did it, Aunty Claire had to do the forfeit, which was to run nudey from the dunes to the sea and back again, with everyone, like, even the strangers on the beach having a right good gawk. And she did it, no bother, because Auntie Claire was always one, at a moment's notice, for whipping off . . .

All right! All right! comes the sudden clamour from below. Keep it PG, for feck sake, Jack Feckin Lord! I can't take any more of these God-awful, rose-tinted memories. Making me sick. You're wreckin me buzz at this hour of the day! And what's so wrong with surfing, ha?

The Clappers rolls out of her sofa bed and over to the bay windows. She is wearing a huge, oversized pink T-shirt that is stamped, on both sides, with the two enormous black interlocking Cs of Coco Chanel. A bit like a sandwich board, Jay will later tease, though The Clappers will tease right back that at least she knows feckin class when she sees it.

For now, she waves up at Jay and Bonnie and tells them not to move a muscle. She disappears underneath the balcony, and reappears, humming the James Bond theme while clutching a small silver remote control in her hand. Grinning, she points to the ceiling, presses the remote, and three thin white covers on three strip-skylight-windows slide back automatically. She presses again, turning towards the bay windows, where the open curtains slowly bunch together and run themselves neatly into the corner. She then points towards a black glass box on the wall, which suddenly blasts into action the thumping sound of a raspy-voiced Caribbean man from all corners of the room.

It's Shaggy! she shouts, above the din. All the rage!

Jay smiles, and shouts back at her, wanting to know, as drolly as he can muster at 120 decibels, whether her little silver friend makes the coffee too.

Funny ye should mention that, says The Clappers, before dashing towards the sink unit, and meddling purposefully with a whirring, hissing, clanking machine.

Cap-A-Chino! says The Clappers, while mounting the shiny steel stairs in her Coco Chanel maxi-shirt, and clutching a tray of freshly microwaved croissants, two frothy coffee cups, and a large glass of orange juice for Bonnie.

Nothing but the best for the top cop in all of Hawaii, she says.

Bonnie launches herself at the croissants and juice. Jay sips delicately from his cup, deftly nudging the tip of his nose through a mountainous splodge of creamy-white coffee top.

The three sit, facing forwards, staring out the bay windows at

155

the long rolling waves. From all around them Shaggy suggests that they watch how his love rocks, how she models it a swing, like me grandfather clock.

The music stops. Then starts again. Same song. Same Shaggy.

The Clappers grabs hold of the bed leg, swings a free arm underneath the balcony and clicks the silver remote. All stop. Silence. The waves crash. Break and retreat. Break and retreat. Bonnie chews. Jay stares. The Clappers fidgets.

So, she says, after an eternity of deafening quietude and pulsing subterranean angst. I suppose we should go and visit th'aul Mammy.

Jay doesn't even flinch. Doesn't make eye contact either. Just sighs, I suppose we should.

13

Moulinex Makes Things Simple

So, so the story goes, Jay's mom has gone berserker with the Moulinex, piling in the foodstuffs like it's the last Friday before Armageddon. Eggs, flour, milk, butter, apples, raw sausages, and even sardines. Literally, everything but the proverbial sink.

The Moulinex?

Food processor. Chip chop chop. You don't call it food processor, though. You say Moulinex. I guess it's that talismanic thing. Brand names as symbols, modern markers of pride. Contemporary saints. The Moulinex. The Sony. The SodaStream.

And the cakes are important?

The cakes are important to Jay's mom, and to Jay. They are the food that they eat, the treats that they consume on the couch, at the weekends, when they sit down and, hour upon hour, do nothing but watch movies.

And this idea appeals to you?

This idea is not the point. The movie watching is Jay's idea, as are the cupcakes. They seemed, he said, both things, to calm and quieten his mom and make her mind less agitated and discomfited. For her regular mental state, he said, joking, but not, was technically described as mad as a hatter, a complete basket case.

And has been, easily, since her early fifties, since, what he called, ominously, the early onset.

And he told you the name of this condition?

At the time, when it first started, he wasn't even ten years old, and he says that it was, initially, bizarre. Totally comical, in fact, to watch her wrapping five-pound notes, hair curlers and telly remotes in old newspaper, and hiding them deep inside the airing cupboard, for fear that the local clergy might come to claim them for themselves. 'Ye mad aul wagon,' he said to her once, smiling but confused, guileless but nervous, baffled more than anything else, still a child, from behind her shoulder, while she was carefully hiding minor household objects. And whenever she felt him there, watching in her the slow creeping emergence of insanity, she'd either ignore him completely, and continue muttering madly away to herself, or else she'd respond coolly, and without a scintilla of affection in her voice, hitting Jay with the incessantly repeated catchphrase, 'Oh, it's well you might be mad! Living in this nut-house!' At other times too, better times, he'd come home from school and find her, together with Bowsie the dog, happily sprawled on the sitting room floor, surrounded by old family photographs, casually ripped from once-cherished albums. She'd beckon him in, pull him down to the floor and cuddle him close, kissing him gently on the forehead, with eyes closed, and heart aching, whispering, my love, My boy, my old *segosha*.

This is you, she'd say, holding up a blurred and faded monochrome baby picture. And even before that, this is you in my tummy, right there in the middle of that two-piece bathing suit. I know. Very daring. Was a grand young thing in them days. I had to practically force your father to take that picture. Morto, he was. Because of the bump.

And this is your grandad Farrell when he was only a couple of years older than yourself, down in the arse end of County Kerry! And this is me at the Christmas hoolie, and you just a dot in the background, in Auntie Maudie's arms, while I'm like a young starlet, like feckin Twink herself, and I'm holding forth by the piano, and telling a *coopla schale*, much to everyone's amusement, I might add.

And she had moments of perspicacity too, including one, crucially, where she stumbled into the kitchen, lightly dusted with attic flecks, and with a classical print in her hands, torn, it seemed, straight from the pages of an old *Reader's Digest*. She announced the painting as *The Madonna and Child* by Guido Reni, 1628, and then asked Jay to examine it closely and tell her the main thing about it that appeared to him unusual. Jay, who was almost thirteen at the time, was deeply embarrassed, because the painting featured . . .

Breastfeeding, I believe. Yes?

Yes, the Virgin Mary, with fleshy breast exposed, and the infant Jesus, in a perfect latch, glugging away contentedly, and her not even wincing, not the slightest hint of swollen nipple or any physical signs at all of early breastfeeding aggravation.

Point being?

Point being, Jay was stumped for an answer to his mother's question and so she leapt about triumphantly, announcing the right, the right, it was the right-hand side. The infant Jesus was on the right-hand side of the Virgin Mary!

This is true.

Jay was unfamiliar with the significance of this innocuous fact. He shrugged again. His mother called him a heathen, and explained to him, just as her own father had once explained to her, that Mary the Blessed Virgin, in classical art, was always depicted on the right-hand side of Jesus, and not vice versa, because this was exactly how she was seated and arranged, so says the bible, within the gates of heaven. Jay's mom announces that she has been in the attic all morning, rooting through the old *Digests*, because she knew, just knew, that it was in there – Not

159

bad for a mad aul wan with no memory, she joked. Because sure enough, she says, 'clare to God, there it is, and here it is. Guido Reni's *Madonna and Child*! Then, overexcited and half-garbled, she delivers to Jay a strange staccato art lecture, read directly from the pages of the *Digest* itself, which informs him of how the left to right switcheroo was not an act of defiance against the Church, but an attempt to humanise both Mary and Jesus and, crucially, the relationship between them. By placing Jesus on Mary's right, Reni was moving him away from religious para-digms and bringing him instead within an earthly fold, to the realm of mothers and sons in this mortal life.

I understand. But—

No, wait, this bit is key. For at the end of the lecture, she turns to Jay and says, This picture is you and me!

And, you just know, for a second Jay's thinking, Holy shit! Where, in God's name, is she going with this? But luckily, his mom puts him out of his misery and tweaks his cheek and says, grinning, You! You are my right-hand man! The nickname sticks.

And the diagnosis?

Just weeks after his thirteenth, when the local parish priest, one Fr Francis, apparently a decent fellow with a white shock of hair, arrives at the house in Cloonavullaun. He has, according to Jay, a right decent posse of doctors and nurses behind him. He announces to Jay, on the QT, in the back garden, under the pre-tence of a parish survey, that Jay's mom has been seen stalking the streets at night in her pyjama top with no bottoms, banging on the shutters of Mulvey's Garage, and asking aloud for ingre-dients for a White Russian plum pudding. Everybody believes, says Fr Francis, everybody alongside him there that day, the whole posse from the medical establishment across the border in Sligo Town, everybody believes, without doubt, that Jay's mom has contracted a fatal dose of Alzheimer's disease. And the nature of the disease is such that it will make, and is making, even right now, Jay's mom progressively weaker, more forgetful, more confused and more insane, minute by minute, hour by hour, until death. Jay, remember, just thirteen years old, feels only the weight, the pain, and the panic-stricken finality in Fr Francis's words, even despite the caring tone. He hears correctly, between the lines, the intimation that his mom will need to be removed from the house, sooner rather than later, and placed into care. And that he, inevitably, unless saved by the last-minute intervention of Auntie Maudie from over the water in London Town, will soon be facing the same grisly scenario.

Of course, Jay, normally shy and quiet, but feeling outnumbered, cornered and threatened, goes bat-shit on the day. He warns Fr Francis, and the rest, to go feck off for themselves, and that they can tell fecking Al Simon (seriously!) and his fecking disease that he clearly hasn't heard of the bold Farrell family bloodline, which was hardy as feck, and had dodged the bullets of British squaddies back in the day, and was certainly not going to be bothered by something as piffling as a dash of memory loss, some missing pyjamas and a couple of quare phrases. They leave. And yet, despite the bravado, Jay, on that very afternoon, and alone in his newly burdened adolescent mind, simultaneously accepts the diagnosis and makes it his teenage mission to upend it. Thus, with occasionally casual tip-offs from a doggedly insistent Fr Francis, he reads library books and health pamphlets, listens, mostly bamboozled, over the phone, to a Dublin-based specialist, and is given the name of a retired schoolteacher, from nearby Derrynacross, who nursed her own husband through the final years of the disease. And from these disparate sources he decides, in whatever way is possible, to fill his mom's life with rhythm and routine. Rhythm and routine. The key to beating it, or at least delaying it. Rhythm and routine.

Which means, from then on in, the same breakfast every morning (scrambled egg on toast – he's already made it by the

161

time she gets down, but leaves the egg in the pan, and lets her scoop it about aimlessly, to give the impression that she's still in charge on the culinary front). Same song on the stereo ('Let's Call the Whole Thing Off' by Fred Astaire and Ginger Rogers, which, without fail, propels Jay's mom into a daily outburst of song, and a tiny mock waltz around the kitchen, crooning along to, 'You like to-may-toes, and I like to-mah-toes!'). Same newspaper in through the doorway (*Irish Indo*). Same daily stroll (her to mass with Bowsie the dog, him to school). Same lunch (cheese sangers, already made, and coleslaw, in the fridge). Same afternoon routine (her, gardening with Bowsie, him, school). Same evening meal (Monday, stew; Tuesday, pasta; Wednesday, pork chops; Thursday, more sandwiches; Friday, fish; Saturday, cupcakes; Sunday, roast; and Monday, stew again, made with leftovers from Sunday's roast). And, of course, same sacred Saturday routine, entirely engineered by Jay, and based on a previously proven appreciation, between the pair, of old movies and sweet sponges. He calls it a Saturday film marathon, and he finds in the films, in their watching, a blank tranquillity that descends upon his mom, a peaceful space that denies completely the twitchy tribulations that can so easily consume her, and drop her into the inexplicable trauma of crackpot selfhood. For without routine and rhythm, those cornerstones of sanity, Jay's mom had the capacity to become an agitated crazy person, flicked like a switch by the slightest provocation – an unexpected visitor, a call from the gas company, a window frame warped, a handy man required – all horrifying surprises, all flinging her into rages of painful confusion, all daily reference abandoned, just the sheer limitless terror of ineffable unknowing stretching out before her.

So, movies were soothing, and cupcakes were easy. The latter required only five handwritten notes, by Jay, her beloved Right-Hand Man, posted above the oven, on which were scrawled huge poster-pen pointers such as 'Flour', 'Sugar' and 'Eggs'. He trusted his mom enough to allow her to make the cupcakes, but watched her carefully nonetheless as she crudely dumped everything, all the ingredients, actual measurements abandoned, into a large plastic bowl and stirred like crazy, arm-breaking stuff, on the sitting room floor, in front of the first movie of the day. He bought her the Moulinex in 1987, at the same time that he bought the video player, affectionately known as the Philips. He was working part time in a gas station by then and, together with her post office pension, he claimed that they had just enough money to surround Jay's mom in limitless video films, oodles of cupcakes, and an unblinking unchanging routine that seemed to stave off the worst symptoms.

And what of Jay himself? He had no life of his own? He sounds, if you would like me to be honest, like a regular true blue Jesus Christ. And this is exactly what you mean, no? This is what this is all about? He was, by his actions alone, the country-boy Jesus Christ of self-abnegation? And I'm supposed to feel sorry for him? You're supposed to feel sorry for him? He plays on your sympathy, no?

No. He wasn't Jesus Christ. He wasn't even special. He was just a boy who loved his mother.

I can see that this moves you, to say this thing. Why do you think this is so?

Because it's sad.

Because it's sad that a boy loves his mother? This is a good thing, no?

This is a sad thing.

Why?

Because his love is not returned.

How do you know?

Because she's fucking nuts.

Can you be sure? That she does not return his love?

No.

163

And maybe this is what he wants? To be the one giving love? The one without receiving love? The one without the life?

No, he had a life. He looked after himself too. His mom, he said, was like a child on a merry-go-round. You just needed to put her on the right horse, set it for the right speed and appropriate duration (in her case, mostly, a weekday afternoon movie on the goggle-box, preferably a biblical epic, something nice and long; a double bill was even better), and you could go off for hours. And he did. And always to the beach in neighbouring Strandhill, always swimming and racing, joking and joshing with a tight-knit trio of buddies, known by the names, and you'll love this, of Mickeleen, The Fox and The Clappers.

Really? These are human beings?

The Strandhill gang knew of Jay's mom's condition, but had absorbed, through precious few doorstep exchanges, only the sense of a smartly dressed woman with a serious face who was otherwise showing few or no signs of total internal meltdown.

So Jay swims. So what?

So he swims, and he grows, and the Strandhill gang grow too, and adulthood approaches, and the allure of real life among the swimmers and the chatters and, yes, the flirters on the beach begins to tug Jay away from his mom and his mom's now maniacally ingrained routine – ingrained into the core of her decaying brain, right down to the exact six spoonfuls of scrambled egg, to every last sung syllable from Fred Astaire, the exact same stroll with Bowsie, the exact number of cupcakes, in the right order, on the right shelf in the oven, and the exact number of video boxes arranged on the table, stacked seven high in the middle, under a sitting horse paperweight, waiting patiently every Saturday morning, or else!

Nor did it help that home life, perhaps unsurprisingly, had deteriorated for Jay. Even within the routine, Jay said that his mom was becoming wildly erratic and almost permanently addled. She was losing weight. Bone thin. Something as simple as a sneezing fit could throw her for hours. Into utter confusion. She could erupt into screeds of babbling nonsense, and then back again into clarity. She continued to refer to Jay as her Right-Hand Man, even though, increasingly, she seemed to find his presence an annoyance at best, especially when she started to half comprehend, via snippets of conversation and pavement exchanges, that his ongoing and escalating social life with the Strandhill gang was boasting a decidedly romantic hue.

So Jay is in love now, and giving his love to someone else, and is still not Jesus?

The girl's name was Mairead, and Jay hooked up with her during a kiss-dare in the early-summer dunes at Strandhill. Jay, who is nineteen, likes her a lot. She is, though not officially announced yet, his first real girlfriend. And for the first time ever, or so he said, he was properly excited at the prospect of living. He was excited too at the prospect of Saturday, 7 July 1990.

An important date?

It was the day when Mairead, who was staying all season long with her family in a beach bungalow in Ballincar, across the bay from Strandhill, was planning to throw a summer party of boundless, booze-fuelled decadence, no parents allowed, all day long. And most importantly for Jay, it was the day in which, at some non-specific point during the highly anticipated and hugely inebriated proceedings, Mairead and Jay, both physically involved, but virgins both, had planned to enjoy their very first act of love.

Sex?

Yes. For the first time. They were going to lose their virginities.

And how do you feel, when you think of them losing their virginities together?

There's just one snag. The party is a Saturday. And Saturday is film marathon day for Jay and Jay's mom. And Jay can't miss that for the world. His mom's life, or at least the last shreds of her sanity, almost, quite literally, depend upon it. And naturally, he thinks about alternatives. He contemplates telling his mom that the day is Sunday, or Monday, when it's not, but it's too risky. The days of the week, repeatedly cross-referenced with the wall calendar, on an hourly basis, are almost all that she has left.

He discusses it with Mairead, and with the Strandhill gang, and the best that they can come up with is a compromise. Mairead, real slow and mellow-like, will get the party started at lunchtime, without Jay. Soon after, with the vibe humming nicely along and her younger brother left in charge, she'll slip out, hook up with the Strandhill gang and swing by in the car of The Clappers to pick up Jay. They'll all crash, the lot of them, on the couch with Jay and his mom for a while, maybe even catch the tail end of a movie. And once everyone's copacetic, and comfortable with the soothing and Alzheimer's-friendly atmos chez Jay, they will gently depart in the early evening hours, leaving Jay's mom in her usual trance, chugging down goodo on the movies till the small hours, by which time Jay and Mairead will have happily danced the night away and, in the words of Jay, found the time to give each other a fierce decent ride. At least that's the plan.

And the reality?

The reality is that Jay's mom fucking freaks from the moment the doorbell rings on that Saturday afternoon. She's watching *My Left Foot* with Jay, but has been irritable with him from minute one. Thing is, she never really watches the movies, Jay says, never 'watches' the movies. They just, kind of, sedate her from the get-go, they douse her with a powerful kaleidoscopic wash of broken images and thundering soundscapes. The moment she looks towards the screen she is sucked inwards, and placed on the loop, for hours on end. Not going anywhere. Not on any journey. Not part of it. Not in story. Just, well, spinning.

Today, though, she seems different. It's as if, from their very first bite of scrambled egg, she can detect a shift in the dynamics between them. As if she is so well attuned to the rhythm and routine of their life that even a break in the intention for that same rhythm and routine is discernible to her in, say, Jay's facial expressions, his breathing pattern, or in the minor adjustments of his wardrobe – long-sleeved shirt instead of T-shirt, and hair deliberately ruffled instead of lying flat, and to the left. In short, and because of the disturbing implications of this interpersonal shift, the sedation doesn't work. Jay's mom turns to Jay throughout the first half-hour of *My Left Foot*, and asks him, repeatedly, for the name of the movie, and the name of the leading actor, and is he really a gom in real life?

It's Daniel Day-Lewis, Mammy, Jay would say. And he's not a gom, he's just brilliant at acting.

But it wasn't soothing. Her growing agitation was evident. She was rocking back and forth on the couch, asking again and again, the name of the film. *My Left Foot*. That's a quare name. And it's called? *My Left Foot*. That's a quare name. And it's called? *My Left Foot*.

In the midst of this the doorbell rang. Almost unbearable in itself. But, worse, what does she see when the door opens? Four large and formidable figures, enormous unannounced bodies, pouring in on top of her, without any warning, or any plan in place, or any ritual and routine to prepare her, on this, her Saturday film afternoon. Naturally, she freaks. She pops up from her chair, looking frightened and drawn, and bone thin, like she's about to dart for the door. Jay introduces the gang. She has met Mickeleen, The Fox and The Clappers before, and they greet her enthusiastically with a rough How-a-ye, Mrs Concannon. But nothing from her. Not even a handshake, or a nod. No recognition at all. Just a nervous grimace.

Jay then turns to Mairead, nudges her slightly forward from

the group and presents her to his mom. And this is my friend Mairead. Jay's mom looks up and makes tremulous eye contact. She looks from Jay to Mairead and back again, and there is, Jay suspects, Jay has said, an understanding of sorts as to the emotional entanglements of this new relationship. Jay's mom stands. And they all stand. All together for several seconds. Jay's mom could melt, and she could scream, such is the level of panic within. But somewhere deep inside, even beneath this, somehow, according to Jay, some last minute doomsday button is depressed in her core, and she goes into what Jay describes as Emergency Mammy Mode.

Go on.

Will yiz have some tea, lads? Some fairy cakes? You'll have some fairy cakes, I know you will. You look like a desperate lot for fairy cakes! My Jay there was always a terrible man for the fairy cakes! You'll have some fairy cakes, ha?

She then, to Jay's absolute surprise, reaches over and snaps off the television, with the muttered imprecation, Enough of that aul shite. She looks around at the guests, without actually looking at the guests, and instructs them all to sit down, and informs them that they'll have a grand hoolie, like the old days, right there on the spot, and if they're really lucky she might tell a *coopla shcale* for their troubles. She instructs Jay to hand round the Cinzano and, for the briefest of moments, is suddenly elated by the company and the sense memory of sociability.

And the guests?

The guests don't get it. They take tiny glasses of Cinzano and smile and laugh and dote upon Jay's mom in the way you'd dote upon a blind dog that ricochets its way through a forest of table legs. And, yes, there is much to enjoy too. Jay's mom is, however briefly, gregarious. Like the host of a comedy club, she moves along the line of guests, plucking names out of the sky, calling them Frank, Samantha, Pixie Dust and Blue Lou Boyle, and tells them that they're a smashing lot, and that Jay's a lucky lad to be surrounded by such a fine bunch of gougers.

And it doesn't last?

No, unfortunately not. Jay's mom is frail, and weak, bone thin. And her efforts to entertain, to converse, and to simultaneously make cupcakes for all, quickly prove to be a huge strain, and in the excitement of suddenly hosting for the first time in nearly a decade, she blanks Jay's handwritten pointers and instead crams the Moulinex, berserker style, with everything from apples to sardines, sausages and sugar. She's in the kitchen for an age, whizzing and stirring, whizzing and adding, until Jay, finally, perhaps, on reflection, unwisely, pops his head inside and casually delivers, hoping against all hope, throwing all caution to the wind, the phrase, Right, Mammy, we're off now!

Jay's mom fucking freaks. She says, No, no, no, and charges into the sitting room, where, horrified to see her guests shuffling towards the door, she orders them back in and warns them that they won't be taking her Right-Hand Man away until she's had her chance to tell a *coopla shcale*! Jay groans. He says, No, Mammy, maybe another time. Secretly, he is happy, unexpectedly delighted even, that his mom has engaged with the very concept of him leaving the building. Not today, Mammy, he repeats, and tries to guide her down towards the couch. Jay's mom appeals to her new guests, all of them, for the chance to tell a *coopla shcale*. Just *shcale awoyne*! she eventually pleads, which means just one tale.

Now there is a moment here, right now, when Jay's own story, and Jay's confession, could've moved off in a radically different direction, and in this moment, in this version, Jay and his friends smile politely at his mom and walk briskly out the door, and enjoy the decadent and climactic highlight of summer 1990, including a spectacular loss of virginity for Jay and his girlfriend Mairead. But no, right now, in this real moment, on a whim, or

169

an impulse of Christian charity, Mairead suddenly speaks up and says, Yes, that she'd like to hear a *shcale awoyne* from Jay's mom.

Jay groans again. The gang sit down again. And Jay's mom, shaking now, leaning into the fireplace for support, proceeds to rattle through, apparently from memory, her memory, an old family story so complex and convoluted that, were it not for the fact that the parameters of her disease allow for occasional ingrained aberrations, any stranger dropping by at that moment would see in her nothing but a master story-spinner in her prime.

And the story?

This is where it gets freaky. The story is a hoary old family tale about Jay's mom's father, who's saved from a bullet in the back by a ghostly visitation from heaven during the Irish War of Independence.

Really?

Yup. The story sounds bullshit now, but his mom's words, and her way of telling it, perfected over the course of, well, her whole life, making that story, in every way, her life's work, casts a magic pall on the listeners, who are glued to their seats and buying every single word of it. The story traditionally ends in 1969, with her father, one more time, getting a visitation from God, who tells him that he was saved, all those years ago, in order to spread the word of peace and tolerance in Ireland, and to campaign against the violence and hatred that had just, less than a year before, erupted again in the north of the country. And he did, apparently, and became a committed peacenik in his old age. Nonetheless, the shocker here, in this version, and the shock that lifts Jay directly out of his seat in horror, is the moment when his mom, suddenly overcome with body-shaking grief, announces that the visiting messenger from God was not interested at all in the northern Troubles, and instead, the actual information conveyed to Jay's grandfather was that he was carrying within him

170

the bloodline of the one living and holy Christ, and that specifically Deirdre, his daughter, Jay's mom, would produce the heir to the kingdom of heaven, meaning Jay.

Goddamn Irish.

There is a moment of utter pin-dropping silence after she hits them with that punchline. Almost immediately, though, and you can blame it on the mood-altering properties of Cinzano, or the giddy anticipation of the evening's festivities, but everybody on the couch, excluding Jay himself, bursts into paroxysms of laughter. Jay's mom is appalled. Jay is upset. Jay's mom is confused. She doesn't understand. She frowns. And in her frown she rolls her eyes and says, Forgive them for they know not what they do. She continues, baffled but insistent. He is the second coming of Christ. It's plain as day, it's even in his name, JC! (The Clappers mutters, *sotto voce*, And in Jerry Connelly the fishmonger – more chuckling.) And it's in me, she adds, dramatically thumping her own stomach. Jay has no earthly father!

Jesus!

I know. The Strandhill gang, and Mairead too, having just about reached saturation point, stand up to leave now. They apologise to Jay, who is still dumbstruck, and torn between the two poles of filial concern and utter repulsion. But Jay's mom, eyes wild with emotion, simply does not stop. He was immaculately conceived! she says. He has the power of Christ within him. The power of God flows through his veins. He can heal us. He can heal you! He can heal the world! The gang nudge each other nervously towards the door. The Clappers is still giggling. Jay's mom retreats into the kitchen, from where she shrieks out the name, Mairead! The gang stop. Feck. Mairead tiptoes tentatively into the kitchen and screams. The gang follow, with Jay at the helm.

Jay's mom has happily placed her right arm, her bone-thin right arm, down through the funnel, and down, firmly down,

171

right down to her bony wrist, right up to her wrist, down, into the non-spinning, non-chip-chopping Moulinex.

Jay says Wait!

Jay's mom looks at Jay and smiles, and says, simply, Be not afraid!

She flicks the switch.

Everyone screams.

And she dies?

No. She doesn't die. She makes it as far as the street, holding her bloody pulsing stump aloft, screaming Heal me Jay, heal me, Jesus! Smearing Jay with her stump, waving it around like a glistening, squirting, Halloween favour, yelling out the name of the Lord, crying out for Jay's assistance, and his miraculous touch, while the neighbourhood emerges and an emotionally indelible, county-wide scandal is born.

And Jay? What does Jay do?

He leaves.

14

London. Wednesday, 7 April 1999

'I got shhhhhumthin to tell ya. I got shhhhhumthin to say. 'M gonna put thishhh dream in motion . . .'

– Fuckin Boyzone! says Darren, inching his van slowly into the Blackwall Tunnel.

Stevie Fitz is holding a camera on his shoulder, filming through the grille, into the back of the van. Darren shouts, at no one in particular.

– Have youze lot seen the video for this? It's gift! Dead funny. All the lads from Boyzone are clowning around with all these comedian lads and shi'. And they're falling all over the gaff. And there's this big red fuckin ball yoke bouncing through the video. Fuckin deadly. Fair play to them. Fuckin gift.

Darren's phone rings. He looks at the number, sighs and answers.

– I'm heading into the tunnel, man, and I've got Boyzone on the tunes, so this better be good, ruy?

Diana says that she's worried. That Malacky has been listless all morning, hasn't touched his breakfast, and is pale, and not communicating.

– Not communicating?! What the fuck, Di? He's a fourteen-month-old baby, not a fuckin spin doctor! Just give him some more Farleys and stick him under the jungle gym, and he'll be grand.

– He is under the gym right now, and he hasn't touched a single dangly.

– Not even the squeaky parrot?

– I'm worried, Dar. I'm worried and I'm furious! I told you not to do those stinking jabs! I told you!

– Not the fuckin jabs again!

– In Morocco we don't do jabs. We never do jabs.

– And look at yiz? Still stuck in the Stone Age! Camels and shi'.

– He could be autistic. Right now. Lying on the gym like a zombie. Our precious baby, our boy? Autistic. Because of you and your bleeding jabs.

– Probably just tired.

– Tired from what?

– From the fuckin jabs!

– You don't even read the papers.

– Tired, not autistic.

– Men of science have said this. Men of learning. They say, don't do the jabs. Because the jabs make them autistic. And what do you say? What does Darren the great Irish scholar, with the inter cert, the Guinness and the potty mouth, say?

– I say fuck that shi', the jabs are grand. Your only man!

– You're not listening to me, Dar! I am worried, and I am scared, that Malacky, our boy, our beautiful beautiful boy, has become autistic since getting the jabs.

– And you're not listening to me. He just needs some more fuckin Farleys and a bit of fuckin shut-eye.

– I hate you, Dar.

– And I fuckin love you, babe. Now, if you don't mind, we're heading into the tunnel, the signal's not worth shite in there, and I've still got ninety seconds of Boyzone left to go, so don't worry,

174

he'll be grand, you'll be grand, I'll be grand and I'll see you tonight. Over. And. Out.

– Fuckin birds, ruy? he says, nudging Stevie Fitz in the elbow, knocking his shot off balance. He shouts out again, directing an enquiry towards the men in the back.

– Any you lads married?

Silence.

– With kids?

Silence.

– Any thoughts on the aul MMR debacle?

He thinks of Malacky, lying beneath the rattling, blinking, brightly coloured gym toys, with his pellucid blue eyes sparkling wide, and his open mouth smiling into a gurgling sideways O, revealing two lone bottom teeth that form the focus of a soft and comical portrait, which in itself gives Malacky the appearance, in Darren's own words, of a fuckin baby tramp. Darren's voice suddenly becomes tight with emotion.

– You can't really catch autism from the jabs, can ye?

He nudges Stevie Fitz again.

– Can ye?

In the tunnel, Darren's heart races. He thinks of nothing but Malacky. The face, the weight in his arms, the warmth, the smell. The light in his eyes. All suddenly fading, faded and gone. He emerges slowly onto the Greenwich peninsula, just as the morning sun breaks through the giant cylindrical skeleton of the gas bell on Dreadnought Street.

– Wakey wakey, lads! he says, thumping the grille with extra frustration, making Stevie Fitz hop with fright.

Darren loops the van swiftly off the main drag and down through a series of strictly coned construction roads, marked by a seemingly random plethora of makeshift yellow signs that announce, in perfunctory black font, destinations as exotic-sounding as Main Dome, Inner Dome, Heavy Use, Light Use,

North Gren, North Gren Main, and North Gren Park. Darren chooses North Gren Park, and joins a chortling line of goods vehicles that are all eventually spewed onto a wide section of scrubland that boasts a variegated sprinkling of double-storeyed, London Underground Portakabins, and a monstrously intimate view of the giant dome itself – a drum-tight arc of brilliant towering white that dominates the morning light, and hides beneath its purity and dazzle a busy world of diggers, lifters, breakers, hoisters and chasers, and a sneaking, creeping sense of push-me-pull-you freneticism unbound.

Darren leaps from the driver seat and slides open the side door. The men who emerge, however, find him doubled over and gasping for air.

– Is alruy, he says, shooing them on with his free hand, while the other clutches at his chest. There's nothing to fuckin see here! You too, Fitz! he adds, waving the camera away.

He has these all the time now. The halted breathing. The tightness under the ribcage. The worry. The soul-crushing worry. And always Malacky. Always Malacky in his mind. Always his boy in his heart.

His phone rings.

Jane opens the thick glass security door, out onto Frith Street in Soho. She takes a tentative sniff of the morning air, a queasily familiar concoction of stale beer and urine, rising freely from the alleyway beside the Dog and Duck. She sighs, carefully clicks the door shut, and begins her short stroll to the *Screen Grab* production offices on Dean Street. She mulls over today's schedule and feels strangely listless. The show hasn't been the same, she thinks, since Stevie Fitz and Jay left. No, same show, but less fun in the making. Less of *the crack*, as Jay might say. Good on them though. Breaking away, out on their own. Making a name for themselves. *Dome Life*. Certainly ambitious. Reminds her of her younger self, way back in the hungry days. Hungry for the career above all else, and at all costs.

Jane walks while holding a home-brewed coffee, and leafing through yesterday's post. The streets are already busy. The catering trade mostly. Metal traps standing open, pavement side. Small men with tired faces, sweeping and splashing about in small streams of roadside disinfectant. Laundry vans too. Couriers. Cyclists. And early-morning winos.

Jane is good with the winos. Gives them cash every time. She crouches down. Eyeline to eyeline. She makes a connection. And where are you from, originally? Ireland? Scotland? The younger ones are Eastern European. She doesn't go higher than a fiver. She once tried a tenner but Matt snatched it out of her hand and told the wino to get fucked. He put the tenner into his own pocket and sneered at Jane, telling her that she was pathological, and that she wouldn't be satisfied until she'd thrown away her trust fund, or mothered the entire world.

This had hurt. The mothering bit. Jane had tried for children with the man before Matt. His name was Terry, an older and modestly successful poet, with long white hair and a penchant for sudden, impetuous holiday breaks. That's it, get your coat, we're going to Heathrow! Terry had suggested children. Jane had liked the idea. She was thirty-eight. Time was ticking. They did everything right. Days, temperatures, and mucosal viscosity. They even talked IVF. But no, all they had to show for their efforts was a single first-trimester miscarriage, which, for Jane and Terry, seemed to be the greatest of earthly tragedies. In grief, Terry and Jane were brought even closer. Matt hated this. He claimed no shared grief with Jane. He had not wanted children. He had short dark hair, and he was not a poet. Terry, however, was eventually revealed to have had another equally powerful penchant – for women younger than Jane, and for making babies, successfully, with them. He asked Jane to understand. He was an artist. The babies were his immortality.

177

Matt and Jane spoke of their life, in company, as the good life. They could travel wherever they wanted. They could eat out in Soho, go to the movies, the theatre, a gallery, or an exhibition, all at a moment's notice. And why, anyway? Why? With Kosovo and Global Warming, the World-Wide Web and Global Poverty, and the G8, and Big Brother and Pammy Anderson's sex tapes? Why would you bring another human being into this godforsaken place? Jane always felt foolish when Matt gave that speech. Others would agree with him. Even those who had children. But she felt humoured and foolish.

Our careers are our children! Matt would continue, briefly elaborating on the effort it takes, the time and attention, to nurture the kind of enviable media spots to which they can, this pair, lay claim. Inside Jane would cringe.

Our careers are our children! She chuckles wryly, snorting to herself, as she pushes open the stiff doors to the Dean Street offices. She walks into the darkened meeting room, blinds down, and stands utterly still while the lights snap, buzz and whirr noisily into action. She leaves her coffee on the desk, wipes down the whiteboard, and yanks up the blinds. She prods her computer stack into life, prods the monitor too. A fax in the corner, overnight from LA, tells her that the interview with A-list megastar Kirsty Jackson is on the schedule, all systems go. Sign and fax back the interview waiver by return.

Pleased, she scans the page. No questions about Kirsty's alleged drug-taking. No questions about Kirsty's previous relationships. No questions about Kirsty's current relationship. No questions about Kirsty's alleged time in rehab. No questions about Kirsty's father. No questions about Kirsty's mother. No questions about *Titanic* and whether or not Kirsty auditioned for *Titanic*. No questions about Leonardo DiCaprio. No questions about *Good Will Hunting* and whether or not Kirsty auditioned for *Good Will Hunting*. No questions about Matt Damon. No questions about *Flubber*, *Face/Off*, *As Good as it Gets* or *Air Force One*. No questions about her brother's childhood car wreck, her guest vocals on Limp Bizkit's 'Counterfeit', or whether she did or did not get ejected from Stella Adler's Los Angeles Acting Conservatory. The interviewer will, at three fixed and agreed upon points during the interview, refer to, respectively, Kirsty's establishment of her own production company, Kirsty's presence at last July's Women in Hollywood ball, and Kirsty's support of the Clean Water Clean Life foundation.

Jane's pen hovers and flits along, over each line, down the page. Her lips move as she reads. She says, Yep, yep, yep, yep, yep, yep, yep, yep, yep, yep. She signs the waiver hurriedly and slips the sheet back into the fax machine. She stands beside it, and stares out the window at a reversing, beeping laundry van. The machine bites, she looks down, and she watches the paper slowly sliding through. She thinks of Mike TV from *Willy Wonka*, and the indubitable power of Wonkavision to break the subject down here, send it through time and space in a million different pieces, and reassemble it over there. She wonders if there's anyone in the office in LA. A lone lady cleaner, perhaps, stolidly working a vacuum through avenues of empty desks, while the brash and brazen vista of city lights blink behind her, save for the long black vein of La Cienega Boulevard, which runs from the giant glass doors below, right down almost to the edge of the ocean. Jane had tried to walk it once, La Cienega, for fun, on her debut work visit during the very first season of *Screen Grab*, back in the day. She stopped, exhausted and sweat-drenched at the first furlong, the Beverley Center, and happily hailed a cab back up the hill to a pristine lobby, a power shower, and a room service salad, eaten alone on the edge of her bed, while a twelve-dollar menu movie played away, mostly unobserved, on the television beside her.

The fax stops. The page falls to the floor. Jane hums the tune to 'Pure Imagination', from *Wonka*. And she chews, one more time, down onto the words of Matt's life motto.

Our careers are our children.

Wendy and Ree are giggling, in fits, trapped under the covers. They will be late for work if this continues. Thirteen stops on the Circle Line for Ree is no small matter, but, according to Wendy, they simply cannot take a single step out into the shared hall space until that noise has ceased completely. It is an ululation of sorts, a long trilling howl of pleasure that is apparently emerging, at regular intervals, from the throat of Roo's latest paramour.

Awwwhh, ula-la-la-la-la-la-la-la-la-la!

Wendy was already awake when it started. Lying awake and thinking, in this exact and very specific order, of Wendy and Ree's summer holidays, Judith Chalmers in *Wish You Were Here*, classic banter from *Blankety Blank*, high-tension hosting in *Who Wants to be a Millionaire?*, the titles sequence from *Hart to Hart*, the similarities of and differences between Robert Wagner and Richard Branson, the beard of Harold Shipman, and the long and lingering, family-wrecking death of Wendy's dad Larry, from non-Hodgkin's lymphoma.

Awwwhh, ula-la-la-la-la-la-la-la-la-la!

Ree pushes himself up onto his elbows. The fuck is that? No? It's not?

Yes, whispers Wendy, deadpan, it's a Hezbollah funeral.

Ree listens. He tuts. He reaches over to the radio, flicks on the power, volume up.

'I got shhhhhumthin to tell ya.'

Boyzone! Wendy gags, diving over Ree and snapping the room back into relative silence. They argue briefly, lightly, and with sleepy, dozy, early-morning affection, about the relative merits of listening to Boyzone over, according to Ree, the sound of his brother down the hall, interrogating the al-Aqsa Martyrs'

180

Brigade, and, frankly, any day of the week, he knows which sound he'd—

Wait! Wendy interrupts, with a sudden scowl of concentration. Listen! It's stopped!

Silence, but for some audible bed creakage, and then . . .

Awwwhhh, ula-la-la-la-la-la-la-la-la!

And on it goes.

Eventually, Ree points to the glass double doors. He mouths silently, What about Jay? Do you think he's—

Gone, says Wendy. I checked.

You checked?

During the night. Stuck my head inside.

Sorry?

Wendy frowns at Ree.

I do it all the time, she says, with a nonchalant shake of her head.

Ree pushes himself up off the pillows, swings his legs round, and drops them onto the floor with a petulant thud.

Wendy explains, entirely unapologetically, that sometimes she goes inside too. And stands there by the door, fingers on the handle, bare feet on the carpet. Looking. And not just at him, mind you. But at the pair of them. Midnight sleepers. The tiny little breaths from her, the dimpled hands close to the face, the masses of curls and the cute, upturned button nose. And him, finally allowed, in the darkened freedom of sleep, to express on his face the sadness and confusion that he otherwise hides, poorly hides, underneath a daily blanket of coy and corny Irish-isms – the grands, fines, no bothers, and you-know-yirselves. Him, there nonetheless, lying down and arcing gently around her, like a fossil that you might see on David Attenborough, an adult and baby hippo together, mysteriously sunk into sediment before the flood, or a mother and child crouching in Pompeii, or crumpled in Hiroshima, all heroic gestures of the eternal in the face of the

181

inevitable. But mostly, though, lying there, broken in sleep, he reminds Wendy of her own dad, before the end. Weakened, but unbowed. Driven forward and dragged along, by ingrained and unwritten currents that defined him first and foremost to his vision of himself and then to the helpless and fractured family around him, as man, as carer, as provider, as father.

Ree pictures Wendy in the darkness of Jay's room. Standing stock-still. The chill midnight air from the Cromwell Road rushing in through the Irishman's opened sash window and whispering swiftly and softly around her naked thighs. Ree stands up, marches wordlessly past Wendy, out the door and down towards the bathroom, slamming himself inside while the remarkable sound from the room of Roo continues unaware, blissfully unabated.

Awwwhhh, ula-la-la-la-la-la-la-la-la!

Shauna carefully carries an over-loaded breakfast tray to the warped wooden door of the smaller, colder, secondary bedroom in the pink-painted palace. This room had previously belonged to Jess, currently belongs to Bonnie, but can also, when needed, transform itself into a last-minute haven for stranded guests, surprise visitors, and unexpected midnight crashers.

Shauna presses the tray edge hard against the door while reaching, at the edge of her range, for the round brass handle. The tray holds fried eggs, fried tomatoes, and a traditional pink-palace indulgence – so-called organic sausages from the high-end food emporium known as Fresh & Wild on Westbourne Grove. Jay always moaned when they shopped there. The same routine every time. Item after item, lifted incredulously from Shauna's basket, and after reading the price aloud, within earshot of other shoppers, staff, and anyone who cared or couldn't be bothered, Jay, with Bonnie nestled behind him in the backpack, would yelp out in a bamboozled falsetto, entirely spontaneously, phrases such as,

Five pounds for a poxy punnet of wild mountain blueberries! What? Were they picked by the feckin Dalai Lama? Shauna would nudge him sharply. You never knew who might be standing next to you, about to splash out a fortune on organic Moluccan mangosteens. They once saw Ralph Fiennes perusing the pastries, upstairs in the bakery corner. Other customers formed a respectful yet keenly observational semicircle around him, as if leaning right up against a force field of fame, desperate nonetheless to take note of the treat upon which he had settled. Jay had said that they should approach him, because they were not just any other star-watchers. They should waltz up to him and say, Howsigoing, Ralph, sorry to disturb th'aul pastry choosing there – although you can't go wrong with an almond croissant – but we were just wondering, what do you think of these feckin blueberries here? Is five pounds extracting the urine, or wha?

Shauna said that money was just energy. That you had to release it into the universe in order for it to come back to you, tenfold. That holding onto your money is called poverty consciousness. And that her father would not have made his fortune in the T-shirt business on Rehoboth Beach without spending a few pennies. And besides, she added, blueberries are brain food. Stop you getting Alzheimer's.

Shauna's tray shifts suddenly, the food lurches precariously forward, as the door suddenly swings open, aided in its action by a helpful hand from the other side.

Well, she says, beaming broadly, how's the patient?

Darren answers the phone, while pushing himself slowly upwards against the van, and releasing his hand from his chest. What follows is a series of awkward exchanges, during which Darren derides the professional decisions and the physical health of the caller, who is, he decides, a whinger, a big girl's blouse, and a complete fanny for copping off over a couple of sniffles.

Flu? he says. Who gives a fuck about flu? Media ponce! There's a hundred different lads around here with flu, and they still have the balls to chuck themselves into the back of the van every morning, that's no fuckin excuse, flu, ye big fuckin culchie bender media ponce!

Darren ends by telling the caller that he'll pass the word on to Stevie Fitz and that they can do today's filming without him, but that if it was him, with the flu, he'd get his arse into gear, and get back to fuckin work before folk starting questioning his commitment, and think about pulling the plug on his precious media gig. Ruy?

Jay gingerly places the mobile phone back down on the dashboard.

So? says The Clappers. Did he buy it?

Sometimes the fillums get it dead right. Because me and Shauna have been having, in the words of Patrick Swayze himself, the time of our lives. I'm tellin' ya, Mammy. Serious *crack*. I've been out of Finula's Kilburn digs since high summer – although there was much hand-wringing there, with Finula all nervous, and rubbing her little 'tache, and telling me that I could be making a huge mistake, because none of her boyos had ever gone as far as the Notting Hill Gate, even to the black end, and that a mick leaving the security of Kilburn was like a UN fella in the Congo leaving the company barracks and heading straight out into the jungle, without a weapon or a clue in his head about how to address the cannibal savages that'd be lying in wait for him behind every bush, tree and godforsaken phonebox. The last thing she does is give me a hefty rib-cracking hug on the doorstep. She asks me not to forget her, like, when I make it to the big leagues, warns me to keep away from pubs with Union Jacks flying outside, and then loads a massive bunch of freshly made ham sangers into me arms, for the trip to Notting Hill Gate, which, at the maddest estimation possible, is near fifteen minutes long rather than, say, a whole feckin sanger-filled weekend.

The moving into Shauna's gaff is gas too. We're like the lads from *Ghost*, only we don't have any sledgehammers, and we're not knocking down walls and running around accidentally on purpose with our muscles out. I don't need a crane either, to bring up any zany statues into Shauna's sitting room. Instead, I drag everything I own, including the electric typewriter, in two suitcases out of the back of a black cab. Jess, by the way, has moved out. No hard feelings. She just said that if she had to witness me and Shauna having one more tongue sanger she was going to throw herself through the sash window. She left us a joke present too, of joss sticks, chocolates and condoms.

The cab driver on the day of the move is a right character. A real cockney lad, with a 'Chelsea Headhunters' tattoo and a thick sunburnt neck and several gold chains around that neck. He grunts when I get in, and asks me if I'm going to 'Heeefrow' or not, and seems like the kind of lad who'd be drinking in pubs with Union Jacks flying outside. So I tell him no, only I try to do my undercover cockney accent, to throw him off the scent, like, and so he won't drive me out to a patch of industrial wasteland on the Isle of Dogs to watch his football hooligan buddies beat me to death with iron bars while singing 'Rule Britannia' and 'Who Put the Ball in the Irish Net'. No, I go, 'No, my! To Noh'ing Ill Guy instead, plyze,' which unfortunately makes him turn full bodily around in the seat, with mouth wide open and eyes on full squint. He utters the single word, 'Irish?'

Turns out that this particular taxi-driving hooligan's aulfella is from County Cavan, and yer man himself is called Sean, and can spot an hiberno brogue a mile off, and it is, in fact, music to his ears, which transforms the brief fifteen-minute trip into a hoot, which bodes well, I think, for the future of me and Shauna's cohabitation. I give Sean the sangers as a gift, and he tells me that I'm a lucky who-er, because the Yank wans are very tasty indeed, and when he sees Shauna at the doorway he goes growly, full-on Sid James, and tells me that Shauna's a dead ringer for yer wan who plays Counsellor Troi in *Star Trek: The Next Generation* and that I'm going to be getting a fierce lot of riding done now

186

that I'm movin in. And, to be honest, Mammy, without wanting to rub it in, as the actress said to the bishop, I have to say that Sean was bang on there, the aul Chelsea knacker.

And I also have to say, Mammy, and I know you've often said yourself through the years, that what's natural can't be wondered at, and because of that, I have to say, we do feckin well everything in the riding manual. Seriously. Shauna has a joke *Kama Sutra* tea towel pinned up in the bog, which is a triffic ice-breaker for dinner parties, because everyone comes out, without fail, going, just for a laugh, Jayz, I haven't done th'aul Weeping Bishop in a long time! And then everyone else laughs because you're immediately talking about sex, but in a safe way, without having to talk about sex.

But, feck sake, Mammy, haven't we done the whole thing, and the rest, in the first five days?! Seriously. The face to face, which is also known as the classico, where we're, like, speaking out the humpy beats, going, I love you, I love you, I love you. Getting faster and louder with each faster and more vigorous hump, until we're like screaming, real window-rattling shite, like two complete randy goms, a big blur of deafening I love yous, like, Lav-ah-lav-ah-lav-ah-lav-ah-lav-ah-lav-uuughhh uugggh, uggh, ugh, uh, uh, uh god, uh God, uh God, I love you.

Or we do the doggie, as the man says. Real Vegas stuff. Or there's the standy-uppy version, the downward doggie, the afternoon delight, or the double crab, the cowgirl, the peg, the toad, the slide, the kneel, the curled angel, the sphinx, the seated ball, the plough, the crouching tiger, the reverse cowgirl and, our own particular favourite, the feckin criss-cross applesauce, over and out. Because in that one, you both make the shape of the cross in the bed, so it's also bit religious, which is a bonus, like, and she's got her legs flung over you, waist height, and you're supposed to start it up, whenever you think the moment's right, although not straight into ramming speed, mind you, just good and slow, like, say, Julio Iglesias on a Friday afternoon, just after he's got his pension book stamped, but then faster and faster, until finally your back is banjaxed and she's howling the head off of her, like a wan who used to have coked-up sexscapades with other women and a couple of lads in letterman jackets but is now totally sold by old-school monogamy and private lovey-dovey doing it, at all hours of the day, thanks be to God.

The rapid-fire sex montage races, comedy style, through the end of the summer, into autumn, and comes crashing to a halt on the afternoon, a Sunday, of Halloween night, with Shauna muttering from behind the papers, the super casual and barely audible phrase, Oh, and I think I've missed my period.

Naturally, Mammy, you'd be expecting a lot of breast beating, hair pulling and *ree raw ogus roola boola*. But no. I'm on the other side of the room, carving a pumpkin for Shauna's window display, when she says it. Halloween, you see, is a big thing for the Yanks, and I don't have the heart to tell her that it never meant more to me than the smell of rotten monkey nuts in plastic bags and a few bent sparklers during a late night downpour, so I play along with the excitement, even buy myself a nylon Batman outfit, which I wear all day, to get into the mood, especially when I'm hollowing out the pumpkin. I'm, like, Halloween! Woo! The business!

So, as it happens, the period line goes down a treat. I put down the pumpkin. Flick off the midi-stereo system (turns out, you can actually have enough Tasmin Archer), and, very gently, while holding my cape, slide down onto the couch beside Shauna, as if she's already gone full term and needs special assistance, and, even more gently, I push down the paper from her face and tell

188

her, scout's honour, no bluffing, that it's the best feckin news I've heard all year.

Shauna, however, is dead calm about it, almost to the point of couldn't-give-a-feck-ness. She tells me that I'm very cute, but I'm not to sweat it, because she has a right manky womb, and the pregnancy, if it is a pregnancy, won't be going anywhere fast down there. Me, still dead excited, and already picturing the three of us rowing across the Serpentine in full-on familial bliss, I go, careful as can be, without wanting to ruffle any feathers, Manky womb? Shauna, whose head is back down in among the papers again, doesn't even look up this time. She gets the *International Herald Tribune* delivered every Sunday from a newsagent on Elgin Crescent. Poor little Asian fella, can't be more than thirteen, skinny arms weighed down with the thing, all twenty thousand pages, comes staggering up our stairs just after eight, like clockwork. Could leave it at the front door, but, in fairness, he knows that Shauna's a serious tipper. Rarely leaves without some decent coinage shoved into his fist.

She's reading about the escalating crisis in California of wild brushfires that were started by so-called penniless 'transients' but are now raging out of control and sweeping down into the populous, super-posh enclave known as Laguna Beach. All that money, Shauna says, scoffing wryly to herself but to me too, all that security, and what brings it down? A tramp with a Zippo.

And the manky womb? I say again, at the very edge of prying.

Oh that, she says, now leafing again. She lets the question hang for a while, before settling on a page about Bill Clinton and Haiti. She then sighs, slightly bored, and explains that the manky womb refers to the usual stuff, her several college abortions, her frequent use of the morning-after pill, and the subsequent suspicion that nothing at all down there, within the actual reproductive engine

189

room, is working towards even half-average levels of satisfaction – suspicions, indeed, confirmed by the three miscarriages she's suffered since moving to London.

Well, Mammy, in the olden days, when I was fresh off the boat, it might've taken the concerted effort of legs, arms and every single fibre of facial muscle not to leap up and off the couch, screaming blue blazes about the horrifying history of Shauna's womb life and the damage she's gone and put herself through for the sake of a few aul rides. But instead, what you'll find in me, Mammy, is a changed fella, who has actually, unlike many actual women I know, read the feckin *Female Eunuch*, a fella who advocates a woman's right to choose, and a fella, most of all, who understands and believes in the transformative power, both in emotional contexts and within the very physicality of the human body, organs and all, of love itself.

So, gently again, I pull down the paper, and look Shauna in the eye, and I'm like, real gooey faced. This time, I think, you'll find it's different. You've never had the seed of an Irish lad inside ye, ha? You've seen what we can do with racehorses?

I don't think— she starts, weirded out.

Breeding! I interrupt her interruption. I'm talking about breeding. It's in the genes. Literally so. I can reel off, off the top of me head, about seven families on the Cloonavullaun Estate alone who have thirteen kids or less. It's what we do best. And I've got a good feeling about this one.

My good feeling, Mammy, lasted until a fortnight ago when, nearly a full trimester into the pregnancy, and just five days before our very first ultrasound scan, Shauna goes seriously crampy at four in the morning, bursts out crying, tells me to fuck off with myself out of the room, and then goes and has a gushy red miscarriage on the bog. As the lads from Take That say, Let me see the wonder of all of you.

It has not been for nothing. Because the days, weeks and months spent imagining the emergence of a little Shauna–Jay cross-breed babby have brought a new kind of calmness, and welcome sobriety, into our lives. Yes, we're still riding like a couple of crack-addled who-ers. But we do less of the applesauce nowadays, and mostly go for the classico each time. We haven't done it since the miscarriage, mind you. Bit like streaking in a funeral home. The mood isn't there.

Instead, we've had Shauna's dad Paul and little brother Chester over for Christmas. Had it planned before the miscarriage. We were going to bring in the pregnancy sticks during Christmas pud and say, What do yiz think of them feckers? But still, Paul's a right aul laugh and a bit of an eccentric, no more than yourself, Mammy. He's a teetotaller too, calls Ireland 'the Old Country', and used to be a serious bollix, and fond of an aul dig, back in the day. He made a fortune from printing T-shirts that say funny American shite on them like 'Help! I've Fallen and I Can't Reach My Beer!' or 'It's Not a Bald Spot, it's a Solar Panel for a Sex Machine!' but he always wanted to be a proper artist, and instead has had to make do with taking pride in Shauna's success in telly.

The brother's grand too. Deadly quiet. And was brilliant at driving up a massive phone bill with the transatlantic calls to the girlfriend in New York. Still, we were glad to be rid of them, and had the best night, the last night, because we all knew that they were going the next day, and so we drank non-alcoholic pina coladas, and played Boggle, and listened to my *Rebel Songs of Ireland* compilation, and watched Paul lip-synch, word perfect, to every single line of 'Come Out Ye Black and Tans', and then stayed up till the wee hours telling spooky stories (I did the one

191

about Auntie Maudie finding the ghost of a suicide priest getting stuck into the jam scones down in the scullery) and talking about how the world's going to end at the turn of the millennium. Paul's a real hard-core enthusiast, full-on Nostradamus nut, quoting quatrains and referring back to great big chunks of the *Mirabilis Liber*, and telling us how brushfires in California and superstorms along the eastern American seaboard were just the beginning. Chester mostly groaned during this, and Shauna, patient at first, eventually told Paul to put a feckin lid on it, and asked him if he had ever thought of going back on the booze.

We've had a grand few days since then, Mammy, mostly in by ourselves, reading, drinking the odd shandy, watching *The Bodyguard* on the box, and cuddling by the fire. Which, incidentally, is where you find us now, on this night of nights. We've both got writing paper out in front of us (with tons of balled-up efforts on the floor), and we're leaning on hardback books for support. Shauna's is the *Times Atlas*, mine is Jane's copy of *The Philosophical Discourse of Modernity* by Jurgen Habermas. We're supposed to be writing a special top-secret letter to each other, which is actually Chester's idea, because he's doing the same thing with his girlfriend in New York. The letter's top secret because the pair of ye aren't supposed to open it until this time next year, and it's special because in the letter you talk about all the things you've done in the year ahead, as if you'd done them already, even though you haven't done them yet. And what's more, they can't just be any aul shite, and this is why it's a bit American, as far as gas exercises go, because you have to write about the things, the best things, that you hope are going to happen in the year ahead, and therefore, so the theory goes, by writing about them to each other as if they've already happened, you are allowing a certain energetic space to open up in the universe for them to happen in the first place, hopefully.

Sounds mad, Mammy, I know, but you wouldn't believe the *crack* we have, me and Shauna, and the amount of pages we go through, fecking crying with the laughter, trying to get it right. And we're reading them out for starters, which you're not supposed to do, but only makes it funnier for the both of us. Because I'm like, Dear Shauna, that was some year! I never thought I'd hear meself saying this, but th'aul boob job worked out a treat!

She tells me I'm an eejit and throws a paper ball at me, and then reads out hers, which is pretty much the exact same thing, only it's all, like, Dear Jay, I'm amazed that we're still friends, what with you going gay for the entire month of July.

We start the letters about ten different times, both of us really struggling to find the right tone, and me thinking that Chester must be a right wet over there in New York, and imagining him filling pages of the stuff, going into great detail as to the fantasy life of perfection he's expecting to unfold once the letters are signed, sealed and hidden away in his feckin My Little Pony lunchbox until next New Year's Eve.

Shauna, thankfully, eventually, takes control, calls me a doofus and says that we should do this properly if we're going to do this at all, and that one year isn't enough, and we should go full Stalin on it, for five years, and aim to open them again in 1998. I tell her that I'll see her five, and raise her two, and that we should go the whole hog, and aim for Millennium's Eve, Nostradamus not-withstanding.

The two of us get dead giddy about this, because it's kind of an audacious plan, but more because there is implicit within the suggestion the idea that we will still be together, in whatever form that takes, as a couple, in a relationship, on Millennium's Eve. The idea, the concept, is like wine to us, and we get kind of woozy. We kiss a little, and I know, I just know, I can feel it, that we're both thinking marriage, big time, when Shauna suddenly snaps herself to her senses, sits back down in the chair opposite me and says that we've got to take this task seriously now, what with the stakes being so high, and that we are to look deep into each other's eyes, and write down on the page the very first thing that comes into our minds, channelled directly from our hearts, and which expresses nothing but the essential truth of our being.

So. Here goes.

Your Right-Hand Man,

Jay

15

The Mother

Ah, sure, here he's on! Mr Dobalina. Mr Bob Dobalina!

That's how she greets him. The Mother of Jay, to Jay. He had been hoping in his heart for something more. He had seen in the movies, had read in the pamphlets, that there were flickers, chances of breakthroughs, complete epiphanies. The patient, in the midst of dribbling, floor-watching catatonic distress, might suddenly look up with alacrity, and greet the blood relative with a phrase or two of such easygoing intimacy that the reality of the entire condition, and the credibility of the diagnosis, might momentarily be placed in doubt. This, for the blood relative, was said to be an anxious, conflicted moment, full of incredulity and fragile optimism, but a tragic moment nonetheless, and one that could be neutralised, only as it inevitably would, by the swift and punishing return of the patient to a state of babbling inconsequentiality.

Thus, when Jay walked into the room, shadowed closely by The Clappers and an irrepressible duty nurse in dark maroon called Heather, he was holding on, deep within, to the secret suspicion that his mother would indeed recognise his face, his voice, his very essence, and throw the nursing home into wild disarray by leaping out of the chair, embracing him fully, and taking him for a rousing comedy waltz around the admittedly spacious and strangely luxurious bedroom. Which was not to be.

Sensing his disappointment, Heather, beaming, tells Jay that Mr Bob Dobalina is quite the achievement for a patient as far gone as his mam. The verbal dexterity required to get that out is nothing less than extraordinary. Most of the others, she says, indicating the corridor outside, simply confine themselves to grunts and groans these days. The Clappers agrees and, from behind Jay's left ear, she makes a few mangled attempts, seemingly deliberate, in order to prove to Jay the veracity of Heather's statement.

Mr Blobaleena, Mr Doll Bolladeena! See! She's a genius, your mammy!

The Mother of Jay lets her head droop down towards the floor again.

Jay, tentatively, kneels before her, gazing upwards, hoping to catch a look, the merest hint of a connection, eye to eye. He is not shocked, up close, by the appearance of the Mother of Jay. He knew what to expect, nearly a decade on. The fact that she is alive at all is the miracle. He had visualised in silence, on the cross-country route in the car, a tiny wizened skeleton in a chair, with lifeless hollow sockets for eyes. That she is even possessed of skin, no matter how translucent, is also something of a bonus. Plus, Heather, he notes, has done her best for the big show, dressing up the Mother of Jay in clean blue blouse and smart grey pleated skirt, in the way you might, perhaps, dress a gormless, weightless, rattle-bag Barbie. There has been make-up applied too, a touch of blusher to the cheeks. The thin wispy hair has been blow-dried into a soft fluffy bob. While Jay is almost sure that they've polished his mother's ancient artificial hand, and slipped a bright golden ring onto the index finger.

Down there, waiting below, Jay notices the richness of the carpet. Spotless too. Hotel class, he thinks.

Mammy? he says.

The Mother of Jay registers nothing.

Mammy? he says again.

Still nothing.

Heather turns to The Clappers. The two women share a look, a smile, and a tiny shake of the head. The Clappers reaches down and gently squeezes Jay on the shoulders.

I'm sorry, Boss Man, she says. You can let it all out if you want.

Jay fires her a quizzical look.

The grief, she says, qualifying.

Jay sighs, shrugs, and continues the task at hand.

Mammy? he says. I've brought a friend. Remember Claire? Claire Connolly? Big boned? The only girl on the lads' hurling squad? Big as a feckin—

The Clappers slaps him across the back of the head, just as the Mother of Jay looks upwards at The Clappers.

Ah, sure, here he's on, says the Mother of Jay. Mr Dobalina! Mr Bob Dobalina!

The Clappers, excitedly, turns to Heather and coos, I got one! I got one!

Jay stays on his knees. He rests his head softly in his mother's lap and tells her that she's a gas wan. He hears the subtle crinkle of plastic beneath her seat, beneath her skirt, and thinks of the Gaelic word *timpishta*, for accident. He used to say that word a lot with Shauna, when they were out with Bonnie, in the closing days of their relationship. They'd visit Jess and her new boyfriend, Jean-François, in Hampstead, bring a kite to the Heath, and then move onwards to the high street, for a high-tension meal, kiddie-friendly, during which Bonnie would duly drop and clank and smash with febrile intensity, much to the amusement of Jess and Jean-François (the latter was fond of repeating the phrase, at no one in particular, that keeds are so

197

vucking cool) and much to the irritation of Jay and Shauna, who were determined, even at this late stage, to rekindle lost hopes of pre-Bonnie privileges.

It was usually around then, as the last straw, with a patient waiter mopping up a strawberry sundae from the floor beside her, and Shauna trying desperately to retain the thread of Jess's giddy account of skunked-up tent-hopping in the best Glasto ever, usually at that point that Jay would look down and see a sudden darker colouring on the seat of Bonnie's pink woollen tights. He'd look at Shauna, hoping not to make a scene, and whisper the phrase, I think we've had a *timpishta*. He would scoop Bonnie up into his arms, grab the emergency pink Bonnie bag from underneath the table and whisk her off into the toilets for the second, third or fourth change of the day.

Paediatricians, me arse! he'd say, later that night. Treat her like a normal kid! Potty train her like a normal kid! They're not the ones up to their elbows in piss and shite seven times a day! They're not the feckers dealing with the *timpishtas*!

He stays like that, Jay, against her lap, for an age, with Heather and The Clappers standing around him, breaths held tight, in respectful silence. He lets his eyes shut slowly and open again. He could be lazing about under Sunday-morning covers on the Cloonavullaun Estate. He remembers a quote from a western she showed him once. The quote says, We all dream of being a child again, even the worst of us. Perhaps the worst most of all.

He reaches his arm up and holds the Mother of Jay by the artificial hand. He gives her a light tug, careful not to pull it off. She leans slightly. The plastic pants creak loudly. He thinks again of *timpishta* and suddenly remembers.

Mammy! he says, turning round and firing The Clappers a conspiratorial wink. We've got a surprise for you.

The Clappers opens the door and beckons Bonnie inwards.

Bonnie lollops inside and crashes straight down into the floor-sprawled lap of Jay.

Mammy, meet your granddaughter! Ta-dah! says Jay, deadpan and slightly droll, half laughing now at the preposterousness of hope, the delusion of the situation, and at his own internal fantasies, even half formed, half harboured, that suggest a profound healing and reconciliation that might result from the magical union of granddaughter and grandmother.

Jay lifts Bonnie up into a standing position, and holds her, briefly, in front of his own mother's face.

Nothing. No Dobalina. The Mother of Jay doesn't even look at Bonnie.

Heather, beaming, blonde, upbeat to the end, announces to the heedless Mother of Jay that she should show Bonnie some of her paintings. Nudging The Clappers, Heather points to a large open leather folder, already pre-placed on the steamed-glass coffee table below the wide bay window. Four large paper sheets, beside the folder, are neatly arranged in fan formation, revealing brash and shapeless squiggles of bright garish paint, which hint, if nothing else, at a creative process defined by a paint-laden brush forced into the unwilling hand of a resentful artist.

Oh yes, she's quite the da Vinci! Heather says, before turning back to the Mother of Jay and bellowing, Aren't ye, Deirdre?

Heather then announces, still smiling, that she will now give the group some quality family time. She adds, without recourse to irony or sarcasm, that Deirdre will take great care of them. And then she suggests that they all meet later in the restaurant for lunch, for the house specialty, Duck à l'Orange.

In the absence of Heather, Jay is almost immediately discomfited. He stands up slowly, lifts Bonnie into his arms, an unconscious gesture by now, and paces around his mother's room. He kisses Bonnie lightly on the hairline, while his free hand strokes the high-specification mirrors, wall-fittings, wardrobes and windows. He steps into the en suite too, and lets out a slow whistle of appreciation. Gold taps. Power shower. Bidet. Skylight.

He leans against the window sill and reminds The Clappers that, if they stick their heads out far enough, they will almost be able to see the dreaded *Collawshta Breen* from there. The name conjures up gruesome memories of a compulsory three-week summer school in the flatlands of Mayo, where the Gaelic language was brutally instilled via threats and intimidation, and was spoken non-stop from morning till night, and where a single sentence of verbal communication in the English tongue would result in an immediate shame-faced expulsion for the loose-lipped *sassanock*. Meaning English-lover.

The purpose of the summer school was, plainly enough, as they were told, repeatedly, to upgrade the Gaelic-language abilities of the so-called faltering students at St Cormac's, and to allow them to experience a deep infusion of traditional Irish culture, free from the pernicious modernising influences of imperialist British voices. The students, en masse, saluted the flag every morning. They learnt an improvised anthem about *Collawshta Breen* and its place at the forefront of Irish Republicanism, and how, in the face of changes in societal mores, the summer school was essentially a brave, bold, native salmon swimming against the foreign tide.

They learnt Irish dancing. They wrote history projects. And they took grammar tests. Naturally, Jay and The Clappers hated it. They'd sit every night at the edge of Lough Flynn, with their trousers rolled up and their legs dangling into the silky black water, and they'd grumble together in English, and yearn for the high jinx in Strandhill, and curse The Fox and Mickeleen for having real parents, who didn't give two fecks about saluting the flag, and learning the *coopla fuckill gaylga*.

And worst of all were the houses. The students stayed at night in random rural bungalows, and supposedly slept, crammed into bedrooms, six and seven apiece, in bunk beds and free-floating mattresses, under the watchful eye of a fearsome farmer's wife who was addressed only as the *ban-on-tee*. The low point, for Jay, came in the last week, during a grocery shortage, when his house and his *ban-on-tee* ran out of toilet paper. The students were ordered to 'go' elsewhere, but nature inevitably called for one, resulting in the misuse of bathroom linens, and a bungalow-wide scandal. *Vee 'shit' air on two-awlla!* That's how Jay remembers the session beginning. The *ban-on-tee* herding every-one into the cramped kitchen and explaining to them, with a face glowing red with rage, sweating so, about the actions of a stu-dent, yet to be discovered, who had clearly, and almost inconceivably, used a hand towel for a job for which only toilet paper was ever intended. *Vee 'shit' air on two-awlla!* she said, again and again, in almost disbelief. *Vee 'shit' air on two-awlla!*

The interrogation lasted as long as it took to ask one simple question. *Kay a rinna ay?* Who did it? The Clappers stepped for-ward instantly, her shoulders shuddering already, face twisted into convulsions of sadness and regret, gagging on the word *Misha*. The *Ban-On-Tee* forgave her, and then quietly asked her if it was a medical urge that caught her. However, Jay was struck, particularly in the light of her matchless bravado and physical prowess, by how quickly The Clappers had folded. Must've been a sporting thing, he surmised. A lover of rules.

He turns to her, to The Clappers, in the room of his mother, the Mother of Jay, and, in the presence of his mother, still star-ing from her seat, Jay indicates with a wide sweep of his hand the room around them and suggests to The Clappers that the Mother of Jay, or at least her legal trustees, or ultimately the solicitors of Ballaghaderreen, must've made a fortune from the sale of the Concannon family home on the Cloonavullaun Estate, in order to cover the cost of this five-star nursing experience for so long.

The Clappers, in turn, unexpectedly blushes. She bloviates wildly about the strength of the market, the region's developmental hot spots and the fortunes to be made from transforming underproductive arable land into commuter-belt apartments, via the aid of a few decent government grants. And yet she never once elaborates on any of the actual finer fiscal details of the house sale. Jay presses, firmly.

And Mammy's house?

Still flushing, now smiling awkwardly, The Clappers, as if deflecting the cost of a trinket, an impulsive gift, tells Jay not to worry about it, and that it's all under control.

Jay sits Bonnie down beside the shadow of his mother. He turns The Clappers towards him and insists, eye to eye, face to face, friend to friend, that she tell him the truth. These are, after all, the rules of friendship.

The Clappers sighs, and spews out, in one great big sentence, that the Concannon cash ran out years ago, and that the payments for the nursing home, and all issues, practical and otherwise, relating to the Mother of Jay, have been handled, for and on the behalf of the Roman Catholic Church, by Fr Francis.

To this piece of information Jay replies with the single word, 'Right.' He then falls into complete and all-enveloping quietude for the rest of the morning. He addresses The Clappers with civility during lunch, and answers Heather's questions cordially, about life in London, the Spice Girls, Oasis, the Millennium Dome and the thrill of meeting famous people from off of the telly. But mostly, and despite the convivial goading by The Clappers (Ask him about Martin Clunes! Ask him about Ulrika-ka-ka!), he is plunged into his own world of silent, sombre, reflection.

The last words from Jay to the Mother of Jay are whispered alone, back in the room, back on the carpet, with the others outside, on his strict orders, on their lives, even Heather herself, not to intrude. He looks deep into the face of the Mother of Jay, and his eyes search her eyes, really search this time, right into the black pupil. He's sure this time, sure and shaken, that he sees only the abyss, and nothing else within, but nonetheless he says it, a whisper from his mouth to her ears alone, in the form of a question, entirely, naturally, rhetorical.

Oh Mammy, he says. What have you done?

Jay remains silent for much of the return journey from Ballyhaunis to the shed. He sits in the back with Bonnie, who is tiring of her seat straps, and wriggling, and kicking, and sporadically stuttering out the gasping, growling half-groan that is her cry. Jay whispers to her, Little darling, little love, *my auld segosha*. He strokes her hair and promises her a swim in the sea, a dance in the waves, when they get back. Just her and him. No Auntie Claire, no Granny Dee. Just the two of them, in the waves, splashing together, in the frothy white horses. He does hand gestures too. The snaky rise and fall of a wave. Bonnie understands. The gasping slowly stops. She snuffles. Jay holds her tiny hand. She grips his tightly. Unspoken in silence, uncreated, they are together.

She will be asleep in seconds, he thinks. Car journeys always the best. Tried and tested. The gradual learning curve after the pell-mell insanity of her first year. Rock her to sleep in the bedroom? Impossible. Gasp-growling for hours. Drive as far as the first roundabout on St Mark's Road and, boom, she was gone. Arms outstretched in stiffened sleep. Each time, every time. So many needless drives for the sake of sleep. From St Mark's to White City, out onto the M4, even as far as Heathrow, driving around the perimeter fence in a zombified loop, watching the planes lift and land in a thunderous roar, right next to her sleepy, dreamy, lullaby brain.

And back home to the flat. Parked outside, engine running.

Him just staring straight ahead, not even thinking. Beaten down by all-nighters, now asleep with eyes open. And the funny looks from passers-by. The censorious frowns at the belching exhaust pipe, on behalf of the ailing environment. But Jay's motto is the motto of many. Let the ice caps melt and run, let the forests burn and the cities choke, let it all go to hell before anyone even contemplates the end of this sleep, this bliss, this precious, precious, baby break.

The Clappers, painfully aware of Jay's silence, and by way of compensation, chatters incessantly, fuelled with nervous intensity, her driving as circuitous as her conversation. She moves cross-country, away from the main roads, through miles of deserted farmland, in great wide loops along single-track lanes, past derelict buildings, sporadic hedgerows and scattered colonies of rusty red pens, adding occasional biographical notes along the way. She asks Jay if he remembers knacker drinking by Lough Nanoge over there, with The Fox and Mickeleen, before the disco in St Michael's? And how, as a joke, she pretended to push The Fox into the water, shouting, Tell yir mammy I saved ye! But she lost the grip on his jacket at the last minute, and watched him plunging in, right over his head, and then sent Mickeleen in after him, for good measure, and for the *crack*. The lads were furious at first. Ruined the feckin disco gear! No snoggin with the dollies that night. Am I right?

She tries again on the outskirts of Sligo Town, and asks Jay if he remembers the brutal GAA match against *Collawshta Ayanna*, on that very same pitch, by the Tullynagracken roundabout, when Mickeleen got sent off for calling Bowsie, out loud, a right hairy little bollocks, because he'd come charging onto the pitch, off the leash that Jay had twisted round their bikes, and had gone straight for this one *Collawshta Ayanna* lad, teeth into his shorts. Was a decent rip and everything, and you half saw the *Collawshta Ayanna* lad's jocks, so he started crying, and his mam had to run onto the pitch for cuddles, while Jay had to drag Bowsie off, and tie him to the back of the *Collawshta Ayanna* goals, and the coaches were furious, and blaming the ref for running a three-ring circus, and so when poor aul Mickster starting cursing at Bowsie it was too much, and the ref, a real gentle sort of a fella, told him that words like hairy bollocks had no place in the national game, and pointed straight to the sidelines. Was gas, wasn't it? Wasn't it?

Desperate, she drives straight on, as far as Drumcliff, instead of turning left into Strandhill. Jay does not comment. Bonnie, as predicted, is asleep. The Clappers knocks on her window, gesturing towards the giant domineering slab in the landscape beside them.

And I bet you won't forget that feckin day in a hurry? 'Under Ben Bulben', me arse! Poor Fr Francis with us lot of heathens, and him with the book in his hand, like yer man, Mork from *Dead Poets*, trying to rouse us all to become artist warriors by listening to doggerel in the lashes of rain. Yeats, ha? What did Yeats know about school trips, wet sangers, and making ends meet on the Cloonavullaun Estate? And when Connor McCourt said as much to Fr Francis he went spare, although only on the inside, you could see it, though, for a couple of seconds, but he did nothing to Connor, and instead, which was mad, and dead embarrassing, he made us walk, all of us, in the rain, while reciting all six verses, off by heart, of 'Under Ben Bulben'. Just reciting and walking, in the lashes of rain, and following him in a seemingly random squiggle, designed, we thought, to punish us all for McCourt's remarks, and to teach us, somehow, through repetition alone, about the magical power of WB.

And, of course, we're, like, on round number fifty, like poetry zombies, when he turns the corner and leads us into Drumcliff churchyard, and right over to this bog-standard grave, with a grey bog-standard headstone on it, and he keeps us reciting, strictly reciting, as he points to the grave, he points firmly to the grave, and we look down, we look down together, and even as we are saying the words, 'Under bare Ben Bulben's head/In Drumcliff churchyard Yeats is laid,' we see, and we twig, and we know, suddenly, horribly, that we're standing by him, beside him, by the man he once was, by the man of these words, and some of the lads are shocked, and some of the lads knew what was coming, and some of the lads' chins start to go, and as they say the final lines, they read the final lines from his bog-standard gravestone, on life, on death, horseman, pass by, and Connor McCourt especially loses it completely, and starts properly crying, and looks like he wants to fling himself into the grave, and hug Yeats, and say sorry to Yeats, and tell him that he was only being a youngfella who didn't know any better, and that he loved Yeats, and that he had sung 'Down By the Salley Gardens' at the school *fesh*, and come second, and got a medal and everything. But Fr Francis just leans down, with his white shock of hair, and puts his arm around him and says, with that gentle caramel voice of his, 'But I was young and foolish, and now am full of tears.'

Jay responds by turning his head towards the window and staring out dutifully at Ben Bulben. He absorbs the view, the massive limestone monolith, flat-top green, utterly dominant and immutable, and a symbol, according to Fr Francis, of Irish art.

Jay finally speaks.

Why am I here?

The Clappers smiles. Relieved.

What do you mean, Boss Man? she says, chirpy as ever. Because of th'aul scenic route!

No, he says, deadpan, eyes unmoved from Ben Bulben. Why am I here?

Because of your mammy! The Clappers replies, with the tiniest hint of a vocal quiver. She adds, however, the jocular coda, Ye know? Up in th'aul nuthouse.

No, Jay deadpans again. Why am I here?

Jay knows this won't take long. *Vee 'shit' air on two-awlla!*

The Clappers twitches in her seat.

Jayz, Boss Man, she says, are ye losing the plot, or wha? Don't tell me it's catching. You'll be calling me Mr Dobalina next!

Jay remains focused.

Why am I here?

The Clappers, seemingly irritable now, voice cracking. Because of London. Because we, if ye had forgotten, are fleeing from the Peelers!

No, he replies, still in his best robot, why am I here?

Because it's better than getting locked up by the Brits.

No, why am I here?

Because of the big feckin bang, how should I know?

Claire, Jay says, suddenly leaning forward into the front and resting his hand gently on the tight bulk of her upper arm. Why am I here?

Ah Jaysuz! she says, flushing with frustration. What is this? Feckin Paxo?

Claire, Jay says again, this time opting for an apparently random change in tack. Is Shauna's father dead?

Maybe it's the relief in The Clappers released by the sudden interrogative switch. Or maybe it's simply her infamously poor resistance, combined with an inability to prepare herself, that speedily, against another line of attack. Or maybe, perhaps most of all, it's the emotional fallout from the trip today, and the sight of Jay next to the ghostly shadow of his mother that finally breaks her down. The Clappers sighs. She turns to Jay, strokes his face, and speaks.

No.

16

Pain with a Purpose

What about your own mother, how did she compare to the Mother of Jay?

I remember my mom only as a silhouette.

Yes, of course, a symbolic image.

No, a real silhouette. From my bedroom at home. That's how I remember her. Standing against the drapes, with a diffuse, low-level glow behind her. In summer it's the setting sun, in winter the street lights. She's looking down at me in bed. With remarkable patience. And steely silence. Iron-willed determination, for her and for me. Because I was a wuss. Did it every single night. A total tantrum at bedtime. Couldn't bear the dark, or the very idea that I might be left, alone in the night, to face the frightening fall into sleep by myself.

And she stayed?

Every night. Must've been for over a year. Or at least until Paul whacked her face out through the back of her head. Paul didn't really have the patience for silhouette duty. He was more of a lights-out, heads-down, and get-over-it, kind of guy. Whereas Mom. She embraced the gig. Big time. She stood there, by my bed, like a sentinel. There was no affection in it. It wasn't about cuddles or hugs. It was about duty, her duty to me, whether she liked it or not, as a mom. To get me to sleep. She functioned like that. Was big into duty, and the done thing, and what they might think on Gibson Island if they found out that everything within the walls of our house was not just fine and dandy. She got it from her mom, I guess. The fear that she might one day be found out. Or that she was found out already, and they were laughing, the right people were, laughing at her behind her back, for marrying a penniless dude with long hair and bad jeans.

The legwear, or the hereditary traits?

Those too.

And so she'd stand there, in front of my drapes, saying nothing at all other than telling me, very occasionally, to calm down, especially if I was crying loudly and begging her to turn the lights back on or, at least, to crank the door open a couple of inches. She had a single line that she delivered every night, which was to tell me to find her voice, and look into the darkness, into the black, and focus, really focus on the space where her voice had been and, for the next ten to fifteen minutes, in total concentrated silence, watch and wait for her silhouette to emerge.

And she said nothing else? No actual conversation?

Once, perhaps unsurprisingly, after Paul had been a drunken dick at supper, and scoffed at her macaroni and cheese, she suddenly erupted in the darkness, scared me to pieces, and all she said, after wailing briefly, was that not every marriage could be *Joanie Loves Chachi*. And then she emerged, as she always did. A miracle mirage, before my eyes. The blackness of night fading quietly away, while a negative portrait of my mom in mid-shot coalesces against the grey, colourless fizz of the slowly glowing rose drapes.

She stayed until you slept?

I never saw her leave. Never once.

She became part of your sleep. An unconscious player in your mind, and a maternal succubus of sorts.

No, she was just a mother. I think she liked it there. In the dark. She might've stayed for hours after I drifted off. Who knows? She was fucked up in her own way. And fucked up by her own mother too. Who was, no doubt, fucked up by hers, right down through a whole unhappy line of motherfucking motherfucker-uppers.

And in Jay you found, finally, another fellow victim of motherfucker-upper syndrome?

Maybe. But I didn't see it like that at the time. I found in Jay a quiet calmness, and a simplicity that bordered, at times, on bemused indifference. He was someone who made no claims on me, who didn't seem to want from me. And that felt good. To be in the company of man who wasn't pawing, clawing, sniffing and licking. Jay, most of the time, was downright elusive. Yes, he told me everything I needed to know about his freak-show mom. And there were times when we'd look into each other's eyes and feel a connection, a total oneness, like nothing else on earth. But there were other times when I'd look into his eyes and see no one at home at all. He could sit on the couch for hours, staring at brick-work and saying nothing. I once asked him, on one such occasion, what he was thinking, in that trance-like stare, and you know what he said? You won't believe what he said. I mean talk about rich. Guess what he said? Can you guess what that tight-lipped spud-muncher said to me?

No, I cannot guess. And though I am very much interested in the intricacies of your relationship with Jay, if you would permit me for a moment, in the few short minutes we have left, to indulge my unorthodox methodology, I would suggest that we try something new. Talking isn't always the answer. The conscious mind can be devious. The superego is strong, no? Instead, I would like to try something physical.

Oh. OK. I suppose. Is it legal?

Very much so. I'd like you to stand up, like this. Good. This is something they teach you in Copenhagen. You've been to Copenhagen, yes?

Once.

And you like?

Lego? *Hamlet*? Carlsberg and Nazi collaboration? What's not to like?

Why is this?

Why is what?

You joke, yes? I like it very much. It's good, the feeling. But why you do this?

I joke?

You make jokes. When I speak. Why?

Why? I dunno. Because life is funny?

You ask me?

No, life is not funny. Life is loss. Life is a succession of losses. It is absurd. Life is a joke. And if you don't have the will to joke about life you might as well slide open that window right now, and let me jump out, face first.

You know the ancient Greeks liked jokes too?

You don't say.

They met, some fifty or sixty men, in the Temple of Heracles in Athens in the fourth Century BC, to partake in so-called joke groups, and to test out their material on each other. Can you imagine it?

Sadly, I can. What did the Philosopher say to the Slave Trader?

I don't know. What did the Philosopher say to the Slave Trader?

No. It's, er, it's not a joke. I was just imagining the kind of joke they'd test out on each other. Although, that being said, I do have a philosopher joke. It goes, like, How many philosophers does it take to change a light bulb?

This is the joke?

Yes, this is the fucking joke.

211

And the answer is?

Define 'change'.

In the context, it means to replace one light bulb with another.

No. The joke is over. It ended at 'Define "change"'. That was the punchline, ba-da-bing!

Of course. And you know that laughter releases oxytocin into the bloodstream, for quick thinking? And then, just afterwards, there's a flood of seratonin too, for calmness. It opens up new neuropathways too, for clearer cognition.

I didn't.

You know what else does these three things?

I have no idea. Boggle? In-line skating? Celine Dion?

Sexual intercourse.

Of course.

Yes, sex. And did you know also that laughter, especially in courtship situations, is the physiological expression of a vital release of nervous sexual energy? And that the reason teenagers giggle is because they have so much of this newly acquired sexual energy that it is building up inside of their bodies and needs to be shaken free, physically, often violently, with laughter?

And the reason I need to know this is?

I am interested in your sexual energy. It's unorthodox, but I have a theory about your sexual energy.

Oh, I love you, Dr Ghert. You're quite the card. You got the beard, the sweater, and the overarching sexual obsessions. I must remember to thank Jess for the recommendation.

Your anger is good. It is energy. And an expression of that same energetic block.

I'm blocked?

Like the teenagers. You have the sexual energy in your body, but with nowhere to go. It builds and it builds. With no expression. And a need to be shaken, violently, free.

212

And I need to be shaken violently free, right?

Your mood is an energetic block. This depression you feel? This is an energetic block. You are stuck. You are not flowing. Flow and block. It's how we live, no? How we all live, through periods of flow, and those of block. And right now, you are blocked.

Can I ask you a question, Dr Ghert?

By all means.

Have you ever had a baby?

I have six children, from two wives.

Congratulations. But have you ever given birth to a baby? Had it pop, as it were, out through your vagina, half alive, half dead, out onto the bedroom floor in front of you? Can you imagine what it feels like?

I have been at the births of four of my children, and thus I am aware of the physical process, and find it very fascinating indeed.

That's not what I'm asking. I know it's fascinating. I find it very fascinating indeed. And I've had a baby. No, the question I'm asking is if you know what it feels like?

And I say, I've been at four births. Yes, I am male, and so have no personal physical experience to draw from, but I have also read thoroughly and widely around the subject, and thus, from what appear to be repeated anecdotal references from post-partum mothers to a sensation approximating extreme physical pain and yet purposefulness in that pain, I can very well imagine, or at least conceptualise within, what the experience is like. Extreme pain, but with purpose.

So you read, Dr Ghert?

Yes, of course, I read. Psychology papers, non-fiction, biography, fiction, newspapers, magazines, everything. In fact, there is very little that I do not read.

And, long shot here, but are you interested in the writings and reasonings of modern French feminism?

I am aware of it, yes. But I'm not sure how this is going to help our little exercise here, so it might be more helpful if you turn and face me, close your eyes and—

Thing is, I love those girls. Cixous. Irigaray. Especially Kristeva. Some of that shit is mind-blowing. I don't get half of it. But the stuff I do? Blows, my, mind.

I know. These are very accomplished women. Impeccable writers, with an understanding of modern mores and the cultural infrastructure that is second to none.

Tell me about it! Though my favourite is when they start talking about birth and babies, and the early years of life. They're brilliant on that shit.

Oh yes, they are. I believe so.

They're amazing on babies learning, and babies growing, and how babies acquire language.

Yes, of course.

On how the baby, who becomes the toddler, has to sacrifice something quite profound, some primal state of wild and natural bliss, in order to enter the world of language, and speech, the world of signs and order and rationality, also known, to our girls at least, as the world of men.

Naturally.

And they're not hard-line here. They don't do bra burning. They're like kick-ass scientists, and they pull shit apart, piece by piece. And they let you know just how traumatic it is for the child, especially for the female child, who acquires language, because they say, our feminist girls do, they say, and, God, I love this bit, they say and they ask, if there are, as there are, actually, and it's scientifically proven, but if there are over fifty Inuit words for snow, and, in fact, while we're at it, over seventy Inuit words for ice, how come there isn't one single fucking word to accurately describe the experience of childbirth? Huh? Pain? Wrong! Agony? Wrong! A strange kind of pleasure? Fucking wrong!

And, my favourite, pain with a purpose? Seriously, hugely, egregiously, wrong!

I see.

Yes, you see, or do you see, Dr Ghert? And if you see, because you say you see, if you see, can you tell me this, smart guy: if there isn't a single word available, within this whole, bullshit, mind-control baloney called language, not a single word available to describe the experience of childbirth, how can you, Dr Ghert, how can you, with your man's words, your man's mind, and your limited fucking man's imagination, claim to have any access whatsoever into an experience that has been locked out of language for the very women who experience it? It's like saying you can imagine what it's like to be an exploding termite, or the aurora borealis! The arrogance is breathtaking.

You would not call your birth experience pain with a purpose?

No I would not.

But it was painful, yes?

I just told you. There are no words to describe what—

No, I mean emotionally painful. It is the moment when you and Jay cease from having intercourse, no?

Yes.

Did you discuss it?

What was there to say? We were in Bonnie Land from then on. Everything upside down and back to front. Jay was lost to me. The working man. Mike TV. Pitching, proposing, living the Soho dream. Gone. And me at home, surrounded by madness, dealing with the repercussions of my sins. And, of course, he wasn't going to say it, because Jay didn't say anything at the best of times, so he certainly wasn't going to say this. But I could see it in his eyes. See it in the Catholic flicker after midnight, when Bonnie was in full spasm. Just an unspoken dagger, fired in my direction. My past, my abortions, my crappy womb, and my

215

non-existent *doula*, all were mixed together and poured into this crazy, head-wrecking mould that we called Bonnie. This crazy experiment, of which we were as much the subjects as she, and we were failing wildly every day. So, no, sexual intercourse didn't seem to register with us. It was something for other people. Fools who had not yet seen through the trap of the physical, and the risible procreative rush that turns everyone into humping, grunting, salivating curs, a debased spectacle of bone, gristle and sputum that's the closest you can get to death, as in the absence of intellectual life, without actually dying.

And what about the life created during intercourse, during this intellectual death?

Ah yes. But isn't that the sweetest irony? You're never more closer to death than when you're creating life.

And Jay never asked for sex?

The subject became, to us, at least, a joke. Yes, another joke, in a long list of jokes. Or, put it this way, Jay invited a friend over once, a real smart-ass – you'd like him. A construction guy from Ireland, Dublin, name of Darren. They were supposed to be discussing business, talking work, about an upcoming TV show that was going to feature Darren and a load of zany immigrants building the eighth wonder of the world. Darren wasn't much into blue-sky thinking, however, and instead he kicked back, drank beer, and told us that we had a lovely life, and a lovely darlin girl, and then joked, in a thick Dublin drawl, in front of us both, about the reason why he was never, ever, going to impregnate his girlfriend. He had heard, he explained, that sex for the first time after birth was, like, get this, sending a wiener up the middle of O'Connell Street. And then he laughed, and, of course, Jay laughed too.

A wiener up the middle of O'Connell Street?

It's very wide, O'Connell Street, it's in Dublin. Like, six lanes wide. A wiener, by comparison, is not. A wiener carried up through the middle of O'Connell Street would experience very little, if any, friction with either side of the street.

Ah, I see, your vagina was wide since the baby.

Not my vagina, specifically. Just vaginas, in general.

And your vagina?

Not everything revolves around my vagina.

I see. Well, as I was saying, this is unorthodox, and something they teach you in Copenhagen. I'd like to try it with you, if you please?

Shoot.

I'd like you to close your eyes. Good. Drop your shoulders. Good. Breathe deeply, slowly. Now open your stance slightly, really carry that weight on your legs, feel your body push down into the floor. Feel yourself connected to the earth. Breathe. Keep breathing. Eyes closed. No peeking. And don't worry, I shall remain fully clothed throughout.

What?

No, no, you mistake me! It's a famous joke, yes? You, of all people, must know this joke? The young beautiful woman takes a check-up with the doctor with the, how you say, roaming eye, who tells her, almost immediately, before she's asked a single question, to strip down naked for the examination, and when she asks him, slightly embarrassed, the simple question, 'Doctor, where shall I put my clothes?' the devious doctor replies with, 'Oh, just leave them on the bed over there, next to mine!' You see?

I get it. And you were saying?

Feel yourself connected to the earth. Yes. Eyes closed. Widen your stance. Yes. Widen your stance. Yes. That's good. Now feel that weight, carry that weight on your bones, feel your body pulling down towards the floor. Feel every muscle in your being, every fibre in your body. And tell me now, really feel it now, tell me, whereabouts in your body do you feel this depression?

I feel it in my stomach.

Good, very good. And how does it feel in your stomach?

Empty.

Anything else?

Dark.

Dark and empty?

Yes.

Like the manhole, yes?

Yes.

Like Plato's Cave?

No, like the manhole.

Your stomach is dark and empty because there is nothing there. Because something has been removed, yes? Something that was there is no longer there, no?

I suppose so.

Something that was there for nine months, perhaps, has been taken out of you.

Bonnie, you mean Bonnie?

This is not my session. Do you mean Bonnie?

I guess.

And if your stomach, if this dark and empty space could speak, what would it say? If it could cry out right now, with all of its might, what would this dark and empty space say to us, right now, in this room?

Help me. Help me, I'm drowning.

17

Welcome Home JC

There is a banner. There is a fecking banner.

This is Jay's first thought. He sees it through the giant bay windows of the shed, before he's even set foot inside. He has marched around the building, from back to front, with Bonnie still sleeping in his arms. He has walked several steps ahead of The Clappers. To make a point. A signifier of fury.

I have a job. I have a life.

He has made these two points, repeatedly, and with passion, on the short trip from Drumcliff to the shed.

You can't just mess with people's fecking lives. It's in-bloody-human.

Jay once made Shauna a banner. Twenty-six sheets of A4 printing paper taped together, and stretching across the stairwell, in front of the security door. Welcome Home, Mrs Concannon! He cleared it with the other tenants first. And he told them not to touch the rose bouquet if they were passing. Twenty-four flowers exactly. It was her first trip back home to Rehoboth since the wedding. She had been gone almost two weeks. He was sick with anxiety about the very idea of her return. Didn't sleep the night before, with thoughts of her, on the red-eye, making her way back across the Atlantic, speeding towards him, every minute five miles closer. He made pancake batter at three in the morning. Reloaded the photo-frames at five. Vacuumed at seven. Had already done the banner, did it at the end of the first week. With loving care, filled in every letter with a different colour, and behind every letter the dark chunks of block shading, to make them stand out, for the wow effect.

They kissed. How they kissed, when she came in the door. One of those historical kisses. Not tongues and heavy breaths, and prodding, and searching, with groping on the side. Just the kiss, the deep, soothing, aching kiss of home. Bodies fallen together, in place, as they were meant. A miracle of emotional design.

Welcome Home, JC!

Jesus. The whole gang's here!

This is Jay's second thought. For, smiling below the banner, and crammed completely into the shed, is any number of local faces, possibly Niall from the butchers, certainly aul Mrs D from Drury's, the Sweetmounts for sure, Mr and Mrs, from Cloonavullaun, a load of faceless aul wans hanging onto shopping bags and a glass of vino, a busy throng of kids and teenagers clutching fizzy drinks, Fintan the Solicitor from next door, and there, dotted among them, notable only by their broad beaming smiles and complete lack of curiosity, is Fr Francis, Mickeleen and The Fox.

Jay stands perfectly still, with Bonnie in his arms. The crowd inside cheer together, an entirety, in unity, perfectly on cue, and seemingly marshalled by some invisible ringmaster. They clap and wave, and make woo woo sounds, and the children jump about, and beckon Jay inwards with clawing hands.

Jay remains motionless. Staring at them all. Like a giant mental experiment or a nutso museum exhibit, all encased in glass. A Damien Hirst Sensation special, he thinks *Paddies in a Box*? *The Impossibility of Lunacy in the Mind of Someone Livid*?

The Fox is the first one out. He slides the door open, and emerges in a glow of open-necked white linen and dazzling, rattling, clinking jewellery. He charges onto the sand-dusted roadway between the house and the sea, grabs Jay by the hand and, according to local custom, reefs the paw off him amid a barrage of welcomes.

Here he's on! Your only man! Jay Feckin Concannon, ye dirty great big gobshite, how's she fuckin cutting?

Jay shakes. The Fox shakes.

Been too long, ye lanky shthreak a pish, hu? The Fox says, before pulling back his upper lip and announcing proudly, Check out them pearly fuckers, hu? Cost a few bob, I'll tell ye that for free. Best falsers in Sligo Town. No flies on th'aul Fox these days. Makin a pretty penny, down the high street, selling the best coastal kips to only the richest, most gullible, fecking Germans. Me and Mickeleen. Some scan, huh? Am tellin ye, it's a gold mine out here. Germans will buy any aul shite. A fuckin coal shed. Tell 'em it used to belong to Michael Collins's sister's nephew's poodle, and they pay through the nose. Paid for my gnashers, I'll tell ye that for free.

Jay tells The Fox that it's good to see him. The Fox is joined by The Clappers. They greet each other cordially, without ceremony or seeming affection.

Fox.

Claps.

They both, Fox and Claps, try to persuade Jay to join them, inside, at his own Welcome Home party, but he insists that the noise – at his best guess, based on the terrifyingly solid vibrations pulsing from the front façade's reinforced glass, a skull-rattlingly loud and suspiciously timely presentation of the popular music anthem 'Things Can Only Get Better' – would be too much for Bonnie, now stirring, now stretching, in his arms.

Instead, Jay turns pleadingly to The Clappers, and says that he just wants to go home.

Home, is it? says The Fox, leaping in, combative as ever, a

221

decade of lost intimacy simply vanished in a handshake. Well, listen to yer man! Home? Have the *sassanocks* got to you already? Ye gone native, Jay Boy?

The Clappers, chivalrous as ever, offers to knock The Fox's dental work through the back of his neck. He, in turn, covers his mouth with his hand, and warns her against trying it, and of the hefty legal repercussions that will surely follow any form of physical altercation between a peace-loving lad like himself and a wan of, well, her stature.

The Clappers had cried in the car, with Jay. A tearful confession.

Vee shit air on two-awlla.

She had, she said, made a mistake. An honest mistake.

I'm a good girl, I am.

She had, she said, delivered a single punch to the nose of the wrong man.

She had no pictures, she said. She should've had pictures for that kind of a job.

How was she, she said, supposed to distinguish one aul fart from another without pictures?

She was, she said, going to take it up with the Big Man.

Because he, she said, the Big Man, she said, had meant no harm at all to come to Jay.

It was supposed to be an adventure, she said. Not a trial.

Like IRA lads on the run, she said. A right laugh.

Excuse me, Claps, said Jay. Who's the Big Man?

Mickeleen soon joins the confabulation at the front of the shed, followed closely by Fr Francis.

Howaye, Jay, says Mickeleen.

Grand, Mick, says Jay. And yourself?

Oh, grand. Can't complain. Making a few bob with The Fox here, from the Germans, like. Has he shown you the gnashers?

Fr Francis, grinning broadly, elbows past Mickeleen and grabs Jay by both shoulders, casting looks back and forth between Jay and his waking, blinking, daughter.

Ah, would you come here to me now, *me auld segosha*! he says, leaning forward in a comically exaggerated style, as if replicating the mien and delivery of a so-called stage Irishman, before referring to Bonnie, genuinely, and with some affection, as a sight for sore eyes, and then telling Jay, with barely a downward shift in conviviality, that the natives were getting restless, and that, more importantly, it was not wise to keep our other guest waiting.

Well? he says, pointing Jay towards the shed, and adding, It is your fecking party, after all!

I have a job, says Jay. I have a life.

Nobody is listening.

They guide him, almost push him, into the shed. 'Things Can Only Get Better' is relaunched. Louder than before. Jay covers Bonnie's ears and signals to The Clappers, with a slashing of the throat gesture. The Clappers cuts the music before it even hits the much vaunted chorus, and instead chokes for ever on the observation that the song subject ain't never gonna know me, But I know you ...

Jay once held the baby Bonnie up close to a loudspeaker that was playing the track called 'Wonderwall' by the band Oasis. The speaker was on the tallest bookshelf in the sitting room. Jay had to reach, on tiptoes, to hold her in place. Bizarrely, pleasingly, proudly, it seemed to calm her to the very core.

And maybeeeeeeeee.

Shauna screamed when she entered the room. They argued. Shauna asked him if he had any understanding of paediatrics at all, or of the considered, thoughtful intent required for parenting Bonnie, of all babies. She threatened to report Jay to the specialist. Why would he even think to do something like that? Bonnie might now, on top of everything else, be deaf for life.

Jay, eyes front and focused, passes under the Welcome Home JC banner, and carries Bonnie in towards the kitchen area of the shed, where he hopes to place her down on the draining board and pull a fresh avocado, pitta bread and milk from the fridge. The sound of light disco playing loudly has been replaced by a low grumble of conversation, punctuated by the occasional high-pitched yelps and screams of chasing, jumping, beam-swinging children.

As Jay moves politely through the throng, some of the older folk, however, touch him gently, a light stroke on the shoulder and back, or a short finger jab. Immediately, repeatedly, he turns to answer their questions, or to face their address, but finds only eerie downward glances, and hands replaced quickly by sides. The children too, and some of the adolescents, giggle around him, and track him across the room, in a ring of wide-eyed ador- ation that circles him completely without making contact or impeding his progress.

Jay puts the pitta bread in the toaster of The Clappers, and begins to slowly slice the avocado. Every move is watched from all angles. Bonnie extends her hand. Jay offers her a piece. She eats it, and grins, a wide grin that creeps wider, and deliberately so, all the better, Bonnie appears to think, to allow her space to push the masticated avocado outwards through her teeth, much to the ersatz shock and outrage of her attentive father. This is something of a game, well worn by now. The crowd, witnessing it for the first time, seem to appreciate it. A general murmur of approval is heard from those around. The pitta pops. Jay cuts it, gingerly, down the middle with a breadknife. Mickeleen warns him to watch for the emerging steam, which can burn like a bas- tard, and adds that he once contemplated patenting his own pair of heat-resistant pitta gloves, for that very reason.

Probably would've made a fortune, he says. The amount of feckin Arabs in this country now. Abrakebabra, me arse!

The grumble of conversation intensifies. The Clappers offers Jay champagne. He refuses. The Fox wonders aloud if Jay has become a teetotaller like The Clappers. Mickeleen hisses, in her direction, teetotal gee-bag! The Clappers feigns a punch. Mickeleen winces. Bonnie bites down hard on the bread. Jay fills her glass with milk. Fr Francis, resting a hand gently on Jay's shoulder, announces that their other guest is on a tight schedule, and is very keen to make a connection with Jay. Fr Francis then physically adjusts Jay's body, and angles him towards the corner where, just below a tasteful triptych of female nudes, a tall dark-haired man in sunglasses stands, seemingly deep in serious conversation with Fintan the Solicitor. The man with sunglasses is also wearing a priestly cassock, without the cape, but bound round the waist with a bright-red silken sash. The man with sunglasses, sensing the attention, nods and smiles in their direction, and beckons them over.

Automatically, organically, a space opens in the crowd, a human passage from the kitchenette to the triptych of nudes, which allows Fr Francis to guide Jay, holding the hand of Bonnie, holding a pitta, back across the room.

Fr Francis clears his throat and lifts a sweeping arm towards the tall man in sunglasses.

His Most Reverend Excellency, Bishop Gannon.

I can't sleep, Mammy. I can't fecking sleep. Haven't slept in a week now. And I'm going feckin mental with it. No worse than yourself, I'd wager, but feck me if it hasn't been a hard aul slog, sitting here, surrounded by silence, with Shauna dead to the world, and outside nothing but emptiness and darkness, save for a few young gurriers running up and down the street, shouting rap lyrics at each other while the occasional drunken couple goes ambling past, her screaming the head off him, calling him a filthy aul prick, and him, even though you can't make out the words, him, by the tone alone, sounding like he's been sussed rapid, and is trying to backpedal while he still has the chance.

And it started off, insomnia, as a bit of a laugh too, night before Shauna came home. She was back in the States, on a visit, and I was bopping around the gaff, sticking up banners, and sprucing up the place something rotten, and redoing all the ancient photo frames with new piccies, mostly from the wedding.

That's another thing, Mammy. We're married, me and Shauna. Now, I don't want you to go getting your knickers in a twist about it, and about not having the chance to buy yourself a grand big hat, and a new *goona* and be the star turn of the day, and entertain a couple of hundered English punters with a few *shcales*, and the Grandad Farrell bit and the like, all in the ballroom of the Tara Towers in Kensington. But we didn't do that shite at all. We're not like that, me and Shauna. Not all commercial and, like, gaudy. Like the tinkers down the back of Kilcoman church on First Holy Communion day.

226

No, Mammy, instead, we decided, or Shauna decided, and I thought it was a triffic idea, so we decided to keep it dead cool instead, real grunge stylee, rock'n'roll and skip the church altogether, and just do the double-header of registery office followed by pub lunch. Yir only man. And don't get me wrong, I know you would've liked a bit of God in there somewhere, and I did, fair play to me, hunt down a Catholic priest in Notting Hill, and told him that I was marrying an American wan with no discernible religious faith of any kind, and he goes, get this, Mammy, he goes, some cheek I'll tell you, he goes, Well, if you want to marry this American wan in the eyes of God, you'll need to bring her here, to the church door, for eight weeks of pre-marital lessons, like, after which you, meaning me, will have to write out a big feckin letter to the higher-ups in the Church, explaining why I had chosen to marry outside of the faith. Then, and only then, would the higher-ups consider sending down an honest-to-goodness priest to put an actual real-life blessing on the day.

And the gas thing was, the priesty fella wasn't blushing when he said all this. He wasn't even going, like, Isn't it mad? Isn't it a bit mental? A bit medieval in this day and age, ha? Instead, he was real snooty like, with a dead posh English accent and everything, which is always a bit of a shock, like seeing a blackfella with an Irish accent, and so he goes, saying it without actually saying it, that I'd be dead lucky to get my American wan in through the front door of this exclusive club of feckin hypocrites, gombeens and pederasts.

So, no, Mam, no church for me and Shauna. The full-on grunge rock'n'roll instead. Just a quick service in the register office at the Chelsea town hall where you're in, like, almost a queue, and this dead nice fella stands you up and gets your witnesses to read out their passages – I chose Corinthians, thirteen, Mammy, on your behalf, for the bit of God in the day. Stevie Fitz read it out for me. Did it beautifully too, the little Scotty scene-stealer. Hitting all the right notes, and really chewing up the 'When I was a child' finale. I know, would you credit it? Me and Stevie have been best buddies since the night he told me about deep-dickin Shauna. He came round the next morning in a mad coke depression, half weeping, telling me about how ashamed he was of what he'd said, and how me and Shauna were clearly meant for each other.

Shauna chose the so-called 'Stay Alive' speech from a fablas fillum called *Last of the Mohicans*, with Daniel Day-Fecking-Lewis. She chose to recite it herself too, which meant that I had to do the other part, live on stage, from the Chelsea register office. So, I go, the first bit, looking at her, gorgeous to the day, in a bright-red silk shirt, skintight black denims, and massive, giant, ankle-breaking runners, I tell her that she's done everything that she can do, and that it's time to save herself, and that if the worst happens, and only one of us survives, then something of the other one survives too. Which is, at best, hopeful thinking. Although I don't point that out in the moment.

At which point she looks down at the ground, and is clearly getting into character, because when she looks up her face has totally changed, and is pained and angry, and very much in Day-Lewis mode, and she goes, top of the voice, No! Which makes everyone, about fifteen altogether, including the entire *Screen Grab* team, right down to the researchers and the two work-experience wans, jump a bit in their seats, and then have a nervous laugh together. No! she says again, before telling me to stay alive, and to be strong, and survive, and if the other lads don't kill me they'll take me up north, to Huron land!

Of course, Mammy, I know that anyone in the register office, including the dead friendly fella at the front, who haven't been lucky enough to see the fillum itself, are all going, What the feck is Huron land? Does she mean Manchester, or Scotland? But me and Shauna are in the moment, and she's topping off the speech by telling me that no matter what occurs, she is going to find me. No matter how long I'm gone for, or how far I go away from her, she will find me.

I will find you! she says, repeating it to herself, dead quiet, and then once more, voice cracking, just for effect.

I will find you.

It's brilliant. And she gets a round of applause from everyone, including her dad Paul and brother Chester. Yep, them feckers got wind of the wedding at the last minute and, even though Shauna strictly banned them from coming, by saying that it was no biggie, and that she was going for cool, dirty and grunge and a bit Oasis, and not a big sickly Waltons family deal, and because I had no family on tap so she didn't want to upset the apple cart, and even though she said all that, the blaggards still insisted on rocking up on the very morning, straight from the airport. With poppers and streamers, and tiny American flags, which they unleashed, the lot of them, as we emerged onto the steps of the town hall. And which Shauna hated, and loved, at one and the same time. She spent the night in the boozer afterwards, calling Paul and Chester bastards, and then hugging them, and calling them bastards again. We ate sausage and mash for the wedding meal, and drank a whole rake of pints, and did shots, smoked a ton of fags, and ended the night, totally Oasis style, mashed out of our brains, linking arms and singing about drinking gin and tonics and feeling supersonic, and being the maddest feckers in the world.

So, as I say, it started a week ago, the insomnia, with me flitting around the gaff in the small hours, like Mary Poppins on crack, dusting and cleaning and jamming all sorts of weddin piccies into the frames, and happy to cruise on through till the morning hours without a wink of sleep, just knowing that one Mrs Shauna Concannon was going to waltz on in, through that door, all tanned and glowy from the Delaware sun, and glowy too from the luvvy-duvvie that two weeks apart, our very first post-wedding weeks apart, had created inside the ache of us.

Of course, I put the second night of sleeplessness down to some serious reverb of glowy love ache, like an emotional echo of the first night. That, and the kind of full force, Olympic-level *seshoon mah*, say no more Mammy, that drives your heart up through your own noggin and out your ears, and takes everything you have left not to just expire there, flat out and wasted, on the *labba* of love.

Third and fourth nights were a right feck, all novelty worn off completely, just staring there, eyes practically burnt open with some unspoken inner urgency, while, naturally, the unfortunate side effects of my nocturnal deprivations were now being felt during daylight hours by everyone on the team. They'd be, like, nudging me awake during brainstorming session, or telling me that I looked shot to shit, or slagging me rotten for snoozing all the way through *Lightning Jack*, *The Hudsucker Proxy* and *Guarding Tess*.

Well, Mammy, as you can imagine, by nights five and six, still sleepless, I'm really starting to panic, and thinking that I'm never going to sleep a decent wink again, and will probably, any day now, go to the grave a skinny emaciated wreck, as the world itself collapses around me, in a devastating psychological implosion that has fatal physical repercussions. Thankfully, Shauna's ex-flattie, Jess, who, it transpires, is also a bit of an insomniac, goes to this shrink fella, a Danish lad called Dr Ghert, who once told her that insomnia was to be embraced, because insomnia was the mind's way of telling the body that there was still work to be done. Insomnia, said Dr Ghert, was proof that the mind had infinite reserves of creative energy, and the only way to respond to insomnia was to respect this creative energy, and to express it in whatever form it wants to take – say a picture, a bit of house-cleaning, some cooking, or perhaps, even, a brief but informative epistle to the beloved mammy of the insomniac in question. Mostly, however, Dr Ghert said that insomnia often arises at times in our lives when great changes are occurring and often, and get this, even before the actual changes themselves occur. It's like the brain is so fine-tuned to the ebb and flow of that strange and ineffable quantum world that surrounds and permeates our dull and clumsy, pig-shit bodies that it can actually anticipate the changes coming to our lives before we get the slightest whiff.

Naturally, Mammy, this piece of news, passed on from Jess to Shauna, and designed to calm me, only freaks me out even more. Because I look around at my life, and my world, and I don't want any feckin change. I absolutely reject change. I've only just got married, for feck sake. What's so great about change, anyway?

But then, of course, I'm watching the news on the box tonight, and suddenly it hits me. The 'RA have gone and declared a ceasefire, and the fellas and the wans on the telly are banging on, like ninety, about a brave new era for these two islands. An era of genuine peace between these two nations. A remarkable era ahead of us. War is over. The Troubles are done. Seven hundred years of it. All them battles. All them killings. All them *shcales* and songs. Grandad Farrell too. All suddenly diffuse and gone, absorbed by the process of life, like so many random deodorant particles in a steamy winter bathroom. Yes, they say again, the era of peace between nations is really and truly, and finally, upon us.

231

And that's when it hits me. The penny drops. I can't sleep because life, right now, life is perfect. And the change that I'm feeling is in that perfection. That's the change. I look around me, and it's like I'm in a feckin dream. Working on the telly. Married to a Yank. Owning an Akai wall-mounted midi stereo. Renting a flat. You couldn't make it up. Like I've hit the jackpot. Big time. And th'aul brain, that for so long has been used to some fierce awful shite that passes for a life, simply can't handle it. Can't handle the perfection. Hence the insomnia.

Well, Mammy, shite and inions to that, is all I can say. I'm going to ride out this perfection for as long as it takes. I'll stay awake for ever if that's what it needs. And in the meantime I'm going to enjoy my life of bliss with Shauna. My life of happiness right here in London. And my life, at last, my life without change.

Your Right-Hand Man,

Jay

PS Shauna says that we should also have a baby, a proper one this time. And have it soon.

18

The Copenhagen Technique

No jokes today?

Too tired.

You lack energy?

I lack everything. That's what I do. I lack. I lack the will. I lack the sleep. I lack the power. I lack the time to have a shower. I stink. I lack the freedom to visit the crapper when I want. I lack the breakfast. I lack the food. I lack the home pride and I lack the clothes, or the self-awareness to give two fucks about the clothes – and don't call these gloomy black duds clothes! And, on top of everything else, right now, I even lack a husband – who is, for the umpteenth week in a row, seemingly locked into an edit suite in the bowels of the city, unable to pay anything but the most cursory trips home to his wife and child, while sharing every breath and flirtatious chuckle he can muster with an older woman that he once half fucked. So, yes, I lack energy. I lack it all.

And yet you are perfect too.

Right. According to who?

To me.

Excuse me?

To me and the world and everyone else. It is objective fact, no? We are all perfect in the eyes of nature.

What about your eyes? What do you see, here, on this couch, laid out before you, tattered rags on a stick? What crosses your mind when you see me now?

Right now, my mind tells me that we should try, together, one of the more revolutionary new techniques that I learnt in Copenhagen.

Another one?

Yes, only this one is quite controversial, as it aims to unblock the pathways of your kundalini energy, and to break down for ever that enormous sexual barrier that is at the root of so much of your current condition.

Oh. Great.

And for this, we're going to need the lights down.

19

A Proposal

Bishop Gannon apologises to Jay about the sunglasses. He says that he suffers from the same degenerative eye condition that afflicts the internationally renowned singer and entertainer referred to as Bono, from the band called U2.

Photophobia, he says, shaking his head lightly in disappointment, before readjusting his precious self-described Armanis. Cost him a fortune, but he needs the best. It's an absolute scourge. One drop of daylight on the retina and I'm weeping all day, like a Carmelite in a cathouse.

Bishop Gannon then grins wickedly, drops his voice to a lock-jawed growl and suggests that Jay, however, could probably fix his photophobia on the spot, with nothing more elaborate than a mouthful of spit and some dry sand.

Jay is confused.

Fr Francis leans into his shoulder and whispers, John, nine.

Go! Wash in the Pool of Siloam! continues the bishop, very much in character. So the man went and washed, and came home seeing!

Jay gives Bonnie's hand a squeeze, instinctively, out of habit. He has done this a lot since the break-up. Finds himself in strange social situations, suddenly surrounded by sympathetic mothers, uncomfortable for the first time as a single parent, with comments passed about resilience and divorce, and then off it goes, his hand, in a series of short, sharp squeezes of Bonnie's. She squeezes back of course, identical squeezes, Morse-code style, and he squeezes to her squeezes. It can last for minutes, but it usually does the trick, and will often end with a surreptitious wink passed from Jay to Bonnie, which, in return, will entice a conspicuous double-blink from Bonnie. Game over.

Jay gets nearly six squeezes in before Bishop Gannon breaks the silence, still smiling from behind his Armanis.

You saw the mammy today?

I did, says Jay, circumspect.

Mad as a bag of hammers? asks the bishop, no offence intended.

She is, says Jay, coolly, honestly, no offence taken.

There is another pause. Jay does four squeezes, to Bonnie's three.

Fine style down there, all the same, says Bishop Gannon, starting up again. Isn't it?

Indeed, interrupts Fr Francis, hoping to lubricate the conversation, on behalf of both men. It's like feckin South Fork!

Costs a fair whack too, adds Bishop Gannon, brows peeking out above the glasses frames, before suddenly softening with, Although, bless her heart, Deirdre, she's worth every penny.

Jay looks from Bishop Gannon to Fr Francis and back again. He suddenly reddens with embarrassment.

Is this about the money? he says, relieved yet mortified. He launches into a haphazard monologue about never checking the accounts and always presuming that the Cloonavullaun home would've bankrolled his mother for a long . . .

Bishop Gannon raises his hand. His face is pained.

Saith he unto them, Render therefore unto Caesar the things

236

which are Caesar's, and unto God the things that are God's! This is not, my dear boy, about money.

Bishop Gannon then turns solemnly to Fr Francis, waves him away with a flicker of his hand, and the muttered, dismissive, Amscray.

He then stretches a slow avuncular arm around Jay, leading him towards the back of the shed, and out through the rear exit. Jay clings to Bonnie for dear life, dragging her at Gannon pace, despite her reluctance to leave the party, signified by a wriggling motion against his hand, and a few tiny raspy whelps. They're brilliant like that, he thinks, kids. Like a human shield. God knows the amount of awkward streetside encounters from which he's been able to extricate himself simply by hoisting Bonnie up into his arms, kissing her on the cheek, puppeteering a friendly wave from her hand, and then marching away into freedom.

Bishop Gannon points to his own car, a large black Mercedes, parked in the driveway of The Clappers. He points to the van-truck-tank hybrid of The Clappers, parked next to it. And he points to the car of Fintan the Solicitor, a large, black, all-terrain vehicle bearing the Range Rover brand name, and parked just beyond the black Mercedes. He asks Jay to tell him what he sees when he sees these cars.

Jay stares, and pauses. If Shauna was here, he thinks, she'd probably say, Tiny Dicks, Massive Egos, and Global Warming, though not necessarily in that order. Instead, he makes do, trying helplessly to appeal to Bishop Gannon's latent vanity, with the single word, Cool?

Bishop Gannon shakes his head and says, No.

He explains to Jay that when Jay looks at these cars he sees wealth. And wealth, he says, wealth is what we're talking about today. Wealth, not money.

Wealth, he begins, folding his arms together deliberately, like an orator at the commencement of his opening address. Jay deftly picks Bonnie up, and raises her into his arms. He might have to do a puppet-dash special. Bishop Gannon explains, with a concentrated frown, that wealth is the scourge of their glorious island nation. That it has always had something of an illusory and unattainable quality for the native peoples of this island, and has been the provenance mostly of foreigners, of the British, the Yanks, and of the Other. And yet, he suggests, for the longest time, this obvious absence of wealth, which, he qualifies again, just to make sure, to underscore the point, is the definitive national lack, has seemingly fuelled in this hard-working, God-fearing people an unparalleled spiritualism that has ultimately served as nothing less than the creative dynamo for an entire race. Think of it, he says, before reciting a long line of notables that bounces randomly from Brian Boru to Maureen O'Hara, Bram Stoker to James Joyce, Wolfe Tone to Padraig Pearse, Packie Bonner to Keith Duffy and the rest of Boyzone. All of them. Every one. Did not. Have. A. Pot. In which. To piss.

Pardon my French, darling, he says, suddenly breaking character, and pinching Bonnie on the cheeks. Bonnie gurgles appreciatively, and reaches for the Armanis. Bishop Gannon refuses the request, apologises, and instead pulls a giant silver crucifix from inside his cassock, loops the chain over his own head, and offers it to Bonnie as a conciliatory gesture.

The wealth lecture continues, much to Jay's disappointment, shifting to the modern era, especially recently, and how, in the light of *Riverdance,* multinational investment, property portfolios and the proposed wedding, on native soil, of David Feckin Beckham, the iniquities and inequalities of wealth have become a visible, and very real problem, for the entire nation, and indeed are apparently threatening to drown the native soul, and certainly the soul of the honest-to-goodness countryside folk around us, in a sea of clamouring hands, greedy fingers, beady eyes and dull, senseless, baseless hearts.

Look around you, says Bishop Gannon, there's no soul any more. It's all about the greenbacks! The greenbacks, the rap music, the chilled champagne, and the four-by-four-feckin-all-terrain-armoured-transport! The churches are empty, confession is practically non-existent as a sacrament.

He says that he did the Stations of the Cross on his own last week, but for a couple of aul wans, and a few drunks. And yet, the one and only place, the only place, where they, the clergy, are having any success at all, where they, the God Squad, are winning, the one place where they can see a sliver of hope, a chink of ancient light coming through the great imposing door of modern darkness, the one place of hope, is in the apocalypse business.

And this, my friend, he says, suddenly blessing Jay, quickly, but with dread seriousness. Is where you come in!

Jay's arm is tiring. He switches Bonnie to the left. He kisses her. He is seriously contemplating the puppet wave, followed by a quick nod of thanks to Bishop Gannon and a return dash towards the back door. He has, Jay has, already heard enough. Insanity. This whole trip. Insanity. He wonders, instead, about Shauna. And if Shauna's been wondering. Shite. The feelings. Such feelings. And him telling everyone, when they ask in the office with sympathetic faces, that he's fine with it. That they are fine with it. They are both fine with it. They're modern. And they're both fine. Jane told him later that fine was an acronym for Fucked-up, Insecure, Neurotic and Empty. He liked that.

He wonders if Shauna's happy with Ghert. Are they still having intercourse? Do they have as much intercourse as Jay and Shauna used to have, and in their bed, in the pink palace? He wonders if Paul's nose has healed. He wonders, too, if he can get back on site, at the Dome, by tomorrow lunchtime, faking the final symptoms of flu, without anyone the wiser. He'll take a few verbal lashings from Darren. A few snide remarks from Stevie Fitz. Nothing he can't handle.

I said it's doing gangbusters! repeats Bishop Gannon, louder than before, snapping Jay to attention. Knock, he says, Knock, the holy shrine, is doing gangbusters. Busier than it's ever been. Because of the Millennium. And because of fear. Fear that this whole, stinking, grubby, money-grabbing cesspool is going to end, once and for all, on the stroke of midnight, 31 December of this very year.

I've heard that, says Jay, nodding wisely.

And this, is where you come in! repeats Bishop Gannon, beaming from beneath his Armanis, reminding Jay, if only for a moment, of a longer-faced, fuller-haired Jack Nicholson.

The bishop explains, with mock humility, that his homilies can only go so far. Much publicised though they are, they can motivate only a limited number of the flock. Yes. They can remind only a limited number of the flock that they are going to die in an agonising fireball of heaven-sent retribution unless they pray for forgiveness with all of their might in Knock, as part of a relaxing sojourn to the region, which might very well take in the verdant surrounding countryside, pristine local beaches, and ever-welcoming public houses that are second to none for the chat, *crack ogus keyole.*

The bishop tells Jay that this is very much a win-win situation. He spreads the wealth around the region, but he does it responsibly. Wealth with fear. It's a beautiful combination. They bring riches to the land, purify the pilgrims, and, at the same time, they reignite the true essence of the Irish soul through the power of religious duty and genuine spiritualism. All they need is the touchpaper.

And this, he repeats once again. Is where you come in!

Jay feigns ignorance but he's getting the picture.

Oh, come now, says Bishop Gannon, you don't have to be coy with me, Jay.

The bishop explains that everyone in the region, and certainly every single person in that shed right now, is aware of Jay's history. Of his mother's claims. She was at it for weeks after he left, says the bishop. She announced that Jay had ascended into heaven. Puff. Into thin air. Instead of to Kilburn. Told anyone who would listen, that you were gone to be with your true father. Told them too about the vision of Grandad Farrell and the virgin birth. She was a laughing stock, yes. Running around in her pants for days, with her awful old stump, still rotten red, and sticking up in the air, and a stream of obscenities flowing freely from her gob. Got pelted a few times for her troubles, I can tell you.

Jay bridles at the notion. He pictures her thus described. His Mammy. His brave, crazy, stupid, life-sustaining mammy. His legs feel suddenly, momentarily, weak. He squeezes Bonnie tighter than ever, bodily, by the waist, in his grip. She gasps, and pokes him with Bishop Gannon's crucifix.

But adopting the philosophy that there's no smoke without fire, continues the bishop, they set Fr Francis to work. Or, Fr Francis PI, as some of the quicker wits down in the rectory were fond of saying. Naturally, all it took was a few pertinent questions, together with a couple of gift-wrapped Jamesons, to discover that there was indeed enough actual murk and ambiguity at the heart of Deirdre's havering declarations to sustain, if not quite the full-value virgin-birth story, then certainly a mood of intrigue, optimism and anticipation around it, one that would, no doubt, be thunderously elevated by the hopes and dreams of the faithful flock around this country, perhaps around the entire globe.

Murk and ambiguity? asks Jay, genuinely woozy now.

Have you heard, says the bishop, deadpan to the end, and only slightly patronising, of such a thing that is nowadays called a lavender marriage?

Cautiously, Jay confirms his awareness of the term.

241

Well, there is strong evidence, in the form of anecdotal accounts of physical appearance, bodily deportment and, most damning of all, nocturnal activities, to suggest that your daddy, or at least the man you refer to as your daddy, was in fact very much an enthusiastic member of the homosexual persuasion. And that your mammy, your beloved mammy, was to him, first and foremost, and perhaps ever only, as they say, a beard.

Jay remains silent. Has nothing to say. Instead, the bishop lays it all out for him, with meticulous precision. The facts, the theory, the plan.

The facts: Jay's parentage was in doubt. His biological father unknown. His mother devout. There is not a scintilla of evidence, anecdotal or otherwise, that points to the existence of another man, fleeting or long term, in Deirdre's life. Not a hint of written correspondence to a former lover. Not a single diary entry mentioning the words boyfriend, lad, fella, shifting or courting. Nothing. Fr Francis PI had combed the house in Cloonavullaun, top to bottom, inside and out of every drawer, cupboard and trunk. Nothing. The only man, it transpired, the only man she ever had in her life, and loved in her life with a passion unbound, was Jay.

The theory: Jay is a virgin birth. Even if the less charitable, the cynical and the downright degenerate accuse Jay's daddy of donating his seed, Fr Francis is in possession of written testimony to the contrary – a letter to a gay lover, male, that may yet be something of a smoking gun for Team Jesus 2, since it refers to Deirdre's pregnancy – albeit ironically, but these things don't often translate – as the 'immaculate conception'. Theories of one-night stands, slatternly behaviour or, perhaps even, and perish the thought, forced penetration by a family friend or neighbour, will all be batted back in the strongest terms, with reference to Deirdre's saintly profile, and her near-ascetic life before the pregnancy, tending to her then already ailing husband – still gay, but now dying and gay – and leaving the house, day in, day out, only for her shift at Drury's post office, some grocery shopping in Mulligan's, and the occasional summer or Christmas hoolie during which she was renowned for her oratorical skills, and nothing else at all.

The plan: Jay will be introduced, slowly at first, by the bishop, at the height of pre-millennial dread, perhaps at the end of the summer, with the nights getting shorter, the chill setting in, and the seasonal gloom compounding a profound sense of communal unease in the shadow of an impending apocalypse. It will initially be low level. A church sermon here or there. A meet and greet afterwards. A rumour of a miracle or two, perhaps. A blind aul wan with vanished cataracts. An aulfella with kidney stones suddenly cured. Certainly, it will be a healing mission, and a permanent presence at the shrine in Knock. And even if he doesn't heal, even if there are no miracles, the appetite for the same is there, and the perception will be moulded to fit the appetites. And there will be talk, lots of talk, about the apocalypse, and the need for devotion at the shrine in Knock. And Jay will be a lightning rod for that devotion. The media will be involved. *Telefeesh*. BBC. ABC in the States. The world will watch. The land will thrive. Jay will be, without a doubt in anyone's mind, the new and risen Jesus Christ.

What do you think? says Bishop Gannon, slightly exhausted, but certainly wound up with his own excitement.

Sound like a goer?

I had this dream last night. It was a disturbed night, Mammy, to say the least. I'm back doing the sleeping, full time, but Sundays are never good. Think it's an ingrained hangover from home days, and school days, with you watching *Glenroe* on the telly, and me at the kitchen table, doing my ecker, with Bowsie at my feet. And no matter what time of the year it is, it's always feckin dark outside, with dead leaves blowing around, and the week is dead, and hope is dead too, and nothing will happen until Monday arrives with the aching predictability of Claps Connolly at the buzzer, dragging us off for another day of soul-crushing tedium in St Cormac's.

The dream was feckin rotten. Although it started off brilliant, with me being the man about town, dragging Shauna, Jane and a whole rake of *Screen Grab* bods with me on a tour of the West. Although when I say *Screen Grab* bods I mean literally that, just the bods, because, in classical dream mode, besides Shauna and Jane, they don't have any actual faces, just blank spaces on their heads, like shop dummies. Anyway, I bring the lot of them down onto a beach that is very much Strandhill without actually being Strandhill. This one's deeper into the ground, with higher dunes and steeper headlands closing in from both sides, so when you're in the water it feels kind of like you're in a bucket, rather than the open flowing sea.

Naturally, Mammy, you pop up too, as does Fr Francis. You're in your heyday, you'll be pleased to hear. In fact, you're younger than I ever knew you, and you're wearing the same two-piece bathing suit from the photo with me in the bump, only in the dream you don't have the bump at all, just the kind of tummy, tanned and muscley, that you see on all the wans in *Baywatch*. I know! Mental, ha? And you didn't even lift a finger! Fr Francis is in Speedos, but you only see them once or twice, thanks be to God, whenever the waves retreat too quickly, and he's caught there, revealing his jet-black bulge to the world. And, honestly, Mammy, isn't it the hairiest thing you've ever seen, like he's gone and put the Speedos on over a pre-existing pair of hair shorts, full on teen-wolf style.

Anyway, the dream's going brilliantly, and I'm being the toast of the town, and have managed, with some effort, I might note, to get everyone down onto the beach, and into their bathing suits and finally, reluctantly for some, into the sea. Jane, in particular, kicked up a big fuss, saying that she didn't want to go near the water at all, because it was chockers with seaweed, which it was, the result of an unseasonal summer dream storm. You know the kind? Waves slamming all night long, then you arrive onto the sand, first thing in the morning, and the sea is positively green, bright green, with seaweed. And even when you, like, go out into it, with a hefty limb-swinging front crawl, it's a right load of arse, because it seems that no matter how far you swim there's always long slithery arms of green pulling at you, curling around you, riding up over your shoulders. You daren't put the head under either, for fear of what may emerge on top when you lift it out again.

So, as I say, Jane is looking at all the bright green seaweed in the water, and is freaking out goodo, having a tantrum on the beach, saying that she's not getting into that water, not on her life. She is wearing a bathing suit from the olden days, possibly even older than yours, Mammy, a bathing suit that features it's own inbuilt frilly skirt that seamlessly joins with the rest of the upper body bit. The suit itself seems to be adding to her sense of discomfort, and she stands there, hands folded in front of her, like the way you do when you're hiding a bit of a bell, until Shauna comes along, and is incredibly unreasonable, and fires a string of eye-wateringly crude expletives in her direction, the very act of which is the greatest hint yet that we are, in fact, in a dream.

After another barrage of Shauna's expletives, Jane finally works up the courage to enter the green seaweedy water, which is the cue for everyone else to follow. She screams a lot as she's going in, yelps at the top of her voice every time a slithery subaquatic tendril makes contact with her ankles, knees, and then thighs. Meanwhile, Shauna, fed up with the histrionics, and the achingly slow progress, takes it upon herself to liven things up by firing a fistful of wet seaweed in Jane's direction. In fact, not just in her direction, but dead on target, full-force, splat into her face, like a big green throwing-pie from kids' comedy telly. Naturally, Jane screams, and cries, and pulls at her face, at the seaweed, and yells blue bloody murder at Shauna, and threatens her job, saying that she's going to be fired from the newsroom when we get back – that's another thing: for no reason other than it's in my dream, we all work in the BBC newsroom, rather than on a fillum show.

Still lost in sheer temper, and forgetting her initial fear of the seaweed, Jane reaches into the water, picks up her own green handful and flings it across the surface, making perfect contact with Shauna, another peerless splat, directly in the face. Instead of screaming, however, Shauna bursts out laughing. She pulls the seaweed away from her eyes, comically, as you would do if parting a tiny green curtain and, still laughing, flings another fistful at Jane. The latter laughs too, this time, and in her laughter there is the signal for a full-scale seaweed fight, involving all personnel in the water, including you Mammy, and Fr Francis, and any number of faceless, dream-filling bods.

And so, for about ten seconds of dream time, it's the biggest hoot ever. The seaweed, big clumps of it, is flying about and splashing down left, right and centre. We're all up to our waists in the water, and we're diving left or right on cue, and plunging quickly down whenever we can, to avoid any unnecessary splatting. And then, something very odd happens. I get hit in the chest by Shauna. I'm up to my waist at the time, so instinctively I reach down to scoop a handful of seawater upwards, to rinse myself clean of the seaweed splat. But, and this is where it gets pretty stinking, Mammy, literally, instead of there being a green blob of seaweed on my chest, isn't there a feckin horrible brown smear of human excrement. I know. You couldn't make it up!

It gets worse, however. Because I try to say, out loud, Hey, lads, what the feck's going on, and when did we start throwing shite at each other? But nothing comes out from my mouth. Total silence. As I say, classic dream stuff. I think for a second that maybe it was just an aberration, a freak throw, Shauna accidentally grabbing some effluent that was bobbing about in the seaweed. But then it happens again. Same place, same splat. Same excrement.

And worse. I look down around my waist and notice that the water has gone from bright green to a dull grey brown, and instead of strands, tendrils, and floating clouds of seaweed, there is just giant swirling ribbons of brown. And in the brown there's all sorts of fierce, sick-making stuff, all the stuff that you'd never want to see, see, see, in the dark-brown sea, sea, sea. Like, saving your presence, menstrual pads, and tampons, and, again, saving your presence, rubber johnnies, and feckin femidoms, and all sorts of unidentifiable objects for wiping, poking, soaking and extracting liquids, flows, sebum, sputum, rheum and phlegm from the secret, the private and the unmentionable areas of the human body.

247

Naturally, the others don't have a clue, and continue, in blissful ignorance, with the filthy flingathon, slowly turning each other into excrement-covered gombeens, laughing and chucking, and filling the air with flying shite. But me, with my detective's hat on, I follow with my eyes the swirling ribbons of brown, and quickly find that they snake directly out of the water and meet up on the sands, where they combine into a single pulsing stream. That dark-brown flow has cut a deep channel through the beach and is easily traceable right back to the headland where it is emerging, niagariously, chock-full of bubbling rejectamenta, from a giant open sewer pipe.

Yes, Mammy, we are all swimming in a huge and noxious stew of Irish shite. Of course, the minute I spot the sewer I double my efforts at th'aul screaming. Mouth torn open on me, brain going, SHAUNA! JANE! SHAUNA! JANE! AND MAMMY! YES! SHAUNA! JANE! MAMMY! CAN YIZ NOT HEAR ME? LOOK AT THE SEWER! WE ARE ALL SWIMMING IN SHITE! SHITE IS ALL AROUND US! EVERYWHERE IS SHITE!

Naturally, classic dream, they can't hear me. They go on tossing the effluent at each other, happily splattering each other, full force, with excrement, menstrual products and prophylactics. And that's how I leave it. That's how it stops. Me, screaming in silence while the world I know, my world, and all the loved ones in it, is reduced to, and defined by, shite in the water.

Penny for your thoughts on this, Mammy?

Your Right-Hand Man,

Jay

248

20

Drowning

I am drowning. We are drowning. In the waters of the West. I say this to myself, repeat it like a mantra, an automatic loop, because I can't quite believe it, and yet I can. There is no drum roll, here. This is not a fillum. No great big orchestral crescendo to let me know just when. Or no super-slow-mo crash-zoom into extreme close-up to signal the moment when I suddenly realise the acutely painful reality of my impending doom, and that of my precious and blameless child.

Instead, there is only the sound of the savage offshore wind smashing wave-tops into spray, and pushing us both mercilessly out, further out than ever, with hints and snatched glances of Maguins Island on the left, the shadow of Dromard on the right, and the formerly wide horizon of Strandhill fading fast, receding, beneath an arcing, breaking, ever-rolling vista of stark consuming sea.

My arm is hooked, at the elbow, into Bonnie's float. I should've known. I should've been faster. The last gesture of The Clappers. A poisoned chalice indeed. Handed over to Bonnie from the back of the van-truck-tank. Didn't even inflate it properly, the eejit – could do with a few extra breaths of buoyancy now. And then she was gone. Off to get a filter bag, for the coffee, so we can do a full Irish before the flight. Of course, she might be back now, bags in hand, sausages on the pan. She won't see us, though. Not from there. Not in this sea. Would've needed a spotter to keep tracking us, in this sea, from the moment we zoomed, like a feckin wind-powered torpedo, past the jetty on the island.

Fierce powerful swimmer all the same, The Clappers. Would've got here if she'd seen us. And then what? Like myself. Knackered. Banjaxed. Bollixed. Bobbing and zooming, out to our doom.

And I should've been smarter when the float came out. Quicker thinking. More, well, parenty. Like the way Shauna would delicately, quietly, remove a juice glass from Bonnie's range, without making a fuss, without even commenting, or breaking eye contact. Just talking, about whose turn it is to hit the Sainsbury's on Ladbroke Grove, or this idea she's had for a dating game show called *Opposites Attract*, or the last chat she had with Paul, and as she does, her hand reaches over, as if acting on its own impulse, slides in front of Bonnie and deftly moves the glass, beautifully so, about four or five inches. Nothing remarkable. Just enough to dodge a wild limb swing or sudden spin.

She's brilliant like that, Shauna. Can stroll into any social situation with Bonnie in tow, and scan it instantly and discreetly, like the Terminator, with a data register in her skull noting down the danger points for a roaming child with gross motor-skill afflictions: solid glass coffee table, corners uncovered; balcony door, slightly ajar; two crystal champagne flutes, precariously balanced; steaming teacup, windowsill; loaded knife block, edge of counter; exposed television wires; and most of all, live fireplace uncovered, with trip-ready sheepskin in front of heavy marble hearth. And then she acts accordingly, Shauna, smiling at the other guests while carefully guiding Bonnie through the hazards, eyes on her at all times, hands ready to catch, legs ready to leap into action, her entire persona, despite affable signs to the contrary, one huge coiled spring of alarm and defence.

You don't understand, she'd say, cold-eyed, red-eyed, staring listlessly into space, with Bonnie dozing, only just, in her arms at midnight. I am on. I am on. I am always on.

Yeah? Tell me about it! I might reply, at my worst. Feckin felt like that for me too, hon, today, down in the edit. Putting together that piece of interview VT with Stevie Fitz really took it out of me. You know? We were missing a whole chunk of audio! Complete nightmare! I told them not to do it on the high street. But no, they had to have the so-called feckin 'vibe'! What are they like?

And she wasn't hysterical with Bonnie, or overprotective, Shauna, no. Wasn't like them mammies you see down Holland Park way, who, like, feckin rugby-tackle their own tots to the ground, with a long, loud, slow-motion Noooooooooo, the minute they see the first sign of a springtime bumble-bee, a stray dog, or a toothless wino by the playground gates. No, Shauna was just there, ever present, like a shadow, always seemingly aware that the greatest tragedies can emerge from nowhere, without fanfare, like the banality of a skull-splitting fireside fall, a coffee-table tumble with fatal results, or, perhaps even a sudden and unexpected punch to the face that has the power to upend the world. Or a drowning.

And I should've been quicker to click, when I first saw the float, a bright-pink dolphin that lit up her eyes, Bonnie eyes, twinkling with excitement, while her throat provided a small simultaneous gasp of rasping pleasure. But I was groggy, dry-mouthed and slow, part of me proudly woolly, like the old days, the Strandhill days, protected from the world by a thick blanket of dull throbbing inertia, courtesy of a hoolie that, surprisingly, ignited, and continued in conversation and in self-created *crack ogus keyole*, continued into the small hours, just hours before Bonnie wake-up.

And I put her to bed in such a fury too. Kneeling next to her on the balcony bed, gripping the mattress with anger, and apologising for the noise below, looking into her wide, blameless eyes, and apologising for everything, and promising, promising a fulsome and long-running polar-bear girl recommencement upon our London return, and cursing, secretly cursing and raging against the lunatic liars, the deluded cheats and the back-stabbing micks in the room below who had engineered this entire sorry excursion on the strangest of conceits. No, I said to Bishop Gannon. Of course, no. And No I said to Fr Francis. Of course, no. What planet? No. I have a job, I said. I have a life. And them, strangest of all, not fecked off, not annoyed in the slightest, just smiling at me, smiling at each other, the giggling goms, and nodding at each other in their smiling, saying, Fine now, grand lad, no pressure now, son, still time to make your decision, no rush, you're a grand lad, a big decision, but we know, me and the father both know, me and His Most Reverend Excellency both know, that you'll make the right decision. In time.

And then downstairs again, grumbling through conversation with Fintan the Solicitor, who calls me a gas man for the Jack Lord deception, but then adds that he understands, from the mouth of the bishop, that I'm to be a major player in the region's Millennium festivities. And I nod politely, with no possible comeback, until I feel a familiar hand on my underwear elastic, yanking it firmly upwards, in a sudden controlled half-wedgie of intimacy, while a heavy chin lands on my shoulder, and the voice of The Clappers tells me that I'm a misery guts, and thrusts a glass of champagne into my hand, announcing solemnly, in parody, Take this, all of you, and drink from it, for this is the cup of my blood, the blood of the new and everlasting covenant, which will be shed ...

I elbow her into silence. Nothing serious. Not even a proper elbow. More of a shove. She does a comedy Oooof. Like you do when a toddler kicks your ankles. She is drinking orange juice. She

252

encourages me to down my champagne in one. If not for me, then for her. To let her feel, vicariously, the buzz of the old days. And she watches, as I do. Fintan drifts off towards the front of the shed. The Clappers refills my glass, and tells me to down it again, in front of her again. I do. Three times in a row. Each time we don't speak. She fills, I drink. She insists, I drink. She stares. I drink.

Naturally, we make love on the sand soon after midnight. At the time I'm feeling woozy. Mairead Ni Davitt, who has arrived, late, with her husband, Fionn, a bearded fella with a rake of guitars, has launched straight into a rousing rebel *seshoon* just as I begin to lose my balance, and any semblance of dignified coordination. I make it up the stairs, however, and rest my head on Bonnie's bed, just below her feet. I decide to sleep the night this way, in this position, like Greyfriars Bobby, perennially on duty at the foot of the master. I want someone to take a photo. For Shauna. Just to prove, you know, that I amn't always totally useless. But then, even through my woozy and blackening subconscious, I hear the stairs creak, and feel the hand of The Clappers on my shoulder.

She leads me down again, guiding me, telling me all the time that I need fresh air. She walks me through the party, and out through the front glass doors, and onto the sand, where we immediately start eating the faces off each other, ripping the threads off, and grunting and groaning, with me saying, like twenty times in a row, that I love her. Perhaps not unusually, The Clappers does not return my declarations of affection, and instead keeps covering my mouth with her finger, and telling me to shut up, that I'll regret it in the morning, and that we are doing this for her sake, not mine, for her past, and for her sense of closure, and, mostly, for her process.

I'm not sure, exactly, what happens once we lie down. Shite tends to get a bit blurry when you go horizontal in the dark after midnight with a feckin Methuselah of champagne swishing around your insides, but I remember some writhing, some rolling, and me freaking out when a stream of sand from behind the white denim collar of the jacket of The Clappers poured freely into my left eye. And I remember trying to wash it out by the water's edge. Then I remember, sometime later, maybe hours, maybe minutes, crashing back into the party, where an entire chorus of 'We Know What You're Up To' continues for an age, until it is widely, and repeatedly, peppered with vocal jokes, from all corners, about the so-called Second Coming. Cute who-ers indeed.

And I barely mumbled to The Clappers, in the 6 a.m. startles, with my eyes clogged shut, and my breath still breathing the brewery fumes, mumbled the fact that Bonnie and me were con-templating a pre-breakfast dip before she was up and over, tracksuit clad, and clinging to car keys, and insisting that she had just the thing for Bonnie, for swimming in Strandhill. And she did twenty rapid breaths and blows, handed it over to Bonnie, who squealed and ran, while I stood opposite The Clappers, and she stood opposite me, and we both tried to refer to the previous evening's writhing in the sand, but decided instead to leave it in silence, until The Clappers announced, loud and precise, that she needed filters. Filters for coffee for the pre-flight breakfast.

The car roared off, Spar-bound, in a cloud of sand and dust, and as it did at one and the same time I had two thoughts. One referred to the way in which the cloud of sand behind the vehi-cle evaporated instantly, pulsed sideways into nothing by a brutal offshore wind, while the other thought was a guttural pang for the whereabouts of my daughter. I turned and, even from there, from the back of the house, with the door open, and an unob-structed view leading straight out through the glass front and into the waves, I could see her, her tiny bodily form, secured within her brand-new plastic pink dolphin, and, simply, sickeningly, gunning it out to sea.

I ran of course, like you do. The potential drowning of your only daughter being an instant hangover cure. I was in denims. Should've stayed in underpants, but didn't want to give The Clappers the wrong signals, whatever they might be, like, hey, by the looks of these mustard-yellow Marks & Spencer boyos you can surely tell that I'm ready for round two, ha? I ran into the waves, into a falling dive, like I had done so many times before, for so many years, so many summers, this action to me, this icy wake-up, the low dip of the sand before the break line, the hazy peripheral headlands left and right, the very smell of the sea, the perfect balance of sickly seaweed with water salt, more salty than sweet-weed, this entire embrace, this raw and stinging icy intimacy, so familiar to me, like a friend to me, carrying me along, willing me along, to get, at all costs, to Bonnie.

Which I do, eventually, further out than I thought, deeper than I thought, far, far out, fishing-boat far, and practically on the last stroke too, the last kick that I have in me, hangover be damned, nothing but The Clappers could beat this stroke or this kick, when I finally get to hook my arm inside the float, and match that hook with a great big throat-gagging gulp of seawater, supposed to be air but the wind's something rotten, and shovelling bucketfuls into my gob at every turn. Try to shout the usual, the help! The Claaaaps! The help, again! But gagging fast, busting a gut, I can barely face Bonnie without choking, let alone bellow to the far diminished coastline. I twist my head, with difficulty, half away from the wave-smash, steal some air, turn back, stare wordlessly at Bonnie, and feel my weight, my useless weight, denim clad, like a stone, dragging her down, float-dipping under, her arms dipping under, waves over shoulders, and facing facts, me facing facts, finally.

I am drowning. We are drowning. In the waters of the West.

And, of course, she would do it now, wait till now, until the end, to let it out.

No, Dadda, no!

If I could fall off my chair, I would, but I don't. Instead, there is amazement in my eyes, which I hope she can see. No words in my mouth. No breath for that. But amazement in my eyes, as I listen again.

No, Dadda, no!

She repeats and repeats. Strangely musical. Like a protest song, a softly squeaking soundtrack to our hellish, and icy, wave-blasted end.

No, Dadda, no!

So sweet for my ears, this voice to hear, on my own way out.

And my eyes say I knew it! My heart says I knew it! She was waiting for the moment, for the chance to erupt.

No, Dadda, no!

But no time for celebrations, back-slapping, or joy. Because her shoulders are dipping down even more, and my weight like stone, dragging her down, deep down, and I can't do that.

No, Dadda, no!

And it can't be my last act, my parting blow to the world, the drowning of this child. So, instinctively, desperately, I ready myself to let go. I ready myself to part. But it's so hard to part. They are so beautiful, these children. They sustain. To leave them is an agony like no other. To leave the orbit of their eyes, their breath and their touch. And so I close mine tight, and I prepare myself in prayer. Because that's what you do. And I say God, whoever, whatever you might be, and however you might make yourself known to me, give me the strength to do this thing, to leave this child of my heart. Please, God, do!

And then, of course, the voice of God, as I imagine him to be, comes back. Because that's what praying is, and it's what we were told in St Cormac's, by Fr Francis himself, straight from the bishops, that praying was allowing yourself to trust the voice you heard inside. Which, in perfect prayer, was guided by God. Not burning bushes from Hollywood epics, not deep stentorian commands from on high, just the sound in you, of what God might say, in perfect prayer.

So the voice goes, I hear you, Jay, son of the Mother of Jay. I have heard you your whole life. But what can I do now, here, at the end?

I need help, I say, in the icy wave-splash, I need help to part from my only child.

Why? asks the voice of God.

Because I'm not ready, I say.

And when will you be ready? the voice asks.

When we're both ready! I say, kind of abrupt, a bit snappy, like, to the voice of God as I understand him to be.

Oh, says the voice of God, then let me try something.

There is an enormous deafening bang in my head, which I recognise immediately as the sound of God, as I understand him to be, clicking his celestial fingers, and I see us back in London, Bonnie and me, living the life as normal, back in the groove for summer '99, one of the highlights of which is certainly Bonnie's third birthday party. Shauna throws it in the pink palace and I am invited. Everyone is. Full house. A roaring success. Pass the parcel, musical chairs, the works. At the end of the evening, I help Shauna with the clear-up, and together we put Bonnie to bed. We kneel beside her pillow, one on either side, while I recite to her again her favourite instalment in our polar-bear girl chronicles. Bonnie looks from face to face, from me to Shauna and back again, and she smiles and gurgles with happiness, and because she can speak now, she says, night night mamma, night night dadda.

At which point the voice of God taps me on the shoulder and says, Well? Now, are you ready now? Is it time?

And I say, Wait! No! Are ye out of yir feckin mind?

And he, the voice of God, says, Fine, dead relaxed, OK, I can wait. And he does, and Bonnie grows, and she learns in school, in regular school, ironing out the developmental creases, quiet always,

257

but never silent, and not a big one for gym either. Still clumsy, but a character too who's the twelve-year-old star of First Year Drama's Christopher Marlowe's *Doctor Faustus*, wailing at the footlights in the final act, crying aloud, O lente lente currite noctis equi! And for the translation bit she stops dead still and turns and faces the crowd, and catches every eye in the room, holds every flicker of attention and sighs, despondently, O slowly, slowly run, O horses of the night! The extra O is her bit. She calls it improv.

She gets a huge cheer. Flowers and everything, and is taken off for pizzas and chat by the school drama teacher. And as I watch her and four other star students pull away in a large Renault people carrier, and wave happily out the back to me, I hear again the sound, straight from my soul, of the voice of God, who says, Surely now, son of the Mother of Jay? Surely you are ready? It must be time?

Not a chance! I say. Still so much to do!

The voice of God, like Bonnie, sighs despondently and turns away, and life rolls along. There are summer holidays in France, through the teen years, with Bonnie and with Shauna, now my wife again, in matrimonial bliss. And there's a celebratory trip to New York to mark the end of Bonnie's college years, after which the voice of God whispers in my ear and asks me if it's time. Am I ready?

Wait! I say, again. No. I'm still not ready.

By the age of forty, Bonnie's forty, the voice of God is furious. Bonnie is her own mammy now, with her own brood. Three of them. Such gorgeous things. Curley mops, all three. The dimples and the cheeky comments. The husband's a bit of an eejit, but that's neither here nor there. Beardy bollix. Bonnie is happy, and a smashing mammy, and a feckin artist to boot. I know, it's not off the stones she licked it, eh?

Then Bonnie has a terrible scare, just before her forty-fifth. A lump. Under the arm. Everyone's up to ninety about it, with worry. The kids find out about it too, and are crying at bedtime. But it comes back benign, and on the positive side, Bonnie is scanned up and down, back to front, and not only is she given a clean bill of health, but she is told, in no uncertain terms, that she's as strong as an ox, as healthy as feck, and with at least another forty-five years ahead of her.

After that, naturally, the voice of God is having none of it. He practically pounces upon me, and hisses, Right, that's it, Mr fecking son of fecking the Mother of fecking Jay! You're done! That's got to be it! You're ready! Right? You're both ready! We are all ready! Right?

No, I say, firm as can be. Not yet, I say. And I stand by her side, stock-still by Bonnie's side, past the aching unthinkable death of Shauna, past time, past growth and decay, and the Bonnie children arcing gracefully into middle age, with children of their own, and teens of their own, while Bonnie herself crumples in size, wrinkles, breaks in places, stoops and falls, and finishes in madness, a ragtag bone sack, with mash mush for brains, like the Mother of Jay herself, in another home, in another place, drooling to the walls, jacked up on drugs, and afloat on a sea of encroaching, inevitable mortality.

Now! says the voice of God. Finally, Jay, the son of the Mother of Jay! This is it! We are, and we must be, ready.

No, I say again.

But look at her! says the voice of God, as I imagine him to be, from his lofty seat of perfection. She is a hideous mound of putrefying flesh, decaying bones, and suppurating, self-consuming organs. She is nothing. A revolting biological mass of insanity. An obscenity.

I don't listen, though. I lean down and touch her ancient head, stroke the last few wiry silver hairs, and whisper in her ear.

Bonnie, I say. Bonnie, I say. It's Dadda. Dadda loves you.

*

Of course, there's feckin murder when I get back to London. Everyone's like, Who in feck's name is The Clappers? And how feckin strong is she that she managed, single-handedly, to swim through a storm, find you underwater, grab Bonnie out of the rubber ring, swim you both, lifeguard-style, back to the shore, give you rapid-fire mouth-to-mouth on the sand, and stick Bonnie into the back of the swanky van-truck-tank hybrid and race her to Sligo Hospital A&E, to be treated, successfully, for shock and hypothermia? She must've been some fine big girl.

THREE

21

Boom

Boom!

Mamma, boom!

Mamma, boom! Boom! Boom!

22

A Hollywood Interview

Jane: And what made you want to become an actress in the first place?

Kirsty: I think I was always acting. Even as a kid, I'd do Broadway in the trailer for my sisters, and sing Billy Joel tunes for my mom. She was a big 'Uptown Girl' fan.

Jane: And did your mother approve of your career choice?

Publicist: Sorry, no personal questions.

Jane: Oh, pardon me. I meant to say, does your mother enjoy your work?

Publicist: Still too personal.

Jane: Of course, my apologies, Kirsty. Now, in your new movie, *Deathfall*, you play Bathsheba Flint, a regular soccer mom who moonlights as a lethal CIA assassin. Did this require much research?

Kirsty: Absolutely. I am a total research nut. And for this I spoke to some high-up guys in Washington, and they put me in touch with some people on the ground, who let me know what it really was like, living the life.

Jane: Wow. I can't imagine. Did they tell you anything specific about that world that you can reveal?

Publicist: Your question puts Kirsty in an awkward position. If you don't mind, please rephrase.

Jane: Of course.

Publicist: And, guys, we can keep that wide for the B-roll!

Jane: Tell me, Kirsty, did the spies give you any tips?

Kirsty: They told me that being a spy was like being an actor, because both are performing all the time. We have a lot in common, as professionals. Except that they don't get to do awards season! Hahaha.

Jane: Hahaha. And you famously changed your appearance, and radically, with muscles, in order to play the more athletic side of Bathsheba. Can you describe the gruelling regime of transformation that finally allowed you to inhabit the very specific space of a soccer mom by day, CIA assassin by night?

Publicist: The question is far too personal.

Kirsty: It's OK, Joan, I got this. Thing is, it's hard for me to talk about it, because becoming Bathsheba was such a personal thing for me. I went to a very dark place. I retreated inside myself. The only people I saw, for six weeks, were my trainer and my nutritionist. I worked out in my gym every day. I ate chicken and broccoli at every meal. I watched spy movies, non-stop, all the greats, *Mission Impossible, True Lies*, and some of the golden oldies, like *Delta Force*, on, like, a loop, twenty-four-seven. I cut off all contact with everyone I knew. I simply, physically and spiritually, became Bathsheba Flint.

Jane: And your friends? What did they think at the time?

Publicist: I'm sorry, ma'am, but you signed the waiver, you agreed to the terms, and yet I find your line of questioning to be unreasonably personal and invasive. Now you need to get back to the agreed terms of the interview or this encounter with Kirsty is over, British television or no British television.

Jane: My apologies. I'm just so interested in what Kirsty has to say that I'm getting carried away by my own excitement.

Publicist: Well try not to. And guys, keep that last wide for the B-roll.

Jane: Apologies again, if I have offended, or overstepped the mark. So, Kirsty. Where were we? Yes, research. This role obviously took a toll on you. Do you find that you bring your work home with you?

Publicist: Excuse me?

Jane: Sorry, do you find that you bring your work away from set with you?

Publicist: Better.

Jane: Do you find, in other words, that it's hard to shake a character like Bathsheba Flint even after filming has finished?

Kirsty: Oh, absolutely. You're so right, Jane. I have such a funny story about that. Because on set, we'd finish a take, and we'd finish for the night, and Steven would be like, OK, everyone, see you guys in the morning, and I'd still be so psyched, I'd almost be ready to, like, karate-chop the coffee boy in the face. Ahahaha.

Jane: Ahahaha.

Kirsty: And it was the same when I got back home …

Publicist: Ahem.

Kirsty: It's all right Joan, I got this. It was the same at home, where, and I can't tell you the amount of times this happened, but I'd, like, totally wake up in the middle of the night, with my pillow in front of me, in a classic shime-waza choke-hold and I'm screaming out, Now! Now! Tell me where the freakin tapes are! Or you die!

Jane: That sounds so very dark, and almost like, during the making of *Deathfall*, your soul was in danger?

Kirsty: You're so right, Jane. It was so dark. I really don't know how I got out of it in one piece.

Jane: And have you always been a Method actress?

Publicist: I'm not sure I like the tone of your question.

Jane: The tone is genuine.

Publicist: Proceed.

Jane: Brando, De Niro, Streep. Is Kirsty the next natural name in that sequence?

Kirsty: Oh, I'm not into naming, definitions, and boxes, and labels. I'm just intuitive. I feel the part. I feel for the part. I read these scripts, day in, day out, and I wait for the part, the one part, that will speak to me. And Bathsheba Flint was one of those parts.

Jane: And what was it like, working with George?

Kirsty: A dream. I have so many funny stories about George.

Jane: And they are?

Publicist: Next question.

Jane: And what was it like, working with Jack?

Kirsty: Fabulous. Jack is the best. Such a professional.

Jane: And Steven?

Kirsty: Incredible, are you kidding me? Totally incredible, like a dream come true for me. I grew up watching his movies, so to work with him was more than I can say. So many good memories, such an honour.

Jane: And who would you like to work with in future?

Kirsty: Oh, them all.

Jane: Like who?

Publicist: You're pressurising Kirsty into potentially alienating some of her closest peers. The first answer will suffice. And, guys, keep that wide for the B-roll.

Jane: Kirsty, you're only twenty-two years old. Do you ever feel that, with one Oscar nomination, two Golden Globe awards, and a blockbusting spy franchise to your name, you might have peaked too early?

Publicist: No, no, no! Are you shitting me? That will not do. Rephrase the question entirely, please.

Jane: Kirsty, you have achieved so much, so early on. How do you do it?

Publicist: Much better.

Kirsty: I have great people around me. My agent, my manager and, of course, Joan here. I wake up every day and I'm just thankful for the beauty I see around me, in the people I see around me, and the opportunities that I have in this wonderful and life-affirming business called Hollywood.

Publicist: Last question, please.

Jane: Kirsty, I wonder if you'd do me a favour, and hold my clipboard for me? Because I think I'm going to jump out that fucking window there if I hear another one of your half-assed fucking answers. I have flown five and a half thousand miles for this shit, and I don't need it. I will be fifty years old in less than twenty-four months, and I have no children, yet I have an Italian specialist who's currently charging me fifty thousand pounds for the privilege of jacking me up with enough clomiphene citrate to fertilise a fucking blue whale. I've spent more years than I care to remember being patronised in chintzy hotel rooms by your entire genus of wonk-eyed, coked-up, cock-sucking, dipshits. And so, yes, I have finally run out of the will, the interest, or the motivation to ask you one last fucking question. Instead, you can take that question, and shove it up your ass, and shove it up the asses of all the beautiful people around you who make your fucking life-affirming, candy-coated existence such a fabulous fucking dream. Now, is that too personal for you, Joan? Or would you prefer to keep that for the fucking B-roll?

23

Tuesday, 5 October 1999, 8.09am

Boom!

That's what Bonnie says, on the day she says it, her best imitation of street sounds beyond, while jumping up and down on the bed, and on the bumpy bodies below.

Boom! she repeats, another jump. Mamma, boom! But still no response, other than muffled groans from the two sleepers beneath.

Mamma, boom! Boom! Boom!

This time she jumps high, the mamma hop, and lets both knees come crashing down onto Shauna's exposed abdomen. Shauna sleeps, these days, with her hands clasped behind her head. She wakes in lock-shouldered agony. Can't decide whether the pose is a sign of complete relaxation or a terrifying symbol of profound resignation. Life arrest, as it were. Hands behind your head, perp. It means; with respect to Bonnie's morning balletics, that her complete body, from torso to kneecaps, is unprotected by low-lying arms, and vulnerable to all forms of fine-limbed fury.

Jeeeeesus! she hisses, clutching her stomach, wincing, and rolling over roughly, making a point to her child, showing her child that a line has been drawn, for once, if just for this day. She then shifts about, exposing only her side to future attacks, and nestles into the spoon position, letting her arm fall lightly over her man.

Bonnie tries Boom again, but nothing. The police sirens don't work either. Not at first. A common occurrence on any week-day morning. Racing up St Mark's Road towards the canal, and to the bridge behind Sainsbury's where the kids always gather, where the drugs are sold, where the tourists are robbed, and where Jay was once propositioned by an ageing prostitute. He took it as a compliment, the big eejit. You better watch yourself now, he said to Shauna, upon his return, beaming with pride, I've got the big fat Afro-Caribbean who-ers after me. I'm anyone's fancy!

The second full minute of screaming sirens, however, does the trick. Shauna pushes herself upwards, and stumbles over to the open sash window. A convoy of emergency vehicles, and a cacophony of sirens. She turns, drops down to the floor, and leans into the other side of the bed.

Ghert? she says. Ghert hon? You need to see this! Something big has happened.

Nearly three months, at least until midsummer. That's how long it took Shauna to re-programme Bonnie out of saying, relent-lessly and on reflex, Uncle Ghert the Pervert. Shauna was furious. It wasn't cute. Wasn't funny. And, as Ghert had gravely warned, after hearing Bonnie's childish slander one too many times, this phrase carried within it the potential to damage intrinsically, and instantly, his hard-won professional reputation, which amounted, he said, without irony, to his life's work. At weekends, for instance, for the entire crisis period, he sternly insisted that his sociable and intensely intellectual *flâneur*-ing around the parks and pathways of West London be conducted with Shauna alone, minus Bonnie on all occasions, for fear that she might yelp out at the top of her voice, under a Kensington gazebo, or else in the presence of a plethora of curious Hampstead mummies, the career-killing phrase, Uncle Ghert the Pervert.

Jay, of course, claimed complete innocence in the face of a series of spitting-fury phone accusations from Shauna. He had used the phrase only once or twice, he said. And even then, it was during the dark and silent times. How was he supposed to know, he said, that Bonnie would suddenly spring into verbal life, and deliver to the world a stockpile of random soundbites and idiomatic non sequiturs that she had accrued inside her wildly eccentric noggin up until that point?

The accusations and the argument, of course, would always wind their way inevitably backwards, sometimes speedily, sometimes not, to the prime fractures, as all arguments of intimacy do, via stepping stones of anger and signposts of sadness. And don't forget, you have me to thank, Jay would say, skating on such thin, so thin, membrane-thin, molecular-thin, ice. Because without me Bonnie would not be speaking at all!

You nearly fucking drowned her, man! was Shauna's reflex response, repeated and repeated in utter frustration. You nearly killed our baby! This would the bout begin, pinging backwards, via a dizzyingly speedy volley of brusquely barked exchanges, to the Irish excursion, to Jay's deception, and, further back still, to Paul's broken nose, Shauna's depression, Ghert's intercession, Jane's interference, Shauna's allegedly chequered sexual past, Jay's apparent inability to get over the same, and ultimately to their blatantly obvious, cruelly destructive and fulminating incompatibility all along.

Of course, Shauna had been extremely tough, under firm and consistent advice from Ghert, and even firmer advice from Ghert's solicitor, with Jay upon his return from Ireland. The solicitor especially, still preening from his record-breaking divorce work, and with barely a tentative nudge from Shauna, had initially threatened Jay with actual arrest and incarceration, but instead, in a flurry of increasingly irate letters, filled with ever more arcane pronouncements, settled for a savage application of Section 5 of the Protection from Harassment Act, which, it was eventually decided, on a hot May morning at Hammersmith Magistrates' Court, would keep Jay at a distance of five hundred feet from Shauna at all times, and would allow him just two visits with Bonnie every month, not overnights either, just day visits, supervised, in the park, without passports.

Jay had wept on the steps of the magistrates' court, thinking of his new life with piecemeal Bonnie. He waited on the pavement, and then tried to tell Shauna, with shouting and gesticulation, that he was truly sorry, and that he had done it only because he thought he had been unwittingly involved in the freak accidental manslaughter of her father, but Ghert and Ghert's solicitor charged him down, and told him that Shauna's ongoing post-natal depression had left her in a very fragile state, and that by his very presence on the pavement Jay had already broken the conditions of his own restraining order, but that he should stop crying and run along, and if, over a period of six to twelve months, he could prove himself dependable and a non-risk of flight, the order might well be rescinded. Jay ignored the men and, driven by something far more elemental, looked over their shoulders at Shauna. Shauna looked back at Jay.

Be not afraid.

Jay continued to look at Shauna, frozen to the spot, through the open passenger window, as his cab pulled away and down Talgarth Road. He thought of Strandhill receding into the distance, beneath the waves, on that day among days, and of the immigrant's dilemma, and the desperate beauty of all things left behind.

God, he said, quietly, under his breath, still keeping her

shrinking figure in focus, right until the junction of North End Road.

She's some wan.

They spend breakfast, Ghert and Shauna, in terse discussion as to the appropriate response of Shauna to the tragedy unfolding at the top of the road. In the background, from just above the draining board, a series of authoritative voices on BBC Radio 4 blast out the rat-a-tat updates on the fire still raging, the number of lives lost, the quantity of carriages decimated and the exact nature, destination, class and velocity of the two unfortunate trains involved in this collision of possibly monumental significance.

Bonnie runs a teaspoon through her porridge and babbles away to herself, repeating, as always, and with eerie accuracy, the snatches of mouth-sounds that filter down from their lips to her ears. Shoot it all, she says, she sings, shoot it all, Mamma. Big crash, death boom, shoot it all, Mamma!

You should shoot it now, like a movie, repeats Ghert, ignoring Bonnie's tuneful mimesis. He is stomping around the kitchen, glancing repeatedly, dramatically, at his watch, and trying to contain his irritation at the sight of unwashed laundry, mounds of it, spilling free from the washing machine, crammed in there since early last week, leaving him burdened beneath a purple paisley shirt for the rest of the day, a shirt that he mostly hates, and can wear only if he's in the mood, on special occasions, or for a private party, indoors, in the dark, with nothing but the closest of friends.

No, he says, shoot it before it's cordoned off.

He tells Shauna that the crash site would seem, from all accounts, to be very intriguing material. Very dramatic, no?

He stomps around some more, eventually muttering a *sotto voce* sideswipe at Shauna's allegedly desultory domestic abilities that culminates in a satirical word-picture of Shauna standing, bemused and beaten, before the 'strange white clothes washing box' in the corner.

Sorry? says Shauna, half missing the mutterings, and yet immediately attuned to the possibility of a barb. Ghert's preferred method of confrontation, she has learnt throughout their crash course of cohabitation, is through the regular non-confrontation of muttered asides, delivered, it seems, to himself alone, and hidden from the listener on the psychologically ratified basis that, if received, they might be deemed too painful to process, and thus prove unnecessarily destructive to the surrounding interpersonal framework.

Nothing, hon, he says, coolly. I'm just late. And you know how I get when I'm late.

He tells her that the new diet, her new diet, for him, recommended by her, in a brief fit of honesty, is not helping either. He needs his bread, apparently. And his pancakes.

He approaches her and cuddles her close, and admits, with his mouth and his voice, while his eyes are elsewhere, that he's a difficult man and one with unorthodox ways, but he suggests still that she should shoot the crash site before the entire place is cordoned off.

Be respectful, yes, he adds. Never exploit. But shoot. Make a short film. Wreckage in close-up! Artful as can be!

Ghert releases Shauna from his grip and stands in front of the tiny cupboard-side kitchen mirror. He buttons, and then unbuttons, the collar of his purple paisley shirt, flashes his teeth and then looks around, suddenly agitated again.

I don't know, says Shauna.

Floss? asks Ghert.

Feels kind of cheap, says Shauna. And creepy.

I'll be late for my nine o'clock, says Ghert.

I might just work on my proposals instead.

Ghert finds the floss, tucked in between turmeric and cinnamon sticks on the spice rack. He sets to work on his upper jaw, at an impressive pace, while lecturing Shauna, through string flicks and pings, about her lack of life direction.

He tells her, with an audible lack of consonants, that she needs to geh ouh ah abouh. May your mah on the worl. This thing, this drama, is lihrally on your doorstah.

Shauna says that her game-show treatment is coming along nicely.

Ghert, despairing, removes the last shreds of torn floss from between his molars with a sharpened index fingernail. He tells Shauna, at a lower register, fakely private, that this is just the kind of thing they've been working on together. Working on Shauna's need to actualise her abilities and to become the change she needs to see in herself. Ghert marches into bedroom and returns trailing cables, with a camcorder in hand. He repeats, again, that he is late, but says that this is Shauna's chance, to find her voice again. It's her chance, more importantly, to get out of the manhole. To finally fight her way, for good, out of this debilitating, ever-lasting, ever-wasting post-natal depression.

Shauna closes her eyes. So many impulses, sparks, feelings and directions. Where to go with this? No, she thinks, remembering the mantra that Ghert had given her. I am perfect in the face of life and I am enough in the universe. Let it all go. Let it all go. She breathes deeply, eyes still closed. Ghert's foot is now tapping. Polished shoe against floorboard.

Listen, hon, he eventually says, I'm late and—

Shauna interrupts, deadpan, I thought our sex life was the key to curing my depression.

It was, says Ghert, taken aback. I mean, it is.

I thought, Shauna continues, still deadpan, that you said, that you said to me, in fact, to my face, or, to be accurate, was it to my ass, that you would not be the first shrink who fucked the depression out of his patient.

Ghert's face bulges, instantly red and bloated. He grinds his teeth, indicating Bonnie at the table, on the last spoon of porridge. He thanks Shauna, with curdled sarcasm, aware now, he says, that the entire neighbourhood is going to hear that particular gem, courtesy of Polly the Parrot there!

Bonnie lifts her face, dotted with sticky splashes of porridge, upwards towards Ghert and grins, Polly the Parrot! Polly the Parrot!

I'm just saying, continues Ghert, looking at his watch again, adjusting his cardigan, swapping his briefcase from hand to hand, that we are almost there with the process work, and, and, he mouths a near-silent reference to the power that sex has been playing in the liberation of Shauna's kundalini energy. The sex and the process work, however, he says, are only part of the treatment. The other part, he explains, must involve Shauna re-embracing the world. And what better way to re-embrace the world than to take that camera, go to that crash site, and make some art!

Shauna equivocates. She says that it doesn't feel right. That nothing feels right. Nothing feels right today, or hasn't done so for some time. For weeks in fact. She feels uneasy in the world. Like there's been an energetic shift that she can't quite compute.

Ghert groans, audibly this time. He breathes deeply, gruffly manoeuvres Shauna down onto the red kitchen chair before him and, in as stern and paternal a tone as he can muster, he orders her to sit tight for the day, to avoid internal reflections, to remember to care for Bonnie, to try to activate the washing machine, preferably with his shirts in it at the time, to walk around the block a couple of times, to take a shower, and just to wait, to sit tight, there in this chair if she likes, sit tight and wait, for him, and when he gets back, they'll talk about it, they'll do serious process work together, then they'll drink some wine, and he'll fuck some seriously solid chunks of depression right out of her system, and then they can work out a coping strategy to get her through the darkness, and to make her mentally healthy, and emotionally stable again.

Shauna clings to his cardigan and tells him that he's not listening to her.

No! Ghert snaps, launching his own voice up into a fulminating register, just below a genuine yell. You're not listening, he says. I have no more time for this. I am late!

No, she replies, quietly, insistently. You don't understand. I am late too.

Shauna is late! I say again, Shauna is late! Repeat after me, Mammy, Shauna is late! Shauna is late! Stop the feckin clocks! Shauna is late! And, sure, can't I practically hear ye saying right back to me, in fulsome reply to that, and ye wouldn't be wrong – Well, about feckin time, ha?

Oh Jayz, I'll tell ya, Mammy, that was some hard aul slog all the same. Month in, month out, I've been waiting there, ever since we began trying for the babby. And each month I've been like, this is the one, this is the one where I tell the mammy, and in me head I'm already going, Guess what, Mammy, Shauna is late! And I've been proud too, imagining how you'd feel when you heard, like, ah Jayz, that's me boy, he's finally gone and made a granny out of us, what more could an aul Irish mammy want from her Right Hand?

But instead I've just been waiting, month in, month out, killing me with the waiting, practically staring down at Shauna's fanny, like the lads in *Groundhog Day*, waiting to see if Punxsutawney Phil would pop his head out and tell us that she's feckin preggers. And you'd think, because of all the miscarriages and the many college abortions, that it would've been easy for her to conceive in the first place, and that her womb would be a magnet for any variety of babby seed. But no, it's agony. A hard aul slog.

And I've got her dates down in the diary, and everything. I just write, dead casual like, a big red 'S', in bright-red ink, on the page where she gets the curse, and so, four weeks and a rake of hot-zone rides later, I'm on tenterhooks – the hot zone, by the way, is the short cluster of hours around Shauna's fertility peak point, during which time, and contrary to the filthy furious images conjured up by the actual name, we have, Shauna and I, several short bouts of possibly the coldest intercourse, saving your presence, that anyone bar a mentally challenged Cistercian might imagine, although I'm sure even some gom nun wan would have trouble comprehending the reality of us there, flat out on the bed, classico style, like two feckin wind-up wooden shagger dolls, clonk, clonk, clonk, clonk, barely a word between us, certainly not a glance, and the erotic dialogue going through both brains never rising higher than, Yeah, that should do it! That's the one! That should be the one to place between 1.5 and 6 millilitres of seminal fluid as close to the neck of the cervix as possible, thereby giving the cellular material contained therein, all three hundred million individual spermatozoa, a head start on the journey to the ampulla, where it will meet the cumulus oophorus mass, and hopefully penetrate via chemical and mechanical means into the zona pellucida and subsequently continue the brief and blissful journey from zygote to blastocyst to syncytiotrophoblast to feckin pure-blood babby in no time at all. Oh yeah! Super sexy, *nock ah*?

And, of course, I follow her around, every month, like a puppy, when it comes time. In and out of the bog, staring down the bowl, looking for hints, or not, of the curse, and givin her the eye, not wanting to rub it in, but desperate to know, or not, whether it's time, or not, to whip out the Boots pregnancy piss testers.

And you'll probably remember yourself, Mammy, but you have to play it dead cool, like, because it's a very sensitive time for the lady. You don't want to make her feel like she's failing some secret and unspoken universal wellness test every time she gets the curse. And so, when she comes out of the bog, and you can see the crumpled strip of maxi-pad wrapper in her hand, you just go, smooth as eggs, Ah, sure, it could happen to a bishop! There's nothing wrong with you at all! Chin up, girl! You did your best! And so did th'aul vag'.

And I won't say that it hasn't been playing havoc with the relationship. In fact, it's been a right divil in that department, and often makes me yearn for the time when we were just two young and mental rider goms, banging the brains out of each other for the *crack*, rather than a pair of dead-serious future parents, who are somehow transforming the great and ineffable pleasures of contemporary lovemaking into something just a couple of heartbeats above blowing your nose, or doing a feckin Airfix.

Naturally, we have a fierce rotten year because of it, punctuated by only a handful of genuinely spontaneous, affectionate and uncomplicated embraces, usually during the arse end of her cycle, when we've convinced ourselves that she's late and that the egg has been implanted in the womb wall and we're all systems go, and cuddling and kissing to feck, which, naturally, usually ends, mere moments after the settling of this very same sensation of giddiness and contented joy, with the arrival of the curse, and the weary return, despite all mutual assurances to the contrary (no, we won't let it get us down this time), to a state of internecine hostilities.

In short, we start to drive each other feckin mad. In work, we sit at opposite ends of the pushed-together white tables, but on the same side, so we don't have to look at each other. It's obvious, of course, that something's up, especially when we drift off in opposite directions at lunchtime, me on me own with some home-made sangers onto the patchy grasses of Soho Square, with just the curious drunks and the friendly benders for company and amusement, while she's off down to Brewer Street, to mingle among the strippers and the who-ers, and have coffee with sound editors and post-production managers, and entertain them, no doubt, with wild stories of college sex and prom-night punch-ups from a Yank adolescence that never fails to tap into and to mystify the mythic imagination of the non-Yank in all of us.

So, whenever they can, when the running order's done and dusted, and when Stevie Fitz's finished pitching the latest roll-call of Hollywood A-listers to the table, everyone's all, like, having a laugh at our expense, with Jiz himself leading the charge, going, What's this? What's this? Trouble in paradise? Oi, oi? Jane joins in too, and lays it on pretty thick, doing a big mock shock thing, going, Say it ain't so, not youze two lovebirds? But me and Shauna handle it cool as ice, like fillum stars when they don't want to answer personal questions, and we go, like, Can we get back to the feckin task at hand, folks? The fillums?

And I wouldn't mind, Mammy, if the fillums were fablas, and if *Screen Grab* was fablas because of it, and we could, like, just lose ourselves in the gig until the babby sorts itself out. But instead, every week it's the same aul shite, another feckin serial killer lad with an ever more outrageous and improbable modus operandi, like, say, murdering a whole rake of wans based on how their surnames match with the periodic table of the elements, and then executing them in reverse order i.e. in decreasing rather than increasing atomic number. Or else it's fillums about gangsters, and cops and robbers, and submarine commanders, only instead of doing their jobs, and shooting and robbing and driving submarines, they're sitting around in diners, smoking and chatting about some ancient Yank telly show or a Japanese karate film that never made it as far as Flannagan's back home. Or else it's just the dead serious fillums, the big award-winning fillums, mostly about mental men. Men who are mental from birth but nonetheless embody the power of the human spirit. Men who

281

aren't mental from birth, but then go mental from boozing, and still have the human spirit. And men who are mental from birth, but go extra-mental from playing the piano too much, but find the human spirit in the process.

I'm telling ye, Mammy, it's wicked stuff, which, combined with a kind of low-level animosity and general discontent that me and Shauna seem to be generating and promulgating among the staff at a hefty clip, starts to take its toll on general morale and the working environment within *Screen Grab*. Jane can sense it too, and she certainly overhears me and Stevie Fitz, whenever we get the chance, talking about the new projects we're planning, as fledgling documentary fillummakers ourselves, when we break off on our own, and blow this joint – first up, we're doing a fillum about the Siege of Sarajevo, and then an artsy observational piece about Soho at night. And I know we're not actually doing them yet. But Stevie says that it's the way you have to talk, in the meeja, because saying things like hope to, plan to, want to, and would like to, makes us sound like second-rate tossers. Do or do not, he says. That's the mantra. There is no try.

Inevitably, the trickle-down result of me and Shauna's discontent, and the growing lethargy among the rest of the posse, is that Jane, the canny who-er, ever attuned to the general vibe, comes marching into the office one morning in late summer and gives this big speech about how she's talked to the channel bosses, and they've agreed to sexy-up the whole shebang, and that it was madness in the first place to make a show about fillums without making fillums in the show, and so she wants us, on top of our clearly dreary daily duties, to make our own short fillums, to become our own fillummakers, and to include these short fillums in the show every week, as long as they're on some subject, any subject, no matter how bizarre, that's related to fillum.

282

My short fillum, you'll be pleased to hear, Mammy, is about romance in the movies. Specifically love scenes. It was kind of Jane's idea, but it's my fillum. I was spitballing concepts by myself at the whiteboard one evening after work, when she comes over and gives it to me. No questions asked. She tells me that I should shoot two actors in Lycra, on and around a bed, copying all the great love scenes in fillum history. Brilliant. We stay late together, at her computer, for about a week, both of us eating pizza and drinking beers while she writes it up, every word of it, and I stand there, just over her right shoulder, as the official script approver. Jane says that she thinks it'll be the best of the bunch, and dead sexy too. Shauna's fillum is about popcorn and obesity, while Stevie's is about the primacy of the male gaze in contemporary horror.

I spend about a month preparing for the shoot. I become totally obsessed, like a real fillummaker, the ones we meet in hotels who don't go to sleep or communicate with their wives and children or think of anything else except their fillum when they're making it.

At home Shauna's getting more and more furious about me being teacher's pet, and getting special tips from the boss, while she's off down the local GP every Saturday. We barely have intercourse, saving your presence, at all during these days. Only when mother nature, and Shauna's basal body temperature, demands it, and even then we're just clonking away, marionette style, like two hopeless feckers from the 'Lonely Goatherd' ensemble.

Naturally, it all kicks off between me and Shauna on the day of the shoot for me and Jane's short fillum. It's early October, and the studio, a converted barrel room in King's Cross, is jammers, and overheating like a bastard. Everyone from *Screen Grab* is there, and a ton from the channel too. Feckin perverts. It's a big draw. And me and Jane are a bit like star fillummakers for the day, like, say, a different gender, age and nationalities version of the Coen Brothers. And we're totally, like, in synch when we're working, using the fillummakers' lingo and the like, like she'd be going to me, Whatcha think, Jay, a two-shot or a close-up? And I'm like, Nah, man, I'd go super-wide with that deal, you don't want to lose continuity with the previous set-up. And she's like, Right you are, boss! And I'm like, Too feckin right. And everyone around us is like, Jayz, them two feckers certainly know their shite, feckin backwards.

Shauna's there too, of course, and for the first couple of hours at least the vibe she's giving off is that she's dead proud of me, because I'm her man, and I'm at the centre of the action, calling the shots, the actual shots. I've even bought a baseball cap for the day, and am wearing it backwards, like the pros. She must be thinking, Well, feck me if he isn't the feckin bees knees up there! And I'm looking back at her thinking, Bingo! I'm definitely paving the way for a proper ride after this, old-school style, none of this fertilisation shite. I'm going to waste meself at least six hundred million spermatozoa tonight!

At least that was the idea, until Jane went all Kubrick on it, and started barking at the poor actor fella and actor wan, telling them that they're supposed to be copying the *From Here to Eternity* snog but they're getting it all wrong, and she just reefs me by the arm and goes, Look! Here!

Next thing I know I'm on the makeshift bed, she's Burt Lancaster and I'm Deborah Kerr, and she's sidled underneath me but is holding my skull in a most arresting headlock and is just drilling into my mouth with her tongue, yet holding the whole head, my head, and her head, stock-still. She does it for about ten seconds, Mammy. Could be ten seconds. Could be a minute. Not totally sure, to be honest. Bit of th'aul dizziness kicking in, ye know yourself. Anyway, at the end of it, I pop out of her, she pops out of me, and all we notice is the silence around us. Not from the channel lads, who weren't really saying much to begin with, but from the *Screen Grab* crew who are, to a man and a woman, dumbstruck.

Jane, thank God, is straight in there with the orders, telling everyone to get on with it, and looking over at her fella, Matt, with a real dismissive glare, and saying, Ah, come on! He's like me godson! We're all fucking professionals here! It's all about the scene. I catch Shauna's eyes and it's like she's been hit with a tranquilliser dart in the head. I stroll over, give my mouth a big conspicuous yucky wipe and tell her, loudly, that it's all about the scene. Jane yells quiet! And says that she's going for a take. Instead of resuming my place over behind the camera, I remain by Shauna's side. Jane yells action! Shauna kicks me in the ankle so hard that, without the power or permission to yell out in agony, my eyes simply well with tears of pure and unbridled pain.

Of course, I know from the kick that there's worse to come at home. And there is. I try to act normal, to downplay the momentousness of the full public snog betrayal, so I stick to my routine, and help Jane bring the gear back to the office, which means travelling home separately from Shauna. In fact, in the end, I take a lift back from Jane and Matt, and sit behind the driver seat and just soak up the sheer arse-rippingly tense silence. Which, as it happens, Mammy, is a feckin hoot when compared to what's to come, once I get inside the pink palace.

Thing is, as well, Mammy, I think there are two kinds of people in this world. The ones who react to a punch in the shoulder with, Hey, what the feck did you do that for? And the ones who don't react at all, or simply say, I'm fine, I'm fine, it's all right, not a bother on me, and then ten hours later suddenly feckin implode with rage, shit themselves, rip out their own innards with garden shears, all the while screaming at the top of their lungs, You hit me! You hit me! I can't believe you hit me!

Shauna was a bit like the second type when it came to the kiss. Because at first, when I get in the door, she's cold enough, but seemingly over it, and talking about any aul shite, about the food she's left in the fridge for me, and the second round of interviews she has to do for her obesity short, and this photo she's just got of Chester and his new wife in Africa, halfway through their round-the-world trip. The niceness, of course, only makes it worse. Like she's a Gestapo officer, making chit-chat before she produces the Luger and blows your face off. It's so tense that it forces me to go, and maybe this was the point all along, So! About that kiss!

And that's it! Boom! It's like I just said, Where's the button to your self-detonation device? Oh, here it is. Let me press it for you!

That kiss!!! she goes. Don't talk to me about that fucking kiss!!!

Of course, all we do, for the next ninety minutes, is talk about that fucking kiss. Me saying that it was just an actorly thing. Her freaking out even more, screaming out for honesty above all else. Honesty, man! she goes, sounding more American than ever when she's angry. Honesty, man! She tells me that honesty is what defines a healthy relationship. Opening up. Telling each other shit. And so she demands that I be honest with her about the kiss, and what I felt about the kiss. And so I go, Right you are, OK, it was a decent snog, in a weird kind of way, and it made me think that doing a porno mustn't be that bad after all.

But Shauna wants more. She's raging at me. More honesty! More truth! Which means, Mammy, that she really starts to push the envelope, and starts grilling me not on what I did, but what I would like to do. Like, you've just been arrested for robbing a

286

corner shop, but you're about to be jailed because you'd like to rob a bank. So, she's going, vicious theoretical like, Did the snog I have today with Jane make me want to have intercourse with Jane? And I try to ask for some clarification of the terms of the question, like, if I was single and I didn't know Jane and that was the first time we kissed? Or if I did know Jane, but Shauna was, like, accidentally dead, and I was a widower and was talking to her at the funeral party and we had eventually kissed at the end of the night like that? Or if Jane was the only woman—

Just answer the fucking question! she screams, real end-of-tether stuff.

So, again, opting for the honesty that apparently defines all the best relationships, I tell her, Yes, it did indeed make me fancy, however briefly, the entirely hypothetical scenario of an incredibly perfunctory and meaningless ride with Jane.

Now, at this point, Mammy, for me, I've run out of things to say on the subject. Yes, the kiss was grand. Yes, it made me think of sex. After that, I am fundamentally stumped. Nowhere to go. And I know, and I've read, that they say, the professors do, that women use roughly twenty thousand words a day, while men use only seven thousand. And though I've always found this extremely dubious, specially after the hours I spent getting the ears chewed off me by Ozzie Titch, the million-word motormouth, I can only guess that a stockpile of excess words has something to do with the fact that Shauna simply won't stop herself, not for a second, getting well bet into the whole kissing and the theoretical shagging debate.

Which is why, perhaps, inevitably, and with due cause, she ends up taking shock, horror, anger and indignation, to entirely new levels when she notices, somewhere around the fifteen-minute mark, that I've started to drift. I can't tell myself, because I can't

287

see myself, but I'm betting that the eyes are probably gone, and certainly the facial muscles will be flat as feck. All I know is that I've completely lost track of what she's saying, and am snapped out of it only by a sudden startling stamp of her foot.

Oh, I'm sorry, she says. I'm fighting for our marriage here, and I'm boring you. Is that it?

Now, maybe it's because I'm feeling a bit hard done by with the whole Orwellian future-sex-crime scenario. Or maybe it's a build-up of interpersonal tension caused by all the joyless, wooden, zygotic, babby clonking. Or maybe it's just the simple fact that Shauna's appeal for honesty above all else has resonated deep within me. Either way, I just look at her and go, If you must know, I was writing a letter to my mammy, but in my head!

Naturally, Mammy, she shoots backwards away from me, almost crying, like she's dealing with some sort of Paddy Poltergeist rather than an average lad turned potentially award-winning fillummaker from Roscommon.

She's like, Oh my fucking God, you are out of your fucking mind!

She tells me that I'm like you, Mammy, and that I'm mad as a coot, and that I've got your disease, and that I might as well go into the kitchen now and whizz my head off with the blender. Whereas I'm, like, looking at her, baffled, and I go, It's not mad to love your mammy. It's not mad to want to tell her stuff. It's not mad to know that feeling within you that wants to reach out to your own mammy. To remember her daily presence around you, as warm and as sustaining as anything since, as natural and unremarkable as the gentle waft of fairy cakes from an oven door in a summer childhood, or as constant and reassuring as the buzzing of her questions and conversation, like the soundtrack around you of the heater humming while you're doing your ecker

288

on the night-time table in winter. No, it's not mad to love your mammy. It's as natural to me as breathing. And then I tell her that I'm sorry that her mammy left her when she was a chisler, but I add that my mammy stayed. And she stayed right here. And when I say here, Mammy, I point to my heart. It's a nice touch, all right, but Shauna doesn't seem to appreciate it.

She goes, Right. And then she leaves.

She stays with Jess for a full fortnight, during which time I fall to pieces without her. I beg, scrape, grovel and bawl, and promise to do anything, anything at all, change my ways as radically as you like, if only she'll come back to me. Turns out, she has just one condition to secure her return, which is that I stop writing to you in my head. Which I do, naturally, quicksmart, and stick to, rock solid, right the way through the winter months, Christmas and New Year, and through all the little things, highs and lows, that would normally send me running to you – like the day Kirk Douglas came into the studio to do a *Screen Grab* special, oh, you would've loved that, Mammy, such a smashing aulfella, really humble-like, and a grand shock of hair on him. Or the big drama when Jane splits up with Matt, when we were all in the Pillars, and this young wan in a tiny skirt and massive heels comes marching over to Jane and, without a word, chucks a full glass of red into her face, because it transpires that the wan is Matt's other wan, who's fed up with him moaning about Jane, and wants to move their relationship on to the next level. Or what about Lady Di on *Panorama*? Or Bill Clinton in the North? Or even the night they showed my love-scene fillum on *Screen Grab*. I'm not sure how well it worked in the end, mind you, because you couldn't really tell, half the time, what exact love scene it was, from what exact fillum, that the two unfortunate actors were supposed to be imitating, so they tended to look like two red-leotard-clad eejits writhing and bashing about like modern dance

289

gone mental, so much so that when they cut back to the studio after it, Jiz and Liz were both, like, curling up their faces, going, What the feck was that?

So, as I say, the writing ban is still very much in place, Mammy. But how often do you find out that you're going to be a granny? Anyway, it's Saturday morning, and Shauna's past the twelve-week mark, pregnancy-wise. We're pretty much through the early miscarriage zone, and while she's nipped out to get us a rake of croissants to mark the occasion, I thought, what better way to celebrate the good news than to sit down, stare into space and write a letter to th'aul mammy.

Nothing major. Just a word or two.

You know yourself.

Your Right-Hand Man,

Jay

24

Dome Life

Jay is standing underneath the giant, half-extended, salmon-pink calf muscle of the Body Zone when he first hears about the crash. He is covering his mouth from the rising cloud of fine white cement dust, the result of a sudden heavy pallet drop in front of him, while holding a mobile telephone up to his ear and bellowing down the line to Stevie Fitz, who is standing some four hundred yards away in the mouth of the still-incomplete North Greenwich underground station. Jay is chewing gum rapidly, and saying 'dude' a lot, an idiomatic tic that he suspects he picked up from his ex-wife, but which has manifested itself only in recent weeks, emerging from a personality that is finally, unequivocally, out of the black hell, free from the trauma of separation, over the agony of diminished visitation rights, and moving on, looking forward, looking up, and wholly embracing, without an ounce of cynicism or irony, the ethos of that sign that sits above the entrance to Millennium Park and bellows to all but the meek and the too timid to notice, 'Time to Make a Difference to Our Future!'

Of course, he has Jane to thank for so much of that. She has been, he says, a dote, and the best friend that a lad could ever want, picking him up, dusting him off, pointing him in the right direction. She, in turn, says, repeatedly, continually, and without embarrassment, even when they're at parties together, and she's introducing him to folk he's never met before, posh folk, like, folk in enormous five-storey Hampstead houses, that he is her special personal project, her own sweet Eliza Doolittle. To which he usually responds, a well-worn routine by now, with a few arch and not entirely ironic bars of 'Just you wait, 'enry 'iggins'.

It helps, Jay has surmised, that Jane quit her job. Blowing up spectacularly in the face of a Hollywood A-lister was the best thing that she ever did. It helped her to remove all the interpersonal and intellectual clutter from her head. To let her see the world clearly again, and to regain focus on the subject areas that truly inspire her – the rehabilitation of the poor, the empowerment of the disenfranchised and the reimagination of the marginalised. And, Jay might often add, depending on the mood and the tone of the night, that Jane was also inspired by the 're-shag-ification of the feckin young Irish lads!' That could usually muster a self-deprecatory chuckle, or a smile at least.

On reflection, Jane suspects that her blow-up might've been a side effect of the fertility treatment, which, as well as triggering shockingly inconvenient and importunate bouts of nausea, including actual vomiting and diarrhoea, tends to push the brain into a state of restless agitation that can manifest itself in a complete and utter intolerance of everything but the most direct and unfussy forms of communication. Hollywood interviews, thus, were the first to go.

The baby, she says, before anyone has a chance to hint otherwise, is her idea. She is strict about that. And insistent too that she and Jay, despite the intensity of their relationship, live apart, in their own separate flats, just to prove the point. This is not about co-dependency, this is not about need. This is her decision. A woman's choice.

She's good with Bonnie too. A natural. Practically overflowing with the plenitude of maternal warmth. A great picker-upper, a hugger and a kisser. And she has helped transform those precious, twice-monthly, paternal park trips into events of near hysterical happiness. She throws everything, Jay says, including the kitchen sink, at the day. Balloons, kites, cake, roller skates, borrowed canines, rabbits in pet carriers, you name it, she's done it, one-upping herself every fortnight, just for the thrill of seeing Bonnie's eyes light up, and her arms swing wide with yelps of pleasure, while she unleashes a delirious and delicious, Auntie Jane! Auntie Jane! I like Auntie Jane!

There are few things better for a mother-in-waiting, Jane has said to Jay, only to Jay, than to sit under a tree, next to the round pond in Kensington Gardens, with Bonnie in her lap, devouring Portuguese pastries from the bakery on Golborne Road, and to watch the contented look on Jay's face as he looks at Bonnie and then at Jane, and then watches Bonnie lollop away, with her own unique dyspraxic gait, with cake crust in hand, towards the mid-afternoon crush of ducks, swans and seagulls.

To any of these people, she once said, trying out the sound of it, but unsure of it, and never again, while she pointed about her, around her, to the rollerbladers, the dog-walkers, cyclists and strollers. We could, she said, pausing, unsure, before suddenly completing, what the hell, but never to repeat again, We could be a family!

Not that she has taken Jay's predicament lying down. No, Jane has raised the stakes there too, at least in conversation. If they want legal? she once said, over rosé and strawberries in the fourth-floor bar of the club. I'm pretty sure that we can show them legal! Her father, she said, in the same conversation, over the rolling din of the Vengaboys and Lou Bega, knew a couple of serious fossils in the high court who could make mincemeat out of Dr Ghert. Two park visits per month, my foot!

Jay got excited that night, and said, How long, how long?

How long before he gets his Bonnie back? But Jane told him not to rush her, or the legal system, and that they should just, for the moment, live in the moment, and enjoy the trips, and the bunnies in the park, and Bonnie's sweet, sweet progress from stumbling toddler to little big girl.

Thing is, she said, in the back of a black cab on the way home to his, at the end of that night, with that same subject preying on her mind. Most blokes your age would kill to have some time away from the kids!

Jay thought about this with the utmost seriousness, while staring out the window at the strangely childish signage, all light bulbs and block capitals, that hung in the arches of the Ritz. He had tried to get in there once, wearing jeans. To shoot some B-roll for an interview with Al Pacino. He was stopped at the door, called sir a thousand times, and then eventually ushered up the backstairs, away from sartorially sensitive eyes, to join the circus in the star's room. Jay turned back to Jane.

For what?

Dude, Jay says, pressing the mobile telephone hard against his head, you've got to come over here, and check this shite out! They've just brought in a giant fecking anatomically accurate heart!

He laughs, and tells Stevie to bring Roger, the sound dude, and not to forget the silver passes. And to bring Pawel, no, make that Esteban, because Esteban is better value. Seriously funny on film. Like Mañuel from *Fawlty Towers*, but with a better tan, and snow-washed denims. The camera loves him. Was fablas last week, Jay says, when he did that bit where he nearly fell down the open stairwell at the service pod. Looks at the camera exasperated and goes, All theees, for the hayth wondair of the whirl?

Jay kept the cameras rolling, but fed Esteban a new line

instead, about it being the first wonder of the twenty-first-century world.

Jay loves that. The buzz. Thinking on the fly. Capturing the magic. That's what he likes to say, when attentions are flagging. We're capturing magic down here, people, in the Dome. The feckin Dome, lads! We're big time! We're going to show the world the men beneath the men beneath the feckers who made the Dome! His excitement is sometimes too much. He calls it motivation. Pawel, Esteban, Ambrus, Burak and Finbar. The five horsemen of the apocalypse, he calls them. The Spice Boys! Chosen, not at random, but with ruthless deliberation, to represent a colourful and telegenic cross-section of a multicultural capital city and to show exactly what happens when the United Nations of sweeping, shovelling, scooping and arse-scratching comes face to face with the most physically elaborate and culturally significant construction project of the old Millennium.

Well, that was the pitch that Stevie Fitz and Jay brought to the table, in early October 1998, for their first official *Dome Life* meeting with Jane, then acting in her capacity as a freelance production manager rather than official *Screen Grab* honcho. Jay, at that meeting, had been unusually quiet, still reeling from the very recent shock of Shauna's tortuous defection into the arms of her Danish psychologist. Thankfully, Stevie handled the meeting like a pro. Batted back all her questions with ease and, more than that, according to Jay, did that thing that only Scottish people can do, which is make any aul shite sound seriously intelligent.

Why, for instance, asked Jane, were there no English people in the five-man line-up for *Dome Life*?

Stevie didn't miss a beat, just launched himself, while simultaneously amping up his normally soft Edinburgh brogue, into a theoretical justification for the absence of English subjects based on the fact that this was the essential English identity at the turn of the Millennium. An absence. A lack. The English identity –

previously defining itself as the centre of the British empire, against which all other colonies had to define themselves – was now without its oppositional function, and thus rudderless as an identity. Hence, in its place, and by its absence, *Dome Life*'s Polish, Mexican, Hungarian, Turkish and Irish builders would articulate this very crisis of identity. And possibly generate reams of scandalised media coverage to boot!

Jane liked that. And she liked also when Jay chipped in quietly, very briefly, a brave face on him, to say that the whole concept was inspired by Jane, and by the short films of workers, real workers, that she'd made when they first met, Jay and Jane. She said nothing to Stevie, and felt that the comment from Jay deserved no further elaboration. But nonetheless, she lifted a hand to her heart, looked at Jay, softly, and mouthed, Thank you.

And yet she was concerned, she said, as she had often discovered herself, when working on the ground, about the possible lack of excitement inherent in the show. The skin on the Dome was already in place. The steeplejacks were done. The high wire work too. And if viewers were shown another shot of Mandy in his hard hat they'd probably top themselves. All yesterday's pizza. What was left to pique the public interest?

Jay leant forward. He inhaled, as if to begin but, thankfully, once more Stevie delivered another barnstormer, about the inherent drama in the human face, and the human story, and about how Jane, of all people, as an award-winning documentarian, must recognise the need to find human dignity in the smallest of gestures. Plus, he added, the installations have yet to arrive. And they, by all accounts, were going to take the entire project to a whole new level of crazy.

Stevie emerges from the station mouth and, free from the deafening cacophony of drilling, screwing, sawing and smashing that reverberates therein, he readjusts his mobile telephone to the side of his head and inquires of Jay his exact location.

Where is here?

The fecking Body Zone, says Jay.

Where is that? asks Stevie.

It's behind the fecking Faith Zone and just below the fecking Journey Zone.

Very funny, says Stevie. And in fecking English?

Here! says Jay, waving wildly with his free hand, just vigorously enough for Stevie to spot him from across the grey sandy concourse. I'm the fecking arsehole waving at you from underneath the giant pink wan next to the giant pink poor truncated bollix with no feckin legs!

Stevie, still phone clutching, starts the walk and talk, closely followed by Roger and Pawel. He begins to recount an explanation for the absence of Esteban this morning.

Hang on! says Jay, flinching at the familiar static drop-out in Stevie's sentences. Got an incoming!

He whips the phone away from his face, presses the space bar, followed by the number three, and then the hash key and the space bar again.

Shoot! he says, to the new caller. He listens for almost a full second before suddenly whooping, Well, speak of the divil and he's bound to ring your swanky Nokia mobile telephone, eh? Esteban! Where in God's name?

Jay's professional joviality evaporates in the subsequent moments, as Esteban explains his predicament. Jay learns that there has been a train crash in west London, near the junction of Ladbroke Grove and Harrow Road, between a big train and a small train. Esteban was in the big train, the back carriage of the big train, *gracias a dios*, the First Great Western from Swindon to London Paddington. The crash was loud, and violent. There are deaths. At least thirty so far. There was fire. Lots of fire.

297

Hundreds injured. Hundreds on fire. And Esteban? Not a scratch, *gracias a dios*. Currently in St Mary's, patiently waiting for the all-clear, and for the precautionary application, on the basis of a tiny muscular tweak in his neck, of a surgical collar.

Stevie, camera in hand, followed closely by Roger, boom in hand, and Pawel, sweeping brush in hand, arrive at Jay's shoulder in the middle of Esteban's testimony. Jay gives them bug eyes, points to the mobile telephone, mouths the word 'Esss, teh, ban!' while making a sad clown face and tracing a single vertical line from his own cheek to his lower jaw to indicate the act of crying on the other end of the call.

Jay instructs Esteban to take a moment to gather himself, during which time, hand over mouthpiece, he engages in a highly accelerated conversation with Stevie and Roger that traverses the current whereabouts of Esteban, the realisation that a train crash would make for a highly compelling *Dome Life* segment, and the tentative suggestion that maybe, perhaps, Jay, Stevie and Roger should hop into Darren's van, race to Paddington, grab Esteban from St Mary's, pop him into a train, any train, film some wide shots, some close-ups, film him looking tense, and then, boom, cut to the news footage, crying relatives, a sunset over the Dome and, shazam, hello, National Television Awards, BAFTAs, Emmys, Golden Globes, the whole feckin shooting match!

Esteban says sorry to Jay, but no way. He has today, no joke, because of this crash, and because of his miraculously unscathed emergence from it – seriously Jay, he says, I've seen bodies on fire – because of this, he is sure that he has felt, for the first time in his life, from on high in heaven, the very real guiding touch of *la mano de dios*. And, as such, everything for Esteban has changed, changed utterly, as the poet Yeats, from the Land of Jay, might say.

Jay is momentarily dumbstruck, but panicking. He knows

what's coming. Not good. No, not good. He hears a voice, a female voice, an intimate female voice, in the background with Esteban. He hears the words, Tell him! Tell him!

Jay knows what's coming. No, not now.

Esteban announces ...

No.

... that he's not ...

No.

... ever coming back ...

No.

... to the Dome.

This is not the películas, he says, by way of qualification. This is my life, and I should be dead. He adds that *la mano de dios* saved him, and because of that ...

The line begins to suffer familiar static drop-out.

Wait! barks Jay. Esteban, just wait! Do not go! Repeat, do not go!

He presses space bar, three, hash key, space bar.

Shoot!

Seen the news?

Oh, fer feck sake! Would you feck right off!

It's The Clappers. And not for the first time that week. And it's only Tuesday.

She tells Jay that he can't keep avoiding it. The train crash is just another sign in a long list of omens and cataclysms that include the Columbine massacre, the earthquake at Izmit, and the breaking up of Boyzone, that, when combined and cross-checked with Nostradamus, all point towards the imminent arrival, on New Year's Eve 1999, of nothing less than the end of all humanity as we know it, *gon doubt awoyne.*

What do you want? snaps Jay, cold as can be.

The Clappers informs Jay that the bishop is offering a hefty retainer, on top of everything else, for the chance to secure Jay's services, effective almost immediately, as the one true and risen Christ.

Not interested, says Jay. Find another fecking patsy.

There is no other fecking patsy, replies The Clappers, almost incredulous, adding, There is only one virgin birth!

I am not, barks Jay, suddenly erupting with irritation, and already reaching for space bar, three, hash key, space bar, the virgin fecking birth!

Stevie Fitz, Roger and Polish Pawel share several quizzical glances.

Shoot! says Jay. But Esteban is gone.

Jay's temperature rises. He can feel the sweat creeping forward below his hairline, right round, forehead to neck. A sodden patch emerges between his shoulder blades. His arm shoots up in the air, a reflex gesture. Rage pulses through his body and seizes his hand. He wants to throw his mobile telephone down to the ground, smashing it on the raw unfinished concrete, hopefully into a million dramatic *smidereeny*.

Stevie, Roger and Pawel gasp. But Jay refrains. He tucks the mobile telephone neatly into the leather holder on his belt, and clips it shut, T.J. Hooker style. He feels a welling up inside of him. A familiar sensation. For months now, a swell of emotion, rising upwards, to seemingly sweep him away in a giant yawn of grief, but manifesting itself only in the tiniest trembles of his lower lip. He could cry, but he doesn't. He thinks, instead, of Esteban. Of Esteban quitting. Their star performer, their leading light. His departure signals not just a death blow to the show's wider ambitions, but, more importantly and more personally, it marks the departure of Jay's only chance of happiness, his daily lifeblood, his calm, his sweet security and his medicine.

His cocaine.

Wait. No. Hang on. OK. This is going to have to be a quickie,
Mammy, because I'm writing to you from the dinner table, with
Shauna directly opposite. We've got a bowl of pasta each, there's
a plate of carrot salad in the centre, and nothing much flying
about in the chat department. But all the same, if it kicks off, you
know yourself. I'm out of here. Never one for the multitasking,
me. Certainly not as a chisler. I'd be, like, gluing the last piece of a
feckin Airfix Messerschmitt into place and you'd go, Tell us, Jay,
is it mashed or roasted ye want with the chops tonight? And I'd
just freeze, with the glue dripping from the nozzle, pouring down
all over me good slacks.

Never understood how you did it. Staring me straight in the eye,
telling me about the new security bars that old man Drury had
just installed in the post office, and what a shame it was, because
the last vestiges of ancient Ireland were falling away and being
taken over by a cold and criminal modern place, and even as
you're talking, and in the flow, you drop down to the oven door,
ballet-style, deft, like a cat, and, still talking, still staring straight
at me, crank open the door and whip out a soda loaf, flick it out
and upside down onto a wire tray, and leave a tea towel neatly
draped over it for the last bit, for the moisture, while you wrap
up the security bars' reflections with the suspicion that it's Provos
from across the border that have spooked old man Drury, him
being a Proddy and all that. Afraid he's going to be targeted,
th'aul miser, for shunning the hoolies in Madigan's, and for
staying open on Paddy's Day. And with that you're down again,

hands rustling through the back of the presses, pulling out all sorts of powders, gels and dried fruits, bowls and pans, for the next gobsmacking instalment in the multitasking masterclass.

Anyway, just the quickie to let you know that, no, it's not a dream, you're still a granny in the making, Shauna's still expecting, and, as if to prove the point, didn't we go down to the maternity wing today and get ourselves our very first, hi-tech, fancy-shmancy ultrasound, with pictures an everything! Oh, Mammy, you would've loved it. Like something from *Star Trek*. They lead you into this darkened room, a young wan does, a young Asian wan, who's guiding Shauna about and treating her like the sacred life-carrying vessel that she is. And in the room, there already, is an older wan, who's Asian also, but Asian Chinese where the other wan was Asian Indian, and she's even kinder and more gentle, and she's operating the machinery, and is sitting, like Lieutenant Fecking Uhura, in front of two big computer screens, as if she's going to be communicating with a land beyond the stars, which is the little baby girl in Shauna's stomach.

Ah, shite and onions, Mammy, haven't I just gone and given it away! The little baby girl! But keep it under your hat, all the same, because it's not official yet. Not until the eighteen weeker. Although the Chinese wan was pretty sure, and certainly very handy with the slippy-slidey scanner bar, covered in Vasers, moving it backwards and forwards, then really deep, dug deep, bet right deep into Shauna's underbelly area swiping left to right, scanning her heart out.

The first time she got the baby up on the monitor was a big moment for both of us, and both of us went a bit weak at the knees, and I can't speak for Shauna, but I will say for myself that I wanted to pop right off the edge of the bed and go, What?!

302

What?! Oh, lads! We're not in Kansas any more! No, sireee! We are in deep shite voodoo country, lads! Because some devious magical fecker has gone and stuck a mini human being with a massive mental head inside of Shauna's belly! And the picture's all crackly and buzzy, and it looks like you're watching the maddest, creepiest, most heartbreakingly delicate telly show ever made.

We don't jump, naturally. Instead we're rooted to the spot, reduced to a state of silent awe, glued to the image of our baby, our mini person, in perfect profile, huge head above outstretched arms and folded legs, the whole shebang. The kindly Chinese wan goes for another angle, which means more swiping, stroking and deep scanning. She catches the image again, quicksmart, only this time, bit of a performer already, doesn't our baby, in crystal-clear close-up, go and give a great big feckin yawn! Yes, Mammy! A yawn! In the womb! Me and Shauna are, like, panic stations, going, Stop! Stop! Stop, Babby! You'll swallow a mouthful of that awful womb fluid, and gag yourself stupid! Stop, Babby Concannon! Quick, Mrs Kindly, Smiley-Faced, Asian Uhura Wan! Do something!

She's dead cool, of course, and has seen it a million times, and is just, like, Relax, folks, it's a reflex, like, the babby's just trying out some skills in the womb, like yawning, and cracking her knuckles, crossing her legs and a whole rake a stuff that you do without thinking. Which calms us down no end, and makes us look at each other like big thick eejits, like we're total novices in the parenting stakes, and know feck-all about wombs, babies and scans, and, boy, do we have some catching-up to do with the rest of the world.

So, after much deep scanning the kindly Asian wan turns around and tells us that she can't see any sign of a mickey at all. Of course, we had to give her our permission first, so we wouldn't have to be going, Blah blah blah, all the way through, with our fingers in our ears in case she mentioned it, accidentally, while scanning around the crotch. And we gave her our permission because we're dead modern about all that stuff, me and Shauna are, no superstitions, no old wives' tales, or no need to be sitting around smugly in front of frothy coffees with all them other NCT mammies-to-be, and going, No, we wanted a surprise at the birth, as if having a baby was the most unsurprising thing you could possibly imagine, like a live human baby would come flying out of your fanny and you'd have to go, Well, so what? This ain't no big deal, lads! I already know the sex, so everything else is kind of downhill from there.

And naturally, Mammy, since we left the hospital, I haven't stopped thinking about the scan, and the size of the little wan in there, called Bonnie now, because we're calling her Bonnie, if she's definitely a girl, and doesn't grow a mickey in the run-up to the eighteen weeker. It's Bonnie as in 'My Bonnie Lies Over the Ocean', rather than, say, Bonnie Feckin Langford – Jayz, she'd try the patience of a saint, that wan – or, say, Bonnie and Clyde, which would be a bit like naming your child after the Don Tidey kidnappers, or *The General*. Which means I'm thinking of Bonnie, just waiting, floating and yawning, so patient, so perfect, just listening to all the humpety-hump sounds around her, must be deafening at that age, the sounds coming through the womb water like voices through cupped hands, but louder still, and felt through the womb fluid, sound as touch, as motion.

I'm thinking of the scan, and I'm thinking of the speaker sound too, in the scan. Yes, Mammy, the speaker sound was the best. Because after she's done with the main scanner, the kindly Asian wan replaces it in its holder and produces another one, this one more like a bog-standard microphone, which she lathers in more Vasers, and heads, yet again, for the belly, only this time, instead of pictures on screen, we get sound, loud sound, serious sound, through the speakers. And, Mammy, what a sound. It's yet another mind-blower for me and Shauna, who aren't expecting anything else after the yawny-face set-piece. And the wan, who's clearly a master at doing scans, and knows how to eke every last drop of drama from every moment, doesn't say a word, or tell us what she's doing until she's well into doing it.

And so, we hear it first. This magical noise.

Wuchoo-wuchoo-wuchoo-wuchoo-wuchoo-wuchoo-wuchoo.

And then she says it, the aul wan. Almost mutters it. Almost lost in the drama.

This, she says. This is baby's heart.

Wuchoo-wuchoo-wuchoo-wuchoo-wuchoo-wuchoo-wuchoo.

Strong, she says, smiling, almost laughing at us both. Strong baby girl. Live long time!

Shauna and I hold hands at this. We both, without thinking, without words or a single exchange, close our eyes, and we just listen.

Wuchoo-wuchoo-wuchoo-wuchoo-wuchoo-wuchoo-wuchoo.

The intimacy of it, Mammy. The privacy. The privilege. And all that potential.

I don't think I've ever been happier.

Your Right-Hand Man,

Jay

25

'She Don't Lie, She Don't Lie, She Don't Lie'

Jane brings Sue Winsley, her thin, cadaverous and ruthlessly efficient production manager, to the third and final *Dome Life* pitch meeting, just before Christmas '98. This time, as a conspicuous reflection of the seriousness with which Jane is regarding the proposal, they meet in the cavernous basement of Mezzo's restaurant on Wardour Street. All the big nobs come here, Jane says, without irony, as they huddle in close over their white-marble four-top. She looks over the menu and scans the room around her, reciting wistfully, as she goes, a list of names that might very well be scattered right there throughout the restaurant, right then, or simply mythical fragments of past conversations. Supergrass, she says, with hushed reverence. Elastica, The Chemical Brothers, The Mock Turtles, and the entire cast of *Cold Feet*.

Jane and Sue have, they say, joined heads, and come up with some queries.

Access?

All sorted, via Darren.

It's an Irish mafia thing, explains Stevie Fitz, speaking, once again, for Jay, who remains visibly, quietly traumatised, still seemingly reeling from the domestic meltdown, and about to move out of Shauna's Notting Hill flat, later that very day, and into the apartment of some posh Kenyans just off the Cromwell Road.

The micks, Stevie says, authoritative as ever, have the Dome sewn up. He turns to Jay and rests a fraternal arm on his shoulder, adding, Which means that, thanks to Jay here, we do too. Access passes, filming permits, release forms, the whole shooting match. Signed, sealed and delivered. No questions asked.

Sue Winsley, unimpressed, jabs at an asparagus stalk and asks for it in writing. Official writing.

And a potential TX date?

Mid-Jan 2000, says Stevie Fitz. Just when Dome fever is at its peak. When the whole nation is craving access to the Dome, when everyone's talking about it, when the entire world, in fact, is jetting into London, to get themselves a piece of the Dome, and to feel that Dome magic, right then, just when the appetite is at its most rabid, when the world is craving, pardon the French ladies, some serious Dome dick, we go and we fuck them with it! *Dome Life!* The story behind the men beneath the men beneath the men who made the Dome!

So it's Fraggle Rock for immigrants, micks and builders? says Sue dryly, not even looking up from her salad.

Jane, however, is impressed and, out of Sue's eyeline, fires both Stevie and Jay an encouraging wink.

It's so much more than that, says Stevie Fitz, apparently affronted and thus launching, unprompted, into Scotty lecture mode, delivering an impassioned account of his concept for the *Dome Life* crew. He asks the table to imagine the documentary format reborn within the pleasure of eccentric personalities rather than the dull reality of dreary old so-called facts. He asks them to imagine, if they will, the construction world's version of the Spice Girls, with the antics of Burak, who's from Turkey, and a Muslim to boot, and quietly opinionated, and will forever be getting into zany theological scrapes with Esteban, the Mexican, who's super Catholic, and will be prodded, wherever possible, with notes and digs from behind the camera, to engage Burak in fiery debates on the essential nature of God while drilling, banging and screwing together the greatest building project of our age.

Stevie says, going full Scotty brainbox, that the men will be like medieval artisans, working their way through the transepts of Chartres cathedral in the thirteenth century, offering their gifts up to God, knowing that they might live a whole lifetime and never comprehend the significance of their daily hammer strikes. And it's not all brain food either, he says. There's Ambrus, from Hungary, for a start, the dark-eyed ladies' man, like early-era Sean Connery, flirting and seducing his way through a high-heeled phalanx of marketing and management staff. And that's not forgetting Pawel, for Poland, the baby of the crew, homesick and heartbroken for the first few episodes, but then reinvigorated completely in a third-show tear-jerker when his even younger wife and child are flown out to join him. And of course, Stevie adds, nudging Jay affectionately, there's Finbar, the mick, for sheer comedy value. A complete gobshite, and a lazy bollix too, who keeps falling over scaffolding poles, and getting lost in the service tunnels, and comes in reeking every morning of booze, and is constantly nipping up into the cooling towers, to snooze off the latest hangover. In a word, in two words, televisual magic. Say the word and they can be up and running by Jan next year. Get the whole twelve months in the can. All they need is the word.

The meal ends with coffees, no puddings. Sue speaks, while slowly removing the paper doily from underneath the sugar bowl. She begins to write upon it, stopping and starting, for effect. She warns Stevie and Jay that the sum, the entire sum, and

308

the balance, must be recouped from the lucky prospective broadcaster, but for now, how does this grab you?

She slides the doily across the table to Stevie, who flashes it to
Jay.

Fifty-five thousand fecking pounds! Jay yelps, the most ani-
mated he's been all day.

Sue, seemingly with great effort, lifts her heavy-lidded eyes up
from her coffee cup, and fixes both men with a steely stare.

Spend it wisely, she says.

De-ne, ne, ne, ne, nuh, nuh, nuh – cocaine!

Jay has been singing the song all afternoon. He gets like that
when there's a hit coming. He's brazen about it too. Effecting a
modest 'Macarena' in front of a giant yellow skip by the shining
silver pier-side service pod, swivelling about in front of Roger and
Burak, and closing each few dainty steps with the de-ne-ne beats
and the deliciously elongated pronouncement of, Cocaaaaine!

And he can't believe his luck either. Thought he was done for,
without Esteban, the back-stabbing, turncoat, born-again bollix.
Really drove him through a hard couple of weeks there. Not
quite *Trainspotting*, he says, but enough sweating and gasping to
fling Jane up onto her feet in the small hours, and get him
shipped off to the Chelsea and Westminster, where, treating his
shaky pallid presence as the real deal, the full ER, they scanned
him, quizzed him, drained him, and even shaved him, sticking a
slew of electrodes to his torso, and a battery pack by his side, and
sent him home with strict instructions from an Australian orderly
to return, battery and electrodes in hand, within forty-eight hours
for the wide-ranging results of this pitiless analysis.

And did he return? Did he, feck! With his life? With his sched?
Everyone on his case. Sue Winsley, that wan, especially. Show us
the rushes! The big boys, they want to see the rushes! Jesus.
Stopped taking her calls months ago. Let Stevie Fitz dampen

down those flames. The rushes! Show us what we're paying for? Jesus, you'd swear we were making a feckin pizza, he'd say, at night, in the club, on the way up to the fourth-floor bar, while getting the nod from Jamie, the maître d' with the unfeasibly large biceps and the sweetly ophidian, nice-to-see-you-again, Mr Concannon, oh-you're-quite-the-raver-tonight, Mr Concannon, come-back-any-time, Mr Concannon, always-a-place-for-you, Mr Concannon. He loves that.

And the coke too. Loves the coke. Just brilliant. He loves the fact that he's taking coke. Feckin magic. Coke. Just the sound of it. Coke. Big time. Feckin *Miami Feckin Vice*. Taking coke. Too feckin right. Just the mythos of it on its own was part of the high. Just to know that every time, every single bump, every line you did, from the moment you did it, you were connected irrevocably, instantly, up and down through a textual chain that included mobsters, millionaires, dollar bills, Ferraris, South American drug cartels, Wall Street traders, Hollywood A-listers, rock stars, Uzis, AK-47s, jungle firefights, street-corner drive-bys, bullet casings, gang-bangers, prostitutes, plastic surgery, white linen suits, endless sunshine and big white feckin mansions with turquoise pools, terracotta tiling and sprawling verandas. Feckin A! It was like Saturday night at the movies, only it was up your nose. And when it's up there, and it hits you, nose to toe to head to heart, an electro whoosh from the wide-awake club, wackaday, wackaday, it's like, suddenly, for once, for now, everything makes sense, everything whooshes sense, and you realise, with clarity, that life is, in fact, a movie, and you are, as you have always known, and always suspected, you are the star protagonist of that movie. And it's a good thing. Feckin A indeed!

And everyone else who took coke was feckin A too. In the club. In the bogs. Ricky Martin on the speakers. Everyone tooting the feckin heads off each other. Doing coke. Down on the cistern. Using fifties. Livin' la Vida Loca. And bouncing back into the room, full of the chat, and the gags, and the plans, and the reasons why *Dome Life* is going to break all sorts of barriers known to man, to art, culture, and reality itself, because it wasn't just some feckin pizza they were putting together. Show us the rushes! Feck that. This is *Dome Life*, dude! *Dome Life!*

And neither did Jay plan to become a cokehead. It was the warmth of Jane's arms, at a garden party in Islington, that did it. The first blast of summer, proper sun, burning red, on his face, in her arms, lying back on the picnic rug. And kids running about, toddlers, younger than Bonnie. And Jay, for the first time ever, not going to pieces, not breaking down at the sight, just happily holding it together, telling Jane that he's cured of heartache, and on the way up, and concentrating on other things, on *Dome Life*, and on the babby that he knows, that he prays, if he prayed, is inside her.

They enjoyed a full body-hugging embrace, but were careful, also, not to overdo it, for the sake of the other guests. The hosts were clean-living Christians, good people, straight-up folk who were not interested at all in visual displays of gropage and frottage, especially in front of their guest of honour, an ageing, dozing matriarch called Margaret, a stage actress from the olden days who was fragile and wheelchair-bound now, and cruising close to her hundreth year on earth.

Jay and Jane released each other, and Jay said again that he hoped that one of them eggs would take, one day soon, for both of their sakes and the sake of the new family that they hoped to create. Jane was touched, and later, as a gift, she introduced Jay to a round-faced giant in a long black overcoat, a man called Peter Feddan who preferred to be addressed, with just the tiniest hint of irony, as The Hooded Claw. Jane said that The Hooded Claw was a famous face around Soho, with no particular media brief other than to maintain the happy smiles and serene countenances of the movers and shakers in the meeja biz. She told The 'Claw that Jay was a future mover and shaker, and co-director of the ultimate Millennium Dome documentary, *Dome Life*. And she asked The 'Claw, while slipping a twenty into the pocket of his long black overcoat, if he could sort Jay out with a first-time picker-upper. As a treat.

The day, perhaps inevitably, ended in scandal, in the night, with Jay, changed, changed utterly, from the ineffable buzz of seven long lines, his tongue locked with Jane's, and stumbling urgently into a darkened spare room at the host's house, drop-ping onto the spare bed, and engaging, almost instantly, in the abandon of intercourse, only to be stopped, barely a minute in, by the wailing and groaning of a ghostly voice, the sudden stark flash of room light, and the agonising realisation that this spare room of sex was, in fact, an annexed granny flat of veteran stage actress and celebrated nonagenarian Margaret, who was sitting bolt upright, toothless, wigless and wailing in horror at the two transgressing humpers at the foot of her bed, with their sun-seared faces, arms and legs, crimson red, and their startlingly comical white behinds.

Jay blamed The Hooded Claw's stash for the clumsy sexual rampage (had a few rotten lines in there, all right), the news of which spread thick and fast via meeja mouths, eventually alight-ing, during canteen whispers, on the ears of Esteban, who approached Jay later that day with the offer of a fresh and uncomplicated cocaine source, namely himself.

And oh, what bliss there was, what a summer that was. The last summer of love. Summer '99. Day in, day out, bumps and lines whenever he wanted, wherever he could, starting with a cheeky line for breakfast, just him and Stevie Fitz, squeezed into a por-taloo in portaloo station, facing out over the Blackwell tunnel, giddy together, fumbling excitedly with Vengaboys' CD cover, not risking a nose-full of piss splash or back-blasted shit-wash by tooting on the grey plastic cistern in front of them. And on through the day, whenever they wanted, whenever they could. Such clarity of mind, such creativity and focus. That extra edge and the hint of genius that you get only from coke, pointing Jay and Stevie in the right way, inspiring them with the right ideas, as they stand back bamboozled and light-headed, happily stulti- fied, while the installations slowly emerge all round them, all summer long, like the garish inner organs of some giant white alien space crab, all the time tended to, cleaned and pecked by a swarm of hard-hatted insects in fluorescent vests.

And it could've stayed this way, blissful to the end, were it not for the Ladbroke Grove rail disaster, and Esteban's subsequent Damascene conversion from drug pusher to Holy Joe. It was touch and go for a while back there. Jay struggled for a source. He was furious with Esteban, and tried to ban him from return- ing to *Dome Life* when the Mexican suddenly reappeared in the back of Darren's van, a fortnight after his initial epiphany, claim- ing penury, and begging for a second chance.

Jay tried to fire him, but Stevie Fitz, yet again, dampened down the flames, and warned Jay, whispered to him, that you couldn't dismiss someone for refusing to sell you cocaine. Plus, he said, and he knew, and Jay knew, that Esteban was the best value in the squad. And sure enough, on the very day after his return, he gave them pure televisual magic, screaming out of the service tunnel, blessing himself and performing all sorts of fidg- ety comedy shtick, saying, practically crying, that he had seen Santa Muerta herself, the Lady of Death, underneath the main stage, and that the whole place was haunted, and evil, and a place of doom.

Even better, Esteban's outburst led to a fabulous talking head, snatched on the fly, from Michelle Rochelle Cachet, publicity spokesperson, who informed them on camera, matter of factly, television gold, that, yes, in the early construction stages, before the skin was on the frame and it was just a startling circular assemblage of twelve yellow masts, workers and security staff regularly reported sightings of a tall ghostly figure, an elderly woman with long grey hair, drifting about around the main stage. They said she might've been an employee of the old gasworks that they flattened, to make way for the Dome. Or, interrupted Esteban, on camera, elbowing Michelle Rochelle Cachet clean out of the shot, or Santa Muerta herself! Esteban blessed himself, and closed his eyes, as if praying. Jay and Stevie Fitz looked at each other. Two words. Televisual magic.

But, yes, it was touch and go back there. Jay struggled, really struggled, to find another dealer. This is nineteen-fecking-ninety-nine! he used to say, railing at Stevie Fitz, at the end of every day, when the sweats and the dreads were kicking in. And we're in the fecking meeja! How hard can it be? It should be like working in Willy Wonka's Chocolate Factory, where you just kneel down and take a big hefty scoop whenever you feel like it. Not phone bashing all day, begging and scraping for a bump from any aul pox-ridden how-a-ye! The shakes and the dreads were killing him too. Although he did his best to hide it from Jane. Only seemed to emerge late at night, to reveal him entirely, in sleep-lessness, chest cramps and runaway palpitations.

He tried Stevie's contacts too. He got a line here or there. Enough to knock the cravings on the head. But no proper supply. In desperation, he even tried Shauna, phoned her and asked her to get the number of that guy she once knew, the English bender in Mayfair, who made her take coke and snog the face off Jess. Shauna told Jay that he was a complete cock, reminded him that he had missed his last play date with Bonnie, that he had disap-pointed her beyond words, and that he should go fuck himself.

It finally hits him in the flat, staring into space, trying to get it together, to pull the jeans on, spray himself clean, and ready himself for a night out with Jane at the club. He's listening to the television that's leaking in from Ree's room next door, where Wendy's watching *TFI Friday* and the hairy guy from Reef is singing, It's your letters, it's your lehhh-ters, and he suddenly notices another sound, a wearily familiar sound, pulsing down the landing from three rooms away. Roo is screwing again.

Roo?

And so, De-ne, ne, ne, ne, nuh, nuh, nuh – Cocaine! He sings it defiantly into Esteban's face, practically, appropriately, nose to nose. The entire team is gathered for a regroup by the skip, where Stevie Fitz is announcing, with some excitement, that the Faith Zone is about to be assembled that afternoon. Jay is waiting for his phone to ring, for the first sign that Roo is on the premises, and that his life-saving coke has finally arrived. And so when his precious Nokia buzzes into life on his belt he picks it with a theatrical sweep of his hand and, looking at Esteban while grinning, ear to ear, says, Shoot!

I'm sorry for your troubles, says the voice on the other end. But your mammy passed away this morning.

Dear Mammy,

Never mind.

Jay

26

Dr Ghert and Dr Ghert

Dr Ghert is masturbating when Shauna says it for the third time.

Hon, we are now, officially, late!

He can normally block her out. The shower helps too. That water hiss, the low humming of the electronic pump. There was an English word for it, that water sound, which he liked. Tintinnabulation. Yes. Like bells. Like tinnitus, he thought, which he's sure he has. He can hear it, hissing away, tintinnabulating, in the quieter moments, with Shauna in the sitting room, reading the papers, or awake at night in bed. Not in the shower, no. Best place in the world, the shower. Soothing, ameliorating. The warm running of water over the body. Energetically perfect. Better than sitting in a stagnant pool of your own decay. Couldn't understand bath people. Shauna was a bath person. So relaxing. So calming. Couldn't understand it. So fetid. A long shower. Works for him every time. Even with the gastric flu that he got from Shauna's undercooked lamb tagine. Vomiting all night, violent cramps, merciless diarrhoea. But five minutes in the shower, the energy running down, around, and off him, and he was a new man.

And he was not to be blamed for the masturbating either. Was only human. All that warm water. Running, tickling, and licking.

What was he supposed to do? He would not be blocked. Stuck. Sexually stunted, like so many of his hopeless cases. He would be free. He would be released. Released from the mental montage, the roll-call of clients, the women, always the women, just sitting there, flapping away, yadda yadda yadda, father-mother-husband-brother, father-mother-husband-brother, no attention, wrong attention, all attention, fake attention, got me, hurt me, kissed me, hit me, fucked me, felt me, left me, loved me. Yes. Of course, poor you. Yes, of course. But the legs uncrossing, and crossing again, and the static swish of nylon, and the gentle waft, imaginary or not, of warm menstrual air, as the legs uncross, and the arms fold, and the breasts rise and squeeze, rise and squeeze, under shirts, under sweaters, open sweaters, open blouses, just waiting, just dying, for Dr Ghert.

And off he goes, into the game of wild release. Dr Ghert and the women, and the women who want it. Only human. On top of those women who want it. Only human to finally fill them up. Only human to want to energetically unblock all over their faces, those women, those women, those hateful—

Hon, we are now, officially, late!

Dr Ghert grunts aloud, to let Shauna know, without irony, that he's going as fast as he can. He used to make her do it. Especially after the pregnancy took. He'd just stand there, in the bedroom, the kitchen, on the stairs, anywhere, and expose himself, and announce that he was a man with needs who did not desire to end his days sexually stultified and lying low on his own therapist's chair, and so, if she wouldn't mind, he would like it if she would release him, now. Easier, now, to do it on his own. Fewer recriminations afterwards. Easier if she'd just keep her mouth—

Hon!

And he wasn't exactly in a hurry either. The *Screen Grab* Christmas Reunion? Really? Was she serious? He had hated the idea then, when he first read the invite, of a *Star Wars* Santa

Claus dripping with party glitter and fake bonhomie. And he hated it more now, just minutes before their supposed departure for the night in question. A night of hare-brained twenty-and-thirty-somethings, preening with vanity and hipster cool, gathered together in a Soho back bar, blasted into submission by sternum-rattling, synapse-splitting dance music, while hopelessly attempting to share misremembered anecdotes about the days when they were all, all, television stars.

They wouldn't talk to him, of course, if they met him on the street. The young people. Especially the women. Look right through him now. With their push-up bras, and their fake breasts, their eight-inch heels, and their shaven mons. Although, God knows, he could teach them a thing or two, several things, in fact, about pleasure. At his age. At their age. Just ask Shauna. Didn't know what hit her. Rocked her world, sexually. Released her completely. None of these young bucks have a clue what to do, or how to harness it. They're all jackhammer drilling and no finesse. He could show those girls, with their push-up bras, yes, he could show them, yes, he could—

Hon! Annie's here!

Right!

Dr Ghert snaps off the water, wraps himself in a blue bath towel, and noisily stomps out of the bathroom, in a state of moderate sexual agitation. Shauna has laid out his party outfit on the bed. Neatly creased denim jeans. Black brogues. White shirt. He hates that. When she calls it his party outfit. He hates the tone in her voice when he emerges from the room, on the night, in his party outfit. And she says something patronising, like, Woo woo, doesn't he scrub up well? Like you would to a child in a page-boy's suit, or someone who's been horribly disfigured in a terrorist bombing or a nightclub inferno, and is making their way to some hotel reception where they're about to receive a medal for bravery and for not topping themselves at the cruelty of it all.

She has already told him not to worry tonight, of all nights, because him, he, the ex, Jay, will not be there. A complete messy cokehead these days. A flake. Works all day, drugs all night. Hopeless on Bonnie play dates. Half the time he's held aloft by the poor, long-suffering and baby-craving Jane. Which is all fine by Dr Ghert. Not that he should be worried. Or need to be worried. Why would he be worried? That was worse than the party outfit. The sheer galling subtext. The old man and the young buck. Don't worry, Grandad, the buck won't be out tonight! You escaped a thrashing. Whereas, in fact, Dr Ghert could show these bucks a thing or two, several things.

At least, he should be thankful for the shirt. Shauna has used the washing machine. Be thankful that some of his lectures are finally sinking in. Finally. And it's not that Dr Ghert wants to be authoritative, or dictatorial. It's just that some people, some women especially, have this energy about them. They have a female energy, random and chaotic, in classical terms it's Dionysian, and it fits perfectly with an authoritative male energy, which is Apollonian. Fits perfectly like a jigsaw. They need, these Dionysian women, they need a stern, domineering voice, a masculine voice, to protect them from their own feminine chaos. Like the washing. The comments didn't work. The humorous asides didn't work. Whereas a few solid shouts, like you would, perhaps, direct at a misbehaving Labrador, was all it took to get her back on track. Neither was it sexist or old-fashioned or chauvinistic, or any of that claptrap. It was just, simply, purely, energetic.

He fits the outfit, naturally, very well. Man of his age. He'll keep the shirt untucked all the same. Let it hang straight down over the belt. Eradicates the paunch, entirely, at least visually. Open the top two buttons too. He's got nothing to hide. More European that way. He should've kept his chain. Would've been perfect now. A conversation starter. A Danish chain, yes? The

320

pendant is a Viking symbol. Meaning ability and versatility. And I am versatile, and, young lady, I am able. Just ask Shauna.

The jeans still fit, though, which is good. Might need to unthread them more at the hem, though. Do it with the nail clippers. He likes that. When the white threads from the hemline spread out all over the shoes, like the mane of a show pony. And the hair too! Quick. He can hear Shauna giving final instructions to Annie, the sitter. He takes a dollop of Shauna's wax and runs it through his hair, while thinking, briefly, about the many things, of a sexual nature, that he could teach Annie the sitter. Great hair, he thinks, staring intently in the bedroom mirror. Man his age? Really, no other way to describe it, but the ace up the sleeve. His mother always said it. Super hairline, never go bald. Might go grey, snow white indeed, but never bald. Says authority and virility in a way that baldness never can. And the bald men, with their scientifically proven theories on excess of testosterone at the root of their problems? Poppycock to that. He'd rather have his own head of hair than a thousand gallons of testosterone coursing through his veins. And so would the baldies.

Wow! Well, aren't you the ladykiller?

That's what she says, Shauna, when she enters the bedroom. Dr Ghert says nothing. He's nearly ready. Just loosening the last few fibres from the hem of his jeans with the extended arm of the nail clippers. He looks, takes a proper look, at Shauna. She is wearing heels, and a short, short black skirt that curves out, not wildly out, but noticeably out, on the camber of her baby bump. Above she is wearing a blue top, glitter blue, no, sequins blue, that's off the shoulders and clinging to her breasts, breasts that are already showing second-trimester swelling, and certainly battling with the limits of that outfit.

He was good about the baby, too. He was authoritative. He sat her down, told her he was late for work, but that he had now, from his previous marriages, been down the fatherhood journey six times before, and really, and truly, had not intended to take that journey again. But if Shauna was willing to do the lion's share of the mothering, and perhaps get Bonnie involved in the changing and wiping, she would find in Dr Ghert a rare and compassionate parent indeed.

Her lipstick, however, is almost out of the question. Cerise pink. He says nothing. Naturally, she doesn't do social events much, Shauna. She's up and down, these days. A propensity for gloom. This one party, thus, a rarity for her. But, he thinks, Really, could she go any cheaper if she tried? What is she selling, and who is she planning on selling it to? These are the questions.

Shauna looks at Dr Ghert with expectant eyes. Well? she says, doing a mock spin from a fantasy catwalk.

Is the lipstick staying? he asks, coldly.

Of course it's staying, Shauna says, spirits indomitable, anticipation for the night overwhelming everything else. Oh, come here, she says, Mr Moody Boots!

She marches towards him, in her heels, waddling in her heels, her breasts wobbling too, almost at the head height of Dr Ghert. She pulls him roughly close, presses him against her, calls him Mr Moody Boots once more, and kisses him on the neck. As she does, and out of sympathy for him, or worry for him, or sadness for him, she tells him, one more time, as quiet as she can, not to worry, because him, he, the ex, Jay, will not be there tonight.

Dr Ghert closes his eyes. He breathes. He stands back a single pace from Shauna. And he smacks her, full force, across the face. He marches to the bedroom door and slams it shut.

Now, look what you've made me do! he says. That's it. We're not going out. The night is off. Look at my shirt, you've got lipstick on my shirt, your slut lipstick on my shirt, my only shirt, and you know I can't go out without a shirt, without this shirt, so we're not going out. End of story.

Shauna, clutches her face, and holds her heart. No words.

You know what I'm like in these situations, he says. I need to be authoritative with you. And you need me to be authoritative with you. I need to protect you from your own chaos, and from whoever it is that you plan to seduce with those breasts. So that's why I'm telling you that tonight is not happening. And that there's no use in crying. I'll send Annie home. I've made up my mind. No whimpering, please. I don't want to shout. I don't want to be hard and domineering. But sometimes, there are some women who attract this type of energy, and it's in the genes, they attract this type of energy, because their mothers before them have attracted this type of energy, because, all along, they need this type of energy around them. To keep them safe. To keep them sane. And in one place. And not falling apart. So stop the whimpering, don't even think about crying, and please, please, for my sake, if not for your own self-respect, go into that bathroom and remove every single bit of that fucking lipstick.

27

A Yuletide Bender

The Tony Blair. Yes, the one and only Tony Blair. The very one.

Jay is saying this, quickly, into the face of the Father of Jane, while trying to peek over his shoulder, around his arm, towards the kitchen door. The Mother of Jane has been gone too long. Something's not right. What's she doing?

The Father of Jane is nodding wisely. Blair? He tells Jay that this is impressive and might swing it for him. He hasn't, of course, mentioned the M-word yet. Chequebook? Donation? Extra investment? Nothing. Money? Forget it. You can't just come out and ask him for it, Jane had said, horrified, during their pre-meeting, prep-session breakfast at the club. Jay had flinched. Jane was making him nervous again. He had already done a cheeky line, but Jane couldn't tell any more. You'll be fine, Jane had said, they're normal people. You've met them before. At dinner. Totally normal. Just nothing too crude. Nothing too explicit. And no swearing. Not even feck. Especially not feck. Just relaxed, just casual. It's Christmas Eve, for God's sake. Everyone's happy. They'll be happy. They'll do the talking. They'll start the meeting, which they did, at the dining room table, just three of them, Jay alone opposite the Father of Jane and the Mother of Jane, and a monumental grandfather clock clanking in the corner, like the strangest, sweatiest job interview imaginable, kicking off with the casually polite, And how is the adventure in television going these days, eh heh-heh-heh?

Jay had always imagined Jane's investors in a different light. Foreign businessmen. Russian oligarchs. Media experts on the move, looking to make a killing, buy-small-sell-big-style. It wasn't like she never mentioned them, or tried to play them down. Deflect attention. Drop the subject. No, instead, she couldn't stop herself. Oh, I'll have to take this to the investors. I'll see what the investors say before I come back to you. I don't think the investors would be happy with that. I definitely think that's one for the investors. And all along Jay picturing a cavernous boardroom in the heart of the city, and Jane trembling before a phalanx of sharp-suited tyros with slickback hairstyles and metallic briefcases.

And then she comes whispering up to Jay on the site with good and bad news, yes, the investors are amenable, but there's just one thing, they want to meet you. And her, sheepish, and he could tell, before she said it, that there was something else in her bag of tricks. And now here he is, on Christmas Eve, face to face with the possibility of a life-saving top-up, double or nothing, fifty-five K, and no questions asked, all answers supplied.

Sue Winsley was dead against it. She was, like, scratching the head off her, looking at the figures, on Jay's rubbish home-made spreadsheet, with biro, rulers and everything, saying, I just don't get it! I genuinely don't get it. Where has all the money gone? And Jane looking at Jay, not wanting to know the truth, not daring to make eye contact or think, but pinning him down afterwards, later that night, in his flat, after crashing home from the club, about the money, all the money, and him breaking down, saying that it was all too much, all killing him, and that he'd had an epiphany and he knew that he'd have to change, and reform, and get better, and get well, because look at the state of him, and what it had done to him, the working and the clubbing, and how it was ruining him, and how he had missed his own mammy's funeral, just tossed it aside, his own mammy's funeral, like it was some feckin lunch date with some meeja nitwit who didn't deserve the steam off his own mammy's piss.

And he had explained to Jane at the time, to make it clear to Jane, that this is what you do, this is the immigrant life, the immigrant's dilemma, that call, that phone call, you prepare for it your whole life, your whole immigrant life, you wait for it, you build yourself up against it, from it, barricade yourself inwards, against it, that one phone call, and you're waiting, and waiting, the years ticking on, and you're waiting, and building, protecting, barricading each year, a race against that one feck- ing call, need to be stronger to take that one call, that hateful fecker, that one fecking call. And it's a wonder that immigrants anywhere ever answer the phone. Looking at that phone, that ringing phone, and knowing somewhere, always somewhere, in the deep subconscious that's not too subconscious at all, that the one fecking call for you, right now, is to tell you finally, all these years upon years, finally now, with your barricades in place, finally now, that you've waited so long for, finally, sorry, so sorry for your troubles, but your mammy, that mammy, has finally passed.

And Jane bought it completely, and the team did too. The Clappers, however, was another *shcale*, chewing the ears on the phone all day. Your own mammy's funeral? Your own mammy? But Jay, inured, protected and angry, let her have it right back, with, Bury her, just bury her, bury and be done, bury the body, that's not my mammy, my mammy died years ago, the mad aul who-er, that body, that one-armed corpse, don't belong to me, now bury that body and be done with it, because we, we here, we us, in the United States of Kingdom, we've got a feckin show to put on!

But that was bluff and bluster, he said, weeping in Jane's arms. That was the old him, he said, promising newness. Just as he was, at the very same time, fingerpointing with blame, pointing everything away, *ree raw ogus roola boola* style, towards Darren. Feckin Darren. The retainer fees are killing us. Rising out of all proportion. Every day. It's an Irish mafia thing. They're bleeding us dry. No fee, no shooting, no permits, no work, no fee, no show.

And nor does he mention the bust-up with Stevie Fitz over steadicam shots that they couldn't afford, but they went and hired anyway, because why the feck not? This was *Dome Life*, meeja who-ers. What a *shcale*. They weren't making a pizza, they said. But the steadicam hire took them over the edge. So they cut Roger's wage in two and they spent it on Roo, on Roo's coke, and Jay blamed it on Stevie who blamed it on Jay, and Roger, with a rake of kids in the bank, threatened to quit, so they could do their own feckin sound if they were that way inclined, so Jay panicked and took the wage off Esteban for the month ahead, and gave it to Roger, and promised Esteban a monster wonga Christmas bonus, so long as he kept his head down and said nothing about the missing wages, and did some more good ghosty stuff on camera.

And he did, was so good, so compliant, that Esteban, a real character, a credit to his nation, such a performer. He comes streaming out from under the stage, this time a feckin show-stopper, almost literally, because there's eighty different acrobats above him, some of them in the air, high-wire style, doing dress rehearsals for this mad New Year's show that has no story at all, other than this wan in silky robes who goes out with this fella in silky robes, and they're from different enemy tribes of lads and wans in silky robes, and when they find out, they have this huge, aerial, acrobatic donnybrook that ends when everyone wraps their silk around each other up in the air, and then lets it all fall down to the ground, where the audience are, to show them how we're all part of one big silky family, and not to be fighting in the future. It's a message to all those who visit the Dome that the year 2000 will be the beginning of the end for global division, and will mark a period of time when former enemies, the blacks and the racists, Catholics and the Prods, the Muslims and the Jews, the Yanks and everyone else, they'll all come together in a great big understanding of each other, and life, and the power of high-wire silk.

So Esteban comes screaming out, going, again, but ten times louder than before, Santa Muerta! Santa Muerta! And this time he's shaking it up a bit, like a pro, mixing it up, adding, El Diablo! El Diablo! for good measure. The poor dancers have to cut the backing track too, because they're recording it on four different cameras, one of which picks up Esteban at full pelt, screaming the head off him. El Diablooooooo! Of course, Jay and the lads are hooting at this, really hooting, and loving the fact that they're finally, if only for a couple of precious minutes, hooting their heads off, and not thinking, or stressing, or fighting or begging, just kicking back and hooting at the sight of a little Mexican fella in snow-washed jeans going completely mental in front of a load of snooty unimpressed acrobats.

And even when they've got the scene done and dusted, Esteban's still at it. Method style. Panting and gasping. Jay tells him, straight up, that he has some fierce strong performance genes in him, and Jay should know, because he's seen the best in the business, A-listers all, up close and personal, though mostly in hotel rooms. But Esteban doesn't bite, and instead remains a shivering wreck, a pro to the end, in character, full time, El Diablo me arse, and everyone around him having a decent go, saying, El Diablo, me arse, everyone, that is, except Burak, of all

328

people, who's like, arm around the shoulder, nodding and sooth-ing, turning to the rest and saying, Shhhhh, praying silence, and telling them, Iblis, it's Iblis, in the noble Quran it's Iblis, meaning Satan. At which point, mood totally kilt, Jay stands up and announces, brazen as can be, that he's off for a toot, and starts singing, on cue, De-ne, ne, ne, ne, nuh, nuh, nuh – Cocaine!

And the wage trick, inevitably, so easy to do, doesn't stop with Esteban. Pawel is next, this promise even bigger, a mega-wonga Christmas bonus, with a cut of the broadcaster fee. Which is genius, Jay decides, because it's almost like proper cash, and would be proper cash if it wasn't built on delusion. And so he begins printing out, on his own home computer, a load of God-awful documents, non-justified, typos galore, that nonetheless boast a pretty snazzy masthead, lifted entirely, oh sweet revenge, from his last legal letter from the solicitor of Dr Ghert, and promise within the body of the text and the cod-legalese, awful stuff, they promise a five per cent cut from the broadcaster's fee of, the fee of, of, and he has to think about this, Jay, with fingers hovering, nothing too rash, nothing too hysterical, his hands over the keys, let's say, the broadcaster's fee of one hundred thousand pounds, making each printed contract worth a cool, clean, five K! Feckin A!

Naturally, he's handing out them feckers to every gom imag-inable. The lads first. Boom. Pay cheques gone for ever. To be reimbursed by the broadcaster. He gives them out, below price, to any aul punter on the site. Even manages to flog one to Michelle Rochelle Cachet, for a grand. She thinks it's a steal, four grand in the clear already, and she can't thank Jay enough, and they both agree that this is what it's like, on the inside, with the hot tips, and the secret deals, living the life, la Vida Loca, in the meeja. Best of all, he gets two of them into the hands of Roo, who instantly wipes Jay's coke slate clean, and lets him know, sink-me style, that Jay is the proud possessor of a full grand's worth of credit at, sniff, snort, El Banco de Peru de Roo! They laugh about this, the pair in the flat, having a cheeky bump to set them up for their respective nights out on the town. Roo is the first to leave, but before he does, before he closes the door completely on Jay's room, the actual door, not the glass doors, he re-enters fully, bodily back inside, with the contracts in hand, with just one more question, *Columbo* style. Who, he asks, who is the broadcaster?

Jay, typically, blanks. His mind, his corrupted, useless, addled mind, gives him nothing. Nothing at all, other than the lyrics to 'Boom, Boom, Boom, Boom' by the Vengaboys. 'Boom, boom, boom, boom, I want you in my room, la, la, la, la, la ...' It's his favourite coke song. Aggressive, repetitive, and to the point. The broadcaster? he qualifies. Nodding slowly, desperate, scraping the inside of his skull for something, anything at all. And then he gets it, thank God, a broadcaster, yes, RTÉ! That's it, Raidió Teilefís Éireann, they're a broadcaster, yes, he'll say RTÉ, that's the answer, boom, boom. Yes, Irish telly are buying the London Dome doc, yes, yes? No! Shite and onions! No! Boom, boom, not now!

It's the Beeb, isn't it? asks Roo, saving him, throwing him a last-minute lifeline.

Of course it's the fecking Beeb! Who else?

He tries to pay Darren's ever rising-retainers in phony broadcaster fees but the Dublin bollix isn't buying. He tells Jay quietly one morning, after Jay's breakfast toot, while holding one of Jay's freshly proffered contracts, that he's catching hell from the missus at home, who's not taken at all to the mothering of the youngfella, Malacky, and is threatening to leave him at the slightest upset. The wrong cup in the dishwasher, he says, one of them hand-washable china cups, and she's on his back for a week. A living hell, apparently, with only the prospect of the Christmas holliers in Morocco keeping them both sane. And, thus, he surmised, if anything at all was to threaten the Darren family holiday kitty, say, perhaps, a phony contract that wasn't worth shite, then this, obviously, would have serio repercussions for Darren's marriage, Darren's business, and mostly for the two fuckin legs of Darren's favourite culchie bogman acquaintance. In short, he concluded, with a whisper in the ear, intimate from afar, but brutal up close, Pay me my fucking money!

And he explained to Jane, on the night of the epiphany, that he was, right then, promising change. Just a start from scratch is all he needs. Ask the investors. Please ask the investors. I'm begging you, please. Shite! He's half crying now, on his knees by the bed, in her Soho flat, avoiding Roo for the moment. Please! What do I have to do? Remember Thales of Miletus, Jane? Remember him? You and me. Henry Higgins and Eliza Doolittle? Well, Thales of Miletus, he made mistakes. He was a right royal feckin eejit. The world made of water? Me arse. But at least he was trying. He was trying his best. And I'm trying, Jane. I'm trying. What you see before you is someone, like Thales of Miletus, just a person, who's going out on a limb, and who's just trying to be a better man. I'm trying, Jane. So, for the sake of us, and for the sake of our maybe unborn baby-to-be, please, just this once, ask the investors!

The Mother of Jane has been gone for too long now. Far too long. What's she doing in there? A monumental shite, or calling the cops, take your pick. Definitely the cops. And this guy, this duffer, the Father of Jane, is clearly bluffing. He's obsessed by Blair, can't stop talking about Blair. All the Tories are like that. Wants to know how long we have him for, how easy was it to get him, had we met him yet, what's he like up close? And all these questions are wrecking my noggin, my aching *kyun*, and nothing's *guheentock, nock ah*? They're tricking me, designed to trick me, to catch me out, and with each further Blair query my eyes go, and my *kyun* freezes, and I'm thinking, What's the real answer? What's the answer he wants? And what's the answer I am not to say, under any condition? And the latter answer is always that, of course, I don't have Tony fecking Blair, there's no time with Tony Blair, and what sort of gom would hand Tony Blair over to a bunch of immigrant eejits being marshalled about by a couple of red-rimmed, sleep-deprived, pale-skinned, etiolated, bombed-out arseholes! No! I don't have Blair. Michelle Rochelle Cachet practically laughed in my face when I asked. Interview Tony Blair? Right.

But tell me this, he says, says the Father of Jane, real slow, like, too slow in the mind of Jay, painstakingly slow, dragging everything down.

The mind of Jay is thinking, run, run away, turn away, like the small-town boy says, run! Before the cops get here.

Why, continues the Father of Jane, treacle speed. Why are you really here?

Holy feck! Rumbled! This is it! Jay's heart starts to go. The stress of it all. Shakes and palpitations. Skipping beats all over the place. Like the feeling of being in love turned inside out. Little half-breaths in his throat.

I'm here, he says, nothing to lose, hand sliding down for a grip, good and tight, on the *mawla*. I'm just here for the cash!

The Father of Jane laughs. The neck. You've got to love the micks.

The kitchen door swings open.

Jay shoots up in his chair, *mawla* in hand.

Where are you going? says the Mother of Jane, carrying in a

332

thin wooden tray, upon which sits a bowl, a plate, a glass and some bread.

Soup, says the Mother of Jane. Home-made. Just now.

She sets the table slowly, and deliberately, before Jay, placing the spoon straight, perfectly perpendicular to the table edge, nestled neatly next to the bowl.

She says, quietly, that Jay looks like he needs the soup, and she wonders if her daughter is feeding Jay, or what she's feeding Jay, and how often. And then she leaves again, without another word.

Jay retakes his seat, and looks at the soup, and at the kitchen door.

The Father of Jane writes a cheque for fifty-five thousand pounds.

Jay asks him to rewrite it, and make it out to cash.

He does.

The Central Line pops him out at Oxford Circus. Jay emerges into daylight, as planned, as expected, a man reborn. The home-made soup is doing the job. The words of his promises to Jane still proud in his heart. His truth back on track. And where to begin the paybacks? Where to begin his own Step Number Nine? With toys, of course, toys for Bonnie, from Hamleys. She loves Hamleys. Yes, he'll go straight to the girly floor and buy the whole place, and deliver it to Bonnie before the night is done, no expense spared. Then Darren, of course, then the boys on site, naturally. God, he thinks. Will be such, fun, he thinks, 'boom boom', stop it! Will be such, 'boom boom', stop it now! Will be such fun to see how they react when, 'boom boom boom boom', enough! Enough! Will be amazing to go down there, and watch their faces, and Roger too, when I hand out, 'Boom boom boom boom, I want you in my room, la, la, la, la, la.'

Ah, feck it! I suppose one little toot never hurt anyone!

Don't really know how to start this, or how to say this, and I want to be gentle Mammy, like you've always been gentle with me, but things they are a-changing here, like. Big things. And not just the size of Shauna who is, by now, as you might imagine, the night before her due date, the proverbial beach ball. She's been good about it, though, with the heat and everything, and her carrying around inside her a turbo-charged karate chopper who seems, at the best of times, even the quietest of times, to be trying to kick her way out of womb, right through the belly, *Alien*-style. She got me in the kidneys th'other night, the little minx. We were spooned together, me and Shauna, as spooned as spooning can be when one of you is carrying a thundering mound of humanity front and centre. And doesn't she go, the little minx, our Bonnie, doesn't she feckin give me a right kick for my troubles, right in the back, a decent wallop, that I can feel, through Shauna's womb, Shauna's belly, and my back! I'll tell ye, that's some belt.

And it's not just that. Or the new tranquillity that we're engineering around this gaff, on the advice from the *doula*. With soothing white walls and soft cream carpets in the bedroom, and nothing but floorboards and a massive feckin birth pool in the sitting room. The *doula*, Mammy, by the way, just in case them wans haven't made it as far as Roscommon yet, is like this brilliant smiley wan, who's not quite a doctor, but better than a midwife, knows all about giving birth, and her whole job is, like, making sure that having the actual baby come out of your body is going to be, like, the most calm and mellow, chilled-out thing

334

you've ever done in your life, bar toking on a monster joint of marijuana. You pay her good money for it, of course, but Shauna says she's worth every penny.

And because of having the *doula* on tap, me and Shauna are already dead relaxed about the birth, and the only time we ever get into slanging matches is when we're fighting over how to make the house even more soothing. I'm like, we should have fecking Buddhist bells chiming, real calm, like, all the way through the birth, and she's, like, no feckin way, because who's going to be chiming them, not the *doula*, who's got enough to be getting on with, and certainly not you, because you, meaning me, will be busy keeping all the joss-stick holders refilled and making sure that the birth-pool water temperature stays at exactly thirty-seven degrees Celsius at all times, via the adding and subtracting of hot and cold waters.

The *doula* even helped Shauna write out her birth plan, which is this plan you write out that describes how exactly your baby is going to be born and what you're going to do when she's being born and how you're going to react just after it, when she's in your arms. And Shauna's plan, with some fablas and pretty much relentless suggestions from the *doula*, goes: low lighting, lots of smiles, everyone in bare feet, plenty of harmony in the air, Andy Williams and Enya on the stereo, soothing glasses of freshly pulped cucumber juice, voices of birth attendees only in whispers, intermittent neck and back massage to be delivered by Jay, the intensity of which will be regulated by Shauna in consultation with the *doula*, and not forgetting the quiet recital of late eighteenth-century romantic poetry until the near-silent delivery of baby Bonnie, out and upwards, to be gingerly rested on the chest of Shauna, which will necessitate a total cessation of all verbal communication.

335

As I say, Mammy, it's dead relaxing and completely terrifying at one and the same time. Like last week, when we went to Brighton, and Shauna, boiling as usual, from the inside and out, decided to have a dip in the sea. Which she did, eventually, after an age of fretting about the size of her, and the amount of people who'd be looking and pointing at her, as if everyone in the world was (a) feckin thick as pig shite and couldn't distinguish between a pregnant wan and a fat wan, and (b) had never even seen a pregnant wan in the first place. So, she goes in, splashes around in heavenly abandon, while I stay sitting on the stones, to make sure that no one whips the gear. When I say stones, by the way Mammy, I mean stones. Brighton is a manky shite pile as a beach, and would make you weep for the sandy climes of Strandhill.

So, out she comes, happy clappy now, clutching her bump and beaming, the very image of the glowing, thriving mammy-to-be. She towels off, we go for a bite, and then start making the long trek home back to London in her ancient red hothouse Clio. Somewhere along the way, however, around halfway or just over, just after we hit the M23, Shauna decides that the baby's dead, our Bonnie is dead, and that she's feckin kilt it by swimming in such an ice-cold sea. It's a block of ice, she says, feeling the tummy. It's a block of ice and it's not moving! I've fecking kilt it with the water.

Naturally, Mammy, we lose the run of ourselves. The traffic, typically, is bumper to bumper, and the two of us are staring, goggle-eyed in panic, too shocked to cry, just gasping, looking at each other, and then down at Shauna's bump, going, Feck, feck, feck! What do we do? What now? Shauna barks that we should have phones, that she said, all along, that we should have mobile telephones, for just this sort of thing, so she can call the *doula*! I tell her that we're not millionaire titans of industry, or secret agents, so we can survive without a mobile feckin telephone for now and I promise to get her off the road at the next service station, which is Shipley Bridge, about fifteen miles away. Before we get there, though, Shauna pushes the limits of horror-movie trauma, screaming out, on more than one occasion, that the baby's not moving, that there's nothing moving inside her. That she's carrying a block of ice! A block of frozen ice! Dead! It's dead! The baby is dead!

Thankfully, Mammy, by the time we actually get to Shipley Bridge Services the imminent threat of the ice-block-death-baby scenario has passed. Everything, in fact, is just grand, Bonnie's kicking away goodo, and the feeling and the heat has returned to Shauna's tummy. Shauna calls the *doula* from just outside Smith's, to be on the safe side, but all she says is that everything will be fine as long as me and Shauna don't raise our voices or listen to loud music for the rest of the journey.

Shauna, typically, bounces back in seconds, and is gabbing away goodo, right up to the front door. She piles inside, has a soak in the bath, and crashes off to sleep, without even bothering to do the teeth or the perineal massage. The *doula* said that we should do the massage together, like, both of us, rubbing oils and creams and all natural organic foodstuffs in and around Shauna's undercarriage, to prevent it from ripping apart in the event of anything other than a super-smooth, hands-down, pass-the-alfalfa-sprouts, chill-out, Joni-Mitchell-stoner birth. She said that we should incorporate it into our lovemaking. Which is a bit like saying, like, hey, Boss Man, did you know that any day now th'aul scrotum is going to get torn to shreds between your legs? But, well, in the meantime this cream can be incorporated into your lovemaking.

Naturally, I didn't sleep a wink that night. Just lay there, like a trauma victim, replaying the incident over and over again in my mind, getting worse each time, lunatic bad, darker and more hysterical, just replaying that one savage moment in the mind, when we thought she was dead, and we're staring at the womb and we're sure she is dead, and it doesn't take long before I start to hyperventilate, big time, a real show-stopper, gasping for air, jumping up out of the *labba*, into the bathroom, out of the bathroom, glass of water, gasping again, lying on the bed, gasping again, and, secretly, it has to be said, just that tiny bit miffed that Shauna isn't awake, or at least responding to the show at her elbow.

So, eventually, sure that I'm on my last legs, I nudge Shauna, a couple of times, a few decent shoulder pokes, and tell her that I'm losing the plot, and that I've been seriously shaken up by the whole ice-baby-death scenario.

I'm going, like, We could've lost her, hon! We could've lost our baby today!

And Shauna's like, dead groggy, and a bit narked, and just says that we didn't, therefore I'm to be thankful, and get the feck back to sleep.

I wait there, in the bed, still wide-eyed and short of breath for what seems like another eternity, but is probably more like, say, five, ten minutes max, and then I give her another aul tap.

Hon? I say.

Yes, she says, trying to sound normal, but actually sounding like she wants to put me through the window.

I don't think I can cope, I say.

With what? she says, running out of patience.

The baby, I say. Because I think I already love her.

I add, starting to have a bit of an aul snivel to meself, that she's not even born yet. What's going to happen when she's born? I don't think my heart will cope. Will probably just tear in two, like a perineum that hasn't been rubbed with oils and cream and all that shite.

Because this is the thing, I say, on a bit of a roll now, this is the secret they don't teach you in pre-natal classes, or write down in pregnancy books, because they can't, because if they did all the mammies-to-be would be, like, running for the hills, or trying to hand it back. But they should, and they should tell them, tell all the mammies-to-be, that the love for their child comes laced with pain. So much pain in so much love. The pain of fear, worry, failure, and separation, laced, utterly laced, all the way through the love of joy, happiness, truth and togetherness. The love of the child, and the pain, the heart-stopping, eye-watering, ineffable, inconceivable pain, at the thought of ever being separated from them, at all, ever, for a single minute. That pain. That love. And I don't think I can cope, because it's too much to ask. To hold this love, and to hold this pain, inside all at once, like feckin Superman, or Mother Teresa, or some ancient Greek deity who could stare at his wife's belly and contemplate the death of their baby without wanting to bash his own brains out against the wandering rocks.

No, I say to Shauna again, just to underscore the point. I don't think I can cope.

Shauna doesn't sit up in the *labba* or anything. Doesn't stroke me forehead and go, you'll be totally grand, *me auld segosha*! Instead, she simply grunts and, in classic American style, says that I am now very much welcome to the world of parenthood.

It's the job, she says, slurring into her pillow, cool as ice, like a *noir* cop, with the kind of finality that tells me that this conversation is ending now, and if I want to continue I need to take it out onto the couch, into the sitting room, next to the birth pool, by myself.

This is what we signed up for, she adds. This is the job.

She then swings around in the bed, quite the procedure, with that bump, and hugs me, and calls me a neurotic aul arse, and says a pointed goodnight. And, right on cue, Bonnie gives me another dig, another dig through Shauna's belly, although it's more of a rub than a dig, a nice, firm, horizontal stroke, like you get when they're curling around on the spot, and it's an elbow, or a knee, or even the head, and it seems to say, this one seems to say, or maybe I'm imagining it, but still, it seems to say, Chill out, Dadda Jay! No worries, Dadda Jay. Me. Me and Momma Shauna! We got this covered! Wuchoo, wuchoo, wuchoo!

So, Mammy, as you can tell, I've got a lot to be getting on with, what with the hysteria, the panic attacks, the sleeplessness, worry, fear, pain, joy, happiness and the all-consuming love that seem to be the parameters of this new feckin job. And I don't want you to take this the wrong way. And I don't want to be like the lad who goes, you know, like, It's not you, it's me, and the wan is, like, crying her head off, going, What have I done? What have I done wrong? And he's like, You've done nattin wrong, darlin, nattin at all, sure haven't you been smasher all along, it's just me, I'm going through some stuff now, some changes, and I think I need some me time. And you just know, and everyone knows, that he's got someone else on the boil, and girls too, when they say it, It's not you, it's me, you know what they mean, and even if they bluff it for the first few weeks, with solo trips to galleries and language classes at night, they'll suddenly produce this fella, an upgrade on the last, and he'll be like, sure haven't I been snogging the face of her for months now, and you all go, Aha, I see, we get it, it's not you, it's me, me arse!

340

Well, as I say, I don't know how to say this, but it's not you, Mammy, it's me, and I do have someone else on the boil and it's called a fecking incoming baby. So, what I'm trying to say, and don't take this the wrong way, because I'm trying to be gentle, like you've always been gentle with me, but what I'm trying to say is that maybe, from now on, just for a trial period, like, just to see how it feels, we should think about trying postcards?

Your Right-Hand Man,

Always.

Jay

28

The Return of the Mick

Hello? Helloo? Helloooooo?

Jay's head is only half in the door. His body still twisted out-wards. Just in case. Might need to run. Hello, again. No return sounds from inside. Nothing at all. The flat is empty. Feckin A. That's how you're going to beat them. One step ahead. He gig-gles to himself. Jay giggles. Can't believe it. Rock'n'roll, ha? A champagne supernova? Too feckin right. He's so rock'n'roll, Boss Man. And he knows it. Feckin A.

And the stairs! He spots it straightaway. The spelling steps! Jane has been in, and done the spelling steps! Ah, would you credit it? Would you credit her? What a dote! What a crather! She loves that aul chestnut. A page on each step. A letter on each page. You read as you ascend, collect all the letters, and by the time you get to the destination, the bedroom, always the bed-room, you have a sentence of love, spelt out just for you, sitting in the sheaf in your hands. Jane is a devotee of the spelling steps. Any excuse, and she's slapping down the letters, folly the spelly brick road style, leading the way to a night of passion in the *labba*. Something a bit teachy about it, Jay always thought. Or, a bit pedagogical, he might say, after the teachy bit was done and dusted. Something *Sesame Street*. Jane's are always, like, kind of rude too. Like, F, o, l, l, o, w, m, e, t, o, b, e, 'b, l, o, w, n', a, w, a, y! And then he'd pick the last one up, right outside the bed-room, and she'd be inside, waiting, on the bed, super-tarted up, just for him, in a mad lingerie-based assortment of straps and belts and lace and zips. Sometimes a rose in her mouth too. Or she's doing this crazy mental sex pose, looking over her shoulder, bum first, a pose that she's just hopped into when she's heard him on the stairs but is pretending she's been like that all day, like his very own personal sex statue.

Or, say, she's slept in on his side of the bed, after a fablas night before, and is stalking around the empty flat in the mid-morning alone, she'll leave one out for his return, and it'll say, T, h, i, s, w, a, y, f, o, r, a, t, a, s, t, e, o, f, w, h, a, t, s, t, o, 'c, o, m, e'. Oh yes, she's a fierce wan for the puns, Jane. And he gets into the bed-room, this time, and there's more paper on the floor, this time just arrows, and they're all leading up to the bed, the middle of the bed, where Jane has left a seriously well-worn pair of scanties next to another sign, small this time, a sign with scribbled love hearts around the words, 'Use Me!' And sometimes, depending on the mood, Jay will indeed grab the pants up off the bed and get right down to business, then and there, or other times, depending on the mood, he'll pick em up with a biro, like he's just arrived at a feckin multiple homicide, and drop them anony-mously into the linen basket.

Today, however, Jay senses a tonal shift after the letter F. He even stops briefly after, Y, o, u, F, u, c, k, i, n, g. He shakes his head and chuckles on the stairs, and says, Crazy wan, couple of times, and contemplates abandoning the spelling steps entirely. Rock'n'roll. Would show her! But, well, feck it. Let's ride this bad boy out. OK, what have we? P, i, e, c, e, o, f, s, h, i, t, w, a, n, k, e, r, c, u, n, t! Oh, charming. Just feckin charming, that is. Just wait, he thinks, just wait until I have a word with the Father of Jane about this.

It gets worse inside the bedroom. All Jane's knick-knacks are gone from the dresser. The ring holder shaped into a dainty ceramic hand. The translucent make-up bag crammed full of toiletries. The beaded gold necklace that she bought impulsively, because she thought it was very Moloko, but turned out to be too bling-bling. The Ladyshave and the headphones. All gone.

The bed is unmade, the mattress exposed and scattered with printed copies of Jay's so-called broadcaster-fee forgeries. He looks down at the collected paper pile in his hand and notices, for the first time, that they are fee forgeries too, each one, and that Jane has written her venomous message on their reverse sides. At the centre of the bed, nonetheless, there is one final sign-off. Another note. This one in marker, thicker than the rest, blacker than the rest. Written with care. Marker, bet into the page. Almost ripped with the effort. Jay, head throbbing now, in need of water, feckin A, rock'n'roll, boom boom and all that, leans onto the bed, kneels on the mattress edge, hand fully down for head-spinning support, and focusing hard, good and strong, on the blackened scrawl. Just to be clear, like.

I'm Pregnant!
You're Fired!
We're Finished!

Grand, he thinks. Is all he can think. Grand. Could do with an aul toot about now, I suppose. Yes, just the jobbie, would be, that would. Your only man. Ye know yirself. Some *shcale*, ha? Crazy wan, eh? Always the same, with the wans. Love an aul scene. A big scene. Like Shauna in her heyday. No, I won't calm down, I won't motherfucking calm down, don't you patronise me, you Paddy prick, you! And I'm all high voiced, as high voiced as I can get, because that's the way it goes when I get defensive, real high, like, goolies-in-a-vice, like, and I'm, like, I didn't fecking say

344

anything about fecking anything, I just said that Jess was doing her best, whether she liked it or not, to both fulfil and propagate the loud mouth Yank stereotype, but then Shauna hits me right back with this roll-call of all the times and places that Jess was there for her, when she needed her, and stood up to the plate, when no one else would, and I'm, like, Well, I get all that, and she's clearly a fablas wan for doing all that, but what I'm saying is that—

Jay! Jay?

The glass doors are open. Wendy is standing there, tired-eyed, red-faced, in dressing gown alone. Late shift last night. She asks Jay if he has yet taken the time to stand in front of a full-length mirror and, well, see the state of himself. She asks him how long he's been kneeling there, on the mattress, over the notes. She says that she's sorry, but that she read the spelling steps early this morning, on the way in. She's sorry, really sorry for his troubles, like there's been a death. And indeed there has been a death, yes there has, 'clare to God, in Mr Otieno Sr, with the whole family, Otienos and the rest, down in the Surrey sticks since Boxing Day. Of course, nothing, no death, no tragedy at all, can out-trump a split shift on the NHS. Eh? Eh, Jay? No rest for the wicked, eh? Or, there was a bit of rest until you came clomping in, jabbering away at the top of your lungs, nonsensical arse. Which reminds me, Jay, oh my word, Jay, now you've done it, Jay, but Roo is furious. On the warpath. Ree said that Roo once killed a lad in Africa for less. You're done for. And have you seen the state of yourself? Going to just kneel there for ever? Going to move? Can you move, that is? Can you say anything? Jay? Anything at all?

The cold shower seems to help. Fully clothed at first. Jay just gurgling, and half groaning. Rasping sounds too. Like Bonnie in her prime. While Wendy chatters as she scrubs. About the trouble of Jay, and the worry of Jay, and the phone hopping off the hook

345

for the whole holiday season. She removes his clothes too, shirt and jeans and Marks & Sparks boxers, as he starts to come round, hands instinctively, even from the black beyonds, covering the groin

Get over yourself! she snaps. Seriously! Spend my life looking at those things, pitiful creatures, alien slugs, so really, Jay, seriously, I will not give your own sorry addition to the collection a single, flipping thought.

She continues scrubbing. Soap now, hotter water too.

You stink, she adds. Jesus, you stink.

Wendy tackles the armpits with sponges and lather. Shifts him around for the neck, the back of the ears, and a vigorous once-over for the groin and the crack. Jay is loose limbed and compliant, legs and arms up and about whenever she needs it. His head lolls too. Eyes shut occasionally. The waking sleep.

He helps Wendy, though. Not totally gone. Helps Wendy help Jay out of the bath, up over the edge. He collapses into her arms, next to the bath. She holds him there for a mere moment, head lolling back, body half naked in an open bath towel, the soft white terry cloth turning down in heavy folds, over Wendy's knees.

Silly, silly boy, she whispers. And now what?

Wendy rubs Jay dry. She grills him about his so-called Yuletide bender. No replies. Eyes still closed.

Five days? she says. Six days? Seven days on the trot? Who does that?

By rights, she says, Jay should be dead.

Mobile telephones, she says, sneering. Does he know that they're invented?

Did he lose his? she says. Or just sell it, or snort it, or swap it? Or toss it away?

She'll call, she says. She'll call Roo, and calm him down. Or try to.

346

And a trip, she says. A trip to A&E might be just the trick.

Fluids, she says. Saline nasal spray. Multivitamins, half a Valium, and food, lots of food.

And some calls, she says. Apologetic calls, are the place to start.

Humble pie, she says. Very cathartic.

Start with the woman, she says, who called this morning. Wants to meet you at the club.

Jay's eyes open.

The Hooded Claw himself! Your only feckin man!

Jay meets Peter Feddan in the doorway, before setting a single foot inside the club. Jay appears clean and refreshed, in a pressed grey suit, white shirt, no tie. It is just before lunchtime, on 31 December 1999. There are rueful exchanges about the 'bad nose-candy in sex-romp granny hell' debacle, followed by the surreptitious passing of a crumpled fifty-pound note in return for a solid paper wrap of cocaine, a full gram, which will provide Jay with four or five substantial lines before a teatime refill, or with just two big juicy fat ones for a post-prandial blow-out. Unable to wait, and decidedly shaky of hand, Jay eases open the wrap, right there on the daylight Soho steps, much to the horror of The Hooded Claw, who dashes into the distance, as if fire had been called, or bomb, or boom. Jay dips deeply with a doorkey, into the heavenly white, and holds and inhales, and holds and inhales, both nostrils. The feckin, the feckin, the feckin, the feck! Sheeeeeeesh! Wuchoo wuchoo wuchoo wuchoo!

Jamie, the maître d' with the unfeasibly large biceps, stops Jay at the cloakroom.

Lovely to see you again, Mr Concannon. Your party is already seated and waiting.

My party?

The priests?

Yes, of course. The priests.

Where the feck have I been? Where the feck have youze been, dude and dudette? Hobnobbing with the big nobs no doubt. As the actress said to the bishop. The feckin lads are all here now, though. Bringing out the big guns. Youze, meez, them lads over there, on the *labba*. It's like feckin Pope Paul in Drogheda in '79 all over again. Where have I been? Where the feck have youze been?

Jay is sitting across the table from The Clappers and Fr Francis. In the background, observing keenly and unimpressed, from the edge of a four-poster bed, sit two more priests. The bed is the glitzy showpiece, and ironically so, of the club's fourth-floor bar. A showpiece place to chill out and canoodle. The priests are silent figures, young, handsome and tanned, in black full-length cassocks.

Them feckin boys, over there, says Jay. The real deal, eh? The papal johnnies, come to collect? The power of Christ compels you!

Jay is talking rapidly, and with actions, directly into the faces of The Clappers and Fr Francis, who, it seems, to Jay at least, are mesmerised by his non-stop flow of insights, theories, anecdotes, worldly-wise reflections, and interstitial performance bites.

The Clappers tries to interrupt with some banter, some chit-chat. How's work, how's life, how's the wee one, how's Bonnie?

But her words seem to bounce entirely off Jay, bounce right out of his ears, as he rocks and rolls through a muddled account of a Yuletide bender that takes in a wild Christmas party in this very club, some raucous all-day debauchery in the Mayfair flat of a posh English bender – a bender on a bender, what are the chances? Feckin A! – followed by a limo to Brighton, followed by, get this, lads, seriously, hold your feckin whisht for this, a feckin plane! Serio! I think I went to the States? Or Amsterdam? Or Inverness? Feck knows! There was a plane, anyway, and a bog on the plane, and a disco after we landed, and a load of Yank wans, then another plane, another bog, and then back to the bender's flat in Mayfair, for the rest of the bender. Feckin telling yiz, boys, thug life, it's the way to be. *Gon doubt awoyne!*

The Clappers presses again, but all she can wring from Jay are confused conversational zigzags through Shauna's latest failed relationship, with the partner, the big nob, the big nob shrink fella, the one and only, who turned out, get this, to be a real Barry McGuigan behind the scenes, biff-bam, ye know yirself, so she's on the way now, packing the bags, planning the return, the eternal return to the daddy in the U, S, of A, and with the wee wan in tow, but don't worry, we've got lawyers, feckin big-time, high-court lads, who'll piss all over that shite, no mercy, so no one's going anywhere fast, no, sir, no one is ordering a code feckin red around here, ha?

You were missed, all the same, The Clappers says, tentatively, unsure. At the funeral.

Again, the words seem to bounce, clean off, away from Jay's brain. If only momentarily.

He looks into the eyes of The Clappers, and smiles, and beams, and sings aloud, so loud, the lyrics, 'Boom, boom, boom, boom, I want you in my room, la, la, la, la, la!' He says that he has problems of his own, another babby on the way too, would you credit it? And not Shauna's this time, no, that would be too easy, no, another wan knocked up, another story to begin, where to start, where to end, I'm torn down the middle, you know yourself?

There follows a sudden pause.

Thing about the funeral, he says, finally connecting, before finally beginning, and launching into a rapid-fire disquisition on death and the immigrant's dilemma, before deciding instead to abandon ship and plump straight for the funny bone with a movie quote that his mammy would've loved, a quote that goes, and he says this standing up, and giving it some serious welly, I am as large as God! He Is as small as I! He cannot above me, nor I beneath him be!

That one, he says, is for the papal johnnies over there on the *labba*. It's what they want isn't it? Isn't it? he barks, in their direction. The second coming! Isn't it? Well, here I am! The word made flesh! Take a good look!

The two tanned priests stare blankly.

Jay turns the rant on The Clappers and Fr Francis. What did Gannon sell them, the Rome boys, this time? The virgin birth, isn't it? Jayz, he has some neck, that boyo! This is my life, lads, we're talking about. Can't just sell me off to the feckin Vatican, for the sake of a few random geriatrics in the gift shop at Knock. Have yiz no shame, like?

The Clappers gently places a large padded brown envelope down on the table, in between two glasses, still untouched, of sparkling water.

Some of her things, she says. Your mammy.

Jay roughly grabs the package and unceremoniously empties the contents out over the cracked marble top. He scans the booty. A necklace. A wedding ring. A large can of Wella hairspray. Lipstick. False teeth. A bottle of Anais Anais perfume. A post office savings book. Two Miraculous Medals. And one beige plastic artificial hand.

Seriously? he says. And this lot is supposed to make me do what? Put on me Jesus sandals and follow you back to the holy shrine at Knock? Heal the sick? Cast out devils? Announce the dawning of a brand-new feckin—

Fr Francis shoots a hand across the table, and holds Jay by the wrist, firmly, with just the tiniest hint of aggression. It's enough to shut him up.

I think you've got the wrong end of the stick, Jay boy, says Fr Francis.

Jay twitches.

We're not here on behalf of Bishop Gannon, he says, still holding tight. We're here because of you. All of us. Fr Francis indicates the two priests on the showpiece bed.

Yes, says The Clappers, smiling for the first time since Jay's arrival. This is the real deal, Boss Man.

This is an intervention.

The Clappers explains, clearly and patiently, while Fr Francis retains the death hold on Jay's wrist, that the young priests are from the Ballycroy Residential Treatment Centre. They are based in a spectacular fifty-five-acre lowland retreat, slap bang in the middle of County Mayo's Ballycroy National Park. And they are committed, above all else, to providing a Christian faith-based solution to life-controlling drug and alcohol addictions.

Jay says nothing. He picks up his late mother's artificial hand, holds it up to the light, strokes it against the side of his cheek, and then sniffs it slowly and deeply, with his eyes closed.

The Clappers and Fr Francis share a look.

Jay opens his eyes and smiles.

In that case, he says, I'll get me coat.

The Clappers beams. Fr Francis marvels at how easy it has been. He releases Jay's wrist. Jay, in turn, sprays half a can of Wella Extra-Firm Hold styling fixative into the faces of Fr Francis and The Clappers, before gripping the underside of the table, flinging it towards the two priests and charging wildly out the door of the fourth-floor bar. He clatters down the wooden staircase and out the front entrance, not stopping, not pausing for breath, until he has left the environs of Soho completely. He makes it as far as Trafalgar Square, and blends in with the Millennium Eve revellers, who are already, even this early in the afternoon, thronging and swaying by the boarded fountain and the giant Christmas tree, clanking blue plastic bags of beer, bravely singing impromptu ditties about the last night on earth, while secretly looking to the skies for fireworks, for signs and for falling planes. Waiting for the end of it all.

We're on, Mammy! We're on! The feckin water's broken! The *doula*'s been called. The pool's filling up! It's action stations Saturday! We're on! We're on! There's a feckin baby on the way! It's all starting now!

Woo woo!

Jay!

29

The Final Countdown

Ten!

Shauna knows that she shouldn't, but she has kept Bonnie up until midnight. The Dalmatian bodysuit has come out for the occasion. Bonnie's cheeks are flushed with exhaustion, but she is smiling. She is holding a large glass bowl of sugared popcorn. She is curled on the couch, next to her mother. The television is on.

Nine!

Live from the Thames. Bodyjammed with revellers. Reports from Westminster, from the South Bank, from the Dome.

Eight!

Shauna's packing is almost done. The cardboard boxes are neatly stacked. Three large boxes sit together, up against the radiator and open, poised to catch the last-minute picture frames, the paperweights, the cushions, the forgotten books, the knick-knacks. All to follow later, by freight.

Seven!

Shauna cuddles Bonnie. Something illicit and conspiratorial about keeping a child up until midnight. Something gorgeous too. A shared story. This is how we live, and how we live now, just you and me. Shauna looks down at her own abdomen, the swelling signs of a baby bump finally, defiantly, real.

Six!

Shauna had cried earlier tonight. She had found letters. Old letters. Buried inside the *Times Atlas*. Her letter to Jay, his letter to her. Written in jest and in love. Like artefacts from another era. Shauna had held her mouth when reading, then placed her hand to her chest. She crumpled. Bonnie lolloped round the room, around her, weaving in and out of the boxes, to the sing-songy chant of 'Momma's had an owee, Momma's had an owee!'

Five!

Paul used to keep Shauna up at night. Every year, on the fourth of July. They'd leave Chester with a sitter, and go plant a rug and a cooler on Rehoboth Beach. Watch the sunset and the stars. Drink chilled Snapple. Paul would cover Shauna's ears with his hands during much of the fireworks display, when the blasts and bangs became innumerable, and rattled her tiny chestbone, and the child she was felt the fear and the danger from the outside world of men.

Four!

Shauna has opened the blinds, and pulled up the sash windows. She wants to be connected to all of London, and the world, when

355

midnight strikes. She wants to scan the skyline and see the small pockets of localised pyrotechnics. From Paddington to Kilburn. Kensal Green to Kensington. She wants to imagine the communities therein, gasping and cheering at the bursting bouquets above, laughing through the emergence of a new millennium, knowing, deep down, in their hearts, that this life never ends.

Three!

She pulls Bonnie closer, steals some popcorn and kisses her. Right here, right now, there is no one else on earth with whom she'd rather share a couch. The truth.

Two!

She has a momentary wobble. A tiny doubt at the back of her mind. It's not really going to end, is it? The world, I mean? Now? She squeezes Bonnie tight. Either way, something momentous is about to happen. She can feel it.

One!

Dear Jay,

*I have to say, it's amazing that we've been together all these years.
What with you being totally gay 'n all. Although, really, when I think
about it, I always felt that the sex change op was one step too far.*

*OK, sorry, I know, it's hard to do this. I promise. I'll do it properly.
Was my stupid idea, after all. The least I can do.*

Here goes. Whoah. Deep breath.

*Jay. Darling Jay. What can I say? How did we do it? How did we get
here? Seven years later, and, er, three, no, make that four kids in the
bag, we are just about the two happiest motherfuckers I've ever seen.*

*How did we do it? How did we build the dream life? Me, with my
own multimillion-dollar recording studio, my albums, my movie
deals and my fashion line. And you, Jesus, you, with your, er, with
your farm? No, with your billion-dollar chain of video rental
outlets that span the globe?*

*And our kids? God, our kids, Jay. Timmy, Tommy, Jackie and
Bonnie? So perfect in every way, the envy of the world. Already
sports stars and school champions. At their age. I know. It's like,
sometimes, I look around and I feel sorry for everyone else. How did
they miss this? How did they not get even a piece of what we have?*

*And when they ask us, What's the secret? How do we keep it all
together? I say, you, Jay. I say, you. I look at you, across the room
from me now, with your head down, and your stupid concentrated
scowl, and I know that there is goodness in the world, there is*

kindness in the world, because it brought us together. I may not go as far as belief in your God, your uptight Catholic God, but if there is a benign, all-powerful force in this universe, I count myself the lucky one who has felt its loving touch, and found you, in my arms, in my hands, and in my heart.

And as I look back on these blissful seven years, I take pride in the fact that we nurtured this love, we savoured it, and we knew always, deep inside, when things got rough, when things got difficult, we knew always, even if we didn't say it, even if we didn't acknowledge it at the time, even if we did everything bar actually spitting in each other's faces, we knew, secretly knew, deep inside, that nothing was ever, or would or could ever, be greater than our love. Our love. This thing that we cling to, that we crave, that we need, and that lights the way forward for you and for me. I love our love. And I love that it's ours.

And so, that's it, Jay. Keep on keeping on. And, in the words of Daniel Day-Lewis, Be strong! Submit! Stay alive, no matter what occurs! I will find you! No matter how long, no matter how far, I will find you!

Actually, sorry. That reads a bit stalker-y on paper. Bit bunny boiler. But you know what I mean.

I think what I mean to say is, I love you, Jay. Let's get married. Let's have children. Let's be happy.

And, God, let us live.

Love,

The future Mrs Concannon? The current Shauna. The always yours.

Me again, Mammy!

What to say, or where to begin? At the end, I suppose. Which is
where you find me. Here, standing outside of Shauna's flat,
staring up at the sash windows. They're open. The lights are on
inside. This is a sign, I feel. So unlike her. At this hour. Even for
the night that's in it. Millennium Eve. Last night on earth.

And for a while back there, it was. I was a goner. A gombeen.
Out of me tree. Pinging my way through the crowds in Trafalgar
Square like a foam-flecked loo-la straight out of Mark five, verses
one to twenty. Remember yer man? The demonic possession from
the region of the Gadarenes? I used to love that one, in school
and at home. Because Jesus handles it dead cool. So suave. Just
spots a herd of swine near by, probably out of the corner of his
eye, and says, handy as you like, to the demons in yer man, Right,
off ye go now, boys. Like the coolest nightclub bouncer ever. And
they leave yer man's body, and inhabit the pigs and then fling
themselves off a cliff. As you do.

But the best thing is yer man himself. He's gone from a crazed,
foam-faced nutjob to this really sorted lad in a suit who thinks
he's going to travel the world with Team Jesus until the boss
himself turns around and says no. He says, Tell your own
people how much the Lord has done for you. Tell them how
much mercy he has shown you. And yer man can't believe it,
but he can at the same time. Because he has told all his friends,
and all the people that he's well and truly fecked off, that
profound human change is possible and that even a slavering

359

arse-faced whackjob is entitled to a second chance, if only in the eyes of God.

So, as I say, Trafalgar Square doesn't do it for me. I'm getting elbowed and shoved from all angles by angry groups of Santa-capped revellers with party squeakers who don't quite appreciate the physical state that I'm in, or the energy it takes to stay coordinated and upright. In my condition. And my condition, Mammy, is not good. I've been having *the crack* for too long. Days into weeks into months. Non-stop. And it's burnt through my entire system, like a taper, or one of them almondy biscuit papers that you light at the coffee end of dinner parties for the wow factor. You watch them float upwards to the ceiling, burning themselves out as they go, and leaving not a trace of their own form behind. But in my case I am indeed left with something after the burn. Nothing major. Just the greatest bout of all-consuming dread, nausea and fulminating, soul-splitting paranoia.

And it hits me all of a sudden, like a truck, after the tenth resentful dig in the crush of Trafalgar Square. As if someone's elbow actually connects with the perfect spot between my shoulder blades to activate the dread, nausea and paranoia mode. And it's normal, I believe, after too much of *the crack*, nothing to be wondered at. But it holds me tight around the chest, and strangles my throat and whispers poison in my ears. 'Run!' it says. 'Run! They're after you, run!' And it drives me down, panic-stricken, in something of a rolling, stumbling rush, to the base of Nelson's Column, across the road to the Strand, and then further south to the Embankment itself and the edge of the river.

From there, of course, the throng gets even worse. Tighter, and more compressed, like my paranoid fit. Hundreds and thousands, slowly flowing east. An enormous living organism of drinkers and chanters with sparklers and smokes, singing songs and smooching, and rolling inevitably eastwards, downriver, to celebrate the Millennium in grand style, in and around the newly constructed, and fully operational, eighth wonder of the world.

I should add, at this stage, Mammy, that I'm dressed in a sweat-drenched suit and clutching your very own artificial hand. It's a reflex thing. I have it in my own hand, locked tight. I can't seem to let it go. And I don't want to. I'm holding on, in fact, for dear life. Your hand, Mammy. Your hand in my hand.

And I'm pushed along too. There is no resistance. I'm strangled with fear, barely breathing. My paranoia tells me that they've got me now, that they have me now, all of them, I'm in the centre, and they've all come here for me. I get wedged well into one gang in particular, boys and girls. They're cockneys, and they're calling each other dozy cans, and laughing about the end of the world, and the boys are trying to scare the girls by saying, Look, look, it's a plane, it's going to crash, or, Listen, listen, that's a siren, definitely, the nukes are on the loose, and the girls are calling the boys cheeky cans for trying to scare them so, and it's all good fun until they see me stumbling about beside them and call me a dozy can and watch as I trip good and proper and fall down and hit the pavement for the first time.

One of the lads, a bigfella but a real softie, says that the other lads are heartless aul cans for the night that's in it, and he bends down and helps me to my feet. As he does the other lads slag him something rotten, and call him Simon the bender, and Simon the mickey sucker, and tell him that he's hit rock bottom if he's now making moves on sweaty-faced tramps with three hands.

As you can imagine, Mammy, I almost have a heart attack on the spot. The dread, fear and paranoia explode in my head, taking me over completely, and I go, Simon? Is your name Simon? And he says yes. I say, As in Simon of Cyrene? And he goes, No, as in Simon of Chadwell Heath. But it's too late, Mammy. My brain goes haywire, I see Simon of Cyrene on the Fifth Station of the Cross, lifting the boss to his feet, and a million different frazzled synapses twist and torque inside me of their own accord, and I decide on the spot, right there by the river, within sight of the Tower of London, that you were right all along, that it all makes sense, and that I am indeed the second coming of Jesus Christ himself.

Seriously, Mammy. Think of it. The end of the world. The devil in the Dome. The Millennium bug. Me just happening, through sheer fate and dumb luck alone, to end up with the one job in the world that gives me access to the one place in the world that's poised to witness the end of everything and the rise of eternal darkness at the first stroke of midnight.

That's the theory anyway. And it makes total sense to a coke-addled loo-la on the cusp of paranoid psychosis. I stand up suddenly, straight on the spot, all the tremors and half-stumbles instantly evaporated by the new terrifying mission in me. I thank Simon and tell him that tonight, truly, he will be with me in paradise. One of his mates, a real smart lad, adds that paradise is the name of a gay bar on Old Compton Street, but I don't mind. I'm already sprinting down Mansell Street, towards Tower Bridge and the East End of London, and an appointment with nothing less than the earthly apocalypse itself.

By the time I get to the Dome I'm seriously flagging. The sweats are kicking in again, I'm still clutching your hand, and there seem to be more rabid feckers crowded outside on the main concourse, trying to fight their way inside, than there was in Trafalgar Square and the riverside put together. I offer it up for the souls, put my head down and join the throng. We shuffle hopelessly forward, sway sideways, and occasionally flow backwards. The front doors are tantalisingly close, yet frustratingly out of reach, with the striplight design on the wall of Work Zone clearly visible inside, hinting and teasing at the manifold bounties contained therein. A woman shouts out to no one in particular that at this rate we are all going to miss the show. There is much grumbled agreement. Panicked, gasping and sweating even more than before, I'm about to bolt from the pack when a minor miracle occurs.

I see Darren.

He's pushing his way back outside, still in his high-vis vest, like a man on a mission, marshalling his troops until the very end. I yell out his name. He spots me and roughly pulls me aside, frogmarches me right round to the Living Island entrance and punches me three times in the face. I fall to the ground, for the second time. He stands over me and says that the punches are for Diana, for snogging Diana way back when, because they've been to couples' counselling and it all came out in the middle of an openness exercise. I tell him that I'm sorry, and that I don't have the time to explain, but that I've come here to save the world from Armageddon because I am the one true and risen Christ.

He punches me again and calls me a mental culchie cokehead bollix. I think my nose is broken. I feel a tiny rivulet of blood running over my lips. I wipe it with your hand. Darren says, What the fuck. I tell him it's yours. He shakes his head and lifts me to my feet, as if the sight of a lad wiping his broken nose with his mammy's artificial hand is too much to bear. He tells me to look at the state of me, and reminds me that I owe him at least five grand and that if I can't pay up within the week he's very sorry, but he's going to have to get some ex-IRA blokes to break both my legs, and maybe even kill me.

But what about the world? I say, more convinced of my holy mission than ever. There won't be any next week unless I save the world! Darren shakes his head again and sighs. He pushes open the staff entrance and ushers me inside, telling me to get lost, and adding that he's only doing it because he has a mammy too, and can't imagine what my mammy must've done to end up with such an unmerciful gobshite as me.

Time goes a bit fuzzy. I find myself a decent spot, nestled behind a plywood wall in the service tunnel under the main stage. It's the sort of spot only a builder lad would know. It's dark, though. And it smells of freshly cut timber and powdered cement. I put my head down against your hand and lie there, contemplating my next move as the sounds from the stage above thunder down around me. I know I'm in the right place, though. Because this is exactly where Esteban saw Santa Muerta, and later El Diablo, and it is the place where it's all going to kick off at midnight, where Satan himself is going to erupt centre stage, on the Prime Meridian, and call time on existence itself. But for now I'm tired. I've got the shakes. And I'm operating on sheer spiritual energy from the pathway of the Lord rather than anything as mundane as muscles, breath and actual metabolic reserves.

Your hand is hard against my face, a terrible pillow. But I don't care. The greater the pain, the deeper the feeling. I close my eyes and I whisper to you. I'm sorry Mammy, I say. I'm sorry I didn't believe you. All these years I should've known. A mammy never lies. A mammy is truth. And a mammy, for me, is God.

And then I do something mad, Mammy. I say something that I've never said in my entire life. You used to whisper it all the time. On the couch. During the fillum marathons. At bedtime. At morning time. And on annual Holy Day shopping excursions. Only for me to shrink back in response, or cringe, or flinch, always afraid that it was a word too much, or the unfortunate revelation of your own desperation, your own sadness and your loneliness. But now I see it for what it is, and I say it back, uncomplicated, unfiltered and truthful. I love you, Mammy, I say, and I snuggle up to your plastic hand and fall fast asleep.

Naturally, the sound of eighty fecking acrobatic arsehole dancers charging and whooping insanely, like the swines of Gadarene, down through the service tunnel is enough to waken anyone. Even the son of God himself. I shoot up in my hidey-hole and clank my noggin against the sharp edge of a hardwood joist, adding an open scalp wound to the broken nose, facial bruising, and overall atrophy and degeneration that define my increasingly deranged physical appearance.

I don't have time to whimper or mollycoddle myself, however. For the dancers are barely down the tunnel when I hear the first chanted 'Twenty!' of the midnight countdown to the end of it all. I fire myself out of the hidey-hole, taking the plywood wall with me as I fall through to the tunnel, and run directly to the trapdoor during 'Nineteen!', 'Eighteen!' and 'Seventeen!' I lift the trapdoor, barely an inch from the ground, and scan the arena. 'Sixteen!' Feckin Blair's there. And Cherie. The Queen. All the New Labour heavies. Lenny Henry and Mick Hucknall too! Boy, are they in for a surprise! Holding back the years, me arse! 'Fifteen!'

I drop back down under the trapdoor, on a small set of sturdy wooden stairs. 'Fourteen!' Think! I order myself. Think. You're the Son of God. What would the Son of God do to stop the apocalypse? 'Thirteen!' What's the one thing I could do that would defeat the forces of evil and the power of Satan combined? 'Twelve!' Confounded, semi-concussed and more than a tiny bit stressed, I turn to my heavenly father for advice. 'Eleven!' God, I say, the Father, the one and only, I'm in a bit of a fix here. 'Nine!'

I'm your only son on earth, the fruit of the womb of Deirdre Concannon. And when I say this bit, Mammy, I wave your hand around, just so He knows who I'm talking about. I continue, and I say, I want to save everyone in the world, Lord, the people, all six billion of them. 'Eight!' I know, Lord, that they're all kind of annoying, these people. Especially when they're being ironic. But they mean well. 'Seven!' And I haven't met one yet who doesn't possess within them even the tiniest atomic spark of divine goodness. Although I'd say Hitler was pushing it. And I met this vicar once— 'Six!' Point being, I've made a lot of mistakes. Fecked off a lot of people. But I'm here for you, Lord. 'Five!'

At which point, Mammy, with my eyes closed tight, and your hand clutched tighter, I ask God to please, help me, help the world. 'Four!' Whatever he needs to do with me, do it now! 'Three!' Show me the way, Lord, I say. Show me the way and I will never look back! 'Two!' Into thy hands, I say, I commend my spirit. 'One!' Please God, I say, desperate now, let me make it right!

'Happy New Y—'

There's a flash of white, Mammy, like you wouldn't believe. White everywhere. Filling space. Even through my closed eyes. Just white. Like some pap has got his flash on sports mode and is just ramming them off in your face non-stop, stunning you into submission from the white, bright, burning light.

I don't move for an age. But then I hear something. Just the faintest hint of a voice. Be not afraid, it says, even lower than a whisper. Be not afraid. And then the rip of a speeding tyre across wet tarmac. I am in London, I say to myself. I am in London. I gradually open my eyes and let the world come into focus, the streets and the buildings. And what I see in front of me is not shop shutters, or tube stations or high roads and side streets, but only the familiar, pink-painted façade of Shauna's flat.

It's after midnight. Well after midnight. And the world hasn't died. My feet are filthy, my shoes in bits. And I may indeed have walked the entire way from the Dome to here, in a light-headed, malnourished brain-freeze, an unthinking whiteout, driven forward and compelled only by the real me, and by the aching within that's been hidden for so long.

Equally I may have felt the hand of God down there in the Dome tonight. Answering my prayers and letting me know, via a cosmic, if slightly time-consuming, trip through the light fantastic, that the trick to saving the world entire is to open your heart to the woman that you love and the child in your arms, and to fill their lives with only your kindness.

30

An Intervention

Jay is wrestled to the ground outside Shauna's flat by The Clappers, Fr Francis and the two young priests from the Ballycroy Residential Treatment Centre.

They had emerged, suddenly, from the back of a blue Toyota Hiace. The Clappers had told them where to park and wait. She had done this before.

Jay screams from the ground, and from the grip of his captors.

Shauna! Shauna!

The two young priests do most of the spadework, with one sitting on Jay's legs, and the other pinning his arms back behind his head.

Within seconds, Shauna appears from above, leaning bodily out of the window.

Jay? she says, squinting down at the commotion on the pavement. Jay, is that you?

The emotion in her voice conveys the sense of startled sympathy.

Shauna! Jay repeats, while he is roughly lifted to his feet.

The Clappers faces upwards and waves a hand at the general window area.

Ma'am, she says, I'd advise you to withdraw your head back

inside. The situation is under control. And this fecker here will no longer be a bother to you. Sorry for your troubles.

Jay is bundled into the back of the Hiace. The Clappers takes the wheel. She races the length of St Mark's Road, roaring into the morning hours. Out of Shauna's life for now, and for the foreseeable future.

31

Rehoboth Beach

The water on Rehoboth Beach is warmer than Strandhill. Good paddling temperature, Shauna thinks. Not quite swimming weather yet. Certainly not for Bonnie. Getting her back in the water? That's going to be interesting.

Shauna walks along the water's edge, keeping Bonnie sandside. They've been here for over a month and already it has become their routine. The pre-breakfast beach walk. Bonnie remains an early riser, so hitting the shore at eight requires very little effort. They usually walk the entire length, right up to the last groyne before the headland. On their return, they buy breakfast from the boardwalk diner and drive home to Grandad Paul, who's usually surfacing in time for a bagel, a coffee and some juice.

Shauna worries, even there in the tranquil bliss of the beach, about the change of scene for Bonnie. The change of rhythm, life-path and pace. And she worries about the coming months, and how Bonnie will react when Shauna starts studying again, when Shauna starts picking up shifts in Paul's T-shirt business, and, most of all, when Shauna gives birth in May, in the maternity ward of Wilmington General Hospital, Delaware, USA. Will the disruption be too much? Will they both bond with the new baby? Will all this overwhelming newness sink Bonnie completely? And will her emotional life be defined, like that of her mother, and her mother's mother, by compromise and failure?

In these moments, on the beach, when Shauna feels the anxiety in her chest, the dryness in her throat, and the growing tension in her jangled nerves, she thinks only of Dr Ghert, and of the mantra that he created specifically for her.

I am perfect in the face of life, she says, breathing deeply, hand on her womb. And I am enough in the universe.

She looks around her, and out over the water, to the Atlantic and far, far beyond.

I am enough in the universe.

14 February 2000

Dear Shauna,

Feckin Valentine's Day, ha? What's that about?

Nearly done in the nutters' prison, me. I'll tell you, six weeks of fresh fruit, filtered water and communing with Jesus and I'm ready to convert Keith Richards, Lucifer and the ghost of Oliver Reed. The view's not too shabby, though. Mountains everywhere. And on a good day, from the highest point on Slieve Carr you can see right out to the North Atlantic, and beyond. I suppose it's like that bit in *Jaws 2* when the boat's drifting out to sea and one of the lads wonders where they're going to end up and another lad goes, 'Ireland!' And it's meant to be a big joke, because Ireland's a rubbish destination to the world of fillum people. But when we saw it, way back in the day, we all went, 'Yay!' because we were so thrilled that Ireland got a mention in a fillum in the first place, especially one with a giant killer shark in it.

There's plenty of therapy too. You'd love it. Lots of grown men and women sitting around in circles, trying to convince themselves, and each other, that they're not the biggest scumbags ever to have walked the earth. It's wicked stuff. But efficacious in its own way.

Point being, Shauna, they say that I'm healthy now, and they say that I'm clear, but really, I'm sick with the longing. For you, and for Bonnie, and for the grand illusion of our second chance.

372

You must tell Bonnie sorry, so many sorries from me. Tell her sorry that I never finished her story, but that it ends beautifully, and when I see her next I'll tell it, and describe how Penny the polar-bear girl is saved, and not a minute too soon, by the sudden shock reappearance of the dadda polar bear who, all this time, has been recovering quietly in the polar bear den, bullet-wound healing, heart on the mend. Tell her too that I'm a sucker for the myth of happy endings. Because without them, well, why bother?

And for you, Shauna? I am truly the penitent man. I have a world of sorrow and regret within, and enough heavyweight contrition to drown the shrine at Knock until well into the next Millennium. But sufficeth to say, what I mean to say, in the language of the nuthouse down here, is that you are my Step Number Nine, Shauna, and I will make it right.

Neither am I expecting a hero's welcome. Or for you to melt at the very thought of me. Instead, best-case scenario, I'm hoping, maybe, for that chance. Nothing major. Just a moment together, where we might sit and talk, or not talk. Where we can be, and where we can look, finally, face to face, and eye to eye. And if we are lucky in this moment, we just might see in the deep black pits of our pupils, if only for that one passing glance, that nothing matters or truly exists without the lifespark of love inside.

Before that, however, I've got one important thing to do. And it's the first genuinely important thing I'm going to do in my new and improved, refreshed, revitalised and rejuvenated life.

I'm going to post this feckin letter.

Jay

Acknowledgements

So many people to thank, so pointless to rattle through them. Sufficeth to say that they begin and end with my Little, Brown editor Clare Smith. Keener of eye than ever, and bigger of brain, she took the daunting word deluge with which I drowned her one bright spring day and, without flinching, she beat the bugger back into shape. A teacher, a collaborator and a bloody good person. Hats off, Clare.